Praise for

The Swan House

by Elizabeth Musser

"[A] beautiful story . . . brimming with touches of humor . . . well-developed characters . . . excellent writing and overall quality."

Publisher's Weekly

"[Musser] is an Atlanta native and keen observer . . . *The Swan House* is a sweet read for 'old Atlantans' and a vivid picture of a young girl living through the history of Atlanta in the 60's for newcomers . . ."

Atlanta Magazine

"A beautifully executed story . . . Highly recommended."

CBA Marketplace

"Musser has written an inspiring coming of age novel set in the segregated South of the early 1960's. Chock-full of suspense, the novel's heroine has an intelligent innocence that searches for truth in the most unyielding of places, the human heart."

Mary Rose Taylor, Executive Director
The Margaret Mitchell House, Atlanta

"The deep wounding of Atlanta by a plane crash in Paris in 1962 and the consequential insight of a questing motherless daughter—a fact and faith-based novel of assuring conciliation and comfort."

Doris Lockerman
Columnist

Books by Elizabeth Musser

FROM BETHANY HOUSE PUBLISHERS

The Swan House

The Dwelling Place

OTHER BOOKS

Two Crosses

Two Testaments

Two Destinies

05A

THE DWELLING PLACE

a Novel

ELIZABETH MUSSER

BETHANY HOUSE
MINNEAPOLIS, MINNESOTA

The Dwelling Place

Cover design by Lookout Design Group, Inc.

Published by Bethany House Publishers
11400 Hampshire Avenue South
Bloomington, Minnesota 55438

Bethany House Publishers is a division of
Baker Publishing Group, Grand Rapids, Michigan.

Printed in the United States of America

Library of Congress Cataloging-in-Publication Data

Musser, Elizabeth.
The dwelling place / by Elizabeth Musser.
p. cm.
Summary: "Sprinkled with humor, heartache and history, this stand-alone sequel to *The Swan House* is a journey of sacrifice, forgiveness and hope that finds a daughter and mother linked by love, but separated by secrets"—Provided by publisher.
ISBN 0-7642-2926-5 (pbk.)
1. Parent and adult child—Fiction. 2. Mothers and daughters—Fiction. 3. Disfigured persons—Fiction. 4. Scotland—Fiction. 5. Secrecy—Fiction. I. Title.
PS3563.U839D89 2005
813'.54—dc22 2004024208

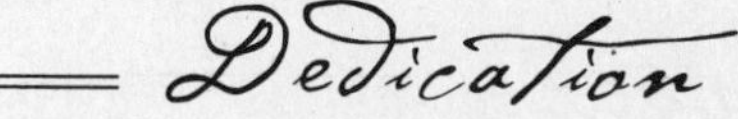

This story is dedicated to my wonderful firstborn son, Andrew. Being your mother has taught me profound lessons about the power of love, and watching you grow into a thoughtful, creative, kind, and analytical young man has brought me delight and pride. You do not yet know who you will become, for now you see through a glass darkly. As you're being crafted into someone precious for God and man, keep walking forward and looking upward to the One who made you with a heart of gold.

I love you,
Mom

About the Author

ELIZABETH GOLDSMITH MUSSER, a native of Atlanta, Georgia, received her B.A. in English and French from Vanderbilt University, where she was a member of Phi Beta Kappa and graduated magna cum laude.

Elizabeth's novel *Two Crosses* was the first of a trilogy set during both the Algerian War for independence from France (1957–1962) and the present day civil war in Algeria. Her fourth novel, *The Swan House*, set in the turbulent years of the early sixties in Atlanta, is the coming-of-age story of a young girl from a wealthy family and her discovery of a love beyond her sheltered existence. Elizabeth's novels have been translated into Dutch, German, French, and Norwegian.

For over fifteen years, Elizabeth and her husband, Paul, have been involved in mission work with International Teams. They presently live in Lyons, France. The Mussers have two sons, Andrew and Christopher.

The Dreary Change

The sun upon the Weirdlaw Hill,
In Ettrick's vale, is sinking sweet;
The westland wind is hush and still,
The lake lies sleeping at my feet.
Yet not the landscape to mine eye
Bears those bright hues that once it bore;
Though evening, with her richest dye,
Flames o'er the hills of Ettrick's shore.

With listless look along the plain
I see Tweed's silver current glide,
And coldly mark the holy fane
Of Melrose rise in ruined pride.
The quiet lake, the balmy air,
The hill, the stream, the tower, the tree—
Are they still such as once they were?
Or is the dreary change in me?

Alas, the warped and broken board,
How can it bear the painter's dye!
The harp of strained and tuneless chord,
How to the minstrel's skill reply!
To aching eyes each landscape lowers,
To feverish pulse each gale blows chill;
And Araby's or Eden's bowers
Were barren as this moorland hill.

—Sir Walter Scott

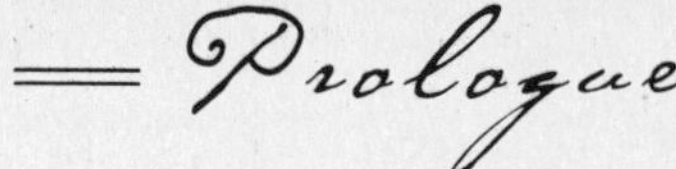

Prologue

Hilton Head, South Carolina

I have never been into journaling. And I am not telling this story simply because it was on my "to do" list from rehab. I'm telling it because, well, it's my story and I need to write it down in case someday I have a rebellious kid who hates me and accuses me of having had an easy life.

At first glance it seems to be about three short weeks in my life. Or three long ones, however you look at it. In reality, the story is much more complicated, as all stories are.

This one is about my mother and me and becoming.

Where I'm writing this story is important too. I'm at my family's beach house. While I am typing on my laptop, I'm looking out the window toward the ocean. This is what I see: one of my sisters, Abbie, with her older son, Bobby, on her lap, sitting by the swimming pool and reading aloud from the Dr. Seuss book *Marvin K. Mooney*. I gave it to Bobby for his third birthday last month.

I'm here for a month, but it's not just a vacation. I brought along my textbooks from veterinary school so I could study. It seems very appropriate that beside me as I write are a cat and a dog who, over the past two years, have forged a wary friendship.

I knew that sitting here at the family room table and staring out at the beach would inspire me. I remember Mom sitting in the same spot that summer, with her easel and palette and the green scarf hanging over the chair.

And the sketch pads. Of course, the sketch pads.

The paintings are still downstairs. And the bikes. I love those old bikes. They're important in my story too.

I think I am writing this also because I want kids who are close to giving up and parents who perhaps have already given up to realize that you can never know the ending in the middle of all the pain.

When I think about my life and Mom's, well, I'm glad we didn't give up. We could have. For a hundred different reasons.

I think about that, and then I see Abbie stand up and take little Bobby's hand as they walk out on the beach. I can picture their footprints appearing—one pair so small beside the bigger ones—and I want to call out to them to enjoy that walk. Oh my. Enjoy it!

There's one other reason I want to tell my story. It's because I've learned that the person you see staring back at you in a mirror can change. It's important to keep observing from time to time, not obsessing over it, but looking, so as not to forget whom you see looking back.

I can't peer into a mirror without thinking of Megan. Then I always think of the mosaic table, and the long Scottish wall with the stones that are crumbling down, and so many other broken things in life. And I say to myself, *Sometimes the breaking of things is cruel, and sometimes it is necessary, and sometimes it is just an accident.*

And having said that, I think I am ready to begin.

Chapter 1

Atlanta, Georgia
June 2001

Where are the songs of Spring? Ay, where are they?
Think not of them, thou hast thy music too—
While barrèd clouds bloom the soft-dying day,
And touch the stubble plains with rosy hue . . .
And full-grown lambs loud bleat from hilly bourn. . . .

—JOHN KEATS, *TO AUTUMN*

From somewhere in my groggy subconscious I heard a persistent ringing. Without opening my eyes, I felt along the bedside table until I located the phone. "Yeah, what is it?"

"Ellie Bartholomew! Are you still asleep? You promised to go to the hospital to be with Mom."

"Chill a little, Abbie," I mumbled. I almost chastised my sister for waking me in the middle of the night, until I realized the sun was shining brightly and my alarm clock proclaimed it to be 9:27. "I didn't get in till after two. You know how it is at Jeremy's."

"It's not exactly the kind of restaurant I frequent." Abbie paused, and I maintained a stony silence. "Well, for heaven's sake, please don't be late. I'm counting on you. So is Dad. I'd go if I could. . . ."

"I know, I know. Bobby's got a fever and you don't want to leave him. You explained it all last night."

With the cordless phone in one hand, I was already out of bed, in the kitchen, opening the fridge, and retrieving a can of Coke. I lifted the tab and took a long sip.

"Don't forget the sketch pads."

"They're right here," I grunted. In truth, I would have forgotten them without Abbie's reminder.

"Call me this afternoon and let me know how it goes, okay?"

"Whatever. Depends on when I get home. I have to work at four."

"Okay, Ellie," she sighed. "Thanks."

Abbie was twenty-eight. She lived in Grant Park with her husband, Bill, and one-year-old Bobby. I imagined her standing by the phone with Bobby on her hip, her hand going quickly to his forehead. She'd have worry lines on her perfectly chiseled face. Worry for Mom, for Bobby, and for the baby she was carrying inside.

Abbie was having an awful pregnancy. She couldn't keep food down and had actually lost two pounds by the time she reached her sixth month. She looked like a skeleton holding a soccer ball at her tummy. I suddenly wished I hadn't spoken so harshly.

My other sister, Nan, was twenty-five and spunky—cute, with short brown hair. She lived in Chattanooga, about an hour and a half from Atlanta. Her husband, Stockton, had just completed his law degree at the University of Virginia and was working with a fairly well known firm. Nan, who taught sixth grade at a girls' school, had recently found out she was pregnant. Big surprise. Nan didn't want kids until she was at least thirty.

And then there was me, Ellie. Twenty and single.

I splashed cold water on my face, swept my hands through my tangled hair, and pulled on a pair of jeans. My cat, Hindsight, wrapped herself around my legs and meowed.

"Oh, hush up!" I said. "You know good and well that I want to go to the hospital about as much as I want an extra hole in my head." I went back to the fridge, took out an opened can of cat food, and spooned the contents into her bowl.

Then, my mind slowly clearing, I rummaged through a drawer for an appropriate T-shirt. Though she hadn't said it aloud, Abbie's unspoken admonition rang in my ears. *And for heaven's sake, don't embarrass Mom. Try to dress decently.*

Don't worry, Abbie, I answered back. *I'll be a dutiful daughter. I won't disgrace you, and I won't let anyone down. . . .*

The sky was already a fierce blue with the sun promising to cast its torrid spell on the city. I glanced down at my watch smugly as my little hatchback Hyundai zipped along Peachtree Road toward the hospital. 10:03. Even with my late start, I was running ahead of schedule. *Ha, Abbie!* She said not to arrive before ten-thirty. The chemo wouldn't be administered until eleven. One thing was sure: I didn't want to be there early. At a red light I let my eyes rest on the two large spiral sketch pads sitting in the passenger's seat.

On impulse, I didn't pull into the hospital parking lot but continued my drive down Peachtree. I looked out on the impressive skyline with its modern skyscrapers, the beautiful multitiered IBM building appearing first in the distance as I rounded the bend past Collier Drive. Atlanta! I passed the spot where a little bar called the Beer Bottle used to stand. It was torn down years ago, and now the newest trend in Atlanta apartments—what real estate agents called *lofts*—lined one side of this section of Peachtree. I rolled down my window and let the June breeze permeate the car as I drove over Interstate 85. The street narrowed and split, the buildings grew taller, the perpendicular street names became numbers. Eighteenth Street, Seventeenth. . . . I pulled into a curbside parking place on Sixteenth and hopped out of the car.

On my right stood the High Museum, a pristine white circular building. Richard Meier had received the world's most prestigious architectural honor, the Pritzker Prize, for its design.

"It's a work of art in itself, something to study and admire, like a sculpture," Mom had often remarked.

I walked in the entrance.

"Why, Ellie," said the volunteer selling tickets, "how nice to see you after all this time."

"Hi, Mrs. Wade."

She leaned over the desk and whispered, "How's your mother doing?"

"Okay. She's at Piedmont this morning. I'm going over in a little while to be with her. You know, during the chemo."

Mrs. Wade smiled sympathetically. "You give her my best. Tell her my ladies' circle at St. Philip's is praying for her."

"I'll do that," I mumbled, my throat suddenly dry.

I walked into the open, airy atrium with the skylight that let in the sun and started up the winding ramp to the second floor, where paintings by both my mother and my grandmother hung. I stared at a self-portrait by my grandmother, Sheila Middleton. She was dressed in a red satin gown, showing off her slender figure at the age of thirty-eight. She held a palette in one hand, and her jade green eyes were somber behind their thick dark lashes. Her auburn hair was swept up in a French chignon. A smile played on her face, but it didn't seem genuine. She looked more aloof or disturbed than happy.

"Your grandmother painted that during the last year of her life, after she'd discovered some things about herself," Mom had told me once. What did that mean?

Beside Grandmom's portrait was a plaque: *Sheila McKenzie Middleton (1924–1962)* and below that were the following framed paragraphs:

> *Sheila McKenzie Middleton, well-known Atlanta portrait painter, perished in the tragic Orly plane crash June 3, 1962. The three paintings displayed here reflect the great diversity of style for which Mrs. Middleton became known posthumously.*

Mrs. Middleton was one of the first Georgian artists to experiment with the concept of art therapy as a way to help in mental illness. Other paintings by the artist may be viewed at a private gallery at Resthaven, a sanitarium in the North Georgia mountains, and at Mt. Carmel Church in the Grant Park section of Atlanta.

I examined the painting called *Joie de Vivre*. It was a landscape painting of an Italian-inspired villa, the Swan House, which was now a famous historical site, located right next door to my grandparents' home and part of the Atlanta History Center. The next painting, *Spring Bouquet*, showed the stately old redbrick mansion called Resthaven. My grandmother had spent quite a bit of time there as a patient.

The last painting was one I have always loved. It showed my mother, Mary Swan, when she was just four or five, swinging on a tree swing behind my grandparents' house. Mom's naked toes are thrust forward in a way that makes it seem they will punch through the canvas as she leans back in the swing. She looks delighted.

Next was my mother's collection: *Mary Swan Middleton (1946-)*. Mom kept her maiden name professionally, though she'd been married to Daddy for almost thirty years.

Daughter of artist Sheila Middleton, Mary Swan Middleton graduated from Hollins College in 1968 with a degree in Fine Arts. She is best known for her bright provincial colors and her habit of painting symbolism into everyday scenes.

The first painting displayed here, Mai '68, *was painted during the student uprising in France in May 1968. . . .*

I was not an artist. At all. There wasn't an ounce of creativity in my bones.

The painting I wanted to examine was the one called *The Dwelling Place*. I was supposed to go with Mom to the field where it was painted, in Scotland, later in the summer. I'd heard a few bits and pieces about Mom's 1968 European trip, the one she never really finished.

Something about riots in Paris and drugs in Amsterdam and self-discovery in Scotland, but a feeling inside told me I hadn't heard the entire story.

The Dwelling Place was a bit strange as paintings go. I guess you'd call it a landscape. It showed grassy, rolling hills in the background and a deep blue sky, and you could tell it was late fall by the leaves on the ground. The main subject of the painting was a low stone wall that ran from the upper left of the canvas down to the center right edge. Mom could explain the whole technique of the way the stones were stacked, with no plaster or cement or whatever, but that didn't interest me.

What I liked best about the painting was the lamb in the far right-hand top corner. Its head was cocked, like a spaniel's, looking toward something in the foreground. The lamb was small in comparison with the whole painting, but Mom painted it in detail, with its legs stiff and braced outward and a surprised or maybe frightened expression on its tiny face; I couldn't tell. It was looking in the direction of the bottom left-hand corner of the painting, where there was part of what seemed to be a brown-and-white ear. It could have belonged to a dog or a cow or another sheep. As I said, it was a strange painting. Still, it intrigued me.

I guess I should have asked Mom to tell me the story behind it, but the truth was I didn't want to know. And of all the people in the world I could go to Europe with, my mother was absolutely the last one I would choose.

I found myself speeding back down Peachtree at 10:28, determined to keep my promise to Abbie. I reached Mom's room by 10:36, out of breath, and hurried inside. Mom was in one bed, and a woman who looked about sixty was in the other.

"Well, here they are, Mom," I said, placing the sketch pads on her lap.

She took the sketch pads and looked at them. No, she caressed them, lovingly, her eyes filling with tears. "What a nice way to pass the next few hours, since I've got to be here anyway."

"Here" was in room number 532 in the cancer ward of Piedmont Hospital. She'd already had seven rounds of chemo. Her hair all fell out after the second. Now a stylish wig, blunt cut, brown with red highlights, sat on a stand by her bed. I had to admit that it looked a lot like Mom's real hair.

But she didn't like to wear the wig, especially when it was muggy outside, so Abbie had bought her a beautiful green scarf made specifically for cancer patients. The green almost matched her jade eyes. She looked dignified, almost, sitting up in the hospital bed with her scarf on. She was wearing a pair of white Capri pants and a hot pink summer sweater. Day patients didn't have to wear the white gowns. Except for the dark circles under her eyes and her weight loss, she looked pretty great, considering what she'd been through.

Mom had breast cancer. It was discovered in a routine mammogram, and she'd had a double mastectomy six months ago.

Her eyes were twinkling. "So nice of you to come, sweetie. You look good. I believe you've lost a few pounds since the last time I saw you."

"Wishful thinking, Mom, but thanks." The words came out more harshly than I intended.

Her smile never faltered. "Well, let's get on with it, then. Start with the first one—your grandmom Sheila's."

This was how Abbie had decided I should get through the last round of chemo with Mom—planning our trip to Europe by going through my grandmother's sketch pad from her trip to Europe in 1962 and Mom's sketch pad from her journey in 1968.

A nurse came in, and we exchanged greetings.

When the nurse inserted the needle, Mom winced a little, smiled, and kept her eyes on me. "Thank goodness your father isn't here now. He'd faint."

We had a dozen family stories about my six-foot-tall father, who often fainted at the sight of a needle. Like the time when Mom was eight months pregnant with me and the obstetrician stuck her ear to see how her blood coagulated. Suddenly the doctor looked past her and said, "Do you need to lie down?"

Mom turned to see Daddy sink to the ground, head in his hands. Then, as she told it, she had to get off the examining table, which was no small feat, and stand there half naked while Daddy lay down.

"I told him not to come today. The last time his face turned an awful greenish yellow while he was sitting right next to me, just as you are, and patting my hand." She smiled. "I told him to play nine holes of golf with Uncle Jimmy after he finishes at the office. I should be home by then."

There was a knock on the door. "Come in," Mom sang out as if she were getting a manicure at the day spa.

The door opened and Rachel Abrams swept into the room.

"Rachel!" Mom exclaimed. "What in the world are you doing here?"

"I wasn't about to miss the party," Rachel replied, her blue-gray eyes flashing mischief. Rachel was Mom's best friend and had been for her whole life. But she lived in New York.

"You have enough things going on without hopping down to Atlanta for my chemo," Mom chided, but I could tell she was thrilled.

Rachel picked up a sketch pad. "I see you brought your work with you. Planning on staying awhile?"

Mom stuck out her tongue, and I suppressed a smile. They acted like teenagers when they were together, these two fifty-six-year-old women. Rachel was still downright beautiful, with soft gray highlights in her shoulder-length blond hair. She wore a pale blue summer suit that showed off her slim figure.

"Ready for treats? I made a quick stop by Publix on the way over." She opened a big Saks Fifth Avenue paper bag, the kind with handles, and plucked out a pint-sized carton of Midnight Cookies and Cream, Mom's favorite flavor.

"Rachel! You shouldn't have wasted the money on it. You know everything tastes like tin to me."

Rachel was undeterred. Producing a plastic spoon, she instructed, "Try it. You'll like it!" Just as Mom was about to take the spoon from her, Rachel shook her head. "Un-uh! You have to answer a question first."

Mom's eyes lit up. "Fire away!"

"Very well, my dear, who said this? 'I love you with so much of my heart that none is left to protest.'"

"Who could ever forget that line? Beatrice to Benedick in *Much Ado*."

It was part of their friendship, throwing out obscure quotes from poems and plays they had memorized in high school. I was only twenty, and I couldn't remember a thing I learned in high school.

"Okay, you've earned it," Rachel acquiesced. She perched on the edge of Mom's bed, removed the top of the carton, and began to feed my mother ice cream.

"Delicious," Mom moaned, closing her eyes. "I can actually taste it. Of course, I'll need to try some more in a few days just to compare how my taste buds work during and after chemo."

Once again Rachel's hand went into the bag from Saks. This time she pulled out a flute case. She opened it and put together her shining sterling silver open-holed Haynes flute. She played a few quick scales before the nurse, looking uncomfortable, whispered, "I'm afraid you can't do that. It may disturb the other patient."

"Oh, let her play," the other woman said. "I'd enjoy it. My niece plays in her high school band."

The nurse shrugged, and Rachel stood and began playing Bach's familiar "Jesu, Joy of Man's Desiring." I'd heard her play it before—at a wedding and at a funeral.

Mom's eyes misted over, and she brushed away a tear. "Really, Rachel, you're too much." Then she closed her eyes and rested back on her pillow as the smooth vibrato from Rachel's flute filled up the room and the corridors of the cancer unit.

As Rachel played, I stared at the chemo slowly dripping into Mom's veins from a plastic pouch suspended from a metal bar overhead.

We all clapped—even the nurse—after Rachel finished. She replaced the flute in its case.

"Marvelous. It means the world to me to have you here," Mom said, reaching out and patting her friend's hand.

"I've got to get you well. Remember that I've already commissioned you to paint my first grandbaby's portrait, if either Ben or Virginia ever decides to get married and have kids."

"I'll paint it—free of charge. *Good price for good friend*," Mom said in a thick, unidentifiable accent. "I'll paint it if it's the last thing I do."

I don't think she meant it to come out that way. I shot Rachel a fearful look.

Rachel didn't miss a beat. "Well, it certainly won't be the last thing you do, silly scatterbrained girl! I'm planning on my kids producing lots of babies in the next few years." She smoothly changed the subject. "So what's with the sketch pads?"

"I've told you. Ellie and I are going to finish the trip that you and I started. Following the sketch pad—Mama's sketch pad. And mine too." Mom's voice was intense.

"Perfect idea, Swannee." Rachel winked at me. She lifted my mother's sketch pad off of Mom's lap and started flipping through it. She found a sketch and held it up triumphantly. "May 1968."

It was a drawing of the Eiffel Tower. Well, sort of. The Eiffel Tower was in the background, rather small. In the foreground was the carcass of a burnt-out car and about a thousand empty crates strewn along the Seine.

"Strikes! Strikes all over Paris!" This Rachel directed to me. "And riots. Wild riots of crazed students. Hundreds of thousands of students." She flipped to the next sketch, and indeed, the page was covered with Mom's feverish sketching of complete chaos. A street filled with men and women, police, overturned cars, people watching and shouting from apartment windows. Smoke in the air.

I scooted my chair closer to the bed so that I could really see the sketch, secretly thankful that Rachel had preempted my role of *getting Mom through chemo*.

"You're looking good," Rachel said to me a few minutes later. "I like the haircut and highlights. I especially like the diamond in your eyebrow." She winked at me.

I rolled my eyes at her. I was far from "looking good," even with the pierced eyebrow and the tattoo on my shoulder. I was five-seven and a half and weighed one sixty-five. Mom and Rachel—they looked great. I mean sleek, together, manicured—and thin. Thin. For goodness' sake, Mom had cancer, and she looked a lot better than I did.

"Well, they've fixed you up just fine," Rachel was saying to her. "Never again can we call you flat-chested."

"Just think, puberty at fifty-six!" Mom joked. "I could make a mint in the tabloids."

"You deserve to look great, Swan, after what you've been through."

Mom looked away, then reached for Rachel's hand and smiled. "Dr. Stern told me he'd make my breasts any size I wanted. I think he did a fine job."

"He certainly did. Pretty soon we'll be calling you Dolly Parton." They giggled like schoolgirls.

I wanted to hug Rachel for knowing all the right things to say to Mom. I, on the other hand, had a knack for saying the wrong thing.

"So you're going to Europe," Rachel said to me.

I nodded. "Yep. If the doctor says it's okay." There I went, saying the wrong thing.

"It'll be okay," Mom said.

I felt awkward again and asked suddenly, "Rachel, why don't you come too?"

Rachel laughed. "We almost killed each other on our first European tour, your mom and I."

"That's for sure," Mom agreed. "But things got better eventually."

"Remember our first day in Florence?" Rachel asked.

"The Piazza della Signoria—my first glimpse of male anatomy!"

They laughed happily.

"I really was hoping it'd be just you and me, Ellie."

I could feel my face go red. "That'll be great, Mom, if I can get off work. It's not that easy, you know."

Mom's eyes were sad for a moment. "I know, dear."

I felt so defensive, even though all Mom had in her eyes was compassion. I didn't want her compassion.

"Jamal is on vacation in late July, and Jasmine has asked for the last two weeks in August. Which means I'd have to take off in early August. And only for two weeks."

"Are you still waiting tables at that trendy little restaurant downtown?" Rachel asked.

"Yeah. Jeremy's."

"That's right. Jeremy's." Rachel laughed. "Jamal and Jasmine work with you at Jeremy's. I'm surprised you didn't have to change your name to Jennifer. But surely you can get some time off, Ellie. I'd think there'd be a passel of kids wanting to work the late shift at one of Atlanta's downtown restaurants."

"The restaurant is okay," Mom offered. "I mean, the clientele is a little different. . . ."

"She means the kids who hang out there have blue hair and pierced navels—which they enjoy showing off. We cater to the dotcom crowd—you know, the brats in their twenties who became millionaires overnight."

"They're fine, Ellie. I'm not criticizing the clientele. It's just that it's not the safest part of town. Remember the murder down there last year. Your dad and I worry, especially when you have the late-night shift."

"Which is five nights a week during the summer," I informed Rachel casually.

"Lovely," Rachel said. "Don't you think it might be wise to investigate another line of work?"

Mom switched sides and came to my rescue. "Oh, now, Rach. Didn't I tell you that Ellie's back in school at Georgia State? She's got a 4.0 grade point average from the past three trimesters. She's planning to go to vet school."

"Well, now, that's good news. When did you decide on that?"

"Whenever," I said, rolling my eyes again. "Sometime this year."

"I'm thrilled to hear it. You'll make a great vet, Ellie! You certainly have experience from all those strays you guys always had around the house. I remember you nursing Mr. Boots back to health when you were just a little kid. And then who was it? Dilly?"

"Daisy."

"Daisy. Poor dog. You and Trixie always had a knack for picking out the ones at the Humane Society who were at death's door."

"And they all lived," I added proudly.

"Exactly. You were born to be a vet."

"I've gotta get home," I said, feeling relieved when the nurse told Mom she was free to leave.

"Oh no you don't, kid!" Rachel said, grabbing me by the wrist. "You and I are taking your mother out for lunch."

"Lunch?" I scrunched up my nose.

"All food tastes like tin, I've told you," Mom protested.

"We're going to the Swan Coach House for lunch, and that's that! No ifs, ands, or buts about it." Rachel glanced at her watch. "Trixie reserved a table and is already waiting for us."

The Swan Coach House is a ladies' restaurant in Buckhead, a ritzy neighborhood in the northwest part of Atlanta. Back in the early 1900s the Coach House was the carriage house for the mansion that was called the Swan House. When the mansion was turned into a historical site in the sixties, the carriage house was transformed into a restaurant, gift shop, and art gallery.

I had begun my "wait staff career" at the Coach House a few years ago. It was a family joke that while Mom was painting the real Swan House and getting paid a bundle for it, I was eking out my living off the tips of the penny-pinching rich of Buckhead.

"Remember that time that Daddy and Uncle Jimmy came to eat with us, and they didn't have on coats? The restaurant made them wear those awful sports jackets from the fifties that they keep on hand just in case!" Mom said, almost giggling again. "Jimmy's sleeves only went down to his elbows."

"And the time the lady came over for your autograph, Swannee, and asked you to sketch a swan on her napkin?" Rachel added. "And you did, but it turned out that there was a stain on the napkin right under the swan's tail, so it looked like your swan had peed all over it."

They were laughing so happily that I volunteered, "Or my first day on the job, when I spilled six strawberry daiquiris! It's a wonder they kept me."

I could still see myself, awkward in my new polyester uniform, bending too far over the table, desperately trying to balance the tray of iced drinks in my left hand. Suddenly the frosted glasses began slipping, and before I could grab the tray with my right hand, they crashed onto the table and spilled all over the startled guests.

When we got to the Coach House—Mom rode with Rachel, and I followed in my car—I saw Trixie waiting inside. Trixie was my grandmother. Well, actually my step-grandmother. She was almost eighty, and today she was dressed in a red-and-white polka-dotted suit with a red hat and matching polka-dotted French-style shoes. She was tiny and elegant, and she was chewing gum. Ever since it became gauche to smoke, Trixie had been trying to stop. She wore a nicotine patch and chewed gum and carried a bag of plain M&Ms in her purse, "in case I get a craving."

"Well, here's a sight for sore eyes!" she exclaimed brightly.

That sentence comprised about twenty syllables with her long, lazy, and delicious Southern drawl. It was becoming a lost art in Atlanta, and I always loved to hear it.

"Ellie, what a treat to see you, sweetie." She turned to Rachel. "I see you made it down here just fine, Rachel. You're looking very New Yorkish. And Swannee, dear, what a lovely scarf! It is just your color."

"Isn't it, though?" Mom laughed. "I like it, even if my roommate at the cancer ward this morning said it was the same color as her daughter's bridesmaid dresses—she called it 'baby diarrhea.'"

The three of them started laughing again, and then, amazingly, I joined in. The other prim-and-proper ladies who were waiting for tables stared at us with disapproving glances.

But it felt good.

I liked eating at the Coach House, even though it wasn't a thing like my typical hangouts. The walls in the main dining room were covered with beautiful material—splashes of bright pink and purple and red and orange flowers—giving the restaurant a happy, feminine atmosphere. I liked the food there too, even though I'd eaten the "Swan Special" probably a thousand times.

"Girls," Rachel said in a mock Southern drawl, "what'll it be? How 'bout the Swan Special? Two of those little pastry timbales full of our homemade chicken salad with those delicious cheese straws and the mouthwatering frozen fruit salad."

"That's what I'm having. No doubt about it," Trixie said, smacking her gum.

Mom was looking over the menu that she knew by heart. "Oh, I suppose I'll have it too. No sense trying something new, since—"

"Everything tastes like tin," Rachel chimed in.

"Exactly."

It was near the end of the meal, when we'd finished our frozen fruit salad and timbales full of chicken salad and munched on the cheese straws, except for Mom, who really *didn't* feel like eating and had left most of the food on her plate, that Trixie asked, "So this was the last round of chemo. What did the doctor say, Swannee?"

"He wants to see me in three weeks. He knows I'm planning to leave for Europe with Ellie sometime in August." Mom gave me a loving glance.

"Well, that's just marvelous!" Trixie said, reaching into her purse for another piece of gum. She popped the gum into her mouth and then pulled out a cell phone from her red polka-dotted purse. "I guess I'd better call Thomas." She held the phone close to her face, squinting behind her glasses to read the numbers, and punched it enthusiastically. Trixie had always believed in keeping up with the times.

"Thomas, yes, dear, be a love and come pick me up now. Yes, I'll meet you out front."

Trixie used to walk home from lunch at the Coach House. Now she had Thomas on call. He was my grandparents' handyman, as Trixie called him. He was twenty-six and had run his own carpentry business for three years before he decided he wanted to get his master's degree at Georgia Tech. So he went back to school and hired himself out to help Trixie and Granddad JJ with driving and "general upkeep"—another of Trixie's favorite expressions.

"Do you want to come by for a while, Swannee?" Trixie asked. "Your father would love to see you."

My granddad was eighty and could no longer drive. He did play golf, sort of. He got out his putter and practiced in the office of his big home on Andrews Drive, which was only a three-minute ride away.

Mom readjusted her wig. "Sure, Trix. I might just take a little nap on the sunporch if you don't mind."

"Absolutely marvelous! Well, we'd better get out front. Thomas will be here in no time. Drives like a maniac," she whispered, glancing over her glasses. "Be careful at that job of yours, Ellie. You know it makes me a nervous wreck with all the crime in that area—and the murder last year." She gave me a kiss on the cheek. "Lovely to see you again, Rachel. Will you be staying in Atlanta for a while?"

"A few days. I'll drop by for a visit. I'm at my parents'."

"I'll count on that."

After Mom and Trixie left, Rachel and I browsed in the Coach House gift shop. It was filled with tasteful china, all kinds of silver accessories, cookbooks with Southern recipes, packages of bright floral paper napkins, pretty soaps and lotions for the bath, and baby clothes that cost a fortune.

"When's Abbie's baby due?"

"September."

"And Nan's?"

"Oh, not until January, I think."

"I should pick out something for Abbie's baby while I'm here. Aren't these just adorable? The smocked rabbits and all? Does your sister know what she's having?"

"Another boy. Sixteen months apart. She's crazy."

Rachel purchased a smocked outfit for some outlandish price. Then she laced her arm through mine. "What are you up to now? Feel like a stroll in the garden?"

I shrugged. "If you want. I need to get home soon, though. I start work at four."

We walked down the driveway toward the Swan House, which appeared as if from another century, serenely standing among the oaks and hickories and tall magnolia trees. It was an "Italian manor house" or something like that. The inside was rather impressive, but I preferred the grounds around the mansion.

Thick woods with lots of walking paths lay to the west. Trixie and Granddad JJ's house was on the other side of the thick foliage. Rachel and I walked past a path leading to the "Victorian playhouse" into the boxwood garden next to the Swan House's screened-in porch.

"You doing okay, kid?" Rachel asked.

"Fine," I said curtly. "Great. Promise."

"That does *not* sound convincing."

"Oh, Rachel, don't worry about it."

She pulled a lipstick out of her purse and began painting her lips a subtle shade of peach, which perfectly matched her fingernails. "Are you excited about the trip?"

"I guess."

She patted my hand. "Not really, huh?"

"No, not really."

"And why is that?" We sat on the stone bench in the garden.

"I can think of fifty other people I'd rather see Europe with than Mom."

Rachel crossed her arms over her chest and leaned forward. "What makes you say that?"

"You know how different we are. Her life is too perfect. I can't relate."

Rachel narrowed her eyes. "Perfect? Perfect, did you say? Excuse me, but what do you know about your mother's life?"

I found the remark a bit odd, but Rachel was looking at me intensely, almost angrily, so I complied. "She's very happily married, she's pretty, she has enough money, she's a famous artist. She travels a lot, and her husband is madly in love with her. She has great friends. And two of her kids turned out perfect too."

"I see." She replaced the lipstick.

I got up and walked away, but Rachel followed.

"Your mother needs you, Ellie."

I looked at her defiantly. "Oh, Rachel. Needs me for what? You know all the crud Mom and I have been through. Life is better when I just stay away from her—I know everything I need to know about her life."

"I don't think you do."

I met her eyes. "What do you mean?"

"I think deep inside, you'd like to know a lot more about your mother's 'perfect life.' You want to know how she did it—how she held herself together and became a respectable, peaceful woman, a blessing to society. Because to tell you the truth, I don't know anyone who's had a harder life. But she isn't complaining, not even with cancer eating up her body." Rachel's voice dropped to a whisper. "There's a lot you don't know about your mother, kid. Or a lot you've chosen to ignore."

I started to protest, but Rachel cut me off.

"I wouldn't wait too long, Ellie. You may not have a whole lot of time left."

Chapter 2

All down the hills of Habersham,
All through the valleys of Hall,
The rushes cried "Abide, abide,"
The willful waterweeds held me thrall,
The laving laurel turned my tide,
The ferns and the fondling grass said "Stay."

—SIDNEY LANIER,
SONG OF THE CHATTAHOOCHEE

Rachel's words were playing in my mind when I got back from Jeremy's after one-thirty, and I woke up with them still echoing in my head. It was after noon when I struggled out of bed, went to the bathroom, threw some water on my face, and grabbed a Coke from the refrigerator. I turned on my laptop, which was sitting on the kitchen counter, went to the sports page of the *Atlanta Journal* on the Net, and checked the score from the Braves game the previous night.

The screen proclaimed a Braves victory over the Mets: 6–3. "Good job, guys," I said. Hindsight perched beside me, and I scratched her under the neck.

Okay, I thought, searching through a cabinet for something to eat, *supposing Rachel is right, how do I get to know my mom?*

I selected an opened bag of Cheetos and shuffled the four steps from my kitchen into the den, where the sketch pads were now lying on the floor. I plopped down next to them and picked up Grandmom Sheila's.

First there was Paris—the Seine River, the Eiffel Tower, the Louvre, Notre Dame Cathedral. Then came Rome and Florence and Amsterdam and other great cities—all set in the midst of flowering trees and blooming gardens and spraying fountains. I could almost smell springtime on the paper. Happiness flowed through page after page of Europe, old Europe mixed with little hints of humor for which my grandmother later became known.

"Grandmom Sheila, bless her tormented soul, was happy when she sketched these," I concluded, closing the pad with the last picture of Versailles.

In contrast, I felt an immediate heaviness when I studied Mom's sketches of a city in turmoil. "You know the French and their revolutions," she had laughingly explained yesterday at the hospital. I didn't have the heart to tell her that I had slept through most of my history classes in high school.

Mom's first sketches were done in Paris. There were the same familiar monuments, but they were all but camouflaged by the action in the foreground. Overturned crates, burnt-out cars, streets jammed with screaming students, air filled with smoke. In one sketch Mom had written *Sorbonne University* at the bottom. The great learning institution was plastered with graffiti, and crowds of students were milling around the courtyard.

My grandmom had felt peaceful on her European tour, I concluded, but my mother had been a bundle of nerves. Even the sketch she had drawn from an apartment building looking out on the Arc de Triomphe at night portrayed menacing figures in the shadows.

Ironic. Life is ironic. Grandmom sketched serenity, but her life ended in tragedy only hours after her last sketch was created. And

Mom's sketches of turmoil had led her to a simple, peaceful life.

I was still on the floor in my pj's, examining the two sketch pads and eating Cheetos carefully, licking my fingers clean of orange powder before I touched a page, when I heard rapping on my door.

"Coming!" I yelled.

I looked through the peephole and saw Rachel, dressed to the hilt, looking like a model for *Vogue*. I drew back the deadbolt and opened the door.

"Well, you're up early today," she said with a grin.

"Give me a break. I got in at two."

"Break granted. I just left your mom's and thought I'd look you up." She peered into my bedroom, then walked into the miniscule kitchen and back out into what I called my "great room." There was nothing great about it, but it did serve as dining room, den, and study. "So this is your place. Not bad."

The whole apartment was a wreck at that moment.

"How's Mom doing today?"

"You should call her and ask," Rachel suggested. "Apparently, the nausea lasted all through the night, and she's got the beginnings of a cold. I offered to stay over, but your dad insisted he could take care of her. Still as protective of his Swan as ever."

There was a little sarcasm in her voice, but Rachel didn't fool me. She was crazy about Daddy. She thought it was *quaint*—I think that's the word she always used—that he treated Mom so well.

"But she looked better this morning. Had a little color back."

Rachel started rearranging some picture frames on a table beside my couch. Then she looked out the window. "You know, you have a great little spot here, a stone's throw from Piedmont Park. You should fix it up. Paint the walls something besides this depressing shade of tan. Get some real curtains."

I shrugged. "I'm not into home improvement—especially when I'm just renting."

"Yeah, I understand. This whole complex needs renovating—someone should follow the lead of the apartments just down the street on Argonne. They're redbrick too, but they look great."

Hindsight came into the room and wrapped herself around Rachel's legs, weaving in and out, tail held high.

"Nice cat," Rachel muttered, petting her, still looking out the window.

"She's a Himalayan Persian." I sat back down on the floor, where I'd left my Coke and Cheetos, and flipped to another page in Mom's sketch pad.

"When I left your mother, she had a new pad propped up so she could draw in bed. She is such a scatterbrained girl sometimes. She had all her charcoal pencils out—on the white comforter!—and then she spilled her cup of tea on the sketch pad. We got to laughing so hard she almost dropped her tomato and mayonnaise sandwich too—" Rachel turned from the window and glanced down at me. "What are you doing?"

It sounded like an accusation.

"What you told me to. Getting to know my mother. I thought I'd start by examining these." I said it in a joking tone, but Rachel didn't smile. "What's with you, Rachel? You look like you've seen a ghost."

"I have," she whispered and knelt down beside me. She fingered the sketch pads carefully. "Forgive me, Ellie. It's just that I found your mother doing the same thing so many times in her art studio. It's how everything started—searching through your grandmother's sketch pads. It's as though I'm watching your mom all over again.

"We used to sit on the floor in the *atelier* at your grandparents' house and look through your grandmom's sketch pads and plan our trip to Europe," she sighed. "And then we went, and Swan lugged these darned sketch pads all over the place. Made me so mad! She was so stubborn, so absolutely sure she was going to visit every last spot your grandmom had sketched and make sketches of her own." She turned to me with a forlorn expression on her face. "And I was so awful to her on that trip. . . ."

"Awful? You?"

"Awful. Me."

"That's hard to believe. Although I can tell just by looking at Mom's sketches that she wasn't having the greatest time in Europe."

"You can say that again. We were two messed-up kids."

I could tell there was a lot of emotion behind her last comment, but she didn't elaborate. She simply gave another long sigh, brushed what was surely a tear from one eye, and said, "I sure do love that mom of yours." Then she asked, "Do you have any idea how much she loves you?"

I gave her an exasperated sigh and said, "All mothers love their children, Rachel. Except the really psycho ones." I closed the sketch pad. "But that doesn't stop her from trying to change me. She's trying to brainwash my emotions so I'll see things the way she does."

Rachel looked hurt. "Do you really believe that, Ellie?"

"Yes!" I said more strongly than I felt. "You know how Mom and Dad are—so religious. So sure God Almighty is working everything out in their lives for good. They succeeded in brainwashing Abbie and Nan. Why can't they be content with two out of three?"

"Brainwashing is a pretty strong word, kid."

I sighed, conceding. "Okay, so it's not brainwashing. I still say they want their daughters to toe the line. Me in particular. Mom wants to convert me to her way of seeing life."

"I think you've got it all wrong."

I didn't answer. I went to my tiny kitchen and grabbed a doughnut. "Do you mind leaving me for now, Rachel? I'm really tired."

She came over and gave me a stiff hug. "Sure, Ellie. Hang in there, kid. If you need anything, I'll be staying in Atlanta for a few more days."

"Yeah, well, maybe. Bye."

When she left, I shut the door, locked it, and collapsed on the couch, the one Mom and Dad had given me when I moved here. It was a lot nicer than my other furniture. Its soft, comfortable dark blue leather pleased me.

Hindsight came up to me, meowing in an annoying way. At that moment, I wanted to be completely alone. Not even a cat for company.

I picked up Mom's sketch pad again and stared at the sketches near the back, the ones she had done of the "Dwelling Place" in Scotland. In one sketch, Rachel was sitting on a stone wall and smiling, almost awkwardly, waving at Mom.

"This is the first peaceful sketch you've done, Mom," I said aloud.

I just didn't understand my mother. Rachel had helped her live her dream in 1968—following her mother's sketchbook around Europe. The proof of that trip was right before my eyes. So why did she need to go again? "You got there already, Mom! Leave well enough alone. And for heaven's sake, don't drag me into it!"

The only reason I had agreed to go was because my two sisters were busy with their families, whereas I wasn't even to the dating-a-nice-guy stage. I was at the can't-we-find-a-happy-medium-between-a-singles-group-at-church-and-a-singles-bar stage.

The last date I'd had was with someone Abbie had set me up with. "He's this really nice guy from Bill's office."

I never should have agreed. Whenever someone strings together the words *really nice guy,* you get one of three possible scenarios: weirdo, never married, midforties, and still living with his mother; divorced and desperate for a wife; or Dr. Jekyll and Mr. Hyde—nice guy at work, maybe even goes to church, porno king at home.

Believe me, I had seen all three types. I preferred the straightforward beer guzzler who was up front with what he was after. Anyway, I hadn't had a lot of luck with men lately, and my sisters had been no help at all. Abbie's "really nice guy" got really drunk and really scared me to death driving me home from a really weird restaurant. I never told her.

But anyway, the sisters were occupied, and Daddy had health problems, which meant he couldn't travel. So I was elected. And we couldn't put it off any longer.

I stretched out on the couch with Hindsight curled beside me, grabbed the remote, and flipped on the TV. The Braves were playing at two. Now baseball, that was something I could get into. I played on a women's softball team, the Panthers. Catcher. We went to the regional championships last year.

When I glanced at the clock much later, it showed the time as 3:30. I cursed out loud. Hindsight jumped out of my lap, surprised.

"It's okay, girl. Nothing big. It's just I don't want to be late for work." *Again.*

I put on my uniform. One good thing about my job: for all the trendiness of Jeremy's, the uniform was very basic. No tight-fitting miniskirt, like so many places around. All servers, men and women alike, wore black pants with a white shirt and a bright green jacket.

I pulled my long hair back into a ponytail, watching my reflection in the mirror. Rachel had said she liked my highlights. They did look pretty good with my thick strawberry-blond hair. But they couldn't change the fact of my face, which, in spite of numerous plastic surgeries, was still the first thing anyone noticed about me. My mouth turned down on the left side, and when I spoke, people had to concentrate a little to understand me. And the skin by my mouth was red and unnaturally smooth from the skin grafts.

I used to be a beautiful little girl. Blondish red hair curling all over my head and the brightest green eyes anyone could imagine. I could say that, because now I was so very far from beautiful. People looked at me, looked away, looked back and stared, and then got this disturbed kind of expression on their faces. It all happened in the course of a few seconds. I was so used to it, I hardly noticed. Hardly.

Before I left the apartment, I dialed Mom and Dad's number. I was relieved to hear the answering machine after the fourth ring.

"Hey, Mom and Daddy. Just calling to check on you. Hope you're feeling okay, Mom. I'll talk to you soon. I work the late shift tonight."

There. Now they wouldn't be tempted to call me or expect to hear back from me tonight. Maybe tomorrow.

By one-thirty I was about to fall asleep on my feet, and I thought if one more person walked through the door of the restaurant, I'd scream. But in spite of my fatigue, I didn't want to go back to my apartment, where there was nothing to greet me except a cat and the sketch pads. I deserved a good time.

I knew I shouldn't have gone there, to this upbeat singles bar with Jamal and his buddies. I was supposed to stay away from bars—or more precisely, as I had learned in rehab, from "potentially compromising situations involving alcohol or narcotics."

But Jamal was a nice guy. I trusted him.

"Want a joint?" offered Eddie, who worked the weekend shift with us.

I shrugged and shook my head

"What's gotten into you, girl?" he muttered.

"Ellie's cool. Leave her alone," Jamal fired back.

I liked the way Jamal was protective of me. He was six-foot-three and probably weighed close to three hundred pounds. Most of it muscle. But on this night, I noticed how his dark skin glowed with perspiration, and I wished he would stop drinking.

As the night wore on, I began to get fidgety. Jamal was stoned. So were all of his buddies. And there was a voice in my head just screaming at me to get out of there.

I ignored it.

"What's up, Jamal?"

I'd never seen the young man who stopped by the table. He was laughing, his eyes red, tattoos covering every unclothed part of his body.

"Doin' all right, Masta'. Don't you be messin' with me none." Jamal punched Masta' and they high-fived each other.

"See you're out with all the boys. Ain't got no lady friends around?" Masta' taunted.

I felt my face go red, then white.

"You ain't got eyes, boy? This here's Ellie." Without consulting me, Jamal pulled off my baseball cap so that my long hair fell down loose.

Masta' looked me over slowly. It was always the same when someone first met me. A quick glance, then an embarrassed look away, then a stare. "How ya doin', Ellie?"

I forced a smile, but inside I was feeling misery and anger and fear.

"Well, you boys *and* girl wanna come kick back wit' me at the crib?" Masta' continued, looking right at me.

"Sho' nuf. What kind of stuff you got 'round?" Eddie asked.

"Crack, X, and some real fly honeys."

"Cool, I'm wit' that," Eddie said with a whistle, and several of them stood.

I didn't budge.

Jamal leaned over to me and slurred, "Come on, Ellie girl. Have us a little fun."

"No thanks!"

Then Jamal did something he had never done before. He put his arms around my waist and pulled me to him, touching under my blouse.

I pushed his hand away and said, "I'm going home. Y'all go on and have fun."

But Jamal put his arms all over me and started kissing me on the neck. "Come on, Ellie. A little fun for your buddy?"

I pushed free of his arms and yelled, "Leave me alone, Jamal! I thought we were friends."

And with my heart beating wildly, I ran to my car, without knowing if I'd paid for my drinks, without looking behind me. I drove away, cursing Jamal at the top of my lungs.

I knew exactly where I was going—to Megan's apartment.

"Ellie! What's up? Come on in," Megan said, rubbing her eyes.

"I know it's the middle of the night—"

"You look awful!" She peered closer. "Have you been drinking? Shooting up?"

Megan knew everything about me. She was the one and only person who really knew. And she cared. She was the closest friend I'd ever had, and we were both trying to recover from hard things.

"No, I just had a Coke. But I was out with Jamal and a bunch of his friends, and he . . . he got stoned and started coming on to me."

"Oh, Ellie. Get real, girl. Jamal's not the right guy for you."

"He didn't mean it. He was stoned. It just scared me. That's all. It reminded me of that other night."

That was all I had to say, and Megan understood. "The night we ruined our lives" was the way we put it.

"Who's there, Megan?" I heard Timothy's sleepy voice from upstairs.

"Just Ellie. Go back to sleep."

"What's up, Ellie? Something wrong at work?"

"She's fine, Timothy. Go back to sleep."

I liked the way Megan's face lit up when she was talking to Timothy. I liked to see life in her eyes.

She turned back to me. "Do you wanna talk?"

"No, I wouldn't make any sense. There's too much in my mind right now."

She gave me a smile. "There's always too much in your mind, girl.

If I had a mind like yours, I don't know how I would stop it long enough to get some sleep."

"Am I a freak, Megan?"

"I thought you didn't want to talk." She shrugged and took my hand. "Why do you always ask me the same question? No, no, no, and a thousand times no! You are Albert Einstein smart and just hiding undercover until it's time for you to make your big splash."

"As a vet."

"As the nearest thing to Dr. Dolittle I can imagine. Now go to bed, girl. The couch is made up from last time."

"Thanks, Megan. You're great, you know."

"Whatever."

"Love you."

"Love you too. Good night."

Megan climbed back upstairs, back to the queen-size bed she shared with Timothy. I went into the downstairs john. My bathroom, we kidded. I kept a toothbrush and a stash of makeup underneath the sink.

I stared into the small mirror and threw water on my face, wishing I could wash away what was looking back at me.

Sometimes it infuriated me the way people looked at me. As if I were dumb. As if, since my mouth curved down on one side, so did my brain, and I couldn't understand things.

One time my uncle Jimmy described how angry and incompetent he felt in Paris when he was trying to speak French. The French got this worried, pained expression on their faces when he would talk, because they couldn't understand what he was saying. He wanted to scream at them and say, "Quit looking at me as if I'm a moron. I swear I'm a fairly intelligent and witty person, if you will only let me speak in English."

When he had said that—it must have been five years ago now—my heart skipped a beat and my face turned red, because that was exactly how I felt with most of the kids in high school. When I spoke, they got a pitiful, confused expression on their faces. Their embarrassed eyes told the plain truth: *Could you please quit talking to us, because you are making us feel uncomfortable. You aren't normal.*

Except Megan. She had never made me feel like that.

Megan was gorgeous. Stop-you-dead-in-your-tracks gorgeous. She had jet-black hair that fell thickly to her shoulders and dark eyes that were the exact color of pure Arabica coffee. Her olive skin made her look as though she had worked on a perfect tan, but she hadn't. Everything about her was natural. No makeup, no sexy clothes. Guys literally followed her around wherever she went.

And she hated it.

Once she said to me, "Ellie, I am so tired of people liking me for my face or my breasts or my hair! It is the absolute worst thing in the world to be out with a guy and see pure lust in his eyes. Drooling over himself trying to make some sort of conversation. I hate it. I'll never meet anyone who looks deeper."

The fact that we were friends showed that Megan knew how to look a lot deeper.

Once in high school we went to see the film *Elephant Man*. I was so thankful that I was with Megan. No one else would have understood my reaction. I think from the very beginning, where this brilliant man was shown locked up like an animal because of his grossly malformed head, I began to bawl. I cried my eyes out during that film. It touched my soul in a way I couldn't explain except to say I understood him. Trapped behind a face.

Granted, my "deformity" wasn't even a hundredth degree of his, nor had I endured a smidgen of the suffering and cruelty that he lived with daily. It seemed presumptuous and selfish to even suggest I could relate to that man, but I could. In my soul, I understood his suffering. I understood the judgment of other people's eyes.

And Megan was so great. During the movie, she periodically squeezed my hand or patted my back, and once we looked at each other, and her face was streaked with tears too.

She didn't say that I was crazy, that I was fine compared to him or that I shouldn't feel that way or that I was selfish. What she did say I will never forget: "It must hurt very badly. I'm so sorry if I have ever contributed to your pain." And then she hugged me.

"Megan, I know it's a small cross to bear compared to other people's problems," I told her one day, soon after we'd seen the movie. "But it feels so heavy. Mom is always telling me about my beautiful soul, but how can I explain the hurt to know that no guy in the whole world will ever want to kiss me? He'll look at my face and my mouth and think I'm hideous."

"Not when it's the right guy, Ellie. Someday we'll each meet a guy who will have different eyes." She said it mournfully but hopefully. "Someday we'll meet someone who looks at the soul. Your mom is right."

But you were wrong, Megan. That's not who we found at all, I thought as I stared in the bathroom mirror. And then I let myself drift back to that other night, the night we ruined our lives. . . .

"Megan, I'm going to James's party tonight. Wanna come along?" I was seventeen, a junior in high school, and this was the first party I'd been invited to.

Megan was unimpressed. "No way, Ellie. James hangs out with all the potheads. You don't want to get into all that."

"Well, then let's you and me do something. There's an old Hitchcock showing at Garden Hills."

Megan looked uncomfortable. "I'd go, I swear, Ellie. But I've got a date."

"Oh. With who?"

"Mick. Mick Anderson."

"That jerk? Why would you go out with him?"

"He's asked me a dozen times. I got tired of giving excuses."

Megan's eyes met mine, and she shrugged.

I felt a terrible foreboding. "Don't go," I begged.

But she did.

And I went to James's party. At first I hung back, away from the rest of the kids. But there was an incredible pressure to smoke pot. No, not pressure. Allure.

"Wanna try it, Ellie?" James asked. He was the only person besides Megan who never seemed to have a problem with my face.

He put his arm around me, and I hardly remember the next few hours. Just a beautiful feeling of floating, of escaping. And laughter. Everyone was laughing. Including me.

And then James kissed me. We were both high and giddy and he pressed his lips on mine and kept them there. At first I tensed. Even in my blurred state, I had not forgotten my mouth. Surely he would draw back, repulsed. But he didn't.

And I discovered a miracle. It felt wonderful. Perhaps my mouth was deformed, but the kiss—I could feel it! I didn't ever want him to stop.

So that was how pot became my friend. Pot, then crack, then the other stuff. When I was high, I fit in. And when James was high, he thought I was sexy. Those first kisses were so intoxicating. They were almost as addictive as the drugs.

I could hardly wait to call Megan the next morning. "Mrs. MacDougall, can I please speak to Megan?"

Her mom hesitated. "I'm sorry, Ellie. She's feeling sick."

"Could I come see her, bring her anything?" I was so excited I was about to burst.

But the moment I walked into Megan's room, the spark fizzled. "Megan, what's the matter? You look awful."

She didn't meet my eyes. She looked lost, or in a trance, or as if someone had reached inside her and stolen her soul.

When her mother left us alone, I climbed onto the bed beside her.

"Oh, Meggie, what is it?" All thoughts of James's kisses had disappeared.

She looked straight ahead and said without expression, "I died last night."

That same foreboding came over me again. "What d'ya mean, Meggie?"

"He killed me. Mick Anderson killed me."

"What did he do? What?" I whispered desperately.

"You don't want to know." Then she buried her head in her hands and began to sob.

I threw my arms around her and cried with her, but she pushed me away. "Don't! I'm dirty. I'm filthy, and nothing will ever wash it away."

I got stoned, and Megan got raped. All in one night. And it was just as Megan had said—she died inside. She started seeing herself only as a thing to be used by boys. She had never wanted that before, but when that awful, cruel thing happened, it sucked all the dignity out of her.

And I watched it happen. I watched her lose hope. And I felt guilty. If only I hadn't gone to the party, maybe I could have convinced her to go to the movies with me instead of going out with that monster.

I guess my "great mind," as Megan called it, helped me get through the prestigious Wellington Prep School without my grades plummeting. But I lost interest in learning, and I didn't care.

Mom and Dad did, of course. They weren't dumb. They saw the changes. But I had a trump card. My deformity. I think they were so relieved that I had a social life of some kind, they didn't ask too many questions.

Oh, I never introduced them to James and the rest of the bunch. They thought I was always hanging out with Megan. And I was, in a way. We were at the same parties, but not really together—each in a separate room with a separate guy. My guy was always James, but Megan never stayed with the same one for long.

I hated myself. I guess it goes to show how parents never really know. Mom and Daddy loved Megan, and they knew her parents pretty well. They trusted us. So when we said we were going to the movies together every Friday night, it was okay by them. Garden Hills was always playing great old flicks that no parent would object to—*The Sound of Music, The Wizard of Oz, North by Northwest*.

I thought I was so clever. And I never would have gotten caught, except for one thing. The cops busted a party during my senior year, and Megan and James and a bunch of other kids and I spent the night in jail. Then several of us were expelled from school.

I will never forget the look of disbelief and shame on Mom's face. Not only did she have a deformed daughter, she now had an expelled-from-school-and-in-drug-rehab deformed daughter.

Mom and Dad forced me to go to a *Christian* rehab center. I think they expected a miracle. Though I hated it at first, I ended up knowing it was the place I needed to be. I stopped doing drugs, but I started gaining weight. Over the past three years I'd put on thirty pounds.

In rehab, there was a girls' softball team, and that saved my life. I smacked so many homers. I was an awfully good catcher too. I felt accepted there, even needed. But after a year, during which I got my GED, well, I had to leave.

Megan didn't have to go to rehab. And she wasn't expelled. She graduated with our class and then she did something pretty brave, I think. Instead of going to college, she moved up east and helped out with her aunt's little kids—kind of like an au pair—and worked part-time in an ad agency. She escaped Atlanta and all those guys. For a year she didn't have one single date, and she was happy. She'd write me at rehab, and I could tell she didn't feel as filthy about herself. The next year, she came back to Atlanta and signed up for classes at Georgia State.

After rehab, I got my apartment in Midtown, with my parents' help, of course, and started waiting tables. And gradually I figured out that I really wanted to be a vet. I guess it was something I had known for a long time, but it took me a while to believe I could actually do it.

I came back to the present, and the same scarred face was still staring back at me in the mirror of Megan's bathroom. I felt so tired. Megan was right. Jamal wasn't good for me. I needed to change jobs.

Jeremy's and softball and school were keeping me plenty busy. I didn't have a lot of time for my family. So why did they have to invade my life right now?

My mind was a jumble. *Mom has cancer*, I thought, *and I'm supposed to go to Europe with her, and Rachel says she hasn't had a perfect life.*

I looked deep into the mirror, into my green eyes, and I watched my mouth move in its awkward way as I whispered out loud, "Well, of course she hasn't had a perfect life, you idiot. She has you for a daughter, doesn't she?"

Chapter 3

The naming of cats is a difficult matter. . . .
When you notice a cat in profound meditation,
The reason, I tell you, is always the same.
His mind is engaged in rapt contemplation
Of the thought, of the thought,
Of the thought of his name. . . .

—T. S. ELIOT, *THE NAMING OF CATS*

It was nearly noon when I got back to my apartment, after spending the rest of the night at Megan's. The phone was ringing as I unlocked the door. I threw my purse down on the couch and picked up the receiver.

"Hello?"

"Hey, Ellie."

It was Jamal, and his voice made my heart skip a beat. "Oh, hi."

"Look, about last night. I'm sorry. Don't know what got into me. . . ."

"I do. You were stoned out of your mind. I'm surprised you even remember what happened. Anyway, don't worry. I learned my lesson. I won't crash your party anymore."

"Ellie . . . come on. I'm sorry. Really."

"Fine. See ya at work." I hung up.

I was always frank; I didn't sugarcoat things like Mom and Nan. Jamal deserved to hear me mad, I argued with myself, secretly hoping that he'd call back. Well, at least I would see him Monday night.

I was concentrating so hard on not caring if the phone rang that it was a minute before I noticed the flashing light on my answering machine. I punched the button and listened to the message. It was from early that morning.

"Mae Mae, it's Dad." That was Daddy's pet name for me, taken from my full name, Ella Mae Middleton Bartholomew.

"We had to take your mother back to the hospital early this morning. Her platelets went way down. They'll be giving her a transfusion in a little while. She's back at Piedmont." He hesitated. "Well, I don't know when you'll get this. See you soon, and . . . and do say a little prayer for your mother."

Daddy's voice sounded tired and crackly, as if he were on the verge of tears. I punched the button to replay the message and grabbed my softball, tossing it in the air as I listened to the recording again.

Daddy always added a little religious phrase at the end, like "say a little prayer" or something. I bristled inside hearing it. I knew I shouldn't have that kind of reaction when Mom was so sick, but it felt like a finger pointing at me. As though I needed to be reminded of my responsibilities.

If Dad had left the message on the answering machine for Abbie or Nan, it would have been completely different, I guarantee it.

Nan—it's Dad. Mom's had a turn for the worse. Bad reaction to the chemo this time and the platelets are dangerously low, so they're going to do a blood transfusion soon. I'm at Piedmont with her. Give a call as soon as you get this. I've called Helen at St. Philip's, and Abbie said she would get the prayer chain at Second Ponce on it right away.

Then he would have sighed.

Honey, just pray that the Lord will have His way. You know your mom. She's not worried; weak, yes, but not too worried. Bless her heart.

A pause.

Thanks, Nan. Love you. The Lord's going to get us through this. You know He always has before.

Bartholomew babble, that's what I called it. Not out loud, of course. Religious babble. That's how my family talked. But they tiptoed around me. They knew I didn't go for all the jargon and "the Lord this" and "the Lord that." Occasionally they slipped into it when I was around, but then they'd go back to the other talk, embarrassed, thinking I wouldn't understand the religious stuff. Which made me feel dumb. And mad. Very mad.

Then the guilt came again. Mom was in the hospital, Daddy had called early this morning to tell me, and I hadn't even given them a sign of life. I changed clothes and washed my face, gave Hindsight a pat, filled up her pan with food and water, and left for the hospital.

Nan and Abbie were there beside Mom's bed, and Bill was holding little Bobby, who was squirming and reaching for his mother. Daddy was seated beside the bed, holding Mom's hand, and Trixie and Granddad JJ and Rachel were on the other side of the bed, talking. Everyone's face was drawn and pale.

Daddy looked up and gave a weak smile. "There you are, Ellie." His shirt was covered in blood. He looked back at Mom and patted her hand. "She's here, Swannee. Ellie's here."

Mom's eyes flickered open, and she motioned with them for me to come and sit down beside her. There was blood everywhere—on Mom's gown, on her scarf, smudged all over her face. It looked like they'd tried to clean her up a little, but I still found it revolting.

Daddy gave me his chair. My throat was dry as I took a seat and leaned over close to her. "How're you doing, Mom?"

"I'm fine now, Ellie." She didn't sound fine. Her voice was barely a whisper. "Thank you for coming. Hope the doctor won't say this little setback will put off our trip."

"Don't worry about that right now, Mom. Just rest," I said, all the while wondering exactly how bad "this little setback" was.

I stayed by her side for at least twenty minutes. At one point, Mom reached over and held my hand. I had never been very affectionate with her, but of course, I didn't object. Then she drifted off to sleep, and I went out in the hall with Daddy.

"What happened?" I asked.

He took a deep breath. "Oh, Mae Mae, we almost lost your mom. She got this little nosebleed at home early this morning—she sneezed hard, you know, she was starting a cold. But the nosebleed just wouldn't stop, and it got worse and worse so that we had to rush her to the emergency room."

I could hardly imagine Daddy dealing with an abundance of blood.

"At one point there were ten different doctors and nurses in the room and alarms going off all over the place. A doctor finally cauterized the nose, and that got things under control. They said it's because of the low platelets. They're at eight thousand, and normal is something like a hundred thousand, I think. Her blood can't clot. They gave her a transfusion—three liters of blood plus a platelet transfusion. . . ."

"Daddy! That's so awful!"

Trixie came out of the room and placed a hand on Daddy's shoulder. "Robbie, let Bill take you home and get you cleaned up. JJ and I won't budge. Mary Swan is resting fine now."

Daddy nodded, as if in a trance. I could barely look at his face. It was a sickly green. He was wearing his eye patch—which he did sometimes at home when he didn't want to put the glass eye in, but never in public. Which meant he had left the house in a big hurry. And when he turned to go, I could see that he was limping a little, which only happened when he was extremely tired.

His hair was a light brown with a lot of gray in it, and it was thinning a bit on the top. His eyes were the color of the sunset. Golden brown, I called them. They matched his hair. Sometimes, when I looked into his good eye, like at that moment, it was as if I saw a little bit of gray there too, as if it were aging along with his hair.

Trixie and Granddad JJ went back into Mom's room. Rachel was still inside, but Nan came into the hall and gave Daddy a hug.

"Get some rest, Daddy. I'll stay too. Take a nap, and you can come back tonight."

Abbie's family left too, and Nan and I walked them to the elevator. When the door closed, I just stood there, staring at the lights flickering from one number to the next above the elevator door. I couldn't think of a thing to say.

Finally I asked, "How long have you been here?"

"Since about eight this morning. I drove over as soon as I heard. Where were you, anyway? Daddy tried to call you at your apartment."

I knew she didn't mean to sound reproachful, but I felt accused. "I was at Megan's—I had a rough night. Why didn't you try to call me on my cell? Gosh, I could've missed seeing Mom. She could've died while I was sleeping on Megan's pullout couch!"

Nan narrowed her eyes. "Are you serious? You really don't get it, do you, Ellie?"

"No, I don't get it. What am I supposed to get? Why do you all tiptoe around me? Do you think I can't handle it?"

"Maybe we 'tiptoe,' as you call it, because when we try to let you walk with us in a normal way, you just trample us down. Or have you forgotten how you yelled at me for 'bothering you all the time about Mom'? That's what you said when I suggested maybe twice in the course of three weeks—three hard weeks of chemo—that you give her a call. Anyway, no one is quite sure *how* to deal with you."

"You're exaggerating," I seethed.

"Am I really? I don't think so. Sometimes I wonder . . ." She stopped herself.

"Go on, say it!" I taunted.

"You're just so darned selfish, Ellie. If you could just for one minute get your eyes off yourself, you'd be a lot happier." Nan sniffed and turned away.

Oh good, I thought. *Here come the tears.*

"Sometimes I wonder if you even care about Mom . . . if it bothers you at all that she might die."

I stared at her as if she had slapped me right across the face. "I've gotta go," I muttered and pushed the button to call the elevator.

Nan tried again. "Look, sis, I'm sorry. I didn't mean to hurt your feelings. Come on back and see Mom."

But I got into the elevator without looking back and rode all the way down to the bottom with my face turned away from the door, staring at the wood paneling on the back wall. When the door opened, I slowly turned around and went out.

I walked toward my car, hating myself, my family, life in general. I was calculating whether I wanted to get a Wendy's Frosty or a dozen cream-filled doughnuts from Krispy Kreme when someone grabbed my arm.

"Ellie, listen to me."

It was Rachel. I hadn't even heard her coming.

"Come back and see your mother. She needs you."

"No, Rachel. Mom doesn't need me. She needs you. Go be with her. Make her smile the way only you can. I don't have anything to give."

"You're wrong, Ellie."

"I doubt it. Look, will you call me in a few hours? Let me know how she's doing? I'll take a shift with her. I promise. Just not right now."

"I'll call."

I opted for the doughnuts and was eating my third one while trying to digest Nan's words. *"If you could just for one minute get your eyes off yourself, you'd be a lot happier."* No one had ever said that to me before. But I think the stress of the moment and Nan's obvious fatigue and worry just got the best of her. She'd "spilled the beans," as Trixie would say.

So my whole family saw me as this selfish person.

"Well, let them! What do I care!" I fumed out loud, sitting on the floor beside the dark blue leather couch. I was relieved that I had the night off from work.

I grabbed my softball and began tossing it in the air, all the while looking out the window at the joggers going toward Piedmont Park. Hindsight perched on the sink beside me, her light brown eyes fixed on the up-and-down motion of the ball. Occasionally she reached out a playful paw to bat at it.

"Families are weird, Hindsight. Really weird. I'm weird, Mom's weird, and my sisters are weird!"

I took my ball and glove, locked the apartment, and headed to the park in search of a pickup game.

By the time I'd played for two hours, I'd had plenty of time to think about my conversation with Nan, and I didn't feel as mad anymore.

That was when I remembered I did have something going on that night, a fund-raiser for the Atlanta Humane Society. For the past two summers I'd helped out at the local animal shelter, cleaning out the cages. It was a nasty job, but I enjoyed it. I felt sorry for these orphans. All I ever wanted to do was make sure they got good homes.

Once a year a wealthy family in Buckhead held a big party on their spacious lawn, complete with a seated dinner, orchestra, and dancing, and invited the Friends of the Humane Society to attend. Volunteers helped set up tables and hand out drinks. Our main role was to mingle with the big brass and hint at how badly the Humane Society needed their contributions. Which was certainly true.

"I don't think I'll go to the fund-raiser tonight," I told Rachel when she called me from the hospital around five to report on Mom's condition. "I'll stay at the hospital."

"Oh, kid, go on. I'll call you on your cell phone if your mother takes a turn for the worse. She seems stable right now. You go on.

You're good at drumming up funding."

This was not true. I hardly spoke to anyone at the parties.

"Tell you what, Ellie. Why don't we meet at Amicos for a drink before you go? We can talk a little there."

"You're a mind reader, Rachel. I'd like that. I'll see you there at six."

Amicos was a little Italian restaurant on Peachtree that was popular among my crowd, and Rachel knew it. I always got the basil bruschetta for a light lunch so that I'd still be hungry for dessert. They offered twenty flavors of real gelato, and I had tried every one. But that evening I simply ordered a Coke.

Rachel was already seated, sipping a glass of Chablis. She looked tired and she was smoking—something she rarely did. I thought for a moment that I saw a hint of mascara on one cheek, as if she'd been crying, but she had brushed it away by the time I got to the table. She was putting away her cell phone in her blue leather purse, which perfectly matched the silk blouse she was wearing.

"Hey, kid," she said, blowing the smoke in the opposite direction. "Hope you don't mind the smoking section today."

I shrugged. "I'm used to it at the restaurant."

She searched for something in her purse.

"Are you okay, Rachel? You look . . . you look tired."

"I'm fine. I just had a nasty little conversation with Harold, but otherwise, life is great."

Harold was Rachel's ex-husband.

"Virginia was supposed to spend the first part of summer break with me in New York. Harold called to inform me that she wants to tour Africa instead. He's paying, of course."

"Sorry." We all knew about Rachel's family problems. When she had gotten her divorce years ago, her husband had dragged her through the mud, brought up all her wild ways of the past, and eventually gained custody of their two children, who were then teenagers. By the time Rachel worked out the legal battles, she was a lot poorer and her younger child, Virginia, didn't want to live with her. Their relationship had remained estranged at best.

"How's Benjamin?"

"Oh, Ben's all right." She smiled. "He still doesn't know what he wants to do when he grows up, but other than that, he's fine."

Benjamin was twenty-seven.

"I remember when I was about seven or eight and he was a teenager, and he'd come over to our house. He was always kind to my animals. I liked him for that. And I liked the quirky songs he used to sing."

"Good ole Ben. Good ole *quirky* Ben." Rachel crushed out her cigarette and took a sip of wine. "Actually, he's doing okay. He's got the band started up again, and they've been hired to do a summer gig at Hilton Head."

"Hilton Head! That's good news. I'm sure someone in our family will see him down there this summer." My family had vacationed on the island for decades.

She forced a smile. "You're right—it is good news. Ben needed a break, and it looks like he's gotten one. He's my artistic kid. Sometimes he reminds me of your mom."

"Well, according to you, that's a big compliment." I took a sip of Coke and said, "So tell me something I don't know about my dear mother."

Rachel ignored me and glanced at her watch. "Goodness, I need to get going. You do too if you want to be on time."

"Now wait a minute, Rachel! You mean you don't have anything to tell me about her?"

She took out some blush from her purse and made a face in the tiny mirror as she brushed on the makeup, a frown creasing her brow. "Let's just say that your mother has put up with a whole lot from me."

"Oh," I said, and disappointment caught in my voice. "That's all you're gonna say?"

She pecked me on the cheek. "Yep. For heaven's sake, Ellie, you don't need to hear it from me. Talk to your mom. She'll tell you the story. She'll tell you the whole thing."

I arrived late to the party. Ladies in fancy long dresses and men in tuxedos were sipping champagne on the long, perfectly manicured front lawn. I sneaked around to the side entrance of the house and found Mrs. Burkes, the lady organizing everything.

As I walked in, she called out in a near hysterical voice, "Oh, there you are, Ellie! Thank goodness! Could you take care of selling the raffle tickets, dear?"

"Sure," I said, unable to drum up much enthusiasm. I scribbled "Ellie" on the name tag she handed me. It was bright red, with the insignia of the Humane Society printed across the top and a little sketch at the bottom of a cat and dog snuggled together.

The raffle drawing was for a seven-week-old yellow Lab puppy. I had won Hindsight at this raffle two years earlier. I'd come with Trixie and had just gotten out of rehab and found my apartment in midtown. The fund-raiser was probably my first social event, and I was actually happy to go. I hated dressing up—I wore an old prom dress of a friend who used to be a lot bigger than me—but I loved being at a function that helped animals.

When I suggested we buy a raffle ticket, I think Trixie was just so relieved to have me out of rehab and functioning as a fairly normal person that she took me up on my desire. She didn't buy just one ticket; she bought twenty-five! So it came as no surprise when I held the winning number and was presented at the end of the evening with a beautiful Himalayan Persian kitten, five months old at the time.

"I bought those tickets on a whim," Trixie had said in her sweet Southern drawl, seeing my delight. "But hindsight shows it was the right thing to do." Thus my kitten was named.

Seated at the table selling those tickets, I could quite honestly tell my story and share how grateful I was for Hindsight. Once I had given my little speech to several people, I didn't feel quite so nervous about repeating it time and again throughout the night.

Halfway through the evening, a handsome middle-aged couple came up to the table. "Are we too late to buy tickets?" the wife asked.

"Oh no. Not at all. The drawing isn't for another hour. How many would you like?"

The woman was short and slight, dressed in a white linen suit that accented her smooth black skin. "What do you think, dear? Should we buy five tickets?"

But her husband wasn't really paying attention.

She smiled cautiously, bent over the table, and whispered, "I would love to take that puppy home to my granddaughter."

"Oh, then you should buy a lot more than five!" I said, and then felt foolish.

She looked surprised. "Really?"

"Sure." And I told her how I had won Hindsight.

"Your grandmother bought twenty-five tickets?" she asked with a mixture of humor and wonder in her voice. "Dear, did you hear that? This young lady's grandmother bought twenty-five tickets at the raffle two years ago, and that's how she won her cat."

Several other men had come up to her husband to shake his hand and slap him on the back. One was now saying, "Well, Dr. Matthews, I should have known the surgeon with the softest heart in Atlanta would be at a fund-raiser for the Humane Society."

Dr. Matthews let out a belly laugh. A large smile spread across his face. Just one look at him, and I could tell he'd have a good bedside manner. He was tall, probably close to six-three, and his eyes were animated, intelligent, kind. I could read eyes. Dr. Matthews's eyes were almost jet black, with a sparkle in them, a touch of humor, perhaps.

Mrs. Matthews was trying to get his attention and repeating, "This young lady says we should buy twenty-five tickets, honey! Twenty-five.

That's how she won her cat two years ago."

He turned away from the men, put his arm around his wife, and remonstrated, "Cassie, I am not about to buy twenty-five tickets at a raffle for a puppy! I could buy a fine purebred at the fanciest farm in south Georgia for less than what twenty-five tickets would cost." He was laughing.

"But this is for such a good cause!" I offered.

"Yes, dear, it is," Mrs. Matthews agreed.

"Oh, all right." He was still chuckling and reaching for his wallet when I noticed that his wife was staring at me. I felt annoyed that *this* woman, whom I had judged as unpretentious, was showing the same rude behavior as any other person.

She stared at me for so long that I almost said, "I was in an accident—that's why I look this way." That was one of my defense mechanisms—embarrassing people.

But she spoke first. "Excuse me for staring," she said softly, "but I just noticed your name tag. Ellie. And your green eyes." She glanced at her husband, then lowered her voice.

"I've only known one other person with eyes as bright and beautiful and green as yours. We were friends years ago. I haven't seen her in eons. We kept up a little bit over the years, and I know that around twenty years ago she had a baby girl named Ellie." She shook her head with an embarrassed smile on her face. "I'm sorry. I'm sure it is just a coincidence."

I think my scowl had intimidated her, and she patted my hand in a motherly way and gathered up the tickets as I counted out twenty-five of them, and her husband paid with several crisp bills. "Thank you. Thanks a lot," I murmured as they left the table.

For the rest of the evening, I couldn't take my eyes off them. I was dying to talk to the woman again. I liked her. And I was thinking of Mom, lying there ill in the hospital, of my selfishness, and of the fact that maybe this woman knew her.

I got my chance near the end of the evening when the drawing for the puppy was announced.

Mrs. Burkes took a microphone and said breathlessly, "Well, we have sold quite a few tickets for the raffle. I've asked one of our volunteers, Ellie, to do the honors. Ellie's number was chosen at the drawing two years ago, and she won a beautiful Himalayan Persian."

I'm sure that my face turned scarlet as I stuck my hand into the box where all the raffle numbers were placed. I was secretly hoping that I'd draw one of the Matthewses' numbers, and when I did, I saw Dr. Matthews put his head back and laugh. Then he gave his wife a little hug, while the crowd politely clapped.

"My mother is Mary Swan Middleton," I confided to Mrs. Matthews when she came up front.

Her face lit up. "I knew it! You've got her eyes, all right." Almost at once, her face clouded. "Well, I'm Cassandra Matthews. It's very nice to meet you."

She glanced over her shoulder at her husband, who had taken the puppy out of his cage and was busily inspecting him with several friends.

"As I said, we haven't seen your folks in a long time."

"You know Daddy too?"

"Oh yes. We know both of your parents. Knew them, I should say. We lost track of each other." She said this with a strange catch in her throat, and something seemed a bit off, as if she were at a loss for what to say next. Her face looked strained. "Is your mother still painting?" she asked finally.

"Yes. Yes, she is. Well, actually, she had to stop for a while. I mean, she's been ill." Immediately I wanted to take back my words.

"Oh, dear. I hope it isn't serious."

I would not have said anything if I hadn't already felt so bad about my behavior earlier in the day—with both Jamal and Nan. When I spoke, it was more to myself than to Mrs. Matthews.

"Breast cancer. She has breast cancer. They think they got it all."

Mrs. Matthews looked shocked. "Dear me, I had no idea."

She seemed almost out of breath. Her husband was talking to someone else, but she grabbed his arm and said, "Carl, honey, this is Robbie and Mary Swan's daughter, Ellie."

Dr. Matthews looked stunned—pained, even. Then he got a smile on his face—although it seemed a little forced—and shook my hand. "Well, if that isn't something. Pleased to meet you, Ellie. I'm Carl Matthews, and I guess you've already met my wife, Cassandra. We think mighty highly of your parents."

As soon as he said his name, I probably looked stunned too. Even I, the renegade as far as family history was concerned, recognized that name. Carl was a very important player in my mother's story. In fact, Carl was the black man that Mom had been enamored with many years ago.

But something about the way the Matthewses were talking—no, looking—something about their body language struck me as odd, so I didn't say a word about knowing who he was. Abbie would have been all over them in a sec. Nan too. But not me.

"Mary Swan's had breast cancer, honey. Isn't that awful?"

Dr. Matthews winced a little, a look of genuine sorrow crossing his face.

"Actually she finished treatments yesterday. If the doctor says she's strong enough, we're going on a trip to Europe at the end of the summer." This was my attempt to say something positive.

"Well, good for you, Ellie. And good for her. Your mother always loved Europe."

We walked over to the table with the finger foods on it. I was starving, since I'd been stuck behind the raffle table all evening. I picked up a plate and began loading it with meatballs and vegetables and dip. I was trying to decide if the Matthewses wanted to pursue our conversation. They ended up just smiling at me while I stuffed my face with food, a habit I was trying to stop.

"I'm glad you got the puppy," I said after wiping dip from around my mouth with a paper napkin printed with the Humane Society's logo.

"He's adorable. Has all his shots and his papers. I can't thank you enough for suggesting we buy those tickets," Mrs. Matthews enthused.

"You're welcome. I'm sure the Humane Society is glad you bought those tickets too!"

"That's for sure," Dr. Matthews laughed. "So you do volunteer work at the Society, Ellie?"

"Yes—just in the summer. But I love it."

They seemed intent on my every word, but almost afraid to ask questions.

"I want to be a vet."

Dr. Matthews held the puppy and let its lower body squiggle about freely. "I wanted to be a vet at one point." He said this more to the puppy than to me.

"What changed your mind?"

He looked up at me, almost as if he'd been taken off guard. Then he said, "The training I got in the army. And what I saw in the war."

"Vietnam?" I pursued.

Dr. Matthews gave his wife a quick sideways glance. "Yes, Vietnam."

"My dad was there too." I thought I was simply making conversation, but when I said that, it felt like a blanket fell over us and snuffed out the light at the party. The Matthewses' faces grew even more somber.

"Would you like me to get you some more punch, Ellie?" Mrs. Matthews asked me. I could tell she was trying to change the subject.

"Sure. Thanks." I decided to comply. "Yeah, well, we're gonna take my mom's and my grandmom's sketch pads from Europe with us and follow them around for a while until we end up somewhere in Scotland called the Dwelling Place. I've seen paintings Mom has done of the scenery, but honestly I don't know why she wants to go there. I think it's part of her family history. . . ."

I was busy filling my plate with meatballs while I talked, so it took me a minute to realize that Mrs. Matthews's face had gone pale—well, as pale as a black face can go—and that she had reached out a hand to her husband, who himself looked stricken. In one gesture, he handed her the puppy, pulled Mrs. Matthews into his chest, smoothed her hair, and regained his composure.

My fork was poised in midair, sauce dripping off the plump meatball. I felt terribly awkward. But I pretended nothing was wrong and finished my bite. Then I set down my plate and said, "Well, it was really nice to meet you, Dr. and Mrs. Matthews. Take good care of this rascal for me." I scratched the puppy behind his ears.

"We'll do that, Ellie. We will." Mrs. Matthews hesitated only a moment, then she touched my arm in that same motherly way and said in a cracking voice, "You tell your parents hello from us. And that we're thinking about your mother."

Dr. Matthews just nodded his agreement. "Good-bye, Ellie."

I watched them take the puppy and the cage and leave the room, pausing to shake the hands of friends who good-naturedly teased them about their raffle win. I went back to the table and started straightening up things. The whole time I was thinking to myself, *What is it that is so disturbing about the Dwelling Place?*

•

When I got back to my apartment, it was well past eleven. A bright pink Post-it was stuck on the door, and in an unstable scrawl it said, *Princess Augusta Victoria has taken a turn for the worse. Please come and help. No matter what hour. Mrs. Rose.*

Mrs. Rose was an elderly widow who lived two doors down from me and had an apartment filled with cats, seven at the last count. She took in all the strays in the neighborhood and gave them names of Shakespeare characters or of European royalty. "It helps their self-image," she told me. We had discovered our mutual love of felines last winter, and when she found out I wanted to be a vet, she immediately designated me "on call" for any of her cats' medical emergencies.

I knew that I would find Mrs. Rose asleep in her rocking chair with Princess Augusta Victoria on her lap.

I had a key to her apartment and let myself in. Just as I had predicted, the mistress and cat were both asleep in the rocker. I cleared my throat softly. Then, receiving no response, a little more loudly.

"Mrs. Rose. It's Ellie."

Her eyes flickered open, confusion registering on her wrinkled face. Then she smiled. "Oh, Ellie, thanks for coming. Poor Princess is just feeling rotten. Not one ounce of spunk in her."

I lifted the black-and-white tabby off the old woman's lap. "What's up, Vicki?" I asked, scratching the feline under her throat. Mrs. Rose had no money for a vet, so whenever the cat in question seemed genuinely sick, I would ask the advice of the vet on call at the Humane Society and purchase the needed medications.

"Tell you what, Mrs. Rose. I'll come by in the morning and take her to the clinic and see what they say. Don't you worry. You get some sleep now."

"Oh, Ellie, you're an angel. I was so worried!"

"Everything will be fine. Just get some sleep." I patted the cat once more and helped Mrs. Rose stand up, accompanying her to her bedroom. "You gonna be okay now?"

"Fine, Ellie. Sorry to be such a nuisance."

"No nuisance," I said and gave her a kiss on the forehead.

Chapter 4

Symbol for the city's seal, the phoenix [is] a vital part of Atlanta's sense of self . . . [celebrating] Atlanta's efforts to create a "brave and beautiful" city from the destruction of the Civil War.

—*ATLANTA: A BRAVE AND BEAUTIFUL CITY*

As I washed my face and sipped my can of Coke the next morning, I was trying to make sense of something. Atlanta had over two and a half million people in it, so I guess I could say it seemed like a strange coincidence to have met the Matthewses at that fund-raiser. But it seemed even stranger, even a bigger coincidence, that my parents and the Matthewses would never have run into each other in the past twenty years.

"It's a sure thing, Hindsight. They were deliberately avoiding Mom and Dad. Don't ask me why, but they were."

Mom and Rachel had seemed to be doing fine in those Scotland sketches—peaceful at last. But something about that place in Scotland had made Mrs. Matthews cringe. It was as if she had heard fingernails scraping across a blackboard. And Dr. Matthews had gotten extremely protective of his wife all of a sudden, and then there had been nothing else to say.

"Isn't that a bit strange? And then there's the awkward way they avoided talking about Vietnam."

I put on a pair of jeans and a T-shirt and went two doors down to Mrs. Rose's apartment. I knocked loudly on her door and called out, "It's Ellie, Mrs. Rose! I'm coming to get Vicki."

"Bless your soul, child," she whispered when she had opened the door. I took the cat from her and placed Vicki in the little plastic cage I used for transporting Hindsight.

"Bless your soul," she repeated. "When you get back, you come on in and have a cup of tea."

Dr. Banks, the vet on call at the shelter, was used to me showing up with one of Mrs. Rose's cats—or any other cat from the neighborhood. He was also used to me showing up at odd hours—like this Sunday morning.

When he had finished examining Princess Augusta Victoria, he gave me some medicine and said, "Mrs. Rose is going to have to treat the whole bunch for worms. And I know she doesn't have any money, and I don't want you paying me either." He wagged a finger at me. "You've done that enough." He handed me a small white sachet of pills. "You make sure each cat gets one in the morning for three days straight. That should take care of it."

"Thanks, Dr. Banks. Thanks a ton. But I can pay. Really I can."

He winked at me and said, "Don't worry, Ellie, I'll take it out of your monthly check."

An hour later I was knocking on Mrs. Rose's door again.

I heard her fiddling with the lock and knew she was looking through the peephole. Mrs. Rose was terrified of being vandalized.

"It's just me, Mrs. Rose. Just Ellie and Vicki."

The door rattled and opened a few inches where the chain caught it. Mrs. Rose's worried, confused face appeared from behind the door. "Oh, Ellie. It's you. I'm sorry to keep you waiting." Mrs. Rose was a bit hard of hearing. "Come on in." She scooped Vicki out of my arms and began crooning to her.

"The vet said it's just worms. But you'll need to give the treatment to all the cats. It spreads."

"Oh, dear, Princess Vicki." Mrs. Rose's face deflated. "How in the world will I pay for medicine for the whole family?"

"Don't worry. I've got the medicine. And this is for you." I showed her a bag filled with cans of cat food that I'd picked up at the store.

"Ellie, you're an angel."

"Not an angel, just a vet in training. Thanks to you, I'm getting some great firsthand experience."

"An angel. Can you come in for a moment? Have a cup of tea?"

"Sure." I smiled and asked, "You wouldn't happen to have a Coke, would you?"

"Certainly not! All that sugary stuff is terrible for you. It's killing all of you young people! What you need is some good, decent, sensible food. Do you ever eat vegetables?"

I shrugged. "Rarely."

"I knew it!" She shuffled into the kitchen.

I followed her with the cans of cat food.

"Now, let me see. Where did I put the tea?"

I had gone through this ritual a dozen times before. I brought cat food, she felt obliged to invite me in, I felt obliged to accept. And then she couldn't find her tea and cookies.

"Let me help you," I offered, quickly retrieving the tin can filled with tea bags.

Slowly Mrs. Rose filled up the kettle with water. "Oh, Ellie, thank you. It's hard getting old, you know. Very hard."

We waited together for the water to boil, and then, when her shaking, gnarled hands could not pull off the top of the tin, I helped her. We each chose a tea bag, and I watched nervously as she awkwardly filled our teacups, splashing hot water into the saucers and onto the counter as well.

We walked into her den. Mrs. Rose was a bit of an enigma to me.

Poor as she seemed, her apartment was furnished with nice, expensive stuff, like the chair I sat down in. *"That came from France—it's genuine Louis the Sixteenth,"* she'd told me not too long ago.

But she also had quite a few knickknacks I would label as tacky, including a cheaply framed print of a kitten that hung cockeyed over the sofa; a collection of key chains from Rock City, Mammoth Cave, Monticello, and even the Eiffel Tower; and a foot-high plastic replica of the Parthenon.

I knew that her husband had died about twenty years ago of a heart attack and that she had two or three grown children. But I don't think any of them ever came to visit.

She slowly seated herself on a worn loveseat next to my chair and took a sip of tea from her fine bone china cup. Her hand was trembling slightly, and she spilled a little of the tea on her dress, a loose-fitting paisley print. She didn't seem to notice.

Out of the blue, she asked, "Ellie, do you think there are terrorists living in this apartment building?"

"Terrorists, Mrs. Rose?"

"Yes, I heard it on the news. They're infiltrating our country. Maybe you should call your friend and have him check out this place."

I knew she was referring to Jamal. Mrs. Rose always felt comforted by his size, reassured that he could stop any thief.

"I am positive there are no terrorists in the apartment building, Mrs. Rose."

"Well, if you're sure." She wrinkled her brow, unconvinced. "I don't understand why they keep talking about it on the news." She reached down and patted a fluffy white cat with blue eyes. "That's a relief. At least one thing is settled, isn't it, Macbeth?"

Macbeth hopped onto her lap. With no transition, Mrs. Rose asked, "Are you and that big black boy dating, Ellie?"

Although Mrs. Rose swore she wasn't prejudiced, I was amazed by the comments that came out of her mouth.

"You mean my friend Jamal? No, we're not dating. Just friends. He brings me home from work sometimes. That's all."

"Well, then. That's all right. I like him fine. And it's good of him to make sure you get home safely. I don't know why you insist on working in such a terrible neighborhood! But I wouldn't want you having any romantic interest in that young man. I just don't think blacks and whites should mix."

"Yes, I know, Mrs. Rose. You've told me that before. Jamal and I are just friends."

"Well, then. That's settled. But I do think you should find a nice boy to date. It's not right for a young girl like you to spend so much time alone—or with an old lady like me." She reached over and set her teacup and saucer on a delicate end table and began stroking Macbeth. "You know, Ellie, if you would just eat a few more vegetables and quit drinking all those soft drinks and eating chips, why, I'm sure you'd slim right down." She chuckled. "Boys don't mind women with hips, but yours have gotten a bit wide."

Mrs. Rose was not an attractive woman. I say that without any meanness. She was overweight and stooped badly, making her look shorter than she actually was. She had dark gray hair that she kept neatly pinned, but her nose was much too big for the rest of her face, and it was not straight. She must have broken it when she was young, because it curved to the right and looked perpetually swollen. Her eyes were small and bluish gray, and most of the time she wore a frown of some sort—except when she was petting one of her cats. Then she got a sweet, peaceful look on her face.

I liked Mrs. Rose. I liked the way her mind worked, or didn't work, at times. I liked trying to figure out what she would say next, because I could never guess. I didn't even mind her telling me I needed to lose weight. She was absolutely right. But the vegetables—they would be quite literally hard to swallow.

"I'll try to cut down, Mrs. Rose," I said, patting her hand. "Now it's time for me to go. Thanks for the tea. Take good care of Princess, and I'll bring her medicine over tomorrow morning."

I had long since figured out that Mrs. Rose could not remember if she had given medicine (or food, for that matter) to her cats, or to which one, so I had begun keeping the medications at my place. Mrs. Rose forgot most things that occurred in the present.

So it surprised me when she called out after me, "I'll look for you tomorrow morning, Ellie. And tell your mother I'm thinking of her. Poor soul. You take good care of your mother, you hear?"

With her words echoing in my mind, I went back to my apartment, dressed, and drove to Piedmont Hospital. When I entered Mom's room, Daddy was there beside her bed. He was wearing a three-piece suit, which meant he must have just arrived from church. "Ellie! What a nice surprise."

"Hi, Mom, Daddy. How is everything today?" I tried to sound upbeat.

"Much better," Mom assured me.

I glanced at Daddy for confirmation, and he nodded, but the worried expression was still there.

"I'll leave the two of you together for a while," Daddy said. "I'm going to find myself some coffee."

"Sit down, sweetie," Mom said, her voice weak. "Trixie said you went to the fund-raiser last night. Did you win another cat?" She was smiling.

"No, no, I didn't. But I sold twenty-five tickets to some old friends of yours, and they won a yellow Lab puppy."

"How nice! Old friends of mine, you say?"

"Yes. The woman recognized me by my eyes and my name. She said the last time she'd seen you, you'd just given birth to a little girl named Ellie. After that, y'all lost touch." I was watching Mom closely for any sign of recognition.

"We lost touch? How strange. Who was it?"

"You really don't know?"

Mom concentrated hard, then laughed. "I'm sure I've lost touch with quite a few friends over the years."

"She's about your age, African-American, a tiny wisp of a woman."

A slight frown crossed Mom's face. "I believe I do know, Ellie. I believe I do. It was Cassandra Matthews."

"That's right. She and Dr. Matthews were there. They were so sorry to hear about your cancer. They send their love to you and Daddy."

My eyes were riveted on Mom's face.

"No, we haven't seen them in years. Years! But I know he's a pediatric surgeon. Very respected. Works at Grady, I believe. And Cassandra is a nurse."

"They seem really nice."

"Oh, they are great people. We lost track of them. She's absolutely right."

"Dr. Matthews was in Vietnam, like Daddy."

"Yes."

"Were they there at the same time?"

"No, not exactly. Carl was there first, then Daddy. I waited and prayed with Cassandra, and then she waited and prayed with me. . . ." Mom's voiced trailed off, and I saw tears in her eyes.

At that moment, Daddy walked back into the room. "Swannee, sweetheart. You're crying. Are you feeling bad?" He was at her side immediately.

"Oh no, dear. I'm fine." Mom sniffed once and recovered her composure. When she met Daddy's eyes with her own, she looked strong. "Guess who Ellie met at the Humane Society party last night?"

Daddy's regard was part apprehension and part reproach. "No idea."

"Carl and Cassandra."

"You're kidding." He took Mom's hand in much the same protective way that Dr. Matthews had reached out to his wife. "What a coincidence. We haven't seen them in years. Completely lost touch."

I was astounded that my parents had repeated the same phrase as the Matthewses—as if they'd rehearsed their lines long ago.

Daddy bent down and kissed Mom gently on the lips. "You need to get some sleep, my Fat Goose." That was one of Daddy's pet nicknames for Mom.

"Don't worry so much, Scout"—her nickname for Daddy—"I'm all right."

I had the distinct feeling that they were trying to shield me from some family secret.

Daddy motioned for me to join him in the hall. "Your mom is still very weak. She doesn't need to be talking much."

He had shaved and the eye patch was gone, and the glass eye was such a perfect copy that you had to study his face to find which one was fake. On the outside, he was strong and kind Daddy again.

I hugged him around the waist, resting my head on his shoulder. "I'm sorry, Daddy. You're really worried, aren't you?"

"Mighty hard to see your mom suffering."

"I shouldn't have come. I just made it worse."

He squeezed me tightly. "No, Ellie. It means everything to your mother to have you here."

"I made her cry."

"No you didn't. You know your mother. She cries at the drop of a hat. She just hadn't thought about the Matthewses in a long, long time. Don't blame yourself for everything, Ellie. Please stay here with me for a while. You want a Coke?"

"Sure, Daddy. Thanks." We found a vending machine two floors down.

But I didn't really want to be with Daddy. I wanted to hide from everyone. Especially from Mom. I had done it again. I had said the wrong thing and made Mom cry. And the worst part about it was that I had done it on purpose.

On most Sunday afternoons, before my softball games, I met with my neighbor Nate to do geeky stuff on the computer, like researching web sites that Nate had found during the week. Nate was thirty. He didn't have a job, and he spent untold hours a day on the Web. He loved to show me new sites, tell me about the newest search engine, and give me up-to-the-minute news on baseball, especially the Braves. I didn't know the "politically correct" term for his handicap, but it seemed to me that part of Nate's brain worked like a genius and the other part like a little boy.

He lived in the apartment between mine and Mrs. Rose's on the second floor of our complex. We'd met last year when he and Mrs. Rose were engaged in a conversation over what to do with a stray cat. Of course, Mrs. Rose had decided to keep it.

"You're a nice lady," Nate had told Mrs. Rose.

"Oh, hush now, Nate, I'm not a bit nice. Ellie's the nice one. And smart. She's a vet."

"You're a vet?" he repeated.

"Not yet. Just in school. Hope to be one day, though."

"Well, you must be a nice lady too. I like people who like animals."

We'd run into each other several times in the following weeks, discovered our mutual love for animals, computers, and baseball, and somehow I'd ended up agreeing to look at web sites with him on Sunday afternoons.

"Hey there, Ellie." On this afternoon Nate had that familiar vacant look in his eyes. He was tall, about six-feet-five, and very pudgy, with blond hair—towhead blond—that was thick and straight, unkempt, and always seeming a few inches too long. His disheveled appearance made me think of my nephew, Bobby, right after his nap. And Nate's eyes.

They were crystal blue and often held the wide-eyed surprised look of a toddler.

"Sorry about the letter," he said sheepishly as he directed me to a web site.

"No problem, Nate."

In his moments of greatest anguish he often wrote me scathing letters, accusing various people of terrible crimes. Most recently, my sister Abbie had been the culprit.

"I really don't see how Abbie could have poisoned that kitten, Nate. She doesn't live anywhere near here."

"You told me once that Abbie hates cats."

I suppressed a grin. "She does dislike them, but that doesn't mean she wants to kill them!"

"Then who was it?" he demanded, his eyes filling with tears.

"How in the heck am I supposed to know, Nate? Why would you think it was my sister?"

"She hates cats, and she sneaked into your apartment the other day. I'm sure it was her."

"How are you sure? You've never even met Abbie."

"No, but I've seen her from a distance. You look alike. You both have that really thick long hair, only hers isn't as pretty as yours. Hers is the color of wheat and yours is the color of the sunset when it's streaked with red." He gave an awkward laugh. "But you have the same nose exactly. I've seen her." He got a miserable look on his face. "She sneaked into your apartment, and then the kitten was dead. It all happened like that. Just like that."

Between Mrs. Rose and Nate, a good bit of the time I wasn't sure what was fact and what was fiction.

"Nate, my sister is not going to 'sneak' into my apartment. She has a key, but why would she come here when I'm not home?"

"She killed the kitten."

"Did you ever get onto that site that talks all about that unsolvable math problem?" I asked, trying to divert his attention. It worked.

Nate laughed his awkward laugh. "Oh yeah, that was a neat site. Cool. I don't think you'd get it, though."

"Don't tell me I wouldn't get it, Nate!"

"All kinds of impossible math problems. You wouldn't be able to figure them out. But it's only because you haven't been to college and I have." He liked to tease me about his superior education.

"I'll have you know I'm in college right now. Show me your paper work. I don't believe you for a second. If you could figure the problems out, then so can I!"

"I didn't bring the paper work, Ellie. I already know it by heart."

I punched him playfully. "You're a brain, Nate. A real brain."

He laughed again uncomfortably. Then his face fell. "They changed my medication."

"Again? That's the third time in six months! Why'd they do it this time?"

"I don't know. I wasn't sleeping and then I was sleeping too much and everything got so complicated." He stared off into space, his face distorted, as if he were concentrating on something extremely distasteful.

"Are you getting used to the new stuff?"

"No. It's not working," he said, still far away in thought. "If I don't do better soon, they say I'll have to go back to that *home*." His eyes filled again.

"But you're doing fine here, Nate! I'll tell them! I'll make them see some sense."

He grinned bashfully. "Thanks, Ellie. I know you. You'll do what you say. Not like my brother, Mark, who promises to come see me and never does. You're a nice lady, Ellie." We searched the Web for a while. Then Nate's face changed again, the vacant look back mixed with a look of pain. "Do you think you could come over and check out my computer?"

I glanced at my watch. "Sure, Nate. I'll come by. I've got softball practice in thirty minutes. Tell you what. I'll change and get my things ready, then I'll stop by your place on my way out. How does that sound?"

"Sounds good, Ellie." He stuffed his hands in his jeans and stood awkwardly balancing from one foot to the other until I walked with him to the door.

"See you in a sec," I said. As I closed the door, Nate was still standing there with a lost expression on his face.

I was in the middle of dressing when the doorbell rang. "Coming!" I called out, sure that Nate had forgotten something.

I flung the door open to find Abbie standing there, out of breath.

"Abbie! What are you doing here?" My sister never stopped by my apartment. I hoped that Nate hadn't seen her, or the list of her criminal activities might increase.

"Mom's taken another turn for the worse. I've been trying to call you for an hour, but your phone keeps being busy." She had an accusing look in her eyes.

"Sorry. I was looking at web sites with a friend. . . ."

"I see."

"Look, I've got to stop by my friend's place, and then I'll be right behind you."

"Come with me, Ellie. I know what it's like when you think you are just stopping by a friend's house for a second."

I didn't hide my annoyance. "Look. I'll be there in just a sec."

"We don't have a sec."

"Why? Is Mom dying or something?" I immediately wished I hadn't asked with anger in my voice.

"I don't know. It's bad."

Even though my family members had a knack for the melodramatic, I could tell that Abbie was truly worried. I threw off my softball jersey and pants and pulled on a T-shirt and jeans, following her out the door. "Just let me tell Nate."

"We don't have time."

I swirled around and snapped, "Look! I have a life too, sis! I have commitments. Nate will worry. I can at least have the decency to tell him, if you don't mind." I pronounced the last four words like knives coming out of my mouth.

Abbie just glared at me and followed me over to Nate's door.

When I knocked on the door, he opened it immediately, as if he had been standing right on the other side waiting. He was smiling.

But before he could welcome me in, I said, "Nate, I can't help you right now. I've got a family emergency. I'll come over later, when I get back."

Nate looked confused, then panicky, both expressions I was used to seeing on his face.

"Relax, Nate. It's okay. I'll come see you in a little while."

"When?"

"I don't know. This evening."

"But you said you'd come now."

"I know, and I'm sorry. I just found out that my mom is really not doing well. Remember I told you she was in the hospital?"

"She's sick?"

"Yes, very sick."

"You'll come back later, then?"

"Later, yes. I promise."

"Mark always promises too."

"I'll be back." I had the sinking feeling that Nate would still be standing in the same spot waiting for me when I returned.

"Who is that guy, sis? He looks really weird," Abbie said on the way to her car.

"That's my friend Nate."

"He looks like he has a screw loose."

"That's not a very *Christian* thing to say, Abbie." I liked to point out her faults whenever I could.

"No, you're right. Sorry. But do you feel safe going to his apartment?"

"Of course. Nate wouldn't hurt a fly." I felt like adding *contrary to what he thinks of you, sis—a kitten murderer!*

"Well, you should be careful about the kind of people you hang out with."

I lit into her. "What a hypocrite, Abbie! I may not agree with most of the Bible, but I know one thing. The people Jesus was most fed up with weren't the people with a screw loose, as you put it. Those are the very ones he hung around with. It was the religious guys he was tough on—the ones who thought they were so pious and holy and were really just a bunch of no-good hypocrites. Nate was born with problems, and I don't think he has one soul on earth who cares. So I decided I would care."

I could tell I had shocked Abbie by my outburst, but she kept her mouth clamped shut. Often my conversations with Abbie turned out this way. One of us would get mad at the other, we'd exchange a few harsh words, and then we'd exist in silence, side by side.

Abbie was speeding, which she never did. She was the model citizen—at least, she always had been. Today she was a pack of nerves.

After several minutes of that stony silence, I asked, "What happened to Mom, Abbie? I was just there a few hours ago. She was doing much better."

"A problem with the platelets again. She's getting another transfusion right now."

"Is Nan coming back from Chattanooga?"

"She wants to, but her doctor said no."

"What do you mean?"

"She's not doing so well either. Spotting. The doctor says she needs to slow down. But you know Nan. She's determined to be here with Mom."

Abbie was using her gift for making me feel guilty to perfection.

On the way to the hospital, I took out my cell phone and called a woman from my softball team. "Sharon, hey, it's Ellie. Listen, I'm not going to be able to make it to the game this afternoon."

Sharon started cursing on the other end.

"Hey, hold on a minute, will you? I'm on the way to the hospital, for grief's sake. My mother is in critical condition."

That stopped Sharon's barrage of angry words, and she said all the right things.

"Thanks, Sharon. Hit a homer for me."

When I hung up the cell phone, I was hoping that Abbie had noticed I did have plans in my life, that she wasn't the only one this medical emergency was inconveniencing.

If she noticed, she didn't say so. Not one other word during the ten-minute ride.

Once again we went to the fifth floor of the cancer ward at Piedmont Hospital. This time Daddy was standing in the hall, still dressed in his Sunday suit, his tie loosened around his neck. He was talking to two ladies whom I recognized from my parents' church. Trixie and Granddad JJ were there too.

The door to Mom's room was shut, and several nurses had just come out, carrying bloodstained sheets and whispering among themselves. One tried to give us a reassuring smile when she noticed that we all had our eyes riveted on the sheets.

"I think the worst is over," she said.

I felt light-headed. I went to Daddy and hugged him. "I'm so sorry, Daddy. Can't they do anything?"

"They're trying, Mae Mae. The platelet count had gone up yesterday, but I guess it went back down. . . ."

"We were all eating at the club when the hospital called and told us to hurry over," Trixie whispered too loudly, smacking her gum. "Another hemorrhage—she's getting a transfusion now—platelets and blood."

"That's what Abbie said," I murmured weakly.

I glanced over at Abbie and realized how awful she looked, even in her cute maternity dress. *Gaunt* was the word that came to my mind. Her face was splotchy, and her long blond hair was pulled back and clipped off her neck. She was perspiring heavily as she talked in whispered tones to Daddy.

It startled me to see her so tired.

"You go on home, sugar," Daddy was telling her. "You need to get some rest. Bill took little Bobby to your house about thirty minutes ago. Go on home."

"I'm staying until they say she's okay."

"There's nothing more you can do here, Ab," Daddy insisted. "The best thing for us all is if you get some rest."

Abbie looked unconvinced, but she turned toward the elevators. "Call if there's the slightest news."

"We will," Daddy promised.

Rachel arrived a few minutes later, wearing a polo shirt and Bermuda shorts, a visor and golf cleats. "Thanks for calling me, Trixie. Any more news?"

Trixie shook her head. "They're giving her the transfusion now."

We sat in the waiting room for forty-five minutes, trying to think of simple, positive things to talk about. But every few minutes the conversation fizzled and we stared down the hall toward the door to Mom's room. Finally a doctor came to see us.

"The bleeding has stopped. The transfusion went well. She's resting." He sounded brisk and confident.

"Thank the Lord," Daddy murmured, and Rachel patted his hand.

"I'm afraid it wouldn't be wise to see her now. She needs to sleep. From the looks of it, so do all of you." The doctor attempted a smile.

None of us budged.

"She's okay. She's out of danger. Go on out and get some fresh air," he urged.

Rachel spoke up. "Look, I'll stay here till dinnertime. That'll give the rest of you a little break. Might as well take advantage of me while you can since I have to head back to New York on Tuesday."

"Call if there's any change . . ." Daddy began.

"Don't worry, Robbie. Now, off with the rest of you."

"I'm staying too," I said, wanting to be with Rachel.

Daddy smiled at me. "That's thoughtful of you, Ellie." He and Trixie and Granddad JJ left us in the waiting room.

"My whole family's in crisis," I said at length to Rachel. "Mom is in critical condition. She may die at any minute. Nan is spotting. And Abbie looks like death warmed over—Daddy too. And I'm just . . ."

"You're here, kid. That's what matters. You're here. And the rest of them will pull through. They've done it before. Many times. You'll see."

I was not very outwardly affectionate, but for some reason I leaned back in the metal chair in the waiting room and rested my head on Rachel's shoulder.

"Is Mom gonna die, Rachel?"

"No, Ellie. I tell you, your mom's a fighter."

"How long do you think they'll keep her here?"

"Not too long. Just enough to make sure she's stabilized. Then I'm sure they'll let her go home, with strict instructions on how to take care of herself."

"Which she won't obey."

"I think she will this time. And I think she might need a personal nurse for a week or so."

"Yeah, maybe."

"I'm thinking of you."

"What?" I sat up straight, and my eyes grew wide.

"What would you think about moving back home for a week or two and helping your dad take care of her?"

"Are you serious?"

"Of course I am. You usually work the late shift, so you could stay with her in the morning and early afternoon—until your dad gets home from work. Give it a thought, kid. If they let her go home in the next few days, you go too."

"I'm not trying to sound selfish, Rachel, but sometimes it seems like the rest of you think I don't have a life of my own. I mean, I do have a job and friends and obligations. Or maybe y'all just think my life isn't really as important as everyone else's."

Rachel started to protest, but I continued. "I mean, Abbie appears at my door and orders me to go with her to the hospital as if I'm a child. Then she makes fun of my friend. And Nan just openly accuses me of being selfish. It's not a whole lot of fun hanging around my family, Rachel. So please don't you start on me too."

Rachel ran a hand through her hair and sighed. "I was seeing it from a completely different perspective. I was seeing it as the perfect opportunity to get to know your mom without even having to leave the city.".

I gave her a half smile and said, "Okay, Rachel. I'll at least think about it."

"You won't be sorry."

It must have been around seven in the evening when they finally let us in to see Mom. Rachel went by the bedside and took Mom's hand.

"Swannee, wake up, girl. You little nincompoop. What do you mean scaring us half to death?"

Mom's lips quivered slightly, and though her eyes stayed closed, there was a flicker of understanding behind the lids. "Sorry, Rach. Didn't mean to . . ."

"Never mind. 'This living hand, now warm and capable of earnest grasping. . . . I hold it towards you.'"

"You silly girl, can't you see I'm tired?" she groaned, but her mouth turned up in an attempt to smile. "Well, never mind, anyway. I'd know Keats anywhere. Such a nice poet." She squeezed Rachel's hand. "When are you going back to New York? Won't they fire you if you keep playing hooky?"

"Probably. Serves them right. Then they'll see how valuable I am. Anyway, I'll go back to my house when you go back to yours." Rachel glanced at me and winked.

"Stubborn girl. You've always been so stubborn," Mom said, her eyes still closed.

"Ellie's here too."

"Ellie!" Mom's eyes shot open and she looked around until she found me.

I gave her a little noncommittal nod, but inside, it hurt to see how thankful her green eyes were that I was there.

"You didn't have to come back. Don't you have to work tonight?"

"Not tonight, Mom. I had the weekend off."

"Yes, that's right." She closed her eyes again. "You told me. Softball game. How did the Panthers do?"

"They're playing right now."

"Oh, dear. I've made you miss it."

"Mom, it's no prob." But my voice wasn't convincing, wasn't full of caring and love like Rachel's.

Mom was silent for a while. Then she whispered. "Did Ellie tell you who she met at the fund-raiser last night, Rach?"

"No, we haven't talked about it."

I immediately shook my head at Rachel and mouthed, *Don't talk about it,* but Mom was already telling her.

"Carl and Cassandra. Can you believe it? After all these years. We'll have to have them over when I get out of here."

I half expected her to start crying again.

But Rachel didn't give her a chance. "Perfect idea, Swan. After you paint the portrait of my grandbaby and go to Scotland with Ellie. Now rest. Rest, 'close-bosom friend of the maturing sun.'" Rachel emphasized the word *bosom*, and that made Mom smile.

"He always said it best, didn't he? Good old Mr. Keats."

Rachel bent over and gave my mother a kiss, and I stood beside her, my hands stuffed deep down in the pockets of my jeans.

Rachel gave me a ride home. I wasn't at all surprised to open my door and find an angry note on the floor just inside. It was written all in capitals in Nate's childish handwriting.

I WAITED FOR YOU FOR THREE HOURS. DO YOU NOT HAVE ANY SENSE OF PROPRIETY? DO YOU THINK YOU'RE OF A SUPERIOR RACE? DON'T EXPECT ME TO LOOK AT WEB SITES WITH YOU ANYMORE, SIMPLY TO INFLATE YOUR FRAGILE EGO! THIS IS THE LAST WARNING!

It was almost eleven at night, but Nate had strange sleep patterns, so I trudged over to his apartment and rang the doorbell. The door opened immediately, and he looked out at me suspiciously, then stepped into the hall to make sure no one was with me.

"Yes?" he said curtly.

I held up the letter. "I just got back from the hospital. So what's with the angry note?"

"You didn't come by."

"I'm here now. I came as soon as I could. Anyway, my mom almost died today."

His face became that of a child. "Your mommy?"

"Yes, remember I told you I was going to see her?"

"Then you still want to be friends?"

"Of course." I gave him a stiff hug and patted him awkwardly on the back. "Now I'm going to bed. I'm beat."

"How's your mommy doing now, Ellie?"

"She's hanging in there, Nate."

"Hanging in there. We are all jus . . . just hanging in there." He stumbled over his words and shut the door in my face.

Atlanta was a beautiful city by night. If I walked outside my apartment building and up the street about a hundred yards, I could see the skyline spreading out to the south, with the lights in the skyscrapers looking like well-ordered stars. But the thing I liked most about my apartment was that when I went out on the little balcony, it was quiet. And sometimes, if it was an especially clear night, like this one, I could look out and see the real stars. I always thought that seeing stars in the middle of the city was like having the best of both worlds.

I liked where I lived. I liked being near downtown, being able to walk outside, down the block, and across the street to Piedmont Park. I especially liked the fact that I was not hidden away from society. In my little world, the nations converged. Businessmen and bums, baseball fans and joggers, little old ladies with an apartment full of cats, struggling students, artists and musicians, drug peddlers and middle-class families with little kids riding their tricycles. On any given day, I could see a mishmash of social classes and nationalities. Young and old, rich and poor. And a grown-up little boy who waited by the door until I got home.

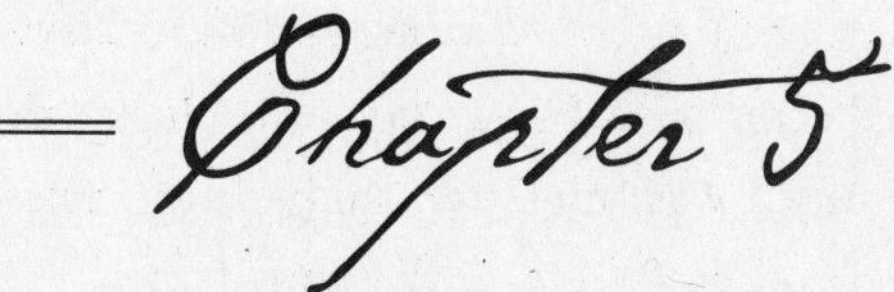

There may be a great fire in our soul and no one ever comes to warm himself at it. . . .

—VINCENT VAN GOGH,
IN A LETTER TO HIS BROTHER THEO

I slept fitfully, waking at two in the morning from the same recurring dream I'd had for the past fifteen years. I'm in a deep chasm and there is fire all around and I'm screaming my lungs out for someone to help me. I'm about six or seven in the dream. Just before the flames engulf me, a ghostlike figure in a white sheet comes and pulls me out of the flames, and I wake up perspiring, my heart beating frantically.

I had dissected this dream step by step during counseling sessions at rehab. It never varied. It was all about the accident where I was scarred for life, all about fear of abandonment and grief and scorching pain.

But as I sat in bed that night, calming myself, I admitted the truth. For the past three years, I had only had the dream once, maybe twice, as compared to the monthly nightmares of my youth. The diminution of the dream corresponded precisely with the amount of time I spent with my family, specifically my mother. It wasn't just selfishness that kept me away from them. It was self-preservation.

And now the dream was back in Technicolor. I stayed awake

wrestling with my thoughts for at least two hours.

I pulled myself out of bed a little after eight the next morning. First I called Sharon and learned that we'd lost our softball game eight to seven on an error by our catcher. Then I forced myself to dial Daddy's number at work. I didn't think I could bear hearing bad news, but I had promised myself during the night that I would be a respectable daughter, even at the expense of the nightmare returning.

Daddy's secretary answered and put me through to my father.

"Hey, Ellie. How are you this morning?"

"I'm okay. How's Mom?"

"She had a much better night. I went by to see her early this morning, and she was smiling and eating cornflakes. Your visits made all the difference in the world."

Sure, Dad, I thought. But I said, "Well, that's great that she's doing better. I work at four. I'll try to go down before then."

"Don't bother. Trixie and Rachel are going to be there most of the day. You've done your part for now, honey. We'll call if anything changes. Promise."

"Do you know when they'll let her leave?"

"Probably by Wednesday or Thursday, if her platelet count keeps improving."

"If they let her go home in the next few days, you go too." Rachel's words pounded in my mind along with my angry response. *No! Leave me alone!*

"Okay, then, Daddy. Hang in there. And don't be afraid to call." A good neutral response, I told myself. I sounded interested, but no commitment necessary. Not yet.

Every Monday morning around eight, Megan and I met for breakfast at a little place called the Flying Biscuit Café on the corner of Piedmont and Tenth Street, only a short walk from my apartment. We loved the fluffy homemade biscuits served with butter and honey and an aroma you could taste before you walked in the front door.

I felt a wave of relief as soon as I walked into the café and saw Megan sitting at our regular table—the one with the bright green vinyl tablecloth with flowers on it. Megan had her silky black hair carelessly pulled back and clipped up off of her neck, and she wore a loose-fitting sleeveless denim top and khakis, but it didn't matter. She looked gorgeous with no makeup and a winsome expression on her face.

She smiled when she caught sight of me. Then she gave a fake frown and chastised, "I thought our rendezvous was supposed to be at eight. It's eight-twenty, girl, and I've already had my second cup of coffee."

"Sorry, Meg. It's been a hellish weekend. I didn't even have time to call you." I filled her in on Mom. "Rachel says I should help out, but you of all people know that I do not want to go back home. Period."

Megan looked thoughtful, started to say something, then stopped.

"What?" I prodded.

She shrugged. "I don't know—just that one of your assignments from rehab was to try to spend some time with your mom. Maybe Rachel's suggestion isn't so bad."

I stuck my head in the menu, though I knew it by heart, and waited for our favorite waiter to take our orders before answering. "Megan, it's too complicated."

We made small talk for at least five minutes until Megan said, "Remember what they told you—one day at a time."

"Yeah, but not today. I would shrink up and die back at that house."

"Quit exaggerating. It's not so bad. I mean, I should know. I spent half of high school at your house."

By now our orders had arrived. We always got the same thing: the "Flying Biscuit Breakfast"—two large farm-fresh eggs served with free-range chicken and sage breakfast sausage, cheese grits, and a Flying Biscuit.

Megan took her biscuit and gently pulled it apart. I watched the steam escape as she delicately spread butter across the interior.

"If you go back home, I'll come by and visit your folks and keep you company too. Timothy's out of town at the end of the week. Think about it, at least."

I shrugged, slopping butter and honey on my biscuit until my fingers were totally sticky. I quickly consumed my biscuit, grits, and eggs while Megan nibbled her biscuit.

Our weekly breakfasts served another purpose—we were each other's accountability partners, something my rehab program had highly recommended and Megan had agreed to. We had a list of questions we asked each other every week.

I started. "You and Timothy—doing okay? He's treating you right?"

She frowned. "Yeah, he is." She took a swallow of coffee.

"So why are you frowning?"

"I still can't forget. Every time he touches me, I shrink back at first." That sad, defeated look that I knew so well was back in her almost-black eyes.

"Do you talk about it?"

"Yeah, and he's great about listening, being patient, all that. But I can't help wondering when he's gonna get tired of me."

"Timothy's different, Megan—I can see it. He's wild about you."

"He told me I was beautiful yesterday. I've begged him never, ever to use those words again. Why can't he remember?"

"You know he means it; he's not like the others."

"I know in my head he means it, but I don't know if it will ever sink into this old scarred heart. Enough on me. How are you? No drugs? No Jamal?"

"Fat and frazzled is all I am. But I can't wait to see him tonight."

"Jamal? Great, Ellie. Just what you need. This is the guy who was all over you Friday night. I tell you, he's not right for you."

"He was out with a bunch of jerks then. He's a good guy."

"What makes you play dumb all of a sudden? Remember that one little word? Drugs? He does drugs. You are *not* going back there. Don't even think of it."

"I'm not sure he does a lot of drugs."

"Go ahead. Change your tune. You're making me mad."

"I'm just being honest, Megan. If he asked me out, I'd go. There's nothing the matter with that. I haven't had the company of a guy in so long."

"I thought I was supposed to be checking up on you, making sure you stuck by your promises."

"I never promised not to go out with a guy."

"No, but you promised not to put yourself in a potentially compromising situation. Something like that. I'd say that a date with Jamal is 'potentially compromising.'"

"Well, look who's talking, Miss Goody-two-shoes. Where'd you meet Timothy? At a bar. It worked out all right for you."

Megan's voice sounded sad all of the sudden. "I guess it's working out. But, Ellie, don't go with Jamal. It's red-hot dangerous. Please."

"He probably isn't interested anyway. No one ever is."

"Ellie, stop the pity party. Anyway, I've already told you—you have a date for this weekend. I'll hang out with you. Put your mom to bed, and we'll watch a video and eat popcorn. Like old times."

"I'll think about it."

"Leave Jamal alone. Promise?"

Later, when I waved good-bye to her, I was thinking that Megan's friendship was the one redeeming relationship in my life at the moment.

It was Tuesday around noon when we got the message about Nan's miscarriage. Daddy had invited me to eat lunch with him at the Varsity, and Abbie had joined us. Nan's husband, Stockton, called on Dad's cell phone while we were in the middle of lunch. His conversation with Daddy lasted only a couple minutes. Right away, by the tone in Daddy's voice, I could tell something was wrong. Then he started whispering and turned his back to Abbie and me.

"Nan's lost the baby," Daddy choked out after he hung up the phone. "She's all torn up about it."

I thought of cute, vivacious Nannie. That's what I called her when I was a kid. I had always gotten along better with Nan than with Abbie, until the whole drug scene. Nan knew about my wild parties, and since she attended plenty of her own, she promised not to breathe a word to Mom and Dad. But when I got arrested and expelled, she was furious with me, and our relationship had been strained ever since.

I never imagined her as an elementary school teacher. To me, teaching demanded a lot of discipline and hard work, neither of which was high on Nan's list. But I guess she'd changed. She had the spunk and creativity for teaching, and she certainly wasn't afraid to be up in front of a classroom of kids. In fact, she was "in her element"—at least that's what Mom always said.

So it was hard for me to imagine my spunky sister all torn up about a miscarriage for a baby she didn't even want.

Abbie looked miserable and held her swollen belly. Her chili dog and french fries went untouched. "It's awful, Daddy. This with Momma being so sick. It's awful."

"Look, honey, you need to rest. Try not to let it get to you. Call Nan tomorrow, but go get some rest tonight."

The three of us sat there in silence for a little while. Occasionally Daddy would take a slow slurp of his frosted orange drink, a Varsity special, and glance at the TV screen in the corner of the room where some sportscaster was commentating on a baseball game.

Finally I thought of something to say. "Well, she didn't want a baby now anyway. It must not have been the right time." I said this because it sounded like some of the Bartholomew babble I was likely to hear. My family always accredited misfortune to something that wasn't the Lord's timing. According to them, His timing was always perfect.

But Abbie was scowling at me in a way that let me know I had missed the mark.

"No matter what the circumstances, a miscarriage is always awful. Nan is broken up about it. She's just devastated," Abbie said through her tears. "You heard what Daddy said."

I kept my mouth slammed shut for the rest of the meal. My family was falling apart and there was nothing I could do about it. Or was there? Now Megan's voice was echoing in my mind along with Rachel's. There was something I could do.

I waited until Abbie had walked out to her car to put my arm through Daddy's. He watched her from the Varsity's spacious parking lot, and I surveyed his golden brown hair with the strands of gray intertwined. He was wearing a dark green short-sleeved polo shirt, so that the deep scarring on his right arm was visible.

In that second, Daddy looked vulnerable, as if whatever had scarred him physically had also reached inside and cut into his soul. I was not used to seeing the look of resignation I now read on his face.

With emotions of compassion and worry mixed together, I made a decision, a very small decision. I picked my words carefully, thoughtfully. "Daddy, when Mom comes home, I'd like to move back in with you for a week or so, just to help out and make sure she's fine—if that's okay with you."

Daddy was quiet for a moment, still staring out to where Abbie's car was pulling away. But his arm tightened around me, and I could imagine the tightness in his throat as he choked out, "Why, Ellie, if you could, if you'd be willing, that'd be a great help. I'm sure your mother would be thrilled."

"I'll do it, Daddy. It's the least I can do." For the first time in weeks, I felt that I had just said the right thing.

Rachel had promised to stop by my apartment on her way to the airport on Tuesday.

"I wish you didn't have to go, Rach."

"If I want to keep my job—and I do—I've got to go."

"Will you come again soon?"

"I'll be back at Thanksgiving. Always come for the big turkey."

"That's five months away."

"Look, if anything comes up before then, I'm only a phone call away, and your mother knows it. Everything's gonna be all right. She's a fighter, your mom. And I think you are too. It'll be good for both of you to be back home together. Have fun. And you'll be in Scotland before you know it."

I shrugged. "I don't see why you think I'm going to suddenly have this great relationship with Mom. She avoids all the issues. Like this thing with the Matthewses—what's the deal there? Obviously something happened to make them all drift apart, but no way Mom will tell me about it. Will you at least give me a hint?"

"No, I won't. We all have painful things in our past, Ellie. I won't tell you all the nitty-gritty details about my divorce. I don't want to go back there. I've survived, and I've dealt with it, but I won't ever be able to talk about it in casual conversation. If your mom and dad don't want to talk about their thing with Carl and Cassandra, they shouldn't have to."

"But I want to know. You're the one encouraging me to get to know my mom."

"Then get to know her. Don't treat her life like a cheap mystery novel with a surprise ending. Care about *her*. Let her let you into her life. Quit thinking of yourself."

"So you think I'm selfish too," I accused.

"Yes, Ellie, I do. Everything still revolves around you. And you're miserable that way."

I think my mouth was hanging open.

"Don't look so stunned. I was the same way at twenty. A jerk. A big jerk, and especially to your mother. I thought I was involved in all these noble causes, but I was really just a messed-up kid being selfish. You'll get over it."

"How do you know I will? Lots of people never do. How did you get over it, Rachel?"

She was stroking Hindsight, her slim legs curled under her on the leather couch. "I hung around your mother."

It only took about five minutes for me to drive from my apartment on Argonne Avenue near Tenth Street to Mom and Dad's house on Beverly Road. They lived in a gray stone Tudor cottage in Ansley Park, an "in town" neighborhood about five minutes from the Arts Center. Most of the houses were old, what they called "fixer-uppers," big homes that had been owned by prominent Atlanta families in the first half of the century and had fallen into disrepair when the wealthy folk left the inner city. Even as early as the seventies, Atlanta was losing tens of thousands of residents in the flight to the suburbs.

Mom and Dad had been "dirt poor" when they married—although I always smiled at that description, since both of their families were what I'd call "filthy rich." But it was true that Mom and Daddy didn't live off their families' fortunes. They had chosen to live in town, which at the time was seen as less fashionable than living in Buckhead, the wealthy neighborhood in northwest Atlanta where both had grown up. My parents liked the Ansley Park neighborhood's location—near the High Museum and the inner city. I guess it fit their dreams—Mom the would-be artist and Dad the struggling city planner.

Little by little, as their careers blossomed, they had joined with other Ansley Park residents in reconstruction projects, so that nowadays these old homes were considered "rare treasures" within the city. Daddy had always taken part in the zoning committee, helping the neighborhood fight off encroaching developers who were looking at Ansley Park as raw land for parking lots or commercial centers.

And it had worked. The neighborhood was a flowering oasis and was listed on the National Register of Historic Places as a historic district and neighborhood. So while skyscrapers shot up and towered around, the residents held their ground and dared anyone to step over the imaginary lines of Ansley Park. Neighbors became excited about renovating and restoring the old homes and developed a strong neighborhood association, complete with a quarterly publication, a civic association, and committees on everything from environment and history to security and traffic control.

In the end, the people who lived in Ansley Park were plenty well-off. Nan once teased Mom and Dad that, in spite of their desire to live in a racially diverse neighborhood, the only thing diverse about the place was the various sexual orientations of its residents. At which Mom had furrowed her brow and said, "Nan!" while Daddy had simply chuckled. For as conservative as they were, my parents had friends of every race, religion, and sexual preference.

I stood in the little driveway on that Wednesday morning, observing their home—I guess I should say *our* home. The steep roof rose to a sharp point, giving the house a small appearance. It sat on a narrow embankment overlooking a golf course. There was a front porch where for years we'd kept our bikes and gerbils. After Abbie and Nan moved out, Mom decorated it with wicker furniture and plants. Mom and Daddy liked to sit out on the porch and sip iced tea on muggy summer evenings, waving to kids who rode by on their bikes and neighbors strolling their dogs.

I walked up the stone steps, carrying my worn Nike sports bag stuffed with clothes in one hand, and the cage that contained a meowing Hindsight in the other, and pulled open the screened door to the porch. To my right was the front door. I had my own key and went inside. Just one step in, my feet touching the hardwood floors and my eyes glimpsing the oil paintings adorning the pale yellow walls of the den, and the memories rushed at me. I walked through the den and dining room into the kitchen. Daddy had left a note on the counter: *Went to get groceries. Be back soon.*

"It's not so bad," Megan had said. She was right, of course. The house

itself was a tribute to my parents' loving and careful restoration, from the antique wood Dad had gotten from an old barn in North Georgia to make the kitchen cabinets to the staircase's Italian marble steps, a gift from Mom's friend Jean-Paul. He'd shipped the marble over, knowing of Daddy's talent and Mom's love of the smooth rock substance, and instructed them to use it as they pleased.

Jean-Paul, a French guy, was an artist himself and a successful one. He felt this great indebtedness to Mom, for some reason, and loved to shower her with gifts. I guess Daddy could have been jealous, except for the fact that Jean-Paul was ten years younger than Mom and Dad, and she considered him as a younger brother.

My favorite addition to the house was the sunroom, located behind the kitchen, with a view out on the backyard. It was actually Mom's atelier, where she went to paint. I loved that room and its smell. For years, before she married, Mom had used her own mother's atelier at Granddad and Trixie's house—a spacious room with one wall filled with nothing but windows. She missed that room when she and Daddy moved into their house, so Daddy had designed the sunroom for his Swannee.

Even unartistic me had always thought it was the perfect hideout for an artist. The glass doors looked out onto "the garden"; that's what Mom always called it. During my early years, it was simply a backyard, with grass and trees and a swing set. And animals. But as we'd grown older, the yard had been transformed into a beautiful hideaway. There was a green bench that sat in one corner, surrounded by flowering plants. In the late morning, the sun warmed that bench, and I had lounged there many times, reading a novel. There were flower beds throughout this informal garden, with flagstone paths leading to the bench and a pond with goldfish. A dark green wrought-iron fountain splashed water into the pond.

When Mom had no pressing orders for paintings, she just sat in her sunroom, threw open the glass doors, and painted the colors of her yard. Those paintings sold really well.

"It reminds me of your Grandmom Sheila—all her paintings of Resthaven—she painted the gardens there," Mom had told me once. "This is my haven. I sit back here and block out the sounds of the world, and paint."

I walked into the atelier and set down Hindsight's cage. Even though it had been months since I'd been out on this porch, I felt at home with the smell of the oil paints and turpentine and the big ficus trees on either side of her easel. Several canvases were covered with tarps. I was about to lift one off and take a peek when I heard a sound behind me.

"Oh, there you are, Ellie." Daddy looked a bit frazzled. "Thank goodness you're here. I'm off to pick up your mom from the hospital."

"Do you want me to come with you?"

"No, no, we'll be fine. But could you put up the groceries and listen to the messages on the answering machine? If it's an order for a painting, here's the notebook to write it in. Some people won't know about the setback. Just note the messages, try to figure out which are the most important to answer, and star those. And could you check your mother's e-mail? She'll have orders there too. If you could simply respond that due to health reasons, she is unable to answer immediately—"

"Daddy, everything doesn't have to be perfectly in order when Mom gets back. Relax. I'll do what I can."

He flashed me the smile I knew so well—the one that showed his dimples and erased the worry lines on his forehead. "Thank you, Ellie. You're right, of course. One thing at a time. It's just that I want everything to be—"

"To be perfect for Mom. I know. But calm down, Daddy! Everything *is* perfect. She's coming home, right?"

"Right." He patted me on the shoulder and turned to leave the room. "Oh, Mrs. Elliott is bringing over a casserole for supper in a little while."

Mrs. Elliott had been our neighbor for twenty-five years.

"And then Janet from Mom's women's circle at church has got a lot of ladies signed up for meals. She may call. You just arrange it with her, okay? I'm off."

He kissed me on the forehead and left me standing in the sunroom.

It felt strange to be back. I had dodged this house for three years, and now here I was—in the middle of my parents' world again. Their little girl, their baby.

I did not want to be here.

Part of my high school madness had been an attempt to flee this house. Flee the frequent visitors who filed through—kids coming for their sittings, neighbors bringing their tales of woe, friends from church and business. And flee the way my parents tried to make me the center of attention. Ellie this and Ellie that. Ellie winning the chess tournaments, Ellie first in the math competition. Ellie figuring out the problems with the computer and the e-mail. "We're so thankful to have a technical genius in the house," Mom often bragged.

You loved me for my mind, Mom. I was a failure in every other way, so you chose to love me for my mind.

I was in the midst of my thoughts when the doorbell rang. It was Mrs. Elliott.

"Ellie Bartholomew! Well, I never!" she exclaimed as she marched into the hallway, headed straight for the kitchen, and set down her casserole on the stove top. Then she gave me a smothering hug.

She was about seventy, rather tall and very sturdy, so that when she hugged you, she pressed you tightly into her ample bosom and held you there until you were struggling to come up for air. I remembered those hugs well.

"Well, it's a treat to see you, young lady. Your mother must be tickled to death to have you here. She's always going on and on about you and Abbie and Nan. You know how we mothers and grandmothers are. I mean, what would we do if we didn't have our kids to talk about? Anyway, she just rattles on. I think she said you may go to vet school someday. That is perfect. When she said that, I knew immediately why she did your painting that way. I think it is absolutely the best thing she's ever done. It is you all over. Don't you just love it? Where in the world are you going to put it? I kept wondering that to myself when she showed it to me. She said your apartment is a little small for it, but she couldn't help it. It needed to be that size—"

She must have noticed that I was looking at her in a strange way, because she stopped to catch her breath.

"What painting, Mrs. Elliott?"

"You know—the one she did for your birthday. . . . Oh my, don't tell me you haven't seen it yet?"

"My birthday is in July."

"Oh, for heaven's sake, I've gone and ruined the surprise! I'm so sorry. Just like me to do that. Well, don't say a thing to your mother, dear." Mrs. Elliott walked out the door, still talking about her blunder. "Sure is good to see you again, Ellie . . ."

Mom had a "tradition" of painting each of her daughters for her twenty-first birthday. I remembered when Abbie sat for her portrait on weekends home from college. She wanted a formal portrait, and I used to watch Mom paint it and feel a little jealous of Abbie's beautiful thick blond hair and her perfect figure as she sat straight-backed in a chair, dressed in a flattering turquoise sweater and silk skirt.

Nan, true to herself, had chosen to be perched on the split-rail fence in the backyard, dressed in jeans and a T-shirt, her dark brown hair bobbed close to her head. She was laughing, and the mischief in her eyes was absolutely perfect.

But I had not thought for one moment about my portrait, even though I would be twenty-one in six weeks. Nor had Mom mentioned it to me. But, of course, the first thing I did after Mrs. Elliott's sudden departure was to go back to the sunroom and uncover the paintings.

Sure enough, there was one of me. It was large, probably three feet by four feet. It showed me close up with Hindsight in my lap. I don't know how she did it, but Mom had made me look pretty, almost feminine.

I scowled at first at what I considered her artistic license. My eyes were a deep, intriguing jade green behind long, dark lashes. I looked peaceful and content and as self-assured as the cat on my lap. I was wearing my favorite denim shirt, and my long blond hair was loose and falling over my shoulders.

It was so startling to see how Mom had perceived me that I said out loud, "Mom, you are still trying to reinvent me. To make me your beautiful little girl again. Well, it won't work!"

Then I noticed a snapshot sitting on the easel right beside the painting. I remembered when Nan had taken it last fall, on one of the rare occasions when she had come to my apartment.

"You better not get me in the picture!" I'd protested. I hated seeing myself in photos.

"Don't worry, sis. You'll be glad one day to have a nice shot of your cat." That was all she'd said as she snapped several pictures.

Well, Nan had obviously lied, and the result was on the easel in front of me. I stared back and forth from the photo to the painting and was dumbfounded. The painting looked just like the photo. I mean, the painting had more warmth, more vitality. My eyes were, as I've said, intriguing. But the rest of the painting was the same. My hair was shining in the photo, and I liked how I'd pulled it over one shoulder. Hindsight was in my lap, covering up my enormous thighs. And my mouth! That was the strangest part of all. From the angle at which Nan had taken the photo and the position that Mom had painted, you really couldn't tell that my mouth was all messed up.

I was astounded.

Mom had painted a chessboard on the table beside me and a novel sitting on top of the board, with a few overturned pawns lying beside the book. And a can of Coke on top of the novel.

So here I was, staring at this absolutely stunning portrait and admiring Mom again for the way she could get into a person's skin. And the thought rushing through my head at that moment was *I don't know you, Mom. I really don't. But you know me. You know me inside and out.*

It had been years since I had lived at home. Years since I'd spent the night in my old bedroom, and I approached the adventure with all the foreboding of a child going off to camp for the first time. Excitement and pure terror. I walked upstairs and into my bedroom. It looked much the same as when I'd left it almost three years ago. I had removed the angriest of the posters and taken them with me to drug rehab, but the walls certainly weren't those of a frilly young girl. In my rebellious years I had demanded cobalt blue walls. Mom had said, "Fine. It's your room. I'll pay for the first coat of paint. After that, if you don't like it, you pay."

One night in the midst of our precipitant decline during senior year, Megan and I had thrown old sheets over all the furniture and the floor and then quite literally paint-balled my room, splattering cobalt blue all over my walls. There was no rhyme or reason to our method, except anger. And it showed when you walked into the room.

I had twin beds, and Mom had put two old family quilts across them for bedspreads. The quilts were a wonderful hodgepodge of colors—red and blue and green and yellow in tiny squares of fabric sewn together by hand. I liked the contrast of that old hand-woven tradition with my teenage hysteria.

"Well, here we are," I announced as I let Hindsight out of the cage. She was furious to have been moved from her home to new surroundings, and she skittered under the bed.

I felt the heaviness immediately. The memory of my hopelessness and fear and anger settled down upon me like the quilts on my twin beds. I flopped down on my bed and switched on the lamp on the wooden bedside table. It was an antique from my grandparents' house, probably worth a lot of money, but it wiggled on two unstable legs, and I used to curse it at night.

I rolled over onto my back and stared at the ceiling, which had not escaped the paint-ball effects. I didn't particularly like art, or just any old art, but I liked Van Gogh and his swirly canvases. As I looked at the angry swirling paint on my walls, it reminded me of his painting *Starry Night* and the song "Vincent" that Don McLean had written about him in the seventies. I hummed it to myself, repeating some of the words of this ballad to insanity in my mind.

I thought of my grandmom Sheila, who painted and struggled with insanity. I thought of Nate, sitting by his phone and hoping it would ring. And I thought of the one-eared painter, taking his life in a field in Arles, France, on a tormented starry night.

My desk beckoned to me. I sat down and unlocked the cover. It was the kind of desk where the top folded down to make the writing part, and there were numerous little drawers inside. I opened one and found it stuffed with letters. I smiled, seeing my childish scrawl of eleven or twelve.

I opened another drawer, which was filled with letters from Mom. She had written them to me when I was away at Camp Hollyhill. I took one out of its envelope. Mom's flowery cursive filled the page. I remembered the month and the year, June 1990. I was almost ten and terrified of going to camp for two weeks.

Ellie, dear,

I am praying every day all throughout each day that you will have a wonderful time at camp. Remember the talks we had and that you are perfect and unique just the way God created you.

Are you having fun canoeing? Remember the first time we went canoeing together and you fell in the Chattahoochee and then so did I? Fall in again for me. And be sure to brush the horses for me.

Have fun, my precious one.

Bundles of love,

Mom

I had hated that camp. Some mean girls had ridiculed my mouth from the start. A couple of girls were kind to me when I cried, but not many. I determined to show the snooty girls I was good at sports, and I soundly licked them in volleyball and swimming, but it didn't win me many friends.

Abbie and Nan had loved Camp Hollyhill. I hadn't really wanted to go, and Mom didn't make me. Reading her letter, I did remember the times we sat together on my bed and she talked to me about my fears. She knew my facial disfigurement was a terrible burden, but she wanted me to be able to overcome it. She always told me God had a plan and that my life had infinite worth. But after that camp, and the taunts of the other girls, I was pretty sure Mom was wrong about God.

And I didn't know how to forgive you, Mom. That thought out of the blue jolted me. But it was perfectly true. I still blamed Mom for the accident, for the resulting disfigurement. Often through the years, we had talked about true inner beauty versus exterior beauty. But never ever did we talk about the accident, the details, the aftermath. It was just too painful. I certainly wasn't going to bring it up.

In drug rehab, the counselors had asked me questions and listened when I occasionally decided to talk. I had a whole list of homework that I was supposed to complete when I got out. During my breakfasts with Megan, we referred to these commitments. Many I had upheld. But I didn't go near the goal that said *talk to Mom about the accident*.

I set aside the letter and picked up another.

Dear Ellie,

We got your letter today. I'm so glad you're having fun at camp! That's an answer to prayer, isn't it? The weather is so hot and muggy here, we spend every afternoon over at Granddad JJ's and Trixie's in the pool. The ladies at prayer group send a big hello. We prayed for you today. I loved reading about the volleyball game and how your team beat the older girls. I'm not one bit surprised. I'm sure it's because they had you on their team!

Nan sends her love—she says to enjoy camp because soon you'll have to work in the summers and it is NO FUN—direct quote. Just between you and me, she likes her job at The Gap and comes home with a new outfit every other day! I doubt she's saving any money.

Daddy left yesterday for the convention. He'll be back on Friday, and then we'll come get you on Saturday! Can't wait!

Abbie sends a big hello too.

Love,
Mom

I sighed and then felt a stabbing pain deep inside. I remembered getting those letters and feeling a bit guilty that I'd lied and told Mom I was having fun. I couldn't bear to tell her how awful it really was. How could I tell Mom that her prayers for me weren't working?

And I had felt angry. If all these people were concentrating their prayers on me, well, why wasn't it working? God worked for Mom and Dad. At least it seemed like He did. And for Abbie and Nan too. My ten-year-old mind had reasoned that something was terribly the matter with me, then, something maybe even worse than facial disfigurement that made God look away too.

And the very deepest wound struck me with a force as I read Mom's hopeful, prayer-filled letters. Always the same. Always talking about God and faith as if she were commenting on the weather. So easy and personal. But the wound inside said—no, shouted—*Mom, it's not fair! It's not fair for you to pray for me. It's too easy. It's your fault I look like this! I hate it when you try to pray it away. I hate you for leaving me! I hate you for this wound.*

I shivered, remembering the nights as a young girl when I had sobbed in my bed with so many confused thoughts churning away. The nightmares always followed. I heard Nan's accusation again. *"If you weren't so darned selfish. If you'd just get your eyes off of yourself. . . ."* It was true. My thoughts did often revolve around me and what others thought of me. I honestly didn't think I was trying to make an excuse. I was trying to make sense. There was a difference between the two, a big difference.

One of the counselors at rehab had taken me aside after I had tried to describe my feelings toward my mother. "Ellie, those feelings are legitimate," the counselor had said. "But at some point you must get beyond them. The only way to freedom is through forgiveness. You must forgive your mother and try to start something new."

It all sounded so easy, but it was a chasm a mile deep and I was somewhere at the very bottom, a little girl, lifting up my arms and screaming for my mother to come and rescue me.

Chapter 6

To bestow on them a crown of beauty instead of ashes, the oil of gladness instead of mourning, and a garment of praise instead of a spirit of despair.

—ISAIAH 61:3B

Here we are, Ellie!" Daddy's voice called out from the hall downstairs. I could tell that he was trying to sound cheerful. I stuffed Mom's letters into the niche in the desk, closed the cover, and came downstairs.

"Hi, Mom!" I said, sounding too enthusiastic. The moment I saw her, I felt the color drain from my cheeks.

One week ago, she had looked thin but well-groomed and ready to continue the fight with cancer. I thought of her laughing at the Swan Coach House. Today she looked weak . . . worse than weak. She looked as if she'd given up.

She was sitting in one of the armchairs in the den, still wearing a robe, and she hadn't bothered to put on any makeup. The robe was an expensive dark blue satin, but it hung all wrong on her emaciated frame. The sockets of her eyes were hollow and dark, and her wig looked completely unnatural, as if maybe Daddy had tugged it onto her head for her. They both looked as though they'd exhausted every last bit of strength to get her into the car and out again.

"Everything's ready," I said, again too brightly, recovering from my shock. "Where would you like to be? You can stay in the den or go up to your bedroom, or we can have lunch if you want."

"Thank you for coming, Ellie," she said in a whisper, and then tried to clear her throat. "I believe I'll lie down for a while."

Daddy gathered her in his arms and carried her upstairs, and I followed. As he set her carefully on their bed, I turned away, unable to watch this gentlest of gestures.

"What can I get you, my Fat Goose?" he whispered, kissing her forehead.

"Nothing right now, Scout," she whispered back. "I think I'll just close my eyes for a little while."

We left the room after Daddy had tenderly tucked Mom under the covers, like a little child.

"She looks awful, Daddy." It came out before I thought about the effect these words could have on him.

"She's lost a lot of weight in the past week. The doctor wasn't overly excited about letting her come home, but she was so insistent. She's had far too much of that hospital. I think she'll do better now. I have to take her to the oncologist's office every day to have the platelets checked. I'll handle that, Ellie, in the mornings before I go to work. I told the folks at work that I'd be coming in late for a while."

Daddy sank into a chair. "Thank you for coming. Ellie, I don't know how I'd manage without you. Abbie is too tired, and Nan . . ."

"Have you told Mom about Nan?"

"No, no, not yet. The thought of little babies is one thing that cheers her up. I can't bear to tell her yet."

To pass the time, I started listening to the messages on the answering machine. There were at least twenty of them. Many were just friends calling to check on Mom; a few concerned her art. I was absentmindedly noting the names and numbers and petting Hindsight when I suddenly sat up straight, intent on the woman's voice on the tape.

"Hello, Robbie and Mary Swan. This is Cassandra." There was a pause and then, "Cassandra Matthews. I . . . I ran into, well, Carl and I ran into your daughter Ellie at the Humane Society party last Saturday night. Maybe she mentioned it. Such a wonderful young lady! Looks so much like you, Mary Swan. But Ellie told us about your cancer. I . . . I'm so sorry to hear it. I . . . I wanted to call and see if there was anything I could do . . . if you needed food or a nurse to stop by . . . I'm in home health care now, and I do visits. . . . I'll try back later. Carl and I are praying for you both." And she left her phone number.

I finished copying down the messages, set down my pen and paper, and scooted the wooden chair back from the kitchen table where I was sitting. Mom was resting peacefully. This was not the time for her to have a heart-to-heart talk with me. I paced the kitchen, opened the antique cabinets, and surveyed their contents. The everyday china that Mom had always used when we were kids was still stacked on the same shelf beside the stove.

I took down a cereal bowl and found myself smiling as I held it in my hands. It was Italian pottery, a gray-blue background with a dark blue strip around the rim of the bowl, and two more dark blue strips along the sides. Inside the bowl were painted three different flower designs—one bright yellow, resembling a pansy or maybe a daisy with a blue interior. Then there was a cluster of three maroon-colored little flowers, almost looking like berries. And finally two dark blue long-stemmed irises. A very happy bowl. Mom loved bright colors and especially flowers. She'd painted a frieze across the top of the kitchen using the same pattern of flowers from the pottery.

But what made me smile was the crack across the middle of the bowl and the chip on the rim. Those testimonies to use and age had been there for years. I smiled, thinking how Mom had never thrown out a bowl, no matter how chipped. Daddy would patiently and lovingly glue back the pieces of whatever pottery hit the tiled kitchen floor, and we'd keep right on using them.

Once, when Abbie, Nan, and I were fairly young, we started dancing with excitement around Mom, who had just returned from one of her first art showings. We inadvertently knocked into her antique Italian faience bowl, which hung on the kitchen wall. It hit the floor and shattered into a hundred pieces. After she got over the initial shock, Mom hugged us and said, "It's no big deal. Just a plate."

But we felt awful because we knew how much that plate had meant to her. She'd gotten it in Florence when she was traveling around Europe with Rachel. She loved to tell us the story of how she had sat on a wall near the Ponte Vecchio and sketched the vendors interacting with the tourists. Then, as she herself was walking across the famous bridge, she'd spotted this large shallow bowl with the familiar Italian patterns and the colors of yellow and blue, tempting her from a vendor's table. But she had only one hundred lira left in her pocket, and the bowl cost four thousand. Rachel talked the toothless vendor into selling it to Mom for a ridiculously low price in exchange for Mom sketching his portrait.

"I cherish this bowl because it came in an unusual way," she said. "We each sacrificed a little to get what we wanted, and that makes it all the more special."

So when the bowl was shattered, we felt shattered for Mom. Each of us helped gather up the pieces, but we knew there was absolutely no way Daddy could glue this treasure back together.

Mom never said another word about it. But one day, months later, she called us onto the sunporch and asked brightly, "How do you like our new table?"

Sitting by her easel was a small black wrought-iron table with a round top made of bright mosaic pottery pieces. On closer inspection we discovered it was the broken bowl, resurrected into a new treasure. We applauded Mom. She blushed.

The memory of that incident enticed me out onto the sunporch. I stood beside that same wrought-iron table and brushed my hand against the spider plant that sat on top, its healthy spindles cascading to the floor. Then I ran my hand across the mosaic tiles, feeling the uneven surface of the grout between the smooth tiles.

It's not so bad. You're exaggerating. Yes, Megan, maybe being back home at this time was an essential piece in the mosaic-in-the-making that was my life.

I discovered that one of my main jobs was answering the door as various friends and neighbors delivered casseroles, soups, and baked goodies. The other responsibility was answering the phone. I picked up the receiver for at least the tenth time in a period of three hours.

"Hello?"

"Yes, hello. May I speak to Mary Swan?"

"She's resting right now. May I take a message?"

"Yes, my name is Cassandra Matthews. I called a few days ago. I'm an old friend of Mary Swan's."

"Mrs. Matthews! It's Ellie." I surprised myself with the enthusiasm that resounded in my voice. I paused, regained my composure, and said, "Yes, Mom got your message."

"Oh, Ellie. So you're playing nurse. How is your mother?"

"Well, to tell you the truth, she's had a really rotten week. Her platelets went way down and she had some bad hemorrhaging—twice. And she's had two transfusions."

"And the doctor let her out of the hospital?"

"I think both Daddy and the doctor thought she might do better at home."

"Yes, they're probably right. Well, listen, Ellie. Is there a time I could come by for a quick visit? I promise I won't stay long."

"She hasn't been up for visits yet, but Daddy said tomorrow she could see a few people."

"Then I'll come tomorrow afternoon."

"Okay. Yeah, that should be okay." I was about to say good-bye when I remembered something. "How's the puppy?"

Mrs. Matthews gave a wry laugh. "That puppy is giving my daughter and her husband a run for their money. A real handful, that little rascal. But my little granddaughter is wild about him—so that makes it just fine."

The first night in my old bedroom felt like a long, torturous trip through my childhood, where any happy memories were covered with dark paint and darker nightmares, broken only by intermittent times of staring at my swirling walls. All the pain of my adolescence, the drugs, the parties, the lies, Megan's horrors, all of this swirled around in my head until I found myself screaming silently in the middle of the night, "Why didn't you do anything about it, Mom? Why couldn't you see my anguish? Why didn't you try to see it? Why didn't you stop me?"

In another flash, I remembered all the times I had been grounded, all the sermons Mom and Dad had given, the muggy hot nights with their one-sided conversations and my defiant stare and silence. I remembered the anger and hate that welled up inside of me and my scornful pride that said, "You'll never get me to talk. No matter how hard you try, I will never talk."

But they had tried.

As I opened the door for Cassandra Matthews the next afternoon, she took my hand in hers in a warm, strong clasp. "It sure is good to see you again, Ellie." She was the same petite woman I remembered from the Humane Society party, only today she was dressed casually, her white linen suit replaced with a smooth-fitting blue cotton dress. She reached down and picked up a large vase filled with daisies. "From our garden—I thought they might cheer Mary Swan up—inspire her to get back to painting."

Perhaps I was imagining it, but Mrs. Matthews seemed a bit on edge. I pretended not to notice and showed her into the house.

"How's your momma doing today, Ellie? Is she resting okay?"

"Pretty well, I think, although she seems so tired." We stood in the entrance hall for an awkward moment until I thought of something to say. "Would you like a Coke? It's awfully muggy outside."

She smiled. "Just a glass of water would be fine."

I motioned for her to have a seat in the den and carried the vase into the kitchen. When I brought her the cold drink, I said, "I checked in on Mom a few minutes ago, and she was asleep."

"Don't wake her, dear."

"She knows you're coming. I'm sure she'll be up before long."

I sat with Mrs. Matthews in the den, a large open room right off the entryway. The furniture in the room was comfortable—a dark green leather couch and two matching fauteuils.

"This is a lovely house. Are all these your mother's paintings?" she asked, indicating with a sweep of her eyes the oil paintings that hung on the walls in the den and the accompanying bright red dining room.

"No, not all, although Daddy insisted that she hang up his favorites. She thinks it's pretentious to have her work displayed, but Daddy . . . well, he wanted it, and Mom would do just about anything to make him happy."

Mrs. Matthews smiled and nodded.

"That's my favorite one there." I pointed to the canvas hanging over the fireplace mantel. It showed a man and a woman standing on opposite sides of Peachtree Street. Cars were going by; the man was standing in front of the Fox Theater, obviously waiting for someone; and the woman was hailing him from the other side, a delighted smile on her face. His expression showed surprise and pleasure.

Mrs. Matthews stood up and walked closer to the painting.

"Mary Swan and her Robbie," she said a bit wistfully.

"Yes, it was when Mom got back from her first art exhibition in

New York. She and Dad had tickets to see *Cats* here at the Fox, but she missed her plane and told Daddy to go on without her. He wasn't too thrilled, until she showed up in a taxi five minutes before the play started. She told him later that she knew he'd be standing outside the Fox waiting for her, and he told her that he knew she'd show up—right at the last minute. That's just how they are."

"Yes, I'd imagine them to be that way. Some things don't change," she said, again with a wistful whisper.

We sat back down, both of us rather stiffly, and I tried to think of a neutral, harmless question to ask. I settled on, "How did you meet my mother?"

"Now, there's a story," Mrs. Matthews said and seemed to relax. "We were at the church down in Grant Park. Have you ever been there?"

I nodded.

"I met your momma on one of the most important days of my life—back in the summer of sixty-two. We were both just scrawny teenagers, about fourteen or fifteen at the time, and I had my new little baby Jessie with me. I was trying to talk to Miss Abigail about something important. Excuse me—did you know Miss Abigail?"

Again I nodded.

"And Jessie was hollering to beat the band, so Miss Abigail asked Mary Swan to hold Jessie. Your poor momma! I don't think she'd ever held a baby before. I'll never forget the look on her face. But Miss Abigail had a way of being convincing, so Mary Swan didn't argue." Mrs. Matthews got a sweet smile on her face. "I thought she might drop little Jessie, the way she was holding her so awkwardly. Fortunately, Carl came to help her. He'd had plenty of experience with babies. And he coddled little Jessie while I gave my heart to Jesus."

In an effort to avoid Bartholomew babble, I asked, "You and Dr. Matthews were married when you were that young?"

"Heavens, no! I was just a messed-up kid with a baby of my own and no man in sight. Carl and I didn't get married till years later, but we were from the same neighborhood and attended the same church. Anyway, your mother didn't quite know what to think of me, this poor black inner-city girl with a baby. And I certainly didn't know what to do with your mother, this rich white girl from that uppity side of Atlanta. I believe the only black person she'd ever met was Ella Mae—the woman who worked for your momma's family—" She stopped in midsentence and said, "Of course, you must know all this. You're named for Ella Mae. I must be boring you to tears."

"No," I said too quickly. "No, I'm not bored." I hoped she couldn't read the embarrassment on my face, nor the intrigue.

"Well, I guess I helped your mother learn about babies, but she's the one who convinced me to stay in school, gave me a desire to get an education, to believe I could get beyond my beginnings."

She set down her glass of water and looked down at her hands, as if she'd said too much. I thought to myself that this woman had the gift of discretion. I could easily imagine her standing behind the doctors, taking their instructions and efficiently acting on them, doing her job so well that she was hardly ever noticed. She was used to being around sick people, used to calming bereaved loved ones, used to caring. But perhaps, it seemed to me in that moment, she was not used to talking about herself and her past.

"Let me see if she's awake," I said.

I found Mom sitting up in bed, sipping a cup of what must have been lukewarm tea. Her old Bible was opened across her lap, and her eyes were closed.

I cleared my throat and whispered, "Mom, Mrs. Matthews is here to see you, if you feel like it."

She turned her eyes to me, a serene smile on her face, and said, "Yes, of course. Of course."

I wondered if she felt the least bit nervous at the thought of being with someone she hadn't seen in so long. But as I closed the door, the only thing I saw in her eyes was fatigue.

I showed Mrs. Matthews into Mom's bedroom, wondering fleetingly if I should leave, but I soon realized it didn't matter. I was all but forgotten as soon as Mrs. Matthews stepped over to Mom's bed.

"Cassie, Cassie, what a blessing to see you. After all these years." Mom choked these words out with difficulty, the kind that comes from overwrought emotions.

"Mary Swan, oh, sweetie." Mrs. Matthews was down on her knees beside the bed, grasping Mom's outstretched hand.

And Mom was crying. I knew I should turn away, should slip silently out of the room, but I could not.

"I'm so sorry, Swan. So very sorry." The way Mrs. Matthews said it sounded as if her sorrow engulfed more than Mom's battle with cancer—as if she were groaning for a lost twenty years. It was such a real anguish I was sure of one thing: my mother and Cassandra Matthews had shared a deep affection for each other.

Finally I turned and left the room, closing the door behind me. As I did, I asked myself what exactly was it about my mother that made people love her so deeply, so fiercely? How did she manage to get to a person's soul, even after decades of absence? Simply by pronouncing Mrs. Matthews's name and telling her she was a blessing, Mom had reclaimed a long-lost friend.

Laughter was floating down from the bedroom. Amazed, I stood by the staircase and listened. A moment later, Mom appeared, her arms wrapped around Mrs. Matthews's waist. "We thought we'd take in a little light on the sunporch," Mom said, leaning heavily onto her friend and grasping the staircase railing with her other hand.

I'm sure my eyes were as wide as two Krispy Kreme doughnuts, but I didn't say a thing. I watched the two women make their way back into the sunroom. Mrs. Matthews helped Mom onto the wicker chaise lounge and fluffed up several pillows behind her, then took a seat beside her in the wicker chair with the bright floral cushion on the seat.

"This is a lovely place, Mary Swan. It seems just perfect for you. The house, this porch. Your garden out there."

"It's home. It's so nice to be back home."

I fixed Mom and Mrs. Matthews a pot of tea, setting the cups on the mosaic table. Then I tried to busy myself in the kitchen, determined not to intrude. As I said, they didn't seem to notice me. But I noticed them, everything about their gestures, the warmth in their eyes, the conversation that started and stopped, like a stalled-out car that needed some prodding. With Hindsight wrapping herself around my legs, I took out one of Mom's old cookbooks and started leafing through the pages. This was obviously a silly façade, since I could hardly boil an egg, but it gave me something to do and kept me out of sight while permitting me to hear their conversation from the adjoining room.

"Where are you and Carl living now?"

"We've been down in Riverdale for years. We're about a twenty-minute drive from Grady Hospital, where Carl works."

"Carl likes his job?"

"Most days he does. He likes working with the kids. I can't get him away from kids—even with ours all grown. On our last vacation, we took a mission trip to Haiti, and he spent every waking hour at a clinic, treating those poor children. I think he would have stayed if I'd have let him."

"You two are something else. I've read about Carl in the paper. He's got quite a wonderful reputation."

Mrs. Matthews laughed softly. "Imagine that! Carl Matthews in the paper."

Awkward silence.

"How's Jessie doing?" Mom asked.

"Jessie is having a time of it!" Mrs. Matthews sounded relieved to find another topic of conversation. "I told Ellie, it's that puppy we won at the raffle—he's giving them fits. He pees all over the furniture and chewed up her son's baseball glove. And he has this pitiful howl at night. Keeps them wide awake. Jessie says he's worse than a newborn." But Mrs. Matthews was chuckling.

"And of course, that rascal has already stolen every one of their hearts. Anyway, Jessie's doing fine—working as a paralegal at a law firm in Marietta, and her husband's in insurance. They're getting along fine."

They talked about their children for a few minutes. I flipped through the cookbook as silence descended on the sunroom. I could hear the clink of the china teacups being set in saucers on the mosaic table by the chaise lounge. For some reason, I wanted to rescue them from the silence. I grabbed a plate of cookies that Mrs. Elliott had brought over the day before and marched onto the sunporch.

"Excuse me. Would you care for cookies?"

"Why, thank you, Ellie," Mom said.

Hindsight sauntered into the room after me, placing herself strategically in my path, so that I had to give her a gentle tap with my toe.

"What a gorgeous cat!" Mrs. Matthews exclaimed. She reached over to pet Hindsight, who glowered at her.

"Yep, this is the young lady I won at the Humane Society raffle. She's not overly fond of strangers," I said apologetically, setting the plate of cookies on the table.

"Come on, Hindsight," I said, and she followed me obediently out of the room. I perched on a stool at the kitchen counter, poring once again over the cookbook.

The conversation resumed, and I felt relieved to hear them talking about their memories from Mt. Carmel Church. Mom said, "Abbie and Bill fixed up a house not too far from the church. The neighborhood certainly has changed. I can still hear Miss Abigail ranting that the yuppies were chasing the poor folk out of the inner city and they didn't have anywhere to go. It seems to get more complicated every year. Robbie's still trying to help out."

"Miss Abigail would be proud of him."

Mom's voice fell to a whisper. "She sure is missed. Hard to believe she's been gone for, what, four years?"

"Five years this coming August. Yes, we weren't ready to let her go, that's for sure. But Carl was relieved she didn't have to suffer."

Mom's voice caught a little. "She lived to a fine old age and died doing what she loved—serving the needy. I guess that was the last time I saw you and Carl—at the funeral. I'm sorry we didn't get to talk that day—"

But it sounded as though Mom was making an excuse.

"We understood."

"It would be wonderful to all get together again, Cassie, wouldn't it?"

"Would you really want to, Mary Swan?"

I must have turned six pages in the cookbook waiting impatiently for Mom's answer. When it finally came, she was talking in a low, hoarse voice.

"I guess it's about time, isn't it, Cassie? I guess it's about time."

I went back to my apartment later that afternoon before work to pick up some other clothes—especially my softball pants and jersey, which I'd forgotten. I also wanted to take some cat food to Mrs. Rose and make sure her cats were doing better. When I had parked my car in front of the row of low redbrick apartments, I noticed pieces of lined paper, the kind school kids used, taped to each entrance door with Nate's scrawl on them. Each paper had the same handwritten warning on it:

BEWARE!! MURDERER IN THE PRECINCTS. INNOCENT KITTEN FOUND POISONED AT 7 PM THIS EVENING. ANY SUSPECTS SHOULD BE REPORTED TO NATE LOGAN IN APT C-12 OR ELLIE BARTHOLOMEW IN C-10. CONDOLENCES TO MRS JEANNE ROSE WHO HAS NOW LOST TWO OF HER BOARDERS TO POISON'S DEADLY HAND.

“Not again!” I exclaimed and cursed under my breath. I immediately knocked on Mrs. Rose’s door. When she opened it, I held the paper out and asked, “This is true?”

She nodded and sniffed. “Poor thing. Found little Marie Antoinette all stiff and cold right over by the trash cans. Murder is what Nate called it, and murder it is! Oh, Ellie, I’m glad you’re back. You can call the authorities for us.”

“I will.” I went to the phone and immediately dialed the number of the local Humane Society and reported the incident. Then Mrs. Rose fixed me a cup of tea. With Princess Vicki and Macbeth sitting on our respective laps, I listened to her sad tale. Moments later, there was a knock at the door. We both knew it to be Nate’s.

I opened the door to see his pudgy, tall, disheveled figure staring mindlessly over the top of my head. Then he stammered, “Why’d you . . . why’d you leave us, Ellie? Are . . . are you mad at me?”

“Of course not, Nate. I told you—I’m just hanging out at my parents’ house temporarily. To help out. Mom’s not doing so hot.”

As usual, his expression changed, becoming forlorn. “Your poor mommy. And what about Hindsight?”

“Sassy as ever. She’s furious that I’ve disturbed her routine.”

Nate got a miserable look on his face, wiped his large hand over his eyes, and blurted, “Abbie was here yesterday.”

“Abbie? Impossible.”

“She was here and then the kitten died. Poisoned. It happened in precisely that order.”

“Nate, for heaven’s sake, my sister has no reason on earth to kill kittens. You are mistaken.”

“Has it ever occurred to you, Miss Ellie-in-vet-school, that you might not always be right? That you don’t know everything? That I am not stupid, even if everyone else thinks so? I am not crazy. I know what I saw, and I know what it means when Mrs. Rose is crying in that awful wailing way and holding her dead kitten. You weren’t here, Ellie.

You're *never* here when we need you." He shut his mouth, pouted, and then his eyes filled with tears. "I shouldn't have said it. Now you'll hate me forever."

I stayed with them for an hour, and when I left, I thought, *I could never hate you, Nate. You and Mrs. Rose are like family. We need each other, and everybody needs to be needed.*

The next morning, I went into the sunroom while Mom was still sleeping. Daddy was already off at work. I uncovered my portrait again, and the first word that came to my mind when I regarded it was *elegant*. If someone had asked me to give three adjectives to describe myself, I would have chosen *scarred, insecure,* and maybe *overweight*. Never, ever in my whole life had I thought of myself as elegant. That word *elegant* was reserved for someone like Mom when she was dressed up for one of her exhibitions, or Megan when she wore what we called her "conservatively sexy" black chiffon dress with the open back and folds that fell delicately to her ankles.

I reached out my right hand, and with my index finger I gently brushed the canvas where Mom had painted my mouth, examining the brushstrokes. Then I slowly took a seat on the fluffed-up cushion on the wicker love seat. The sun's rays highlighted my face in the portrait. When I looked at the painting, I felt Mom's love reaching through to me, arguing against the cynicism that said, "Oh, Mom, you're just trying to make me beautiful again, recreating a daughter in your image."

Mom's love had transformed Daddy's scars. I was absolutely sure of that. Never once in all my memories of childhood could I recall being afraid or repulsed by the uneven welts on the right side of his body, welts that covered the length of his arm and his torso. Nor had I ever felt embarrassed by his glass eye or the patch he sometimes wore to cover the missing eye. Mom had always presented Daddy to us girls as the epitome of strength, virility, and good looks.

Her eyes could flash impatience or even occasional anger at Daddy, especially when he was caught up in a Georgia Tech football game and oblivious to her questions. But never had I seen cruelty or condescension in her emerald eyes when she looked at him. Mom loved Daddy, completely and purely and unreservedly. She loved him for who he was, and that love transformed him, I thought now, into someone even stronger.

For many years after my accident, I had longed to be called beautiful by my peers, especially because that word was used *ad nauseum* about Megan. Once a girl in my class had asked me, "What's it like to be best friends with the most beautiful girl in the whole school? Don't you ever feel jealous?"

I had fleeting feelings of jealousy and plenty of private self-pity sessions, but something that happened soon after we began partying cured me forever of comparing myself to Megan.

I was seventeen, waking from a long night of being stoned to a persistent ringing. I lay on my bed staring at the cobalt ceiling in my room and finally realized that the sound was coming from the phone by my bed. "Yeah," I mumbled into the receiver.

"I've shattered all the mirrors, Ellie." Megan was sobbing. "Every single one! Every single mirror in the whole house!"

"What are you talking about, Meg?" I tried to clear my mind. "Are you okay, Meg? Are you hurt?"

"The mirrors," she moaned. "Every one. What am I gonna do now?"

"I'll be right there." It was then that I realized it was only six A.M., and the rest of the house was still asleep. I sneaked out of the house and started the car.

A chill shot through me, imagining the scene at Megan's house. We called her parents' house the "house of mirrors." If she had shattered every one of them, there was going to be a big mess. And why was she at her house anyway? Her parents were gone for the weekend and

Megan was supposed to be staying at my house. I must have lost her at the party—or had been too stoned to care.

I found her on the floor, blood on her hands and face, shattered glass lying all around, a hammer in her hands. "How did you get home, Meggie?" I asked. I grabbed a washcloth and was wiping the blood from her hands and face, looking to see if she had any real gashes.

Megan was holding herself and rocking back and forth and moaning, "I hate being beautiful. I hate being beautiful. Don't tell me I'm beautiful ever again. I never want to see my face in a mirror—never again. Please, Ellie. Never again."

I wasn't sure if she was still stoned. "What happened, Meg? Tell me. Why are you here? Why didn't you come to my house?"

"I was pretty bad off, Ellie—stoned, you know, and was traipsing around the upstairs, looking for my purse, when Joel's dad suddenly appeared."

The party had been at Joel's house.

"I was petrified to see the man—I mean, we all thought Joel's parents were gone. Mr. Johnson was stern and mad. He called me into his room and started lecturing me about drugs."

Megan bit her lip and wiped her eyes with a sleeve. "But then he kept saying I was so, so beautiful. The most beautiful woman he'd ever seen in his life. I realized that he was stone drunk too. And he kept grabbing at me and pushing himself on me, groping. . . . It was awful, worse than awful . . . a grown man who couldn't wait to get his paws on my body. How can you call that beautiful?" She let out a low-pitched moan that faded into sobs.

I felt a sharp pain in my gut, as if someone were taking a knife and turning it there. "Not again," I cried. "Not again, Meggie."

I held her in my arms for a long time. Gradually when I could think more clearly, I said, "Megan, I'm taking you to the hospital. You need help—you know. And we're gonna file a report."

"No!" She grabbed me fiercely. "It won't help. He didn't do it—I screamed and someone came upstairs. He slapped me and told me he never wanted me in his house again."

She heaved a sigh, clutched her stomach, and ran to the bathroom. I could hear her retching.

Later, after she'd showered, we went through every room in her house and swept up the broken glass. I kept staring at the piles, thinking this was my friend Megan lying in pieces at my feet, fragile and destroyed. I never wanted to be beautiful after that.

Three years later, sitting in the sunroom and staring down at Mom's mosaic table, I could still see those piles of shattered glass in my mind's eye. I thought of Megan's tortured face and of the way Mom's faith seemed to make brokenness into something beautiful, and the one word that came to me was *How?*

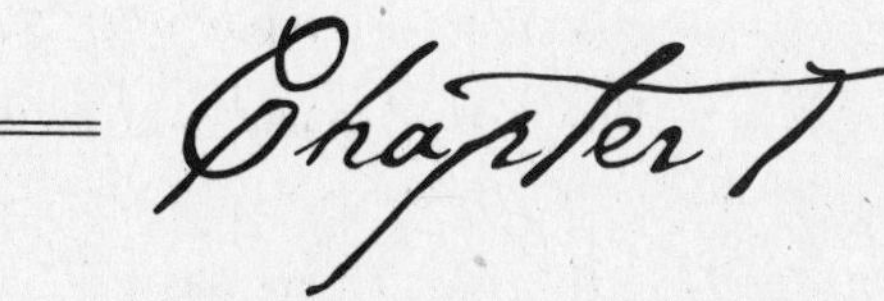

Pure and undefiled religion in the sight of our God and Father is this: to visit orphans and widows in their distress, and to keep oneself unstained by the world.

—JAMES 1:27, NASB

Lissa Murphy had lived her whole life in Grant Park, the last ten years of which she had been caring for her elderly father. Mom used to talk about how Lissa had pulled her family out of poverty and stayed in Grant Park, fixing up their little house. I'd never met her, but I'd heard the story, so that when she came by to visit on Friday afternoon, I could quite honestly say, "Hello, Lissa. I'm Ellie. I've heard my parents talk about you."

Lissa was probably around forty. She was dressed in a comfortable pantsuit and shook my hand confidently. "Oh, Ellie, I'm so glad to meet you. Must mean the world to your mother to have you home like this. Your mother is one amazing lady."

I invited her in, and she assured me, "I won't stay but a sec. Just brought by a roasted chicken and some cream of chicken soup. One of your mom's favorites—I'm sure you know that."

I took the Tupperware container of soup from her, and she followed me into the kitchen. "How's Mary Swan doing?"

"Weak. Tired. She sleeps a lot."

"Well, I won't bother her."

"Um, I can check and see if she's awake. I'm sure she'd like to see you."

"No, no. Don't bother her."

I turned halfway around, unsure what to do next. "Okay. Well, uh. Would you like a Coke? Or iced tea? Somebody brought over some delicious fruity iced tea yesterday."

"Why, iced tea would be great, Ellie. It's over ninety degrees out there—in the shade—and the humidity! 'Bout wilts you just walking from the car to the house."

I gave her a tall glass of iced tea and fixed myself a Coke, and we went out on the sunporch and sat down. I knew the next line in my role as keeper of the house. "How'd you get to know my mom?"

It worked like a dream, and Lissa spent the next twenty minutes talking about Mt. Carmel, Miss Abigail, and Mom.

"Well," she said, standing up and handing me her glass, "I'd better go. You tell Mary Swan we're all praying for her recovery at church. They put it on the prayer chain."

I smirked inwardly at the mental image from my childhood: a bunch of metal praying angels hooked together and hanging around a devout believer's neck.

"Babble, babble, babble," I said aloud when she had left. But as I stood at the bottom of the steps looking up toward my parents' bedroom where Mom was sleeping, I didn't feel like smirking. I was looking through Lissa Murphy and every other visitor, trying to get a glimpse over their heads of my mother, my real mother, the one everyone claimed was an angel or a saint. I felt as though I were straining on my tiptoes . . . but she still remained just out of sight.

When I opened the front door later that day, the pinched face of poverty was staring back at me from the front porch. The woman standing before me was skinny and angular, her face an assortment of wrinkles, straggly gray hair falling down her back, teeth uneven, her eyes hollow, and her skin a yellowish gray.

"Hello, Ellie. Sure is nice to see you again. Heard 'bout yore momma and we hadda come. Got Louella's boyfriend ta drive us up."

"Hello, Patty," I answered, holding the door open wide so that she and her daughter Louella could come inside. The boyfriend, who seemed not to understand English, refused my offer and stayed out on the screened-in porch. He did take a Coke, though. Louella's belly was swollen with pregnancy. She was no more than a teenager, seventeen or eighteen at most. She held something in her hand.

"I done this for yore momma," she whispered. "I done it in her class, and now I want her ta have it."

She handed me a small unframed piece of canvas on which she had painted with oils a little furry black puppy sitting in front of a dilapidated trailer.

"Louella was in one of yore mother's classes—you know. When we lived ova by the church. She went by every Wednesday afternoon, and your momma gave her those oil paints, taught her stuff. When they evicted us last year, well, your momma made sure Louella had her some paints and a canvas or two, and she been workin' on this paintin' for months. When she heard about yore momma, she was bound an' determined ta give it to her. I said, 'Louella, she don't need no more paintin's, but Louella insisted."

Louella looked down, her skinny arms crossed over her belly.

"Thanks, Louella. Mom will really appreciate it. Please sit down and let me get her. You've made the effort to come here. She'd be sick to miss you."

My parents had known Patty for years. As I climbed the steps to Mom's room, I thought of the first time I'd met this family. I was fairly young, probably eight or nine, and had gone with my mother to Grant Park to help Miss Abigail. But I'd been totally unprepared for the poverty we encountered that day. It was Patty's family that always stayed imprinted in my mind, the lean-to house not far from the church, three or four dogs inside, the strident smell of their urine, the TV blaring out an old Western movie, and the way the children, three or four of them, sat on a scrappy sofa and watched the screen with sad eyes. I thought the children looked hungry and cold.

"Mama," I'd said when we'd left them food and wood for their stove, "their house looks like the junkyard where Daddy got that old car part. Why do they live like that?"

"Poverty, sweetie. That's what poverty looks like."

Ever since, Mom and Daddy had kept up with Patty and her family. At different times they'd helped out by giving them money and food and Christmas gifts. Last year, I remembered Daddy telling me how Patty's family had been evicted from their house in Grant Park. Daddy and Mom had hired a moving van, helped her pack up her things, and driven Patty and her grown children and the grandchildren way down south of Atlanta near Flovilla, where they'd found an old run-down house to live in. Mom had cried at how hopeless their situation was, how they'd been completely uprooted from their Grant Park community and were living isolated with no church, no contacts, no hope.

Mom loved Patty, so I knew what she would say when I knocked on the bedroom door and told Mom she was here. "I'll be right down, sweetie. Get them something to drink, and could you prepare a bag of food for them while we're visiting?" And I knew that before she came downstairs, Mom would reach for her purse and empty it of all her cash, putting the money in an envelope that would be tucked inside a brown grocery sack that I'd filled with canned goods and fresh produce and the roasted hen that Lissa Murphy had brought over that morning.

Late that afternoon, I sat on the flagstone tiles on the sunporch, with Mom's sketch pad opened across the floor and Grandmom Sheila's beside it. The paintings from the sunporch, the ones on the easels, had been removed, including my birthday portrait. Maybe Mom hoped to keep the painting a secret. I decided to look through the two sketch pads again. Just in case we ended up taking that European trip, I'd be familiar with the places my grandmom had visited and also would know just how far Mom and Rachel had gotten on their little adventure.

So I took a piece of computer paper, and at the top I wrote: *Sketches in Sheila Middleton's Sketch Pad From her European Tour, May 1962*. I wrote down the name of the town or city where each of Grandmom Sheila's sketches was drawn—those I could recognize, at least—with a brief description of what was in the sketch.

PARIS: By the Seine with the Eiffel Tower in the background

PARIS: Notre Dame with the gargoyles leaning over with their wicked expressions. Uncle Jimmy's face on a gargoyle and Mom's as Virgin Mary

PARIS: Little girl in the Jardin des Tuileries feeding a pigeon with lines of people waiting to get in the Louvre in the background

I did the same thing for all the sketches from Vienna and Rome and Florence and Madrid. Then I came upon the first of Grandmom Sheila's sketches from Amsterdam and I wrote:

AMSTERDAM: Prostitute in window in red-light district

This one I stared at long and hard. It made me feel a tiny shiver of pity for this middle-aged woman sitting in an opened window in nothing but her bra and panties. She didn't even have a good figure. Her face was pretty enough, but it was a hard kind of pretty, and she was smoking.

I studied the details of the sketch and said out loud, "Hey, Sheila, do you mean you just plopped down in front of this prostitute and started doing her portrait? How long did it take? Was she flattered—or mad? Did your presence keep customers away?" I made a mental note to ask Granddad JJ about that sketch.

I kept noting the other sketches until finally I came to the sketches of the Borders. I'd looked up its location on the Web and found out that it was an area in southeast Scotland that surrounds Edinburgh. I was in the middle of writing down, *SCOTLAND, THE BORDERS,* when the telephone rang.

"Hello?"

"Hi, yes, this is Ben Abrams—I know Mary Swan and I was wondering if I—"

"Ben! Ben Abrams. Hey, stranger. This is Ellie."

"Ellie-o!"—that was the nickname Ben had given me when I was a kid—"What are you doing home?"

"Answering phones, screening visitors, warming up food, stuff like that."

"It's good to hear your voice. I haven't seen you in a decade."

"Half a decade. It was a decade ago that you taught me to smoke, remember? My first cigarette while Mom and Rachel were chatting away inside."

He laughed.

"And about four years ago you gave me a joint. That wasn't my first, though."

"Now I remember." This was said with a good-natured chuckle. "Hey, look, Mom told me about Swannie. I'm heading down to Hilton Head for the summer and will be driving through Atlanta on the way. I thought I might stop by and say hello to your mom tomorrow. Bring her some flowers or something."

Mom liked Ben Abrams. No, she loved him, like the son she'd never had. When we were young, she had baby-sat Ben and Virginia often, as Rachel was developing her career in publishing. Then, when Rachel and Harold divorced, Ben and Virginia's time with us doubled. They were at our house so often that some neighbors thought they were Mom and Daddy's newly adopted children. Virginia was about thirteen at the time, and Ben was fifteen.

But with the divorce, Ben had gone off the deep end. He started hanging out with really strange people—the dangerous kind. So Rachel had leapt at the opportunity to move to New York to help with a brand-new publishing company—she was evidently a very well respected editor—and get Ben away from the wrong crowd. I don't think it helped, though, because I remembered his coming down from New York for weekends and staying at our house—smoking and screaming and just being crazy and insolent to Mom and Daddy. But they let him keep coming.

I think Ben loved Mom too. Sometimes I'd suspected he felt closer to my mom than to his own. That was one thing we had in common—we liked each other's moms better than our own.

"Sure, Ben. She'll be glad to see you. Do you still have a ponytail?"

"Yeah, is that a problem?"

"Oh no. Are you kidding? I have a diamond in my eyebrow. She almost flipped at first, but now she doesn't make a peep. *Your* mom thinks I'm cool."

"That doesn't surprise me. My mom is a leftover tree-hugging hippie."

"Well, maybe, but she's a very sophisticated one. Anyway, see ya tomorrow."

"Tomorrow, then."

Looking back, I think that the reason Ben and I had gotten to be friends was that deep down I felt sorry for him. He was what Trixie would call a "late bloomer." Somehow, despite having fantastic-looking parents, he'd picked up their traits in a combination that really didn't suit him too well as a teen. He had his father's wavy black hair, but he wore it too long and couldn't seem to control it, so he had an unkempt air about him that wasn't in style. He had Rachel's gorgeous blue-gray eyes, but whereas hers flashed mischief or wry humor, his were just plain cold, frozen, expressionless. And he had Rachel's "bone structure," another of Trixie's favorite expressions.

According to my grandmom, bone structure was vitally important in the choosing of a mate. Ben was slim with small bones, not effeminate, but certainly not muscular and manly. And he was a half inch taller than I at best. Otherwise he was the spitting image of Harold Shantley, and Harold was quite good-looking. But Harold's high forehead and prominent aristocratic nose looked sharp and jutting on Ben's thin frame. The combination did not lend itself to making Ben Abrams handsome.

Then there was the psychological part—the family dynamics that were against him from birth. Rachel was not exactly what I'd call a doting mother. She was, in fact, the exact opposite of my mom. Practical, stern, and expecting her kids to toe the line. She didn't have time to encourage them with fluffy words. She was busy developing her career and trying to hold together a marriage that had been doomed from the start.

Gradually I came to understand that Harold Shantley was a big, fat, charming liar and womanizer. He'd run off with some lady and done a lot of other awful stuff to Rachel. After their divorce, Ben was furious with his father. In fact, he hated him so much that when Rachel took back her maiden name, Ben insisted on changing his too.

It was when I was around ten that Rachel had gotten a "big break" and moved up to New York. Ben's parting gift to me was a pack of Camels and a kiss on the cheek—which meant a lot because by then I was, of course, disfigured.

After that, I only heard bits and pieces of Ben and Virginia's lives—and they never sounded very promising. I was actually looking forward to seeing Ben the next day, though I told myself that I'd have to turn down the joint if he offered me one.

Neither Daddy nor I was a cook, by any stretch of the imagination. My normal daily intake consisted of Cokes and Cheetos and pizzas and doughnuts, with the occasional yogurt thrown in as a nod to good nutrition. So I felt totally inadequate to deal with the culinary needs of my parents. Fortunately, friends and neighbors had sent plenty of food.

But by the second day there, I realized that most things would do better being frozen, because none of us were eating. Mom had no appetite, Daddy usually had a big lunch with clients and didn't want much for dinner, and I, amazingly, had lost my appetite.

Up until rehab, I'd always been proud of my figure. I couldn't be proud of my face, obviously, but my figure was just fine. I was pretty tall—five-seven and a half—and on the thin side. Not pencil-thin like a lot of girls, but slender, with a well-developed chest. That had definitely not come from Mom's side of the family, we joked. Nan used to lament that she got Mom's flat chest—back in the days when we could still laugh together and every word she pronounced didn't seem like a judgment call on my life.

When I stepped on the scales now and they registered thirtysome pounds heavier than in the "old days," I truly didn't believe it. So I stopped stepping on the scales. When I was hungry, I ate. When I was wishing for a fix, I ate. When I was angry or sad or excited, I ate. So it came as quite a shock to discover that when I was around my emaciated mother, I didn't eat. I just woke up one day and had no appetite. As I looked at Mom's shriveled-up body, I felt perpetually sick to my stomach.

On Friday night, I didn't have to go in to work until eight. Daddy suggested that we eat an early dinner together. I was much less than enthusiastic, but I agreed.

Daddy got home from work at six. "How was your day, Mae Mae?"

"Fine."

"What went on at work last night?"

"I dunno. Same ole stuff. Nothing much." I could feel my body stiffen, my tongue grow thick and heavy in my mouth.

"Any interesting people come to the restaurant?"

I shrugged. "The usual. Two redheads, two blueheads, a guy with a purple Mohawk, and three girls with pearls in their tongues." I glanced up, caught his eye, and we both grinned.

"Lovely. I'd fit right in—I should come over some night, pluck out my glass eye, and toss it around the room!"

"Dad!"

But he said it so happily that I couldn't help but chuckle.

"Anybody come by to visit your mom today?"

"Oh , sure. Plenty of phone calls and a few visitors. Several ladies from some prayer group—I think that's what they said. They stayed an hour—I tried to get them to leave, but they were in the room with Mom, *praying*." I rolled my eyes. "Then Lissa Murphy brought some soup by—but she didn't stay long and she insisted that I not bother Mom. And three ladies from the High Museum came—they barely stayed any time at all. Brought some lemon pie and freshly baked bread and a huge bouquet of flowers—it was from all the volunteers at the High. And Patty and Louella came. That was weird and good too, I guess.

"And then, of course, there was Mrs. Elliott, who said, 'I consider myself more like family,' and proceeded to rearrange everything in the fridge and the cupboards. She also wrote up a menu for the week, based on all the stuff she found in the kitchen. And at the same time she managed to give me the complete history of her family from her ancestor Charlemagne right up to the present."

Daddy smiled. "She's an interesting woman, indeed. And yes, she can talk!"

"Talk . . . she can leap from one century to another in a single sentence without taking a breath."

"You've got to admit, she knows a lot about a lot of things."

"Admitted. For whatever it's worth."

"And I for one don't mind her culinary advice. . . ." His dimples were showing, and I thought he looked relieved.

"You don't have to say it, I know I'm a rotten cook. No—not rotten—my culinary skills are simply nonexistent!"

He reached across the kitchen counter, past the loaves of freshly baked bread wrapped in tin foil and the plate of fried chicken, and touched my hand. My first reaction was to draw it away, but I didn't.

"I'm just so thankful you're here, Ellie. Your mother and I are both just so thankful that you are here."

Mom made an effort to eat with us that evening, but she was not herself. Pale and gaunt, she barely had the strength to lift the fork from one of her happy Italian flowered plates to her mouth. She definitely had no strength for conversation. And so we sat in silence. Then Hindsight meowed, and Daddy thought of something to say.

"Seems you had quite a stream of visitors today, Swannee."

"Yes, it was lovely to see the girls from the prayer group, and Lissa and then Harriet and a few other girls from the High . . . and precious Patty and Louella."

"But maybe they wore you out." Dad said it tenderly, softly, his hand covering Mom's.

"Maybe so." It seemed that even the effort it took for Mom to move the muscles in her mouth to form a smile was too much for her. "I'm not very hungry," she added with an apologetic shrug.

"That's okay. I've got just the thing for you, my Fat Goose." Daddy stood up hastily, left the kitchen table where we were seated, and retrieved something from the freezer. Then he stood behind her, covering her eyes with one hand while simultaneously placing a kiss on the top of her head and setting a pint carton of Midnight Cookies and Cream in front of her. He uncovered her eyes and stated proudly, "Just happened to find this on the way home from work."

She smiled up at Daddy and reached for his hand. "You're too much, Scout. I should be ashamed of myself, with all this delicious food around, eating ice cream."

Daddy sat back down, removed the top from the carton, and spooned out a chunk. He brought it to her lips and she took a bite.

"Dear me, you're having to feed me just like a two-year-old." But they regarded each other with delight. "Mmm. That just hits the spot."

I watched stiffly as Daddy spoon-fed Mom the whole small carton.

I cleared away our plates, plates filled with half-eaten chicken breasts and untouched scalloped potatoes. I scraped a little of the left-overs into Hindsight's bowl and put the plates into the dishwasher. I could hear Mom and Dad talking cozily in quiet tones. I felt like an intruder.

But when I came back to the table to remove the other dishes, Mom whispered, "Thank you for coming, Ellie. I know it's not always easy to come back home."

I was surprised by how completely devoid of emotion came my reply. "It's okay, Mom. Really. It's okay."

"Doesn't it ever bug you to wait on Mom hand and foot?" I asked Daddy later, after he'd helped her back upstairs to bed. "She is so darn dependent on you. I don't mean now, Daddy. I understand it to an extent now. But she's always been that way."

"We're dependent on each other, Ellie. That's what marriage is about—completing each other, accomplishing more because we're together, each doing our part. Yes, sometimes one of us is called on to make more sacrifices for a period of time." He was standing in front of the fridge with a tub of margarine in his hand, trying to find a place to put it. "Your mom has sacrificed plenty for me, Ellie. So very much . . ."

He found a spot, closed the fridge door, and added, "And Ellie, it's a pleasure to care for your mother. She is strong, but in a fragile, delicate sort of way. She's going to get through this with a bit of pampering and lots of love. She'll fight."

"She doesn't seem like she's fighting. She seems like she's just lying there, pitiful and weak. Why doesn't she try harder?"

"We're each different, Ellie. Your mom wasn't created to be tough and strong on the outside. She was created to observe beauty and reflect it back for the rest of us. She has taught me how to appreciate that beauty, how to embrace creativity, how to let life fill me up with ideas. I told her long ago I'd never get bored following her around, and I haven't."

I listened to Daddy's loving explanation, all the while saying to myself, *Well, that's certainly not what I want. I'll be independent. Any kind of relationship I have will be based on individual freedom. You are way behind the times, Dad.*

But out loud I only commented, "How has she helped you? Beauty and creativity are just words. They don't make money or build houses."

"Of course they do." He put an arm around me and hugged me and said, "Ellie, it's okay to be angry with your mother, but someday I hope you'll figure out why you're so angry, and then you'll be able to get over it."

Oh, I know why all right, I thought. *I know why.*

Daddy's blind to Mom was my thought as I went upstairs to my room and changed into my uniform. *He's so terribly naïve and enchanted by her that he lets her get away with everything.*

I opened my desktop and looked in the cubbyhole where I'd stashed the letters from my mother, thought about taking another one out to read, decided against it. In the adjoining cubby were all the poems and stories I'd written as a child—silly, syrupy stories about sick horses and cats and dogs. An occasional squirrel or rabbit also made it into my tales. The common denominator was the vet who cared for and rescued these poor suffering strays. There was nothing particularly impressive about the stories, nothing to point toward a career as a writer. But as I looked through them, reading my childish scrawl, I could feel a smile creeping across my face.

This was me. In spite of my anger at my mother, I felt a pleasure at thinking, *I have found what I was supposed to be doing all along. Even at six and seven and eight, I knew I wanted to help animals. I just didn't know how to express it. So it came out in stories.*

I thought of the hours I had spent alone in my room as a child, inventing stories about my animals. I had even given the stories titles: "Sally Squirrel Finds a Home," "Toby, the Gentlest Dog in the World," "Small Fry—the Pony With the Big Heart," and had scribbled childish pictures on the opposite side of the lined paper in the spiral notebooks. Beside my desk was a small bookshelf filled with other evidence of my love for animals. Crammed inside were all of James Herriot's stories about his life as a vet, Walter Farley's series about the black stallion, Marguerite Henry's horse tales, and Enid Bagnold's wonderful classic, *National Velvet*. I even had Garfield comic books and books devoted to Snoopy.

I guess those books and many others had contributed to my desire to be a vet. I hadn't thought of these things in so long. Hadn't remembered where the inspiration came from. But now, seeing my beloved books lined up in the bookshelves of my room, remembering the feel of the worn covers and seeing the Cheetos-stained pages, I lay down on the bed and looked at the swirling walls.

"Is this what you felt when you painted, Mom? A certainty that you were doing the one thing you were created to do? It feels so right, so good, at last, to see it." For the flash of a second, I felt a kinship with Mom, something so sudden, but it disappeared instantly. It was replaced by thoughts of my after-dinner conversation with Daddy.

Daddy and Rachel talked about my mother as if she were someone larger than life, a courageous saint who had survived life's most difficult circumstances through love and faith. But I saw her as a coward. As a woman who, when that stove exploded and I was on fire, abandoned her child . . . abandoned *me*. Why did she always get the accolades?

Abbie and Nan had come through childhood and their teenaged years unscathed. But for Mom, it must have hurt way down inside to have a scarred husband and daughter. Daddy was scarred "in Vietnam."

I didn't know if he'd been blown apart by a grenade or had been in a plane crash. And I had been scarred in "the accident." That's all they ever called it. The accident.

Another fleeting thought tempted me. I could go downstairs and find Daddy and ask him my questions. I could sit him down and say, "Listen, Dad, I'm a big girl now. Maybe I never wanted to know about things before, but now I do. What happened to you in Vietnam? And how did Mom help you after you got back? Was it hard, Daddy? And what is the matter with the Matthewses? Why did you lose touch?"

These things were in the front of my mind, on the tip of my tongue, as Trixie would say. But in the back of my mind, in the darkest shadows, hidden like my stories in a drawer of my desk, was the real question, the real secret I had to find out. "Why, Daddy, why did my mother, my very own mother, leave me to die when the stove exploded in my face?"

Of course, none of these questions was asked. They remained stuck in the back of my throat, suffocated with polite talk and raging emotions, pushed to that deep dark corner of my room where they could cohabitate with Vincent's swirling sky.

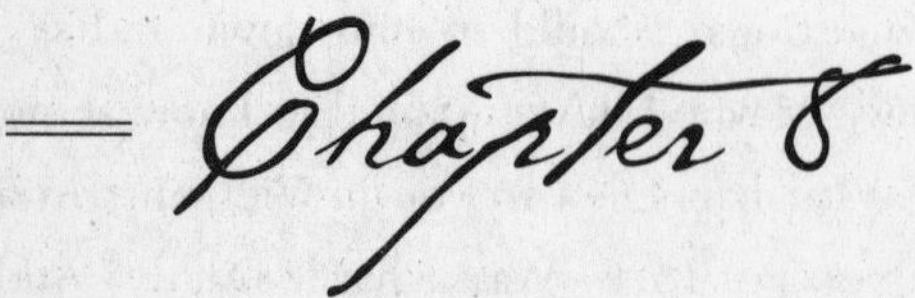

"What's happened to the animals?" I blurted out.

"Oh, they're in the garden," she said calmly. . . . "They're here for good. . . . They'll have a good home with me as long as they live."

Old people and their attachment to their beloved animals. . . .

—*JAMES HERRIOT'S DOG STORIES*

I was looking forward to seeing Ben on Saturday, but as luck would have it, I got called in to work early and wasn't at my parents' house when he stopped by. I didn't get home until around midnight, so Mom and Daddy were already asleep, but the next morning, Mom was up and dressed for church.

"You must be feeling better," I mumbled as I rubbed the sleep from my eyes, standing in my pajamas while Daddy bustled around the kitchen, fixing Mom hot tea and an English muffin.

"Having Ben come by made my day. It was a wonderful blessing to see him," Mom said softly.

"So he's doing okay?" I asked, suppressing a yawn.

"He's doing just fine, great, really. So mature and at ease with himself."

Her comment irritated me deep down. I felt like yelling at Mom,

"Well, I've never made your day by being myself! You're always out to change me. Being around *me* doesn't seem to wake you up and give you a zest for life." But, of course, I kept my mouth clamped shut.

"Mature" and "at ease with himself" were not expressions that immediately came to my mind for Ben Abrams. Then again, I hadn't seen him in ages, and Mom did have a way of working her magic on kids. Ben wasn't the only young person to be swept into her circle of admirers. Many of my sisters' friends just loved Mom and Dad, and still came back to visit. Megan had often told me that she felt closer to my mom than to her own.

Still, I had to admit, I was more jealous than proud of the way others viewed her.

As they were leaving, Daddy added, "Your mom feels like going to the Club for lunch. Isn't that great? The table's already reserved. Twelve-forty-five. Nan and Stockton are coming too. We'd love for you to join us."

I nodded stiffly, pasting a smile on my face while a big fat frown settled down into my heart.

At one o'clock we were all seated in the formal dining room of the Capital City Country Club. Little Bobby was in a high chair and was at the moment smashing the Club's famous buttered saltine crackers onto the metal tray and then putting them in his hair. He was wearing some outrageously expensive toddler suit that looked like it was meant for a little girl.

"Ellie, darlin', you are a real sweetheart to help Robbie with Mary Swan. I know it just means the world to him," Trixie said loudly. She was wearing a hot pink linen summer suit, complete with matching straw hat and pumps in the latest style. She was still chewing her gum and had a bony, tanned hand resting on Granddad JJ's arm.

"Glad I can help," I mumbled, feeling out of place in my tight jeans.

"Mighty fine of you, sugar plum. And an extra treat to have you with us today." Granddad JJ had leaned over to say this. He was wearing his favorite gray suit, the one that made him look like Colonel Sanders, with his bow tie. He smiled, patted Trixie's hand, and reached for the crackers.

Abbie was sitting by Granddad, patiently removing crumbs from Bobby's hair. She had a little more color in her face, but I doubted she had gained an ounce in weight. She sniffed at Bobby, made a face, and said, "Bill, honey, can you take Bobby to the men's room and change his diaper? He smells awful."

Bill laughed in his raucous manner and said too loudly, "Sure will, punkin'. When ya gotta go, ya gotta go." He swung Bobby out of the high chair and tickled his son, cooing, "Need a diaper change, buddy boy? Well, your ole man is a thoroughly modern papa, and he'll do it for you!"

When Nan and Stockton showed up a few minutes later, Abbie smiled for the first time in weeks. "Well, we're all here. Isn't that just perfect?"

Everything had to be perfect with Abbie, from her painted nails to Bobby's smocked suit to the topic of conversation. She had this annoying oldest-child syndrome of thinking that the care of the family rested completely on her shoulders.

"How are you feeling, Nan?" Mom asked gingerly a few minutes later. Dad had finally told her about Nan's miscarriage.

"I'm okay, Mom. Really, everyone. I'm fine." Nan looked down at the table, and her dark bobbed hair swung in her face.

I thought she sounded like she was sniffing back tears. Stockton took her hand, and she wiped a tissue across her face and looked up.

"I'm trying to keep busy. That helps. The doctor says they'll have the lab results about the miscarriage in a few weeks." She flashed her familiar nonchalant-Nan smile, but I wasn't convinced, and I doubt anyone else was either.

I took the cloth napkin that was folded in a fan shape across my plate and placed it in my lap, all the while jiggling my leg under the table. All I could think about was that in two hours I'd be free. I'd be off to visit with Nate and then play in the softball game. With these things to look forward to, surely I could get through one family meal.

As soon as I had finished my last bite of strawberry cheesecake—my appetite had miraculously reappeared enough for me to enjoy my favorite dessert—I wiped my mouth, stood up, and said, "I need to run by the apartment before my softball game, so I'd better be going. Great to see everyone. Thanks for the meal, Granddad." Granddad JJ always footed the bills at the Club.

Then I added, "Bye, Nan. You take care." She gave me a little nod.

As I left, I heard Mom talking about Ben's visit. I'm not sure what she was saying, but I could tell it was something that elicited oohs and aahs of joy from my family. I almost turned around to listen, but there I was again, on the other side of the fence, looking over, not at all sure that the grass was greener. And not willing to find out.

I was already in the parking lot outside the beautiful sandstone main building, walking toward my car, which was parked by the tenth hole of the golf course, when I realized that Abbie was following me.

"Look, Ellie, can't you stay just this once, now that we're all together? You know it means the world to Mom."

I didn't even look her in the eye. "Sorry, sis, I've been with Mom all week. I've got things to do at home. Y'all are with her. She's plenty happy."

"Please stay. Just this once. Don't be selfish."

I'd reached my little Hyundai, unlocked the door, and climbed into the driver's seat before I said defiantly, "Why is it 'selfish' to spend a few hours at my own apartment? I've been away since Wednesday, you know!" I started the ignition, so that Abbie stepped back.

"I just thought, just this once . . ."

"Look, Abbie, I have a lot of people in my life who need me. Mrs. Rose needs me. Nate needs me. Megan does. And so do the people at work and the girls on my softball team. They count on me. But y'all don't. I have never felt needed in this family. What I feel like is a burden. Someone who causes problems and doesn't fit in. Someone who makes everyone else embarrassed. So it isn't exactly fun to be around all of you."

Abbie didn't say a word as I drove away. When I looked in the rearview mirror, she was standing in the middle of the parking lot, long blond hair glistening in the sun, her arms folded across her swollen belly, looking miserable.

Nate was waiting outside of the apartment complex when I drove up. He waved to me like a little kid. "I knew you'd come back! I just knew it, Ellie. I told Mrs. Rose you wouldn't leave us forever."

"I'm back. Don't worry." I fished in my backpack for the keys to my apartment.

"There's something you need to know, Ellie." He shuffled his big feet, looked down at the sidewalk, and said, "Abbie was here again yesterday."

"Impossible, Nate. She knows I'm staying at Mom and Dad's."

"No, I swear, she was here and sneaking around."

I almost asked if another cat had been poisoned, but refrained. "Well, did you talk to her, ask her what she needed?"

He shook his head with a wicked little grin. "No, she didn't see me. I just observed her."

I could imagine. Nate had a habit of sitting right by his front window and staring down into the street with a glazed expression on his face.

The idea of Abbie secretly poking around my place aggravated me. Both she and my folks had keys, just for backup, but I certainly didn't expect them to use them without my knowledge.

"Maybe she decided she needed to clean this place up," I said, half to myself as we climbed the stairs together to the second floor and I unlocked my door. "She's a real neat freak, and she loves fixing things up. You should see all the work she's put into the house she and Bill bought in Grant Park. Restoring things, old things. She calls it a hobby.

I call it nuts. Anyway, I'll bet she got all worried seeing my mess when she rushed through last Sunday."

But when I entered the apartment, I found it in exactly the same disorder as when I had left. Several dirty shirts were strewn about the den, there were two unwashed plates in the sink, and the crust from a piece of pizza sat on the counter.

"Well, isn't that just my luck? She didn't even come by to clean." I threw down my backpack, kicked off my sandals, and plopped down on the blue sofa. "Never mind, Nate. It doesn't matter. Let's just say my sister's weird and leave it at that."

He nodded, towering over where I was seated on the sofa.

"Sit down, silly. How's the computer going these days? Found any new web sites?"

Nate smiled, producing several pieces of paper. "Sure did. Look at these beauties—wild kittens from Africa, baby panthers. You can even adopt a baby ocelot."

We looked at the pictures and then visited the Web. As we sat drinking our Cokes, with Nate eating a piece of cold, stale pizza, he said, "I sure am glad you're back, Ellie. I hope you never go away again."

"I'm sorry I didn't get by your parents' place this weekend," Megan said. "Things ended up being a little crazy. So how are you surviving?" She took a bite of a biscuit as she sat across from me at the Flying Biscuit.

"You'd be proud of me—I'm being a real good daughter. I even ate lunch at the Club with the whole family yesterday. First time in years."

"And?"

"And what?"

"Well, is it as bad as you thought, being back home and all?"

"Let's just say it's rather annoying. It's like I'm remembering all this stuff from the past and, as you may recall, they aren't exactly happy memories—"

"What in the world are you doing?" Megan interrupted me when the waitress brought my breakfast.

"Nothing. Eating."

"That looks like tofu. And green and red peppers and spinach. Are you feeling all right, El?"

I laughed at Megan's horrified expression. "I thought I'd try something different—you know, healthy. Anyway, I probably won't eat it—I've lost my appetite."

"Sure."

"No, I'm not kidding. I can't eat—that's one good thing about being home. No one is hungry. I think my stomach is shrinking. Hey, quit looking at me as if I have a screw loose. I'm just not hungry anymore. Aren't you glad?"

"I think you're acting a bit odd, Ellie. Anyway, how is your mom? Is she getting better?"

"She looks pretty rotten and spends most of the time in bed. She did manage to make it to church yesterday and then lunch at the Club, but I think it about did her in. She was already asleep when I got back from my softball game last night at seven. Dad takes her to see the oncologist every morning—he insists on doing it himself—so we'll know more about her condition when they get home."

"And what about Jamal?"

"Well, now that you mention it, um, he kinda keeps coming on to me. He invited me out and I said no. For now."

"I think you should get another job. Your hours are crazy and it's not all that safe—even Timothy says that, and he's not nervous about much. He said he wouldn't be walking around down there at midnight."

"Look, Megan, can you please quit harping on me about that? I'll think about it, okay? I'll think about the whole thing with Jamal."

She was frowning at me, unconvinced.

"Anyway, what about you?" I asked as I swallowed a bite of tofu—which was actually quite tasty.

"I'm okay. My boss wants me to apply for a managerial position. She says I've got good people skills. And the salary is better."

"Do you want to do it?"

"Maybe, but it's a full-time job, and I don't know if I'd handle that and classes very well."

"What does Timothy think?"

"This is what Timothy thinks." She stuck out her left hand, where a diamond ring glittered on her third finger.

I grabbed her hand and stared at the ring. "Megan! Megan, are you serious? He proposed? And you said yes?"

She was beaming. "I did. Last night. The surprise of my life."

So we didn't talk about Mom or me anymore. I kept staring at the ring and the way Megan's eyes were dancing and how the sun coming through the window of the Flying Biscuit made her black hair look like smooth dark glass. I felt a tinge of sadness inside, as if I were about to lose Megan, and I felt a fear too, that she was still way too fragile for marriage and that as soon as the sun set, that smooth dark glass might shatter into a million pieces. It had happened before.

I arrived back at Mom and Dad's around nine-thirty after breakfast with Megan. Daddy had left me a note on the kitchen counter.

Ellie, there's a mini-crisis at the office, and I need to go down for a few hours. Can you check on your mom when you get in and give me a call? Thanks. Dad.

Mom was sleeping soundly when I peeked in the room. I called Daddy with the news and then asked him, "Well, what did the doctor say?"

"The platelets are coming up slowly, so that's good."

"Yeah . . ."

"But Dr. Marshall said she is much too weak to do any type of trip . . . you know."

There was an awkward pause until I said, "So we won't be going to Europe, Daddy?"

"No. No, I'm afraid not. Not right now. Maybe when she's stronger."

I couldn't explain the mixture of disappointment and relief that rushed through me.

"Daddy, tell me the truth—has the cancer spread?" This I whispered, as if saying it out loud might make it come true.

"No, Ellie. Dr. Marshall isn't saying that. But your mother's terribly weak, and we do have to keep a close eye on everything. And after seeing her today, he said that she's not really resting. One look at her and he knew that."

"She sleeps a ton!"

"Yes, but think of all the visitors. She isn't very good about saying when she's too tired."

That was true. "I can tell people to stop coming."

"Dr. Marshall had another idea. He suggested we send her to the beach. To Hilton Head."

"When?"

"As soon as possible. She can hide out at the beach house, and maybe she'll even feel like painting a little. He says long walks on the beach after the sun goes down will do her a world of good. He says to take her to the beach house and make her comfortable."

"*Make her comfortable!* That sounds like he expects her to die!"

"No, no. Not at all. She just needs a lot of rest. Your mother is tough, Ellie. You may not see it, but she is. She's been through a lot and survived. Don't worry. I'll take her to the beach and it will do her some good."

"But you can't leave work now. You're in the middle of the inner-city project."

"I've gotta do what is best for your mother, honey."

I didn't say anything for a moment, because I was thinking of Mom and the two weeks of vacation I'd just cleared at Jeremy's and how much I loved staying at the beach house. Hilton Head Island, South Carolina, was one of my favorite places in the world. It had turned into this chic spot for vacationers, especially in the area where Granddad JJ and Trixie had their home, but we'd been going there as a family for almost forty years, long before there was anything chic about it.

Suddenly I surprised myself by offering, "I could go with her, I guess. I was planning on taking off two weeks for Europe. I could try to get off earlier."

Daddy sighed heavily—a good kind of sigh. "Oh, Ellie, are you serious?"

He sounded so incredibly relieved that I said, "Yeah, sure, Daddy. Sure. I'm heading to work in a little while—I work the lunch shift today—so I'll talk to my boss."

"Thank you, Mae Mae. Listen, I've gotta go—we'll talk about this more tonight—you'll be off early, won't you?"

"Yeah. I'm done at five."

"How 'bout going with me to a concert at Chastain Park? I got the tickets hoping your mom would feel like going, but I think yesterday's activities and the doctor's visit this morning have done her in. Abbie offered to come over and stay with her, if you want to go."

"Who's playing, Daddy?"

"Burt Bacharach."

I made a sour face. "Um, well, yeah, I guess I could go, if it would make you happy."

"Call it a date."

When I entered Mrs. Rose's apartment after I'd finished my shift, the familiar smell of body powder and cat urine greeted me, causing me to rumple my nose involuntarily. Mrs. Rose was stroking Princess Augusta Victoria, rocking slowly back and forth, back and forth. *The Price Is Right* was playing on the TV, the audience's canned applause occasionally breaking the silence of the dark room. I sat down on the love seat, remembering too late that my black jeans were going to pick up every cat hair on the cushion.

The feline's contented purring matched the slow back-and-forth motion of the rocking chair. Two other cats, Hamlet and Macbeth, came into the room, meowed, and curled around my legs. I sat with Mrs. Rose and the cats for at least an hour, gingerly broaching the subject of my upcoming beach trip about halfway through the visit.

"It looks like I'll be leaving for the beach tomorrow," I started. "When I explained how bad off Mom was to my boss, he encouraged me to take off now. June is never as busy as July and August, so I think it works out better for him this way too."

Mrs. Rose just listened without commenting, but gradually the frown on her face turned into a full-fledged scowl. Finally she sighed and spoke. "So you'll be away for two full weeks. I hate to hear it. I just pray I won't have any medical emergencies during your absence. I just don't know what I'd do."

"Of course you'll know what to do. You'll dial the shelter's number—remember, I've written it on a Post-it and stuck it on the fridge—and ask for the doctor on call. I've already told them to expect it. It won't be any problem."

"Thank you, Ellie," she said, looking nostalgic and sad. "I hope everything goes just perfect with your mom. Take good care of her. There's nothing in the whole wide world that can replace the joy of a mother having her kids come back and take good care of her." The expression on her lined, chubby face was nothing but wishful thinking that her children might come for a visit. I wanted her to believe it so that the hope would carry her through the lonely days with cats on her lap and the TV playing a constant drone of soap operas and game shows that she didn't listen to anymore.

Nate pouted like a three-year-old when I told him my plans. I half expected him to throw a fit. Or cry.

"You said you wouldn't go away again."

"No, I said I was back. Nate, some things in life are way past my control. This is one of those things. I'm gonna help with Mom. We can keep up over e-mail. I'll have my laptop down at the beach."

His eyes brightened. "Can we chat together?"

"Sure, whatever. Just hang a little. It won't be that bad. I'll be back before long. But I need you to help Mrs. Rose with the cats. You know sometimes she forgets to feed them. Can I trust you to do that?"

Nate nodded solemnly. "Sure. I'll check up on her. And I'll watch out for Abbie-on-the-prowl too."

I suppressed a grin.

He got an aloof expression on his face and said, "Anyway, Ellie, I won't miss you much because my brother Mark is coming to see me. He promised. He said it would be sometime soon. Probably tomorrow. I'll be so busy with him that I'll hardly notice that you're gone."

"That's great, Nate."

But we both knew beyond a shadow of a doubt that no one would be visiting Nate in the near future. It gave me a squirmy, sad feeling to acknowledge that for as long as I was gone, Nate would stay behind the sheer curtain in his den, looking out on the world that had so completely shut him out, wishing that the phone would ring, checking his e-mail five times a day, alone.

Cassandra Matthews sent a cheery little card, which arrived in the mail that afternoon. Inside the card, she gave information and phone numbers for cancer recovery groups. She had also called to check on Mom twice. As a professional, a nurse, she handled her job perfectly: thorough, thoughtful, upbeat. But I wasn't sure she had quite gotten the knack of simply being Mom's friend again—as if the professional distance was a safeguard that kept her from treading on ground that was filled with the mines from Vietnam.

"You call me from the beach if you have any questions, Ellie," she told me at the end of a phone conversation. She gave me her cell phone number. "Any time day or night. I'll call you right back. I know you've got loads of people to count on, and I'm sure the doctors have given you all the necessary information. But sometimes it's not easy to get in touch with them. If you're worried, or just need to talk, please call."

"I will," I said, feeling relief wash over me, the way I used to feel when I took my first bite of a chocolate cream-filled doughnut. *You don't know it, Mrs. Matthews, but there's no one else I could call with your medical savvy and perfect diplomacy.*

With Cassandra Matthews's phone number entered safely into my cell phone, I was ready for Hilton Head.

"Hello?"

"Hey, kid! It's Rachel. I hear that you and your mom are heading down to Hilton Head tomorrow."

"Yeah. It looks like it. Did you talk to Dad?"

"Yes. He gave me the whole scoop. You call if anything gets worse, and I'll be there in a jiff."

"What's gonna get worse? She's just supposed to rest."

"Right. You do have to take her to get her platelets checked. But Robbie said they're up to fifty thousand—so that's great."

"Yeah, there's nothing to do for right now, except to wait and make her comfortable."

"Why so cynical?"

"Because it sounds like a death sentence to me."

"It's not. Hang in there with her. She'll fight. You'll see. Hilton Head is just the spot for her to be . . . to rest."

"Whatever. I hope so."

"Hey, I promised your mom that I'd give her Ben's phone number down there—I'm sure Swan has it somewhere, but she's so scatter-brained. He's playing a few times a week at the Quarterdeck Lounge in Harbour Town. He's staying in my apartment there—lucky kid. He can watch the sun set over the harbor every night. And it's free. Anyway, he knows the way to the beach house."

That was for sure. How many dozens of times had Abbie, Nan, Ben, Virginia, and I ridden bikes from our house on Spotted Sandpiper to Ketch Court in Harbour Town, where Rachel had a third-floor condominium?

"He really wants to see you both."

I wasn't even aware that she was doing it, switching the subject so effortlessly, until she started dictating the phone number to me. But I was glad she did, glad that Mrs. Matthews and Rachel knew how to lessen the pressure and responsibility I was feeling for Mom.

"Ben's visit with Mom the other day made her week," I told Rachel. "She was thrilled."

Rachel gave a little chuckle. "That doesn't surprise me. Swan and Ben have always had a thing for each other. Second-mother syndrome—you know."

"I know, Rachel. I know just what you mean." I hung up the phone with a smile on my face. *Second mom*, I said to myself. *Well, look who's talking*.

Chastain Park, located in northwest Atlanta, gave great outdoor concerts throughout the summer. The Atlanta Symphony Orchestra played at many of these concerts, along with well-known singers like Liza Minnelli, Amy Grant, Reba McEntire, and, well, Burt Bacharach. The concerts helped support the symphony, and Daddy loved to attend.

We spread the blanket out, and I unwrapped the tin foil on some leftover fried chicken. Picnic blankets dotted the lawn as people settled down to their dinners. The smell of cold cuts and fried chicken drifted through the air. A murmur of conversation could be heard throughout the park as daylight turned to dusk. Burt Bacharach came on stage and started singing his first song, "I Say a Little Prayer for You."

Well, that's just great, I thought. *Even Burt Bacharach has joined in the babble!*

Daddy and I talked about the family and Ben Abrams and Rachel and my softball team. I scooted next to him on the blanket and laced my arm through his. When Daddy was really enjoying a concert, he had an embarrassing habit of humming along with the orchestra. This used to mortify us girls, because not only could he be heard, but also he hummed terribly off-key. But tonight I would have given just about anything to hear him humming. Instead, he kept checking his watch, spreading his long legs out in front of him, and shifting his weight.

When the orchestra stopped for intermission, I said, "Daddy, I'll take good care of Mom. You're right, you know. Two weeks at Hilton Head will be perfect for both of us. She'll paint, and I'll learn to cook, and you can come down and join us when you've got the project wrapped up."

Daddy squeezed my arm. "Thank you, Ellie. This means the world to your mother and me." And seeing Daddy's relieved expression made Burt Bacharach's last two songs much more bearable.

So instead of going to Europe with Mom, I drove five hours southeast to the South Carolina coast, to an island that had my family's footprints all over its beautiful beaches. Late on Monday night, as I was packing the bags in my old bedroom, I glanced over at my desk with its top hanging open, like a panting dog. On a whim, I gathered up several old letters from Mom that I hadn't reread the other day, as well as the childish stories I'd written. I even grabbed *National Velvet*. With these and my laptop, surely I wouldn't be too bored.

And with Ben. For the strangest reason, I couldn't wait to see Ben. If he had sprouted into a mature, confident adult, I wanted to be there to witness it. And I wanted to prove to myself that Mom cared as much about me as she did about him.

I phoned Megan, who kept apologizing for never having come over.

"You've had other things on your mind," I teased. "Have you come down from the clouds yet, Meggie?"

"I'm telling my parents tomorrow night. Cross your fingers for me. They like Timothy, but you know how they feel about me finishing school."

"Well, you are gonna finish school, aren't you?"

"Yeah, of course. Don't worry, silly. I've already registered for classes next fall. I just keep staring at this ring, and I can't believe it's so gorgeous and it's on my finger."

"You take care of yourself—and of Timothy, okay, girl?"

"That'll be my pleasure," she giggled. "You keep eating now—even if it's just stuff that's good for you."

"Don't worry, Meg. Like I told you this morning, I just don't have much of an appetite. But there's no danger of my wasting away anytime soon."

"You hang in there with your mom. It'll be cool. And I'll call. Promise."

"Thanks, Megan. Say hi to Timothy. Talk to you soon."

When I hung up the phone, the dark, lonely feelings settled on me, the ones that haunted me in the night, that reminded me that I didn't really belong in my family, the ones that tempted me, in spite of what I'd just told Megan, to grab a box of doughnuts and fill up on a huge dose of self-pity. I was jealous of Megan having Timothy, jealous of Mom feeling great because of Ben, jealous of the rest of my family so comfortable in their Bartholomew babble. I hated the jealousy. As I placed one last T-shirt in my suitcase and closed the lid, I admitted something as obvious as the scars on my face. For the past two weeks, I had been thinking that there were two villains in this story about my mother and me: cancer and time. But gradually I began to get a glimpse of the third villain, the one that didn't want to be named, that hid and sulked: my own selfish pride.

Chapter 9

Hilton Head Island . . . a place where man [can] commune with Nature and enjoy the Sea and the Sky, the good Earth and the Forest and all things that dwell therein.

—COMMEMORATIVE PLAQUE LOCATED ON POPE AVENUE, HILTON HEAD ISLAND

I could drive to Hilton Head with my eyes closed. We took Mom's car, the little Mazda with the sunroof, and I was glad I'd brought my Walkman to keep me occupied during the five-hour drive. I could have made it in four hours, really—I'd done it before. But for Mom's sake and because of the ever-watchful eye of the south Georgia state trooper, I stuck faithfully to the 65 mph speed limit as I drove south out of Atlanta on I-75.

Hindsight sat in the backseat, pouting in her cage, while Mom dozed beside me in the front seat, her head jerking ever so slightly as she settled into an openmouthed sleep. This was not a new thing. Every family vacation we'd ever taken started out with Daddy at the wheel and us three girls spread out in the backseat, popping bubble gum and arguing and calling out insults while Mom slept. It was a family joke that once Mom had done the hard work of getting everything ready for vacation, she was too tired to enjoy it.

An hour and a half down the road in Macon, we slipped over to I-16, and soon after, the sophistication of Atlanta vanished into one long, drawn-out Southern sentence where men with big bellies and red necks flirted with women wearing skimpy tops and shorts that looked more like underwear. This, to me, was Georgia, which had nothing much to do with Atlanta: country folks minding their business, simple and honest and satisfied. This drive from the perfect lawns of Ansley Park to the seamless shores of Hilton Head Island was the only glimpse of reality I'd have for two weeks.

Mom stayed awake after Macon, but our conversation was like a car puttering out of gas.

"How's Megan?"

"Fine."

"You still meeting on Monday mornings at the Flying Biscuit?"

"Yeah. Yeah, we are."

"They do have good biscuits, don't they?"

"Yeah."

A silence.

"Is Megan still seeing the same boy, Timothy?"

"Yeah."

"They've been going out for a while. How long now?"

"I dunno." A pause. "Six months, maybe."

Then Mom, worn out with the effort, turned her head to look out the window. Her eyes eventually closed, and I turned up the volume on my Walkman.

It was true what everyone said about Hilton Head. The island's outline resembled a shoe, a giant shoe that someone had walked out of and left in the sand. It wasn't a very big island—maybe ten or twelve miles long in all. Its wide beach of white sand extended from right above the shoe's toe, which pointed southwest, all the way past the heel. Traveling up from the toe to where make-believe shoelaces began, one came upon one of my family's favorite parts of the island: Harbour

Town, with its yachts and lighthouse, golf course and shops. The Broad Creek crept in from the Atlantic Ocean halfway up the laces. Several posh retirement plantations with private golf clubs were built around the creek. And due south about a third of the way from the shoe's toe, on its sole, was Spotted Sandpiper Road, where our beach house was located.

There was no center of town on the island, although numerous shopping centers and outlet malls had sprouted like trees over the past two decades. Hilton Head was no longer just beach and sun, sports and seafood restaurants, but the perfect place to "shop till you drop." There was even a Blockbusters Video not too far from my parents' place.

About thirty thousand people resided permanently on the island, with as many as two million guests visiting annually. I was glad we were arriving before the main tourist rush, because somehow I felt as though Hilton Head belonged to our family. We were not vacationers. We were property owners who'd discovered the island long before the rest of Atlanta and others who came from Ohio and New York, and we loved that island almost as much as we loved Atlanta.

For a softball-playing city girl, there was something about Hilton Head that filled me up better than doughnuts or Cheetos or a hard game of any sport. Its landscape was a wild, vibrant canvas of unspoiled nature: vast sparkling beaches, sweeping marsh vistas, abundant and varied flora and fauna, more than two hundred fifty species of birds, and in some places, trees that grew right up to the beach line. Mom and I shared a love for trees, and there were plenty on Hilton Head: tall pines, genteel magnolias, gnarly moss-draped live oaks, and the unmistakable palmetto, which was so important in the history of South Carolina that it became the state tree. The image of this palm tree with its fan-shaped leaves was even on the state flag.

Most of all, Hilton Head was the one place in the whole world that held happy memories for me. The island was just beginning to be developed in the early sixties when Trixie's family, the Hamiltons, had bought a piece of property near the end of the island in the private resort called Sea Pines. When Granddad JJ married Trixie, they had inherited together the beach house on Spotted Sandpiper Road. For most of the summers of my twenty years, I had spent wonderful, relaxing weeks at that house. A number of other Atlanta families had bought property at Hilton Head in the early sixties. One of those families was the Bartholomews. So both sets of my grandparents had big old beach houses within a five-minute walk of one another.

The Hamilton House, as we called it, was exactly what a beach house should be, a sprawling house made of the gray clapboard known in the region. It had five bedrooms and a swimming pool, and best of all, we could walk out the back door and be on the beach within minutes. It had been remodeled several times in the past forty years, though from the outside, it still had the look of the 1950s. On the main floor, which was actually the upstairs, there was a big sunny family room, and the side that faced the beach was made up completely of sliding glass doors that led out onto a screened-in porch. The walls in the family room were decorated with seashells and Mom's canvases of kids making castles in the sand. The kitchen, which Trixie had redone last year, opened directly into the family room, with only a countertop and tall chairs separating it, so the whole upstairs had an airy, light-filled feel to it. Then there was the bedroom that Trixie called "the master bedroom suite," except that she said "suweet." Downstairs in what had originally been like a basement were the other bedrooms, four of them, and a den with the TV and other electronic stuff for the grandkids. There was also a pool table. And the garage was behind the den. Outside, there was the yard with the swimming pool and then a sandy path that cut through prickly herbs and led onto the beach.

We had six old-timey bikes—the kind with big thick tires and no gears—stored in the garage. They were perfect for long rides on the perfectly flat bike trails—miles and miles of trails that wove around lagoons with white cranes and lazy crocodiles poking their heads out of the water, forests with deer and squirrels, and wide residential streets where turtles lethargically crossed the road at any given time while patient motorists waited.

"You take this one," Mom said, leading me into the upstairs bedroom. "You'll enjoy it, and I need to stay downstairs where there's less light."

The room had a really high ceiling and doors that opened out onto a little covered balcony where a round wrought-iron table and chairs welcomed anyone who wanted breakfast outside.

"Are you sure, Mom?"

"Positive."

Trixie had bought a bunch of bright, flowery pillows of all different sizes and arranged them to her liking on the bed. I was tempted to hop onto the bed and start tossing the pillows on the floor. A long, low chaise lounge sat by the window, and on the other side of the window there was a white wicker bookshelf filled with paperback novels and old *New Yorker* magazines. It made you want to lie down on the chaise and read. Right then.

But Mom said, "You should get out on the beach before you waste the whole day."

Mom's oncologist had given her very specific instructions. No time on the beach during the day. She could only be out before 9:00 A.M. and after 6:00 P.M.

"I'm not leaving you in here alone."

"Oh, go on, Ellie. I thought I might do a little sketching. I'll be fine."

"Okay, but then tonight we can go hear Ben play at the Quarterdeck. This is one of the nights he'll be there."

"Oh, sweetie, I'd love to, but I just can't tonight. Can't bring this body of mine to manage it. But you go on. I'll be fine. And when you see Ben, you set up a time for us to get together."

I fixed supper for Mom. With none of the friends' casseroles and breads and soups to heat up, Dad had told me to order a big batch of clam chowder for Mom from the Crazy Crab. So I warmed that up, along with some fresh rolls, and rented a movie for her to watch. *To Catch a Thief*. Mom loved any Hitchcock or old, sappy romance.

"You sure you're gonna be okay, Mom?"

"Fine. Go on out and have a wonderful time. Give Ben my love."

It took me fifteen minutes to ride my bike from Spotted Sandpiper to Harbour Town. I locked up the bike in a rack that was crammed with dozens of other bikes, looking exactly alike—big wheels, red metal, thick black seats, no gears. I walked out to the harbor, admired the yachts sitting lazily in the water, and felt tears well in my eyes. I stared up at Rachel's apartment on the third floor of Ketch Court and could easily make out the little balcony with its table and chairs and its view of the harbor. I remembered sitting on the balcony with Daddy—we were always going back and forth between the condo and the Hamilton House—summer after summer, watching the sun set and talking about boats and boys and baseball.

"There's nothing more beautiful in all the earth than the setting sun. And we are blessed to be able to enjoy it here." Daddy was forever reminding us of our privilege, begging us never to take it for granted. Sitting there, I could tell Daddy was content, and as a child, I'd crawl up in his lap and feel content too.

In the late summer, around eight o'clock, the blazing sun would start its descent in the western sky behind the lighthouse. There, perched together on the balcony of the condominium, almost holding our breaths, Daddy and I would wait and wait, hoping that tonight the orange fireball would work its particular magic in the sky. At just the right moment on the correct night in the earth's rotation, the sun would set behind the lighthouse in the exact spot where the lighthouse's window was, so that the sun gave off its own warm light, its own welcomed warning to ships, blazing out for us to see. For just a moment, the orange ball was suspended in time. Then it descended, so fiery and alive that I could almost hear it sizzle as it touched the water.

When this happened, I would applaud, and Daddy would say, "Isn't that just like God, to create something so magnificent that it replaces every one of our man-made imitations?"

Later, the sky turned pink and the ripples of colorful horizon mirrored themselves on the ocean. Occasionally we could see dolphins leaping in semicircles across the pastel-colored water.

On this night, around eight thirty, as I stood below and leaned on the railing beside the water, I watched for a repeat performance of the sun's gymnastics—knowing full well that I would not have the same breathtaking view as from that third-story balcony. Still, I applauded again to myself when the sun's light shone in the lighthouse and the incandescent orange flame sent a host of colorful ripples across the water in the sound. I was unconsciously holding my breath as the sun set, and then I let out a relieved sigh. Hilton Head was still the same.

I continued walking around the harbor, past the Crazy Crab and the half dozen red rocking chairs on the sandy sidewalk outside. I browsed by the windows of the shops that lined the harbor, gift shops and dress shops that stayed open until ten o'clock during the busy summer months. I remembered shopping there with Trixie when I was about twelve or thirteen, on the verge of puberty, still slender and flat-chested. She bought me a lime green Lily skirt splashed with yellow seahorses and sand dollars. It was short and sassy and yet very innocent. I tried it on with a bright green T-shirt, and when I stepped out of the changing room, Trixie drawled, "It's puhhfect, Ellie. You look like a million bucks."

I had needed to hear that at thirteen, when my body was threatening to explode into change, when every girl's dream was to be beautiful and when my scarred face kept me from ever really hoping that the dream could come true.

The Quarterdeck Lounge had been around ever since I could remember. I think it opened in the early seventies, originally as a spot for fishermen to gather after a day at sea. It sat right behind the lighthouse, and although it was popular with tourists, its most faithful customers were the locals who lived on the island.

I walked in the main door and through the entry hall into the lounge. A fancier restaurant was housed upstairs. The lounge had wooden paneled walls, giving a warm, casual atmosphere. The band must have been on break, but the small stage on the left side of the room was set up with a drum set and two electric guitars. I went over to the long bar on the right and ordered a Coke.

"How you doin'?" asked the bartender.

"Good. Beautiful evening. Great to be back."

"You come here often?"

"Not to the Quarterdeck—this is my first time. But to Hilton Head, yes, every summer. An old friend is playing in the band here."

"Is he? Good for him. They'll start up again in a sec. Have a look around while you wait."

He pointed to a black-and-white photo on the wall, and I went over for a closer inspection. It showed crowds standing outside the lounge.

"In April, during the Heritage Golf Classic—which is played right over there on the Harbour Town Golf Links—the traditional nineteenth hole is at the Quarterdeck. All the best have played at the Classic—and had their drinks here afterward." Again he nodded to the walls where signed photos of pros were framed. "And many a couple has met here," he said with a twinkle in his eye.

Tonight the lounge was only half full. I took a seat at one of the small square wooden tables and smiled as I noticed Ben coming onto the little stage with two other young guys. He noticed me and nodded my way with a smile. His long wavy black hair was pulled back in a ponytail. I guess the past few days in the sun had tanned his body, because he looked healthier than I remembered.

I settled back to enjoy the music as the band began to play a typical beach tune. Ben had always loved to play guitar, and he had started up several bands in high school. I remembered him singing "Blowin' in the Wind" to me when I was eight and he was fifteen. I had been mesmerized by his soft voice and the strumming of the guitar . . . and it was happening again. I think I was unconsciously smiling as the band sang "California Girls," "Desperado," "You Light Up My Life," "Take It to the Limit," "Surfin' Safari," and a few medleys of great songs from the fifties, sixties, and seventies. In between several of the songs, Ben would say something funny, and the audience laughed. I found it hard to believe that stiff, sour Ben was singing songs and cracking jokes in public. I guess he had changed, just as Mom had said.

Then he began to sing a sad, haunting, yet simple song, a song I wasn't familiar with and suddenly didn't want to listen to. It was about a woman who was hard to love—who was stiff and stuck in her hardness, and the lyrics—especially the refrain—sung so softly, felt like a finger jabbing into my chest.

I try to hold your hand,
You pull away.
I wanna brush your cheek
In a gentle way.
But you're hard, you're hard,
So hard, a hard woman to love.
But you're hard, you're hard,
So hard, a hard woman to love.

He finished the song on a sad minor chord, as if nothing were resolved, as if the story were not over.

But I wanna love you
I wanna love you. . . .

Then Ben said, "Now we'll take a fifteen-minute break. Don't go away!" He set down his guitar, said something to the other band members, and headed toward me.

"Ellie Bartholomew!" He broke into a smile. "I haven't seen you in an eternity." He gave me a big bear hug. "How are you? Hated missing you last Saturday."

"Yeah. I got called in to work early. I'm cool, okay."

"So when did you and Swan get here?"

"Just this afternoon. She sends a big hug—her exact words—and wants me to set up a time when you can come over."

"I want to. How is she today?"

"Like every day. Exhausted—although she perked up for a while after her visit with you last Saturday. Most of the time, though, she's resting. Always resting."

"Must be what she needs. Otherwise I wouldn't say your mom is one to hang around sleeping. Hey, can I have a seat for a sec?"

I blushed. "Of course." I could hear Trixie scolding me. *For heaven's sake, Ellie, offer the young man a seat. What has happened to your Southern upbringing?* I recovered from my embarrassment and said, "I like your music. Who was that last one by?"

"Yours truly."

"Really? You're writing songs?"

"Yeah. Once in a while I throw an original in between the beach tunes, hoping it'll pass."

"That was a sad song."

"When I wrote it, it was, but things are getting better."

"So you had someone in mind when you wrote it?"

He laughed. "You bet I did. My mom."

"Are you serious? *Rachel?*"

"Absolutely. Don't tell me you've forgotten the knock-down drag-outs we had."

"No, no. I can understand what you mean, now that you explain it. It's just that the way you worded the song, well, it sounded like you were talking about a lover."

"That's the great thing about songs, isn't it? You can sing your heart out, and no one has to know the real truth behind it."

"So are you getting along any better with your mom?" I asked.

"Are you getting along any better with yours?"

"You're still the same, answering a question with a question. Contrary to what Mom said—she said you were, I don't know, different."

He grinned and looked like a little boy. "Actually, I have changed. Did she explain what she meant by 'different'?"

"No, she didn't. So you can."

"I'm okay about life. I've got a direction. A purpose. A faith."

I held up my hands. "Don't tell me. You've found God. Is that what you mean?"

He narrowed his eyes. "And what if it is?"

"Not you too! Please don't tell me you do the babble like my family."

"Babble?"

"Oh, please. You know what I mean. Religious babble. Bartholomew babble."

He grinned again. "Hey, I like that. Bartholomew babble. Tell me what it sounds like."

"You know. 'God this' and 'the Lord that' and praying about everything and using little trite religious clichés. And giving God credit for good things and letting Him off the hook for bad things. Babble. Doesn't make a bit of sense."

"Why not?"

"Because life can't be wrapped up in a neat little package, that's why."

"And your family is trying to wrap things up neatly? Forgive me for saying it, Ellie, but that has never been my impression of them."

"You're just playing the devil's advocate."

"Maybe I am." He was still grinning, and crossed his arms over his chest. "Keep going. I'll listen to your side."

"Look, I don't know exactly what the babble means or says, because that's the whole point. My family knows better than to babble when I'm around. But I read the Bible and went to church for years, and Mom had me memorize a bunch of Bible verses when I was little. I even went to *Christian* rehab."

Ben knew about my high school problems.

"It never worked. Life just didn't fit into those easy packages."

He was concentrating on what I was saying and nodding. "Good point, Ellie. I hope we can talk more later. Anyway, I'm doing okay." He leaned toward me. "And are you?"

"Am I what?"

"Are you doing okay?"

"Well, I'm not doing 'okay' the way you might define it. Not religious or anything, but yeah, I'm doing pretty well. Off drugs, back in school, want to be a vet."

"That's what Swan said. I think that's great. You were born with a kitten in your lap. Remember the big fat fluffy one I used to sing to?"

"Mr. Boots. He was the sweetest cat of all time."

"And Shadow? She was a witch, that cat. Those yellow eyes and her perfectly gray fur—beautiful. A beautiful witch. You'd think she'd have acted more civilized after you and Trixie rescued her from the shelter, but all she could do was hiss and scratch."

"Yeah, well, wait till you meet my newest friend, Hindsight. She has an ornery disposition too."

"Well, I'm glad for you, Ellie. You'll make a great vet." He glanced at his watch. "Hey, gotta go back to the songs. But if you want to hang around, I'm getting together with some kids after I finish here around midnight."

"Are they all weird?"

"Pretty weird. Weird, great kids. Hang around afterward and you'll see."

I ended up at a small Baptist church on the island that Tuesday night. It turned out that Ben was what he called "the youth leader" at the church for the summer. I was surprised to see that about twenty kids turned up. Some were young teens, but there were a few who looked nearly my age too.

And Ben was in his element, I could tell. He laughed and joked and strummed his guitar and sang crazy rock songs and jazzed-up hymns. He looked as if he was loving every minute of it, and so did the kids.

"I want you dudes to meet Ellie," he said during a pause between songs. "We go way back. Our moms are best friends, and we used to hang out together."

"Hey, Ellie," a few kids said, and I felt myself go tense. I remembered my experiences with past youth groups and their syrupy sweet attention to the poor disfigured girl. But these kids didn't seem to notice or care.

We hunted crabs at one in the morning and then played touch football on the beach, and once I slid into Ben and he knocked me over. When he reached down to help me up, I took his hand and smiled.

"So do you know that half those girls have a crush on you?" I asked him when he drove me home, my bike in the back of his car.

"Nah, you're wrong. I'm way older than most of them."

"So? You're a nice guy. That's what happens. A guy is just nice, friendly—maybe he doesn't give two hoots about a girl—and then she starts thinking there's more to it and off she goes. So don't be too nice, I'm warning you."

"I'll try, but I have to warn you, I have a habit of being nice." He smiled and winked at me, reminding me of Rachel.

"You haven't stopped smiling since I saw you at the Quarterdeck. What's with you?"

"Babble, babble, babble," he teased.

"Very funny."

"Just substitute whatever words you want in there—you know, the words your family uses. That's what's with me. Lighten up a little, Ellie. Life is full of great things, you know."

"Yeah, I guess I missed out on them."

"Come on, Ellie. You're a great girl. Plenty smart, pretty, all of life ahead of you."

"You forgot disfigured. . . ."

"Everybody has some type of scar. I bet most people don't even notice yours. They're too busy worrying about themselves."

"You don't seem to have too many glaring faults." As soon as I had said it, I wished I could take it back. I suddenly remembered the nickname Ben had in high school: Benji of the Big Nose. And it was actually rather large. "Doesn't anything bother you?" I asked, hoping to cover up for my mistake.

"Oh, sure. Some things bother me. Break my heart. But not what people think of me. I just don't put a lot of stock in other people's opinions. That's what's so great about starting over. You learn not to care in the same way you used to. I also learned to like myself, in spite of my *glaring* faults." He raised his eyebrows two or three times and puffed out his nostrils obnoxiously.

"Now that's profound," I said with mock admiration.

"Can't figure it out, can you?" He shrugged, then laughed again. "You should give yourself and your family a break, Ellie. Look deeper."

That last comment really bugged me. "At the risk of sounding like a school kid, look who's talking. You said yourself that you and Rachel don't get along too well. Is she jumping up and down about the way you've changed?"

"No, Mom isn't all that thrilled with the twist my life has taken. She's a hoot. She clings to your mom, to her Mary Swan. I think she's thought all these years that if she stays close enough to Mary Swan, her faith will bring good luck on Mom too. But she won't embrace it for herself. She's been too hurt by Christians, and she's too doggone smart to grab faith in the emotional sense.

"And so when I did, well, she found that really hard to swallow. And I can understand. I mean, she's seen me go off the deep end for several other causes. And all she wanted was for me to get a half-decent job, bless her soul. So I don't think she's oozing pride over the fact that I play in a bar at Hilton Head and lead a youth group at a Baptist church."

"The two don't seem to go together very well, I'll admit."

"Oh, but they do, Ellie, they do! How can I understand those kids unless I can see what they're up to most of the time? There are a bunch of those kids who come to youth group but hang out at the bar the rest of the time."

"I bet they don't hang out at the bar where their youth leader plays."

"Not yet, but give them a few weeks."

"Whatever. So when are you going to come by and visit with Mom?"

"I can come tomorrow if you want. I don't work in the days."

"All right. She'll be thrilled to death."

"Call it a date."

"It's been good seeing you, Ben. Even if you have gotten a little weird." I grinned.

"It's great to see you too, Ellie-o. I'll drop by tomorrow." He gave me a quick hug, and as I was preparing to leave, he added, "Hang on. Here, take this with you." He scribbled something on the back of a calling card from the Quarterdeck and handed it to me.

"What is it?"

"A reference to some of my favorite babble—when I need to give myself a break." He winked at me again. "In case you can't sleep."

Back at home, in the wee hours of the morning, I fixed myself a cup of herbal tea and climbed into the king-sized bed, setting my teacup on the bedside table. I stared at the wicker bookshelf across the room. Paperback novels, magazines, and a Bible. A big white Bible. What Ben had scribbled on the back of that calling card was a reference to a chapter in the Bible. To the uninitiated, the scrawl would not have made a bit of sense. But I knew every abbreviation for every book. He'd written *Ps. 91:1–2, 9–10*.

Reluctantly, I crawled out of bed, retrieved the Bible, and got back under the covers. Sipping my tea, I looked up that psalm, keeping the white Bible hidden in my lap as if I thought some ghost were going to whoosh in and laugh at my reading material. When I located Psalm Ninety-one, I read the verses he'd jotted down.

He who dwells in the shelter of the Most High will rest in the shadow of the Almighty. I will say of the Lord, "He is my refuge and my fortress, my God, in whom I trust. . . . If you make the Most High your dwelling—"

I frowned and said out loud, "Good grief! Not that 'dwelling' word again. Then I finished the passage: *"—even the Lord, who is my refuge—then no harm will befall you, no disaster will come near your tent."*

I stopped right there and again spoke aloud. "Well, that is obviously not true! That promise has been broken a hundred times in my family alone. We've had plenty of disasters! Sometimes I think that is all our life has been—one disaster after another."

This was just another example of why the Scriptures irritated me so much. But for some reason, I kept reading the psalm, maybe wanting to get fuel for the fire—my next conversation with Ben.

"Because he loves me," says the Lord, "I will rescue him; I will protect him, for he acknowledges my name. He will call upon me, and I will answer him; I will be with him in trouble, I will deliver him and honor him. With long life will I satisfy him and show him my salvation."

Immediately all thought of argument was swept away by a memory that made me laugh out loud. I was five or six, I guess, and Mom had a little set of boxed memory verses that she made each of us girls memorize each week.

Abbie and Nan were dutiful. I hated it, even though the memorizing was a cinch. But one time, Mom had given me the card for Psalm 91:15 from a new translation of the Bible. I learned the verse and proudly recited it to my mother one afternoon. "This is God talking," I stated matter-of-factly. "'He will call upon me, and I will answer him. I will be in trouble with him.'"

What a great verse! It had delighted me to think that God would get into trouble with me!

Mom chuckled at my innocent rendition, but my sisters cracked up.

"It's 'I will be with him in trouble,' you dope, not 'I will be in trouble with him'!" Abbie had scoffed.

When Mom told Daddy the story, they had a good laugh together. I laughed too—I understood the joke. But inside I still thought I had it right. The only kind of God I was interested in was one who would climb right in beside me and enjoy my mischief.

Chapter 10

But you'll look sweet
Upon the seat
Of a bicycle built for two.

—HARRY DACRE

My alarm was blaring at me at nine o'clock and I got up with difficulty, yawning and rubbing sleep out of my eyes. I checked on Mom and found her propped up in bed reading her Bible, the one with the smooth leather cover, almost as thick as a dictionary, and crammed with all kinds of papers—church bulletins and old letters and even a pressed rose petal in the middle of the Psalms.

"Morning, Mom."

"Morning, Ellie. Did you sleep okay?"

"Not enough, but fine. And what about you?"

"Better, sweetie. Better. Being here is doing me a world of good. I'm fine. Go back to sleep for a while. There's no rush."

"No, that's okay. Anyway I'll get your tea ready, and orange juice and toast."

"That sounds great. Thank you, dear."

I brought her breakfast on a tray that could sit on the bed, then I opened the shades and let in the light. Mom closed her eyes and smiled.

"Ben wants to come by this afternoon, if you feel up to it."

"I'll be ready, Ellie."

I stood there, suddenly wanting to sit on the end of her bed and ask her questions, questions about Ben and Rachel, about Daddy and Vietnam. I was surprised and terrified. But as I hesitated, the phone rang. I ran to get it. Daddy was calling.

Mom's face lit up when I brought the cordless in for her.

"Hey, Scout. How you doing? I miss you too. Oh yes, we're okay. Ellie's taking good care of me." She smiled and nodded my way, and I left the room.

I opened the door at eleven to find Ben Abrams standing there with a bunch of daisies in his hand.

"Mornin', Ellie-o. How'd you sleep?" He looked like one of the kids from the church, standing there in his long, baggy shorts, unshaven, his wavy hair falling loosely to his shoulders.

"I slept okay. But not enough. A little sore where you tripped me on the sand."

"Hey, you're the one who tripped me! You'll not get any pity from me, Miss Athlete."

"Come on in. Mom's getting dressed."

"This old place looks great. What'd you do to it?"

"Trixie's touch—you know. Yeah, it's not half bad. Want anything to drink? A Coke, lemonade, iced tea?"

"Is it freshly squeezed lemonade?" he teased.

"Are you kidding? I'm allergic to anything that requires me to be in the kitchen."

"Well, give me some nice out-of the-can stuff. Tomorrow I'll bring you some that's fresh squeezed. And some homemade cookies."

"Are you serious?"

"Sure. No one else is gonna fix anything for me, and I get tired of TV dinners."

Mom came into the room, dressed in a pair of jeans and a summer sweater. Ben leapt to his feet.

"Hey, Swannee girl. How ya doin'?" Ben had always talked to my mother more as if she were his big sister than his mom's best friend.

"Today I feel just fine. Everything is fine here with Ellie, and the beach and the ocean at my doorstep. And now you're here too. Have a seat and tell me another one of your stories. What beautiful, amazing stories! Has Ellie heard them?"

"Not yet. Someday I imagine she will." He held out the daisies as he sat down. "I know you like them fresh cut. I thought maybe they'd inspire you to paint."

"How thoughtful, Ben. Yes, I'm sure they will." Then a frown crossed her brow, and she cocked her head toward Ben. "I was just remembering the last bouquet of flowers you brought me, at a party we gave for you in high school. Do you happen to recall those flowers?"

Ben hopped off the couch, knelt on the carpet in front of Mom, and grinned up at her. "I certainly remember those beautiful roses. And I remember that they were fresh cut from Mrs. Cunningham's garden—in the middle of the night. But never fear, fair Swannee, I did not steal these flowers. I paid for them one by one. I promise."

Mom smirked and patted his hand. "Well, that's a relief. My, you were a rascal back then! At any rate, the daisies are lovely. Just set them in the sink and we'll get them in a vase later."

"I'll do that, Mom," I said. In the big open kitchen, I busied myself with the daisies and then began to put the breakfast dishes in the dishwasher. I could hear the ease of their conversation and the lilt in Mom's voice, and as I listened, I felt that familiar stabbing again.

"How is the youth group going?"

"The start is always rough—the kids are silent as stone, feeling you out. But they seem to be warming up. We had a blast out on the beach last night. Ellie was there. Did she tell you?"

"Yes, she mentioned something about touch football at midnight."

"Your daughter was the star of the show. Where'd she get that competitive spirit?"

"Not from me, that's for sure. But she came by it honestly. You should have seen Robbie in high school and college. He's the kindest guy in the world, except when he's playing football. That's the only time I see fire in his eyes, and maybe even a little bit of hate."

She actually giggled—*giggled* after five minutes with Ben, when her first twenty-four hours with me had been practically passed in silence.

"Dear me, Ben! Well, those kids are blessed to have you for the summer."

"Blessed or not, they're stuck with me. . . ."

They must have talked for an hour. A real conversation. Granted, Ben said a lot more than Mom. He told her about the band, the kids, his life, and even his faith, but he talked naturally, without all the babble. And somewhere in that hour, I got a tall glass of lemonade-from-a-can and sat down beside my mother and listened.

"Well, I'm going to have to take a little nap," Mom said after we'd each had a tuna fish sandwich prepared by Chef Ben. "But you're welcome to stay awhile."

"Thanks, Swannee. I may just do that. Keep resting."

He gave her a peck on the cheek, and as I watched, I couldn't quite figure out what had happened to introverted and angry Ben Abrams. Could faith make that big of a change? Ben Abrams, who had once proclaimed he was a hater of mankind, seemed genuinely happy with himself and those around him.

"Do y'all still have all those old clunker bikes in the garage, Ellie?" Ben asked when Mom had gone downstairs.

"Yeah. All six of them."

"Wanna go for a bike ride? I've found some new trails."

"Sure, I'd like that a lot."

"Good. If you want to see wildlife, I know the exact place to take you. Yesterday I saw a gator, a deer, and half a dozen cranes. Maybe with a little luck we'll find a wounded duck that you can take home." He grinned at me.

We left Spotted Sandpiper and biked side by side past roads with names like Whistling Swan, Red Cardinal, Snowy Egret, Black Skimmer, and a bunch of other streets named after native birds of the island. The live oaks and the palmettos gave shade to the paths and, sure enough, once we saw a deer and at another place, the tip of an alligator's snout poking out of a long pond.

It was easy to talk to Ben, with him riding just ahead and no eye contact necessary.

"What miracle stories was Mom talking about?" I asked.

"Oh, just stuff I told her about some of the kids I'm working with in New York."

"Are you a youth pastor there too?"

"I was this past year. Part of an internship program with my seminary."

"You're in *seminary*?"

"Yeah. My mom didn't tell you?"

"No." I made a face, which he couldn't see.

"Well, I am. In fact, I'm halfway through. Anyway, I'm working in a church in the Bronx. The complete opposite of Hilton Head in every way. Actually, I take that back. In some ways, the kids are exactly the same. Everyone's looking for meaning to life."

"So tell me a miracle story, Brother Ben."

He glanced back at me, lifting his eyebrows as if to say *Are you serious?* When I nodded, he said, "Okay. If you want. I'll tell you about Stacy. Fifteen years old. No father that she's ever met. Her mom's a heroin addict who brings in a new guy every month. Stacy started selling her body at thirteen to earn money to keep her and her little sister alive. I met her in one of the worst bars in the Bronx. She was strung out on drugs."

"Hey, wait a minute. What were you doing in a bar?"

"Meeting kids, like I told you last night. You don't expect them to come to church, do you? She was so desperate for something that she soaked up every word I told her about the Lord, started coming to church, gave her life to Jesus, and converted her pimp! She's off the streets, back in high school, and living in a foster home."

"Cool." But I wasn't enthusiastic. I felt almost threatened by the story, suspicious and yet strangely drawn to it. We parked our bikes at South Beach, and as we licked ice cream cones in the shade of a big pine, he told me three other miracle stories of kids like Stacy.

I didn't know how to explain Ben Abrams. He was the first person I'd ever met who had become someone else because of his faith. My family had always been that way—religious and babbling. I could not see any big changes in them. But Ben was a whole new person, and I couldn't help asking, "Now tell me *your* miracle story. What happened to change you?"

We walked out to the very tip of Hilton Head's big toe, what was known as Land's End Drive, and stared out at the lagoon with its fishing boats slowly making their way to the ocean. As we walked, he tossed a conch shell up and down in his hand and wove his true tale as if he were a wizened old sailor and I his young apprentice.

"Three years ago I was the saddest kid you ever wanted to see. Twenty-four and dried up—no direction, hanging with the wrong crowd, hating my job, eaten up with worry. I didn't see any reason to keep on. Not one reason."

He took a long swing and threw the conch shell into the water with such force that it splashed water back onto us. "I wanted to get the heck out of Dodge and quick. I felt stuck and dried up and miserable, wasting away. I was angry at everyone, especially at my dad for leaving us, and at Mom for not knowing how to help Virginia and me. I hated my family. I even hated *your* family, your picture-perfect family."

"Why?" I said as my mouth turned dry.

"Because you were all doing okay, and I didn't fit in there either. I felt welcomed by your parents when I'd appear on their doorstep every few months, even loved by them. But mad as hell at their feeble attempts to get me on the right track." He looked over at me. "The Bartholomew babble bugged me big time."

"*I* wasn't perfect."

"No, I realize that. But you weren't around. You were off in some rehab place up east. And the rest of them were 'coping through prayer.' That really bugged me too. Anyway, everything I did and everywhere I went, I just felt hollow and angry. So I decided I'd just skip town, leave this little shallow earth and head straight to eternity. I figured it might be better. I didn't think it could be worse."

"Suicide?" I picked up a pebble and tossed it into the lagoon, feeling my heart beating in my chest.

He was quiet. Then he said, "Yeah. I had it all planned out."

"You really, really did?" This time I looked him straight in the eyes.

"I'd written a note, and I knew exactly what I was gonna do." He ran both hands through his bushy hair, pushing the sweat off his face, squinting into the distance and grimacing, as if reliving every detail in his mind.

I kept quiet.

"And okay, I know this sounds like a big cliché, but it's really what happened. There was this church I'd pass all the time on my way home from work. And that night, for some reason—you tell me why—I just stopped in. I guess a youth meeting had just finished up, because there were all these kids leaving. And this guy, Larry, was there—he turned out to be the youth pastor. He had a way of getting me to talk, and I ended up staying there half the night.

"Before I could even tell him what I was planning to do, he said, 'Ben, you look awfully sad to me. I know you don't know me from Adam, but I'd like you to promise me something. I'd like you to promise me that if you ever have self-destructive thoughts, you'll find someone to talk to, just like tonight. Can you promise me that?' And then he gave me a book and asked me to read it before I went to sleep that night.

"Well, that jarred me a bit. Especially because when I looked at the book, its title seemed vaguely familiar. So instead of killing myself, I went to my room and got down a little book your mom gave me a few years ago. It was called *From Screwed Up to Awesome*—and it was the same book Larry had just given me."

I did not want to hear this. That was just the kind of stuff that made my family babble about "no coincidences" and "God at work." But it got worse.

Ben grinned. "Great title, huh? I'd never looked at it before, but I'd also never forgotten what Swannee said when she gave it to me: 'Ben Abrams, you're enough to drive anyone crazy, but I love you and so does your mom, and I want you to know that things are going to get better. Promise me that you'll call me, any time of the night or day, if ever you get too low, if ever those dark thoughts get way too dark. Do you promise?'

"The same book and the same promise. It was pretty weird, Ellie. Like God was after me.

"So on the night of my planned suicide, I stayed up all night and read that book, which turned out to be a very teen-friendly version of the Gospel of Mark. And about halfway through it, I started crying—something I hadn't done in a long time—because I realized how much I wanted what the Bible had to offer. So I took it—faith, and Jesus, and I begged God to do something.

"And He did. Not all at once. It took me a while to clean up my act, to get away from the dangerous kids I was hanging with. I thought I'd have this easy ride—you know, once I was 'saved.'" He grinned at me and said, "Now *that's* a babble word . . . so I just call it 'going from being screwed up to being almost awesome.'"

We talked for another couple hours, the conversation real and easy between us. We talked by the lagoon, with our shoulders getting burned by the sun, talked as we rode back along the trail to Harbour Town, talked until Ben had to go to the Quarterdeck and I needed to check on Mom. When I left him, watching him park his bike and disappear into the condominium complex, I thought about that book, *From Screwed Up to Awesome*. I hadn't told Ben, but Mom had given me a copy too. I too had never once opened it. It had stayed stuffed in my desk, beside Mom's letters to me at camp, forgotten and gathering dust.

If I'd had it with me at the beach, I would have gone back to the beach house, settled in a big chair with an ice-cold Coke, and read it straight through, just to see what could have possibly grabbed on to Ben enough to change his whole life. I'd never felt this way with my family, never wanted to be infected with the germs of their faith. But that afternoon, pedaling back to the road called Spotted Sandpiper and watching for cranes and alligators, I wanted something. I wanted Ben's faith to be contagious so that I could catch it too.

The phone was ringing when I walked into the house. I grabbed it, hoping it hadn't bothered Mom, and was surprised to hear Rachel's voice on the other end.

"Hey, kid! How's it going?"

"Fine. Pretty good, I guess."

"I talked to Swan earlier today. She said that Ben had come by, brought her flowers, and taken you on a bike ride."

For some annoying reason, I felt my face grow hot with embarrassment, as if I'd done something wrong. "Yeah, we rode around for a while. Mom loved seeing him—they get along like two peas in a pod. He seems to be doing well."

"You think so, huh?"

"Sure. He likes his job. His jobs," I corrected.

"Well, let's hope that little church at Hilton Head can pay him more than the big ole poor church in New York."

"He doesn't seem to be complaining. And his band is good. I really like their sound."

"Yeah, beach tunes," she laughed.

"Hey, give him a break, Rach. He's got some original stuff too. I think he's doing okay. Heck, at least he's working. And he's in school. You didn't tell me that."

"He's not in school, Ellie. He's in *seminary*. There's a difference. School—let's say law school or med school or any of a hundred degrees—prepares you to earn a living. Seminary will just plunge him further into debt, with not much hope of digging himself out."

"You're not being very fair, Rach. I bet you'd be singing Daddy and Mom's praises if they chucked everything and went to seminary. You'd say they were brave and devout."

"Ben is *not* your parents. He needs a good dose of reality before he jumps into another one of his wild ideas. Anyway, forget it. I'm glad he seems happy and that you two got to see him. And I was hoping I'd get you on the phone. I want your take on Swan. How is she?"

"Tired. Sleepy. Lethargic."

"Is she eating?"

"Not a lot, but she manages to get down the clam chowder I bring her from the Crazy Crab."

"And are y'all talking?"

"No. She talks fine with Ben, though. Good ole Mom. I seem to have a gift for putting her to sleep."

"Give it time, kid." Then she added, "And a little effort on your part."

I started to protest, started to list off all the effort I was putting into this venture, but then I thought it wasn't worth it. For the second time recently, talking to Rachel was not making me feel better. "I'd better go," I said.

"Yeah, hang in there. Thinking about you both."

"Thanks."

I hung up the phone and went to check my e-mail.

Dear Ellie,

Missed talking to you today. Mom sounds chipper. Said you and she were planning on a walk on the beach this evening. Great idea. She even mentioned taking out a sketch pad. I'll call tomorrow. Thanks for all you're doing.

Love,
Dad

P.S. Heard that Ben came over. Tell him hi from me.

Hey there, Ellie,

Guess what? Mom and Dad were thrilled with the wedding plans. They simply adore Timothy, and Mom is in a flurry of nerves reserving the church and thinking of a thousand things that need to be done. If I let her run with the ball, she'll be out of our hair for a while.

Okay, now the questions you'd ask if we were sitting across from each other at the Flying Biscuit. No, I haven't had a drop of liquor, not even at the restaurant with Mom and Dad. Yes, we plan to keep the apartment. Yes, Timothy is still treating me like a queen. Okay, I'll admit I did go on a spending spree yesterday. No, I haven't told him about that little vice. I mean, he kinda knows. We have lived together for six months. No, we haven't talked about premarital counseling, but this one church where Timothy wants to have the ceremony—the one he went to as a kid—requires premarital counseling with the pastor. Sounds a little far out to me. We argued about that last night. It's not like we don't know each other. I can't see the point. . . .

Now about you—talked to your mom yet? How is she? How are you? Are you bored stiff? Any cute guys around? Are you still eating vegetables and stuff like that? At this rate, you'll be in a bikini before long.

Gotta go. I'll call you on Saturday.

Lots of love,
Megan

Dear Ellie,

My brother Mark is coming tomorrow. I'm cleaning up my apartment.

I don't have another bed or mattress or anything. I guess he can sleep on the couch. He might even bring his girlfriend. Is there anything I should do?

Worried,
Nate

P.S. No need to panic, but Abbie is hanging around again. Twice now she's come by your apartment, let herself in, and stayed for over an hour each time. What should I do? She saw me yesterday and said hello, but not in a very friendly way. I've warned Mrs. Rose to keep the kittens inside.

I quickly typed a response to Nate and sent it through cyberspace:

Hey, Nate, hang cool. All is well.

Mark will be fine on your couch. Maybe if he brings his girlfriend, she could stay with Mrs. Rose—she has an extra bed. I bet she'd be thrilled to help out.

Don't worry. I'll deal with Abbie when I get back. How are Mrs. Rose's cats? (Hindsight is acting sassy.)

Speak soon,
El

As I walked by the big mirror in my bathroom, I noticed with satisfaction that my jean shorts were hanging on me, looser than usual. Granted they were size sixteen, but to feel anything loose around my waist, well, it was exhilarating. It was motivation in itself to stay away from Cheetos and Coke. I decided to fix Mom and me each a tomato sandwich with mayo on whole wheat bread for a light supper. And I decided something else. I would start walking. I would walk for miles and miles down the beach while Mom sketched and the sun sank into the water. And I would start this very day.

At six o'clock precisely, I helped Mom out to the beach. I carried a beach chair for her and a bottle of chilled water, and she hung on to my arm, watching her feet as she stepped through the sand. I set up the chair and helped her remove her beach cover-up, making sure she kept her big straw hat securely on her head.

When I saw her there, in her bathing suit, I involuntarily turned away, stunned. Mom looked worse than emaciated. It gave me a creepy feeling to see how loose and wrinkled the skin was on her arms and legs. I turned back and helped her into the chair.

"Thanks, Ellie. Go take your walk."

And I did, a long, brisk walk beside the ocean, watching the white bubble-bath-looking foam wash over my feet and noticing the tiny clams burrowing into the sand until a little bubble popped through and dodging the jellyfish that sat, transparent and jiggling, in the tide. When I got back, I spread out a beach towel beside Mom's chair and lay down on my stomach.

We didn't say a thing for a while, but eventually she whispered, "The tide, Ellie, is constant. Everything can change. When I come back to Hilton Head, the houses are bigger, there are more people, but I plant my easel here in the sand and look at the ocean, and it hasn't changed."

But there was no easel today. No strength in her arms to hold the palette. Today she simply let her arm dangle in the sand, pushing it absentmindedly through her fingers.

"It is certainly comforting to know the ocean will never betray you."

I couldn't imagine why she had said that, but it kept repeating itself in my mind until I decided to ask. I could feel the pulse beating in my temple. "Have you ever felt betrayed by someone you love, Mom?"

At first I thought she hadn't heard my question, that maybe she was asleep, this wisp of a woman in the lounge chair with the tide at her feet. But then she said, keeping her eyes closed, "Oh yes, Ellie. I have felt betrayed. Betrayal is one of the most horrible wounds—I think it's worse in a sense than grief. Grief is pure and terrible and deep, but grief isn't bitter. Betrayal left me bitter and full of hate and despair."

"Who betrayed you, Mom?"

A single tear dropped down her cheek.

The tide reached my feet and lapped over my toes. I scooted my towel back a foot or two.

"I suppose I have felt betrayed by each of those I loved the most," she said at last.

"By me, Mom? Have you felt betrayed by me?" Then I added quickly, because I couldn't bear that question and the way she might turn it back on me, "By Daddy and Nan and Abbie?"

"Oh, Ellie, I suppose I have felt betrayal by each of you—I'm not saying I *was* betrayed, sweetheart. But you asked if I had ever *felt* betrayed. And I have, many times. Sometimes it was real, sometimes it was mixed with my own self-pity, sometimes I just completely got the facts wrong. I felt betrayed the most by the Lord." Another tear slipped down her face.

I swallowed hard. I had felt that way—still did, in fact—but I couldn't imagine Mom having those feelings toward God.

"When things were going so wrong, sweetie, I blamed Him. I was sure He'd left me alone or worse, betrayed me. He wasn't a God of love. Oh, I felt such incredible guilt to feel that way. I was supposed to be a good Christian." She shrugged. "And I felt betrayed by Rachel."

"Rachel?" Impossible. Rachel was her best friend from forever. But I remembered that Rachel had made comments about their European trip—laughing about how they almost killed each other, and then telling me she was "awful" to Mom on that trip. "When did you feel betrayed by Rachel, Mom?"

"It was a long, long time ago. Why do you ask?"

"I . . . I just wondered, that's all."

"Never mind, dear. You don't have to tell me." She let her arm fall to the side of the low beach chair again, scratching one finger in the sand. "Mmm, isn't it nice to have that cool touch at your fingers and the ocean running over it to keep it moist?"

A breeze picked up and blew her straw hat down the beach with a strong gust. I chased after it, retrieved it, and placed it delicately back on her head.

"Thank you, Ellie." She looked up to the sky. "Storm's brewing."

"I'd better get you inside, Mom."

"Yes, maybe. I think I need to take a little nap."

I helped her stand up and held her tightly around the waist as we walked back to the house. We walked slowly, as if Mom couldn't make her legs work any faster. As if it took every ounce of concentration for her not to collapse right into my arms. It began to rain, big slow drops. Soon it became a downpour. By the time we stepped inside the house, both of us were dripping wet.

"Shall I fix us a cup of tea, Mom?"

"No, dear. I'm just going to lie down for a bit. Afterward, maybe."

I felt surprised and disappointed. Mom was always up for a cup of tea and conversation. And finally, finally we were beginning to talk.

A cold fear prickled my back. She was more than tired, more than exhausted. She was shriveling up, as she had described my namesake Ella Mae doing before she died. I helped her to the downstairs bedroom, the one she had picked because it was small and dark when the shades were drawn. She slipped off her swimsuit, unembarrassed by her nakedness, her fragility, the incongruity of her perfectly reconstructed breasts against her skeletonlike figure.

I turned away, went into the adjoining bathroom, and grabbed a dry beach towel. I wrapped it around her and, remembering Daddy's admonition to be sure she didn't catch cold, carefully patted her dry, as if I were Abbie drying little Bobby after his bath.

I expected her to refuse my help, to tell me she could do it herself, but she didn't. Suddenly, it was as if an eighty-five-year-old woman had come to inhabit her body. A tired toddler or a worn-out old woman. Mom was both.

I tucked her into bed, blinking back tears. "Rest well, Mom."

"Oh, I will, Ellie. There's nothing nicer than a nap at the beach when the rain is pelting on the windows and I'm snuggled warm under the covers." I turned to go and she said, "Thank you, dear, for being here with me. I can't think of anything more lovely than this time with you. I'm sorry I can't be much of a conversationalist right now. . . ."

She let that phrase dangle, and an expression of extreme frustration crossed Mom's face—or maybe it had been there all along but I'd never wanted to see it. Now I saw—her weakness, her fragility, her cancer screamed at me, and that same cold fear raced through me again.

Mom knows she's beaten. She knows, and she can't make herself find the strength to pull out of it. For the first time in her life, Mom is beaten.

"Later we'll talk. Later we'll plan the trip to Scotland."

"Okay, Mom." I left the room and shut the door after me. The wind was howling, moaning, the rain popping against the window, but I think Mom had already fallen asleep. Just like a child.

Chapter 11

Velvet, dressed in her own clothes, went up the road. . . . The Piebald was flashing his colours under stars by the gate. . . . "Do you know what you've done?" said Velvet to the Piebald, but he shook his head suddenly as though a night gnat was on it.

—ENID BAGNOLD, *NATIONAL VELVET*

I had forgotten to put my bike back in the garage, and since I was already sopping wet, I ran outside where I'd propped it against a pine tree and rolled it back inside, more to give me something to do than for the bike's sake—it had certainly sat through many a rainstorm. Instead of going back out through the garage entrance, I opened a door that led from the garage into the downstairs area and walked through what had become a type of hallway-closet combination. It had been a few years since I had used that passageway, mostly because it was very narrow and I was not, and on either wall hung Daddy's tools, long rows of every imaginable tool, all arranged in perfect order. Whenever I walked through, I'd inevitably knock a shovel or a rake or something off the wall.

I flicked on the light switch and looked around. I noticed what seemed to be an addition to the narrow hallway. Above where the tools hung on the left side of the wall was a long shelf, which ran the length of the passage. I could walk under it without bumping my head, but I imagined Daddy might have to duck a little. The shelf was draped with thick old white sheets, draped in such a way that I knew there was something underneath. So of course, I got a stool that had been hung on the wall, set it on the ground, and stepped up, pulling a sheet up at one corner.

Underneath were canvases of every size—unframed painted canvases that had to be Mom's. They were stacked sometimes two or three thick, standing up, all along the shelf. I reached for one, a small square, no bigger than a coffee table book, and brought it down. I smiled. It was a portrait of my aunt Lucy—Trixie's daughter and my mom's half sister. Mom must have painted it years ago, because Lucy was still a young teen in the picture and now she had teenage kids of her own.

Suddenly, I had a great idea. I'd take all these paintings upstairs and set them out in the family room so Mom could see them again. I carried the first three upstairs and carefully set them on the floor, propped against the low wall between the family room and the kitchen. I kept making trips, propping some paintings against the walls, laying others down flat on the coffee table or kitchen counters. There were thirty-eight in all, and I thought a lot of them were really good—some not at all the style I had grown accustomed to from my mother.

I could hardly wait for her to wake up.

Hindsight appeared and twisted around my wet legs, disapproved, and scuttled under the table. I needed to take a shower, but I was afraid of leaving the paintings to the mercy of the cat's claws. What if she suddenly got the urge to sharpen them on Aunt Lucy's face? I brought Hindsight into the bedroom with me and shut the door before she could slip out.

After I'd showered and changed into dry clothes, I went back into the family room, sat on the couch, and stared at the different paintings, trying to imagine why my mother had painted some of these canvases. A few were downright strange. I felt restless, so I got back up, fed

Hindsight, checked out a few web sites, read the *Atlanta Journal* online, and grew impatient.

Mom finally woke up around eight-thirty and came upstairs. When she saw the paintings all spread out over the room like that, she froze, then she looked perplexed, then she glanced over at me with a look of anger and disappointment and maybe even betrayal. At least, it seemed that way to me.

And then she started crying. She just burst into tears. She stood there in her blue satin robe and cried.

I was dumbfounded, my eyes as wide as those doughnuts again, unable to say a thing. In my mind, I'd imagined her delightedly saying, "Oh, Ellie, sweetie, you've found these. Thanks so much."

Instead, she was crying those silent tears she was famous for. And then she started to cough, a dry little pitiful cough. That shook me into action. Daddy had said at least ten times, "Don't let your mother catch cold."

Maybe Mom was going to start another nosebleed, and it would all be my fault!

"Mom! Hey, Mom! I'm sorry. I found these paintings in the closet and I think they're great and I thought you'd like to see them and gosh, I'm sorry! I didn't mean to upset you. So hey, sit down and chill. I'll take them back downstairs. Don't worry. I'll do it right now."

Mom did sit down, on the couch, and then she wiped a finger under her eyes, and I ran to get her a tissue. As I picked up two or three paintings, she managed to sniff and then said, "Oh, Ellie. Forgive me. No, don't take them down. It was just a shock to see them. Silly me—I'm extra sensitive these days."

Which sounded like a feeble excuse to me, but I didn't say anything. I just stood there.

"It's okay, Ellie." Now she was perfectly composed. "Your dad moved these paintings down here about three years ago. We just ran out of space at the house on Beverly. So we stored them here."

That sounded like another feeble excuse, because the house on Beverly had a basement and an attic, but I wasn't about to contradict her. Instead, I said, "But Mom, these are good! Why haven't you framed them, put them out? Or tried to sell them?"

She shrugged. "Just because something is good doesn't mean it has to be displayed. Anyway, most of these paintings are just stuff I did for assignments at Hollins or rough drafts of paintings I did later. They weren't meant to be framed. Exercises, you know. But, of course, sentimental me couldn't bear to just throw them out, so your dad fixed up that place in the downstairs closet for them."

I brought her a cup of herbal tea, eyeing her a bit suspiciously, afraid she might start another crying/coughing fit. But she didn't. I picked up a canvas that was about two by three feet. My eye had gone to it immediately because it was what I'd call abstract—or maybe not that, because you could tell what was in the picture, but it was, I don't know, really weird.

"Um, do you mind telling me what this is all about?" I was trying not to smile, but then Mom did, so I figured it was okay.

The painting had a huge baby diaper—which she'd painted red, of all things—safety-pinned between two flagpoles. I wasn't sure, but I thought the flags were of the former Soviet Union and China. Inside the diaper were a bunch of naked people—grown adults, men and women with their bosoms and other body parts showing—they were actually climbing out of the diaper and sliding down the flagpoles. And there were a bunch of normal people, men dressed in suits and hats, and women holding babies, and also American soldiers, in the foreground running for their lives with expressions of pure terror on their faces.

"What in the world is this?"

Mom said, "I got an A+ for that when I was a junior at Hollins. It's called *Red Diaper Babies.*"

She said it as if that explained everything, so finally I said, "And . . . what's that, Mom?"

"Oh, you don't know about the red diaper babies?" A frown creased her brow. "Didn't you learn about that in American History?"

"Nope. At least not that I remember."

"Well, anyway, I painted that because I was furious at Rachel."

"Really?"

"Oh, gosh yes. We went our separate ways in college. She went up to Columbia University in New York and became what I would call ultra liberal. She started smoking pot and then a lot of other things—you know about that—and she joined the SDS—Students for a Democratic Society—and she was always talking about 'red diaper babies'—the kids whose parents were favorable to Communism. So that was my rendition of Rachel and the rest of those babies growing up and trying to infiltrate the country. And my art teacher thought it was extremely clever."

I scooted closer to the painting. "So Rachel was ultra liberal. Cool."

"It didn't seem very cool at the time," Mom said.

"Like what did she get into?"

"You name it. Drugs, free love, Communism. And of course, she was a staunch hater of the Vietnam War. She was always quoting statistics to me about what was going on and how awful America was and that our government was lying to us and we were bombing innocent villages and on and on. . . ."

"A regular Jane Fonda."

"Exactly. I don't know how many marches against the war she helped organize, but it was definitely her passion."

"And you hated her for that? Everybody's got a right to an opinion, Mom."

She sighed. "Oh, Ellie. It wasn't that simple. Not at all. Two of my closest friends—Carl Matthews and your father—were going to Vietnam. Actually, Carl was already over there, and your father was getting ready to go into training. And Rachel kept making it sound like he was going to be a murderer. Nothing patriotic about it to her.

"She tried to convince him to dodge the draft. She had all these connections in Canada and Sweden, and she kept telling him that he was going to get killed, that he didn't have a chance. . . ." She let out a long sigh.

I picked up the painting and said, "Okay, let's not talk about that anymore."

"It's okay, Ellie. Don't worry. Just a lot of memories. Rachel and I went through a lot during those years." She nodded over to another painting, almost equally as strange as the *Red Diaper Babies*. "I was just as messed up as Rachel was. Just in a different way. That was me. Right there," and she nodded again at the painting.

It was of a monster, a genuine, bona fide monster, with its mouth wide open and a woman falling into its mouth. Actually, there were five different figures of the same woman. In the foreground of the painting she looked normal, but gradually, as she approached the monster, she got more and more distorted, her body becoming huge in comparison to her head. She looked like she was falling into the monster's mouth, or being sucked in was probably more accurate, because her head was going in last, and she looked horrified and creepy and you could tell her whole body had already been swallowed because the body of the monster had taken on her form, the way a snake does when it swallows a mouse.

"That's kind of gross, Mom."

"Yes. Yes, it was gross. I called that painting *Addiction*."

"What's it about? I mean, what kind of addiction?"

"Food." She said it like that, plain and simple, as if she were talking to herself, not to me.

But when she pronounced the word, I suddenly felt my heart skip a beat. *Addiction* and *food* were way too close to home for me to be talking about them with my mother. But I don't think she saw it that way. Mom was always sensitive, trying not to hurt people's feelings or bring up delicate subjects. I called her the master conflict-avoider. But all of a sudden she just didn't seem to remember I was there, or that food and addiction were two of my biggest problems, and she just started talking.

"Being addicted to food was one of the most awful things I've ever experienced." Then she looked at me. "And I've experienced some pretty awful things. But food . . . It was just like the picture. It was a monster swallowing me alive, and I felt completely helpless."

"What kind of addiction do you mean? Like anorexia?" I asked in a voice that sounded small and full, as if I needed to clear my throat.

"It was definitely an eating disorder, although no one called it that back then. I guess it was bulimia—although I didn't make myself throw up all that often. I just binged in secret. I gained a lot of weight, and I guess you'd say that food controlled me. I knew something was very wrong with me. It wasn't normal to skip meals with friends and then gobble down a whole bag of chips or cookies or a half-gallon carton of ice cream alone in my room.

"And I think the guilt was the worst part. I felt guilty for bingeing, and then I felt guilty because I thought a Christian shouldn't have such a problem, and then I felt guilty because most kids my age were struggling with things that seemed a lot more serious—drugs and alcohol and being drafted—and here I was, trapped by this kind of monster."

She reached over and touched the painting. "And Rachel was no help. Once I tried to broach the subject with her on the phone, to tell her about what was happening to me and how I was depressed about gaining so much weight.

"And she said, 'Oh, Swan, you're so skinny, you can stand to gain weight.'"

"'But I can't stop eating,' I told her."

"And she just laughed and called me a silly, scatterbrained girl, the way she always had. I tried to explain how depressed I was, but obviously Rachel couldn't relate. She said, 'Swan, for goodness' sake! Please don't tell me that the biggest struggle you are having right now is whether or not to eat a doughnut! Get real! Do you know what I worry about?' And then she listed things like wondering which guy in the SDS she should sleep with and what her next trip on LSD would be like and how she was going to organize the next big march against the war."

Mom's face looked kind of pasty white. She just kept staring at her monster painting while she relived the whole conversation. "I felt so much anger toward Rachel, I wanted to kill her. And I knew I'd lost her—lost her as a confidante and soul mate. After I hung up, I literally hid in my bed and stuffed doughnuts into my mouth, trying to make the pain inside go away. And then I painted this painting."

She looked over at me, patted my hand, and said, "I'm sorry, Ellie. I've shocked you. You see, that's why I was crying. Some of these paintings represent hard memories."

"I'll put them away, Mom. Never mind."

"Hard isn't necessarily bad, Ellie. Sometimes it's just . . . hard. Leave them here. I'll tell you about the others another time. That's one thing we've got down here. Time." She got off the couch slowly. "But right now, I think I'll turn in for the night."

I followed her downstairs, made sure she was tucked in and warm and had a glass of water and some Kleenex by the bed. As I switched off the light, I looked back at her and said, "Good night, Mom. I hope you sleep well."

She gave me a weak smile. "Good night, Ellie. Thank you, I'm sure I will."

It was getting dark by now, and with the lights off in the family room, *Red Diaper Babies* and *Addiction* looked sadder and weirder than before. I put those two paintings on the windowsill and then stood across the room, flipped on the light, and stared at them long and hard.

It was very obvious that Mom was hurting when she painted these things.

I wanted her to explain to me how a Christian could have an addiction to food. Now *that* was an interesting subject to explore. I just couldn't quite imagine my devout, disciplined mother bingeing on food. I thought about how flippant Rachel had been with Mom's food addiction and then I thought about what she had said the other day: *I was so awful to your mother on that trip.* I'd imagined their European trip as this blissful getaway for two college grads, the trip of a lifetime. But if Mom was already that ticked off at Rachel before the trip, why'd they go in the first place?

There was something else that kept creeping into my thoughts. I was thinking about how mad Mom had been at Rachel, and how I could understand that anger, even just from the little bit she'd shared. And then I remembered the way Megan had looked at me the other day with big, sad eyes when I'd tried to defend Jamal. *You're making me mad,* is what she'd said.

I liked the fact that Megan "spoke truth" to me—that was the way they put it in rehab. You needed people in your life who dared to speak the truth. Well, Megan did. But I had brushed it off. I didn't want Megan and me to go through all the bitterness that Mom and Rachel had—even if in the end it turned out okay for them. I knew Megan cared about me and really wanted my best. I thought about it for a long time—about my addictions and my promise to stay away from "potentially compromising situations," and I decided right then and there that I was going to quit working at Jeremy's.

Finally, I had to admit that there was one other thing exploding in my head: anger—anger erupting from out of nowhere. It throbbed so loudly in my temples I was sure it would wake up Mom from her sleep. Impossible that *that* was my mother: cramming food in her mouth, judgmental, angry, depressed, overweight. Impossible. Because it sounded way too much like me. Faithful, pretty, talented Mom had felt this way? Not only had she felt this way, she had felt this way at twenty-one.

I tiptoed into Mom's bedroom. She was sound asleep, and though the rain had slowed, it was still hitting the windows. She looked peaceful as I watched her chest rise and fall, that skinny body with its made-over chest. I bit my lip and looked away.

Somewhere inside I felt relieved. Mom was resting okay, and I was fulfilling my daughterly duty by caring for her. And I had days in front of me to figure out the sketch pads and the paintings. That was what I wanted to do. Maybe I didn't know the weak woman in the bed in front of me, but I felt I was just beginning to get to know the young woman who had painted her soul on these canvases. One thing was for sure. I knew all about having monsters eating me up inside.

I went back to my room. Hindsight was curled up on the chaise lounge, so I decided to stretch out on the floor, leaning my back against the chair. I turned the TV on—the Braves were playing the Phillies—and watched the game without interest. I felt tired—mentally tired, anyway, or maybe I should say emotionally tired. But my body, the physical part, was wide awake. The paintings were calling to me, but I didn't want to respond. So I sat there, feeling as if the family room and the bedroom were two competing teams playing tug-of-war with my emotions. The bedroom gave a yank and said, *Braves baseball, Hindsight, sleep*—admittedly three of my favorite things. The family room team gave a yank and said, *Mom*. Mom with a food addiction. Mom the guilty Christian. Mom with breast cancer. That last yank did it, and I went back into the family room.

When I switched on the lights, it was like my own private art showing in the middle of the night. I had never been to the High Museum at night, of course—it wasn't open—but I had never even been there on a winter afternoon when it got dark at five. The paintings, with the windows and glass doors as a backdrop, seemed to take on a whole new life at night.

In this light, I kept thinking, *Mom has completely changed her style. She doesn't paint like this anymore*. And that was too bad, according to me. I liked these paintings. In them, Mom had a clever way of rendering a familiar subject so that it bothered you or got under your skin, in a good way. Some of them looked like sophisticated cartoons—they almost seemed to be hinting at political commentary. I liked Mom's strange sense of humor exhibited in these paintings—nothing sentimental or devout. At least as a young woman, no matter how messed up she claimed she'd been, Mom was also smart and sassy. Controversial. That was the word I was looking for. Some of these paintings were downright controversial. So why did she end up mainly painting portraits and scenery, when this stuff was great and would surely make people think?

There was one that showed three big churches on Peachtree Road. Everybody knew that spot—where the Episcopal church, the Cathedral of St. Philip; Second Ponce de Leon Baptist Church; and the Catholic church, the Cathedral of Christ the King, sat within a few hundred yards of each other. Mom had painted an aerial view, kind of; from above, you could see the churchgoers all walking into their respective sanctuaries, heads held high, eyes straight ahead, each person intent on entering a particular church.

But then she'd painted the same people walking out of the buildings on the other side, only they were no longer walking along Peachtree Road, but on one road that merged together, a gold road that I guess was supposed to be heaven. They were all going in the same direction, intermingled and smiling, talking with each other, drawn toward a very bright light in the distance.

"I like what you're trying to say, Mom," I whispered to the painting, and I got a little tingling along my arms, so that when I looked down at them, they were covered with goose bumps.

I didn't want to feel anything at the moment, so I turned my attention to a painting of the Fulton County Stadium, which housed all the baseball games before Turner Field was built for the 1996 Olympics. This painting, I knew, was Mom's rendition of the way the Braves had come to Atlanta. She showed the Atlanta Crackers—Atlanta's minor league team—leaving a brand-new stadium (she'd painted a big blue ribbon on the stadium entrance gate). The players on the team were walking away, so you could read their names on the backs of their uniforms. Then the new team, the Atlanta Braves, was coming into the stadium. The players were waving their caps and the crowd was cheering and a man on a ladder was changing the name on the scoreboard. Being the baseball trivia queen that I was, I knew that the stadium had opened in April 1966.

Mom cared about baseball? That was a revelation. Daddy and Uncle Jimmy loved the Braves, but I'd never thought of Mom having the least bit of interest. But this painting had so much emotion and, I don't know, such a feeling of celebration, that anyone viewing it would say that the artist really liked baseball!

And I got goose bumps again on my arms.

As I studied the other paintings, I realized that a few of them did look familiar. Some were indeed rough drafts of other paintings I knew well. Like the one of Trixie and Granddad JJ's wedding day. It showed Trixie walking down the driveway of the house that sat directly across the street from Granddad JJ's. She was dressed in a beautiful white winter suit and was carrying a gorgeous bouquet of red roses, and my aunt Lucy, who was about twelve at the time, was beside her in a red satin dress. On the other side of the street, standing in my grandparents' front yard, were my mother, Granddad JJ, and Uncle Jimmy. My mom was wearing the same dress as Lucy's—so you could tell they were meant to be bridesmaids—and Granddad JJ and Uncle Jimmy were dressed in tuxes, and all three of them were waving to Trixie and

Lucy. It was the happiest painting, and it was the perfect representation of what had happened in real life.

After my grandmom Sheila died in the Orly plane crash, Granddad JJ married Trixie, Sheila's longtime best friend and across-the-street neighbor. And the way my family always told the story, so sweet and sentimental like, I knew there had never been anything between Trixie and Granddad before Grandmom died. Their getting together later was what everyone in the family called a "wonderful answer to prayer"—and since I adored my grandparents, I could agree with that particular bit of Bartholomew babble.

There were probably ten portraits among the paintings—the one of Aunt Lucy, and then one of Rachel wearing a lime green shirt (no bra) and very low hip-hugger jeans with a patch proclaiming, "Make Love Not War." She had a string of love beads around her neck, and her thick blond hair fell to her waist, with a little braid on either side of her face. The painting made me smile. No doubt if Rachel were a teen now, she would have several body piercings—surely in her perfect little navel and probably in her nose. At any rate, hippie or not, she looked absolutely stunning.

There was a painting of Dr. and Mrs. Matthews. Dr. Matthews was wearing his army uniform, and Mom had painted it decorated with stars and a Purple Heart—which I guess was true. His face was an enigma—joy, pride, sadness. I wondered if all Vietnam vets looked that way, even on their wedding day. Mrs. Matthews was wearing a really simple wedding dress. White, of course, with a nice heart-shaped neckline and no frills or long train. But the dress appeared to be made out of satin, the way it shone, and Mrs. Matthews was smiling so big you'd just about expect her to start belting out, "Glory, glory, hallelujah!" Everything about that painting, even if it was a rough draft, seemed to suggest, "These are two really neat friends of mine!" So I told myself one thing. My parents and the Matthewses were still good friends on Carl and Cassandra's wedding day.

I really liked the portrait of Miss Abigail. The original, or maybe I should say, the final copy, hung down in the fellowship hall of Mt. Carmel Church. From the stories I'd heard about Miss Abigail and what I'd observed, Mom had done a great characterization. Miss Abigail looked about sixty in the painting, with her long gray hair pulled back in a ponytail. She was kneeling by an old beat-up station wagon, with the back door open. Bags of canned food and clothes were lying all over the back of the car, and there was a line of people receiving food and clothes. But Miss Abigail was focusing her attention on a little black girl who was no more than five. She was kneeling down to the child's height and holding her shoulders, and she had so much love in her that it just flowed out to this little girl.

And there was a painting of my mother's mare, Bonnie, whom Mom had owned ever since she was a young teen. The painting was of Bonnie's beautiful head and neck, showing her flaming chestnut coat and mane and the tiny white star slightly off center on her forehead. Her ears were pricked forward and her nostrils flared, the perfect representation of a high-strung Thoroughbred. Bonnie had lived to be thirty-three years old, which is really old for a horse, and Mom had kept her at Rachel's parents' house right up to the day she died, which I remembered in vivid detail.

I loved Bonnie. As a young girl, I'd sit on her swayed chestnut back while she ate grass and hold on to the coarse tufts of her mane that grew on her withers. Mom, of course, was always holding on to a lead shank that was attached to Bonnie's halter. I loved the feel of the horse's fat belly and my skinny legs wrapped around her.

As I looked at the painting, I got this pinching in my chest. Mom had said some of the paintings held painful memories for her. This one held them for me. After my accident, I got lost even deeper in the world of animals, and I loved going to the barn and brushing Bonnie. Mom even taught me how to ride her. But Bonnie was so old by then that all I could do was walk and trot on her because her fetlocks were almost always swollen and she wasn't surefooted anymore—once she actually fell down when Mom was riding her. I remembered how carefully Mom had bandaged her old, swollen legs, and the stench of the thrush in her hooves and the way her beautiful chestnut coat started getting all rough and scabby.

I remembered the day we went to see Bonnie and she was lying in her stall and couldn't get up. She scrambled a little, almost like a newborn foal, but she couldn't get that old body up out of the shavings. So we sat there in her stall, Mom and I, petting her and brushing her and feeding her oats from our hands. I knew Bonnie was suffering badly, but Mom knew she was dying. I wouldn't believe it. I spent the night in the stall, with Bonnie's big head in my small lap, an old horse blanket wrapped around her and another one around my shoulders, and I sang songs to her.

The next morning Dr. Hammond came to the barn. When I saw his face all serious and sad—he'd been Bonnie's vet for years—I knew what was happening. They had to practically pry me away from the horse, I was crying so hard. Mom was crying too, and she wouldn't let me stay with her. Trixie took me to her house, and I remember Rachel coming to the barn and hugging Mom while they both just sobbed.

They buried Bonnie in the spacious woods behind the riding ring at Rachel's parents' house, which was probably against the law, but none of us cared one iota. And I'd take flowers over and put them on Bonnie's grave.

It's funny how an image or a painting can make you feel things. My fresh, unexpected tears flowed so freely that by the time I'd wiped my eyes dry, I felt exhausted myself. I scooped up Hindsight and brought her into the bedroom, shutting the door. I sat on the bed, with Hindsight beside me, petting her till she purred and thinking about Bonnie and then about how much it had hurt me when Bonnie died. I was surprised by my next thought. If it had hurt me that much for Bonnie to die, how much more must it have hurt my mother? That was what I wondered as I sat on the bed, staring out the window at a black sky.

Chapter 12

Oh, young Lochinvar is come out of the west:
Through all the wide border his steed was the best;
And save his good broadsword he weapons had none;
He rode all unarmed and he rode all alone.
So faithful in love, and so dauntless in war,
There never was knight like young Lochinvar!

—SIR WALTER SCOTT, *LOCHINVAR*

When Mrs. Matthews called the next morning, the phone by my bed woke me from the sound sleep I'd finally fallen into. "Hello, Mrs. Matthews."

"Ellie, I hope I'm not waking you up?"

I glanced at the clock. It was after nine. "No, no, it's fine. Thanks for calling."

"I got your phone number from your father. I just thought I'd call and check up on the two of you. How is your mom doing?"

"I guess she's okay. Is it normal for her to sleep all the time? I mean, she rested most of last week—even with the visitors—and now down here, that's all she feels like doing. It's a little scary."

"Is she eating anything?"

"Yeah, a little bit. And she drinks a lot of water and fruit juice. But she isn't painting or even sketching—I don't know if you remember, but that used to be her favorite thing in the world."

"Oh yes. I remember. And Ellie, your father has already talked to her oncologist, who thinks it'd be a good idea to have her blood checked. Your dad said it's been three days. We usually recommend having it checked at least that often after chemo—and especially considering her recent problems with the platelets. Knowing your father, he's probably already made an appointment for this afternoon." She chuckled a little, as if she was trying to make Mom's health issues not so serious.

"Well, I'll talk to Dad. Thanks, Mrs. Matthews. Thanks so much for calling."

But Cassandra Matthews wasn't quite ready to hang up. "What about you, Ellie? Are you doing all right? It isn't too hard on you?"

"No, not too bad. I guess I'm getting used to it."

"I hope you can just keep telling yourself that you're giving your mother a gift. It will be worth it, Ellie. I guarantee."

"I hope so. I really do."

I called Daddy right then, and sure enough, he'd made an appointment for three o'clock that afternoon with an oncology specialist on the island whom Dr. Marshall had recommended. He also gave me precise directions for how to get there. I could just see him with his map of Hilton Head spread across his desk in his roomy office with the glassed-in walls on the eighteenth floor of the Pinnacle Building that looked out on Peachtree Road. He'd have pushed all the other papers, the ones dealing with building projects in Grant Park and Summerhill and the renovations for Oakland Cemetery, to the side and would be tracing the roads with his pencil, leading me to my destination. Daddy had always loved maps.

"I'll get her there," I promised him. "I'll get her there on time."

I went straight to the shower and stayed in for at least fifteen minutes, relishing the hot, pelting water against my skin. I put on shorts and a T-shirt and stepped out onto the little balcony as I towel-dried my hair. The sun was out and had already pretty much dried up the pavement from the previous night's storm. I went downstairs, a little embarrassed to be checking in on Mom so late in the morning.

She wasn't in her bed.

I looked in the other rooms, went back upstairs and felt a tiny shiver of worry as I went outside, squinting in the sun. I ran out onto the beach and there was my mother, standing at the ocean's edge—it was high tide—her head covered with her big floppy bright pink straw beach hat. Her white cotton Oxford was tied at the waist and her baggy jeans rolled up to the knees. She caught sight of me and waved and started taking tiny birdlike steps in my direction, reminding me of an elderly woman I used to visit in a nursing home. I felt silly to have worried and relieved to see her standing there. She met me at the end of the little trail.

"Hey, Ellie. I was just coming in—sun's getting a bit hot now. Ah, but the ocean air smells divine."

"Do you feel better this morning?"

"Much better. Just have a teeny sniffle—nothing to worry about. I must have slept for half a day. And what about you, sweetie?"

I shrugged. "Fine."

Then I told her about the appointment at the clinic. I thought I saw a frown crease her brow, but she wiped it away immediately.

I had rushed outside so quickly I hadn't noticed that Mom had rearranged the paintings in the family room. When we came back inside, she took a seat on the couch and waved her arms around the room. "I put them in chronological order," she said matter-of-factly. "Thirty-eight paintings from 1963 to 1972. A visual diary. They're very valuable to me because they show my progression as an artist, how much work and discipline it takes to become good at something."

"I think they're really good. Admittedly, your style has changed. These are bolder or gutsier, something. Different."

She shrugged again. "Many, many things have changed since I

painted those things. The world is a different place."

"So tell me about *this* world, Mom," and I let my arms sweep around the room. "Chronological order, you said. Well, I got the first one there—Granddad JJ and Trixie's wedding."

"December 1963, one month after the president was shot."

"And that's Mt. Carmel Church, and then portraits of Miss Abigail and Lucy and Rachel. And 'Church Corner.' I really like that one." I turned to look at her, all skin and bones with her bald head and green scarf. "Do you still feel the same way, Mom? That all those people in churches are arguing over petty issues which don't matter when they're all going the same place in the end? At least—that's what it looks like you're saying to me."

"I guess I went through a cynical phase, Ellie. I doubted my faith and I doubted the faith of most other people. I thought a lot about hypocrisy—dear Rachel kept me on my toes with that issue too. There was controversy not only over the war, and drugs and free love, but about Jesus freaks and traditionalists, and I just hated it all. I felt like shouting, 'Get over it and show some love!'"

"Good for you, Mom. I agree with you on that." We met eyes, each of us with a suspicious, surprised look on her face.

I pointed to the next painting. "And there's Daddy in his red convertible. He seems kinda sad."

"I didn't think he was too sad, at the time. But I sure was." She had a little sarcastic tone in her voice.

"Why?"

"Because we agreed to date other people. He's waving good-bye to me as I head off to Hollins, and I am just heartsick."

"Y'all stopped dating? I thought you dated all through college."

"Oh no. We didn't date *at all* in college. He wrote me, though. Every week. Long, informative, break-your-heart letters about his classes and his dates and his dreams."

"He wrote you about other *girls*? That was mean!"

"I agree!"

"Was he trying to make you jealous?"

"I don't know if he was or not, but it sure worked. I was green with jealousy."

"So why'd you agree to date other people if you liked Daddy so much?"

"He was the one who brought it up. On prom night of our senior year, of all things." Mom's face got a little red, and she hesitated and looked down at her hands. "He thought we were getting a little too serious." Now her face was scarlet, as if she'd just admitted that she and Daddy had been having sex.

I couldn't let that pass. "How serious?"

"Oh." She was flustered. "We didn't . . . um . . . 'go all the way' or anything. But we were going beyond the limits we'd set for ourselves."

I'm sure I was smirking, but I didn't let her see. "So what happened? How'd you get back together?"

"I've told you that story."

I wrinkled my brow and tried to remember. "Are you sure?"

"The beach? Right here at Hilton Head?"

I felt myself getting defensive. "Sorry, Mom. I must have missed that family meeting."

"It doesn't matter."

"Yes it does. Obviously it matters to you and Daddy, and it matters to me because I wouldn't be here if you and Daddy hadn't gotten together."

Mom was nibbling on her lip. I think she was nervous.

I tried again. "I'm all ears. I *want* to know the story."

She stopped nibbling her top lip and started nibbling the bottom one. "Well, for one thing, your dad had graduated a year early from Tech—he was ROTC, skipped his junior year and became a second lieutenant. After graduation he went to boot camp at Fort Benning, Georgia, and then he was supposed to do a thirteen-month tour of duty in Vietnam."

"Hold on a minute! Daddy skipped his junior year so he could finish school early and go to Vietnam? He *wanted* to go to the war?"

She gave me a funny little smile and said, "That was my reaction exactly. But to him it was logical. You see, by 1967, so many young men—even boys—were being drafted. Robbie thought his chances were better to go as an officer than as what he called a 'grunt.' He said they always were sent to the front line first and got killed."

"Yuck."

"Oh yes. Big yuck. Anyway, your father was bound and determined to get all this war stuff over with, and Rachel was bound and determined that he was an idiot, and I was just scared stiff and madly in love with him. I'd always been in love with him—it had never changed. The only thing that had changed about me was that I'd gained twenty-five pounds and I was miserable.

"Anyway, I finished my last exam in early May of 1968 and had a week before graduation, so I went to Hilton Head. Your father had finished up his training at Fort Benning, and I'd heard that he was going to be here on the island too—so it was my last chance to see him before he left for Vietnam.

"So I was both scared to death and excited to see him when I walked down the beach to his house and knocked on the door."

It seemed like my mother was drifting back in time, almost as if I weren't really sitting across from her, as if it were my dad as a young Army recruit, there with her. . . .

Robbie greeted me at the door, wearing a pair of Bermuda shorts and a white polo shirt. His reddish brown hair was cut in a very short crew cut, and he looked very muscular and handsome.

"Swannee. Great to see you! So glad this worked out." His face erupted into dimples and his eyes lit up as he hugged me in a big-brother way.

I was wearing a beach cover-up, a brightly colored floral print that wrapped around me and was tied with a yellow rope belt. Nothing in my wardrobe fit anymore, but I desperately wanted to look attractive for the last time I saw Robbie. I was embarrassed by my weight gain, and somehow hoped he wouldn't notice.

"Well, how does it feel to be done with school, Swan? A college graduate!"

"Almost a college graduate," I corrected. "Anyway, you beat me to it. It feels good. Yeah, pretty good, I guess."

He brought out a couple of Cokes, and we sat on the screened porch that overlooked the beach and the ocean. "I'm glad you came by."

"I had to tell you good-bye."

"Thanks, Swan. You've always been so thoughtful in that way. It means a lot." He did seem genuinely pleased.

"Well, spit it out, Robbie Bartholomew. How are you feeling?"

Poor Robbie. I never was one for small talk.

"Ready, I guess." He shrugged.

"You don't want to go, do you?"

"Who wants to go to war, Swannee? But it's okay. I've been training for this for a long time. Like I've told you before, I'm just ready to get this over with so I can continue on with life." He looked at me when he said it and gave me a half smile.

"I want you to write me, Robbie, when you're in Vietnam," I said suddenly, breaking the silence as we sipped our Cokes. "Tell me the truth about the war. I can handle it."

"Are you sure, Mary Swan?" he asked, arching his brow. He knew all too well that details tended to bore me, making my eyes cloud over.

"I am serious. I want to know."

"Fine. Have it your way." He set down his glass of Coke and crossed his arms over his chest, and I thought he looked rather pleased. "You know that I'm a second lieutenant. That basically means I'll be in command of an infantry platoon. I'll be the officer platoon leader, in charge of about fifty soldiers. At full strength, the platoon will have four squads of eleven men and a platoon sergeant—kind of like my right-hand man. He's supposed to have a lot more experience than me. Let's hope so, at least." He gave a wry smile. "Three of my squads will be rifle squads, and the fourth will be a weapons squad with two machine guns, a couple of grenade launchers, and possibly a couple of small mortars."

"Sounds awfully dangerous. And you'll have a bunch of responsibility, Robbie, won't you?"

"You bet. I'll be one of the main men in the war; it'll all depend on me." He gave me a wink and a smile. "Do you wanna hear more, or am I scaring you?"

"I wanna hear."

"In the field, I'll be shadowed by an RTO, radio telephone operator—an enlisted man. And every move of my platoon will be coordinated and reported to my company."

"Your 'company'? What does that mean? You'll be having guests over while in Vietnam?" I stuck out my tongue at him, an old habit from high school days.

"Very funny, Swan. What it means is that I'll have a boss who is a captain, commanding a company of four platoons, one of which is mine."

"Gotcha. I understand."

"Do you really want to hear all this?"

"Of course, silly guy. You happen to be one of my closest friends, in case you've forgotten. I care about you. A lot." As soon as I'd said it, I wished I hadn't added the *a lot*. This wasn't the time to be getting sentimental.

"Wanna take a walk on the beach?" he asked, out of the blue.

"Sure, why not?"

We took off our shoes and headed outside. The day was cloudy and windy, but the air was warm. We walked to the ocean's edge, stood there for a while in silence and let the chilly water trickle over our toes when the surf came in. Robbie started digging in the wet sand with his toes.

"What're you doing?"

"Nothing." He kicked a little sand onto my feet. "We've talked a lot about me. Now it's your turn. Are you feeling okay these days, Mary Swan?"

"I'm no swan," I spat out way too quickly. "I'm a goose. Just a very fat goose."

Robbie kept fiddling in the sand with his toes, not looking me in the eyes. "Lots of girls gain weight in college. That's no big deal. You're too hard on yourself, Swannee."

"Sure." It came out sarcastically. "I'm sure you're right."

He looked up then. "Something's really the matter, isn't it? What's up?"

My heart started racing, the way it always did when I realized how much Robbie cared about me. As if I were his sister.

"I have no idea. Nothing works, Robbie. Not prayers, not action, not even painting. Nothing is working these days. Except being a fat goose."

"All right now, lighten up a little, Mary Goose," he teased and then punched me playfully.

"It's not funny, Robbie. I don't know what's the matter with me, and I know it's ridiculous to feel this way when really important stuff is going on, and gosh, you're about to leave for war. It's hard. Life is hard and nothing makes sense and I can't figure it out."

"Don't talk like that, Swan! We've got all of life ahead of us. Look at you! You're an up-and-coming artist. Heck, why I bet by the time I get back from Vietnam, you'll be having all kinds of exhibitions. And you're getting ready to go to Europe! It'll be wonderful."

We were sloshing our feet in the water now as we strolled along the beach.

"I know I've got everything to be happy about. I should be excited, but I just feel kinda numb. And then if you start reminding me of why I should be happy, well, it only makes me feel worse. Guilty. Never mind all that. I'm sorry to bring it up."

"Don't be sorry, Swan. I didn't mean to joke about something that's important to you."

The way he was looking at me made me feel uncomfortable. I knew he meant every word. He cared, as a big brother. But, of course, the problem was that I didn't want a big brother. I had never stopped loving him. I knew for a fact that there was a long line of girls waiting for him. I'd saved all of his letters and guarded them preciously, trying to read between the lines, to see if there might be anything that hinted at feelings for me as more than a friend. But there was never anything except great kindness and that big brotherly concern.

"Are you bummed out about not dating anybody? Do you think that's the problem? If it is, Swannee, don't worry about it. There just hasn't been anybody good enough for you yet."

I shook my head. I was too embarrassed to bring up the weight issue again, so I just said, "You're sweet to say it, but that's not true. There are lots of nice guys out there. I don't know what it is. I guess I'm just too serious for the boys. Or too strange. Something."

"Not too strange, Swan. Maybe they feel intimidated. You're smart, pretty, talented. You know."

"I don't think that's what they're thinking." I shrugged. "But it's okay. I never expected to marry right after college. What about you? How's Cindy?"

He laughed. "Cindy? Oh yes. The girl from New York. Nice girl. Got a little bored with me, I think. Anyway that was a long time ago. I haven't had a date since I finished school. It's been nearly a year."

"They work you hard, don't they?"

"Grueling. Not a lot of fun."

"Yeah, I gathered that it was kind of a bummer from what you wrote."

He had his hands thrust deep into his pockets, and the wind from the ocean was blowing hard. We had our heads turned into it. "Might storm," he said.

"Should we go back?"

"I guess, if you want." But neither of us made the slightest move to turn around.

"I hate it that you're going to Vietnam," I said suddenly.

"Do you?"

"Of course."

"It means the world to me to know you care. Thank you."

"Of course I care, silly guy. That's a crazy thing to say! Don't worry. I'll write you in 'Nam. I'll even send you cookies."

"Thanks! I'll count on that."

It irritated me that our conversation was so flat. Then it began to rain, the kind of rain that stings when it hits your skin. *It figures,* I thought. *This rain is symbolic of our relationship. It stings. Why do I have to love this man who only sees me as a friend?*

"Wanna go in, Goose?"

I stuck out my tongue at him. "Not really. I like walking in the rain."

So we walked along in silence. I had my head bent down, and the wind was whipping my hair in all different directions. Robbie's steps seemed measured, as if he was concentrating on something far off. I tried to imagine what a soldier would feel on the eve of his departure for war. It made my heart hurt.

"Robbie, are you okay?" I asked after we'd walked a long way.

"Not really."

"Stupid question, I guess. Who would feel okay when he's heading off to war in three days."

"It's not just that." He looked over at me with this miserable, worried expression on his face. "It's . . . I have a problem."

"Whaddaya mean?"

"Something I'd like to have resolved before I leave for 'Nam."

"With a girl?" As soon as I said it, I knew I had guessed correctly, but I did not want our last conversation to center on a new love in his life.

"Yep."

I felt that familiar clutching at my heart. "Someone you just met?"

"Oh no. Someone I've known for a long time."

I racked my brains, trying to remember which girl at school he'd seemed particularly fond of. "Does she know there's a problem?"

"I doubt it."

"Does she like you?"

"I honestly don't know."

"Well, you'd better spit it out to her, Robbie Bartholomew! You don't have a lot of time left."

"You think I should talk to her before I leave for war?"

"Are you nuts? Of course you should. I'd want to know that a guy loved me for sure before he took off."

"You would? Honestly? It wouldn't make everything harder?"

"Good grief, Robbie! You can be so pigheaded! If you love her, and you think she feels the same way, you're crazy to say nothing." I was still trying to figure out who "she" was. "This is someone you used to date? And now you like her again?"

He glanced over at me and gave me the strangest sad smile. "You're a good guesser, Swan."

"Well, I still have no idea who it is."

"Really?"

"Promise." I was growing annoyed with him. Couldn't he see he was breaking my heart once again? "Why don't you just tell her how you feel and give the poor girl a chance? For all you know, she's madly in love with you too."

He stopped dead in his tracks. This time his eyes met mine, and I shivered a little. "I'm afraid to tell her, Swannee. She's the best friend

I've ever had, and I don't want to lose her, even if we'll only remain friends." He regarded me closely. "I've wanted to tell her for ages, but I always chicken out."

My heart started racing crazily, shocked and petrified and excited by the hints he was giving me. And there was that look in his eyes. . . .

"Robbie, what are you trying to say? Please tell me!"

"I'm trying to tell you that my problem is you." He took my hand in his and started walking again, with the wind whipping his shirt, making it billow out. "My problem has always been you, Swan. Couldn't you tell? Don't you remember how I told you that all I wanted to do was follow you around for the rest of my life? Don't you remember?"

My hand was suddenly very sweaty. "You mean you like me? You want to date me, Robbie Bartholomew?"

I guess he could hear the astonishment and wonder in my voice, because he got awfully brave and shouted above the wind, "No, Mary Swan Middleton, I don't like you! I love you! I love you with everything within me, and I want to marry you!"

I stepped back, hands on my hips, eyes wide open. "What?" Then I burst into tears. "How can you say that? Look at me? I'm fat and crazy."

"I mean it, Swan."

"I don't believe you!" It was true. I, the dreamer, the romantic, had not anticipated this scene. I'd dreamed of many others, but not this one. "I can't believe it." I was shaking my head back and forth. "I can't believe it!" I wiped my hand across my face, brushing away the tears. Then I put my face within inches of his. "Are you sure? You're not just saying this because I seemed sad? Not trying to cheer me up before you fly away?"

"Of course not, Swan. I'd never do that." He looked genuinely offended.

"There are things I've wanted to tell you about me. It might make you change your mind."

"Never. I love you. Period."

"What if I told you that I've got problems, Robbie?"

"Who doesn't, Mary Swan?" He grabbed my hands again and pulled me close. "Anyway, I've known you long enough to know that I love you. No matter what. Whether you're a swan or a raven, or . . . or a goose, for that matter. Just as you are."

I could barely force myself to look into his eyes, but as soon as I did, all I could see was love, deep love. Not just the kind that makes your heart run—not just passion, or desire. Something that hurts when you see it. Something that is hard to accept—because it is so true.

He cupped my chin in his hand. "I only have to know one thing, Swan. Do you love me?"

I bit my lip. Here it was—what I'd been longing to hear. What could I say? The truth. "Always. I always have and always will."

He got this great smile on his face, complete with dimples, and then he kissed me hard on the mouth. The tingles went from my head to my toes. He let out a long sigh. "Then it's settled. You tour Europe and paint to your heart's content and write me, and I'll come home and follow you around for the rest of my life."

I let go of his hand and pretended to pummel his chest with my fists. "Oh, Robbie! You're doing this all wrong! This isn't like you! I don't know if I believe you or not! You usually plan ahead. How can you spring this on me like this? You're answering my prayers and breaking my heart in the same sentence. Don't tell me you love me and want to marry me and then leave for Vietnam. Please don't do it! Why in the world did you wait till now to tell me?"

"I'm sorry, Swan. I know it's rotten timing. But I didn't think you loved me. I was scared to say it. I tried to tell you in my letters."

"No you didn't. You talked about Julie and Cindy and a bunch of other girls, which didn't make it sound much like you loved me."

"They weren't important. I was trying to get your reaction. I wanted you to be jealous or show something."

"Well, you got a reaction all right. You broke my heart. A bunch of different times. I told you how I felt about life and guys and my struggles. I think I was pretty honest with you, Robbie."

"But we'd decided not to date. I couldn't believe you'd want to change that. . . . I should have told you sooner, Swan. I was just so sure you weren't interested. I mean we talked about it three years ago."

"You talked, Robbie. I listened with a broken heart. Didn't you ever notice that that's when I started turning into a fat goose?"

He shook his head with a sad smile. "No. No, all I noticed was how much I missed you. How every other girl I dated bored me to tears. But then you were pursuing your dream, you were happy painting, and I was so afraid to stop you and make you follow mine."

"I'd gladly follow you to Vietnam instead of Europe, if you asked."

"Oh, Swan. Gosh, the timing is all wrong in this. I don't even have a ring for you."

"I don't need a ring to prove you love me and want to marry me. Just come back to me, Robbie. That's all I need."

We had two days together at Hilton Head. Two days as unofficial fiancés. Two of the most wonderful days in my entire life. I even tried to convince him not to go. He had a whole year to survive in Vietnam. An acquaintance of mine from college had a brother in Vietnam and he'd only lasted two weeks—two weeks before he was killed by a mine. Stepped on one his first day on the field. They had shipped his body back in a casket with glass over the top.

At that moment I had no faith in God's protection. I felt no patriotism. I was simply a young woman surprised by love, reeling from the sudden turn of events. I would have given up my citizenship and maybe my faith on that day if it could have kept Robbie at home.

But he was going to go. I knew it. He told me, "I'll be back before you know it, Swan. You go to Europe. Complete your studies. Take it all in. Pick your favorite spot and we'll go there on our honeymoon."

"I'll feel guilty studying art when you're in the middle of combat."

"Swan, you're the one who is always explaining to me how the artists are rebels in their way, ahead of their time, protesting. Let your art speak. But don't give up your dream. I won't give it up either. I'll be back. We'll have a blast making a bunch of babies, and I'll build you the prettiest house that Buckhead has ever seen."

I started crying. He kissed me, pulling me tight against his chest, holding me there. He was running his fingers through my hair and came upon the gold chain I always wore around my neck. Suddenly he took his class ring off his finger, unfastened my chain, and slipped the ring onto it. Then he fastened the chain back around my neck. "Keep this ring, Mary Swan. When I get back from 'Nam, I'll replace it with a big diamond, I promise."

Two days later he was gone.

Mom let out a long sigh and closed her eyes, and I couldn't help but scoot closer to her on the couch and say, "That was an amazing story, Mom. A really, really good story."

"And every single bit is true." We sat there in silence, me trying to imagine the episode she had just described in such loving detail. After a while, she got up off the couch and said, "I think I'm going to take a shower."

"Sure, Mom."

I looked again at the painting of Daddy waving good-bye to Mom from his red convertible. Then I tried to imagine him waving good-bye as he left for Vietnam, and I almost *could* feel it, an aching deep inside my chest, like the ache I'd had for Megan when I'd found her sitting in the middle of a room full of broken glass.

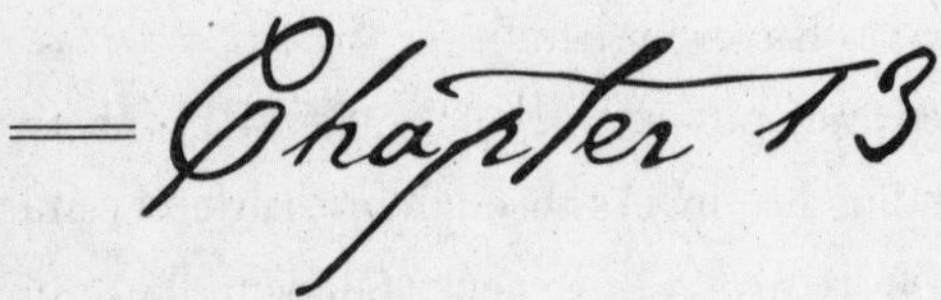

About suffering they were never wrong,
The Old Masters: how well they understood
Its human position . . .

—W. H. AUDEN, *MUSÉE DES BEAUX ARTS*

Ben stopped by to see Mom and have lunch with us again, as he had the day before—although to me, it felt as though years had passed in between. Years long gone, painted on Mom's canvases, had rushed in to interrupt my vacation at the beach. Having Ben there seemed strangely out of place. But I did not want him to leave.

As I was clearing the table, Mom explained to him the reason for the "private art gallery" in the family room, and then she said, "I think I feel like sketching a little."

I almost dropped the plates.

Ben shot me a smile and said, "That's the best news I've heard in a week, Swannee!"

"Yes, it's wonderful to feel like doing something constructive. I guess my paintings have inspired me."

"Can we help you set up the easel, Mom?"

"No, I'll just do a few sketches—no need to bother with paints. I'll sit right here by the window with the view toward the beach. It will be perfect."

Ben and I went to the basement and got out the bikes without consulting each other. As we peddled out of Spotted Sandpiper, I got a silly smile on my face. Peaceful, happy, simple—these adjectives popped into my mind while the sun warmed my head and shoulders. We must have ridden for almost an hour in complete silence, a perfect, natural silence with Ben leading the way beside the marshes and the golf course, pointing occasionally toward a lagoon where a white crane balanced on one skinny leg or an alligator's snout protruded from the murky water.

On our way back toward the Hamilton House, I called out, "Hey, Ben, did you know that our mothers were really screwed up when they were young?"

"What makes you say that, Ellie-o?"

"Mom told me about it—she was explaining those paintings to me." I caught up with him and said, "You should ask her about them. It's hard to imagine your mom as an ultraliberal hippie high on dope and mine with an eating disorder."

"Well, I didn't know about Swan's problems, but I've heard some things about my mother."

"If you want to know the plain truth, it makes me feel not so awful to realize that their lives were messed up too. Like maybe we could have something in common after all."

He hesitated, then said, "Well, I guess that's encouraging—to realize that your mom had problems too. That's your common ground."

"That's not what I mean. It's just that I always thought Mom had a perfect life and that she wanted me to be perfect too."

"Define perfect."

"You know, religious and, well, doing the right things."

"Yeah, well, she probably *does* want those kinds of things for you, but to me that isn't a definition of perfection."

"What do you mean?"

"I think she's just always wanted you—all her children—to

embrace faith and watch it work in your lives. But faith isn't perfection. Faith is trust in the only One who is perfect and an admission that we are far, far from it—"

"Ben Abrams!" I screeched to a halt, let my bike fall over on the path, and walked right up to where he'd brought his bike to a halt and sat on it, looking bewildered. I grabbed him by the shirt and shook him. "Stop babbling!"

Slowly a grin spread across his face. He placed his hands over mine, gently pulled mine off his shirt, and stood there, our noses almost touching. "You're right, Ellie-o. I was babbling. Sorry." Then he let go of my hands, quickly, and said, "Hey, I gotta get to the Quarterdeck. See you Saturday night at the church?"

"Yeah, Saturday night." I realized that my palms were tingling and sweaty as I watched him ride away.

When I got back to the house, I flicked on my laptop to see how the Braves had done the night before. "Way to go," I said aloud when the computer screen proclaimed that they'd won.

Mom was ready and waiting for me to take her to the clinic, which I did without any problems, thanks to Daddy's instructions. After she had had her blood tested, the nurse told me that she'd have the results the next day, but that I should plan on bringing Mom back in on Monday. "And watch that sniffle," she said to Mom. "We don't want you getting a cold—not after what happened in Atlanta."

The short outing had exhausted Mom. She sat down on the couch in the family room, and I brought her some lemonade. True to his word, Ben had left us some—freshly squeezed—along with a batch of chocolate chip cookies.

"Some of these paintings look like statements about civil rights," I commented, nodding toward two that must have been painted around the same time.

"I guess you could call them that. I painted those two in 1966 for a summer class I was taking at the Atlanta School of Arts. The High Museum was under construction at the time—they were adding on, creating the Memorial Arts Center in memory of the Orly victims. So our classes were held in an old warehouse on West Peachtree." She grinned.

"What?"

"Oh, nothing. It's just that there was this repairman who kept having to come over to fix the elevator, and he'd hang around, trying to get a glimpse of the nude models."

I tried to imagine Mom sketching nude models, but I couldn't quite make it work.

"Anyway, that first painting is all about the march in Selma in the spring of 1965." She looked at me hopefully. "Did you study that?"

I shrugged and said, "I know about the civil rights movement, Mom. But I'd rather hear it straight from you."

"Did you know I was in Washington when Dr. King gave his 'I have a dream' speech?"

"Really?" I made a face, concentrating, and then said, "August 28, 1963. Joan Baez sang 'Oh, Freedom,' and Bob Dylan joined Peter, Paul, and Mary, singing 'Blowin' in the Wind.' And Dr. King gave his famous speech."

Mom was pleased. "Good for you, Ellie! Robbie, Carl, Rachel, and I went to take part in the March on Washington for Jobs and Freedom. There were more than a quarter of a million people there. It was unbelievable. I think a third of the crowd was white. Dr. King's speech was so moving."

"And what about this painting?"

"This is about what went on in Selma in 1965."

"Marchers crossing the Montgomery Bridge on March 7, 1965, demanding the right to vote. Bloody Sunday." I said it almost reverently.

Mom seemed surprised.

"Mom, even if I hadn't studied it in school, the history lesson was thumbtacked on Miss Abigail's bulletin board in her office at Mt. Carmel. She explained the whole thing to me—a lot better than my history teacher, I might add—and so did you."

We both looked surprised at that comment.

"No, it's true. I remember asking you why all the people who were getting lunch at Mt. Carmel were so skinny and poor, and you took me on your lap and told me about civil rights."

Mom's painting, again almost more like a cartoon, showed whites beating up the blacks as they crossed over the bridge.

"They were using tear gas, billy clubs, wet bull whips. I saw it all on TV." Mom whispered this. "Then a little later in March, several of us from Mt. Carmel—Carl, Robbie, Cassandra, Miss Abigail, and a few others—took part in the big march from Selma to Montgomery. They say that only three thousand people started the march in Selma, but by the time it was over, there were probably twenty-five thousand of us. It was peaceful, even though all those awful KKKs and red necks kept shouting obscenities along the road. But President Johnson had sent lots of National Guards and other people to keep the peace. And everyone was so inspired by Dr. King's speech.

"But then the next day, we learned about the murder of a white mother of five who'd felt she should go on the march. After the march was over, she was helping drive different marchers back to their homes, and some Klansmen pulled up beside her car and shot her in the head." She shook her head slowly. "What hate can do," she murmured.

I regarded her canvas more closely and realized it had been splattered with flecks of red. It looked like the whole painting was bleeding.

"And that's Mayor Allen standing on the car," she said, pointing to the next painting in her chronological line. "That was in the fall of 1966. There was a riot brewing in Atlanta right down near Grant Park—a crowd of a thousand blacks or more—and Mayor Allen started walking through the crowds urging people to go home. I don't know if he was afraid, but Miss Abigail was there and she said he didn't *look* afraid.

"But the blacks were furious and didn't want to negotiate with the mayor. Earlier that day, a white policeman had shot a black man who'd resisted arrest. Anyway, it set everybody off. The blacks started throwing bricks at the policeman, and then Mayor Allen got up on top of a police car and yelled at the crowd to calm down. They jeered and rocked the car and he fell off, but he wasn't hurt, and then an armored car arrived and the police started using tear gas and everything broke up. Miss Abigail said there were a hundred thousand blacks just waiting to riot, but Mayor Allen's courage saved the day. He kept Atlanta from boiling over.

"And that one is called *Assassination*. It was the last thing I painted at Hollins, right before I graduated."

The painting was big, and every inch of space was covered with people walking behind a mule-drawn cart. The line went on and on for so far that the cart was just a small rectangle in the top right corner of the canvas. I knew immediately what this was. "Martin Luther King's funeral, right?"

"Exactly."

"Were you there?"

"Yes, I was. I skipped three days of school to be there. And Mayor Allen was once again instrumental in keeping the peace. It was like a miracle when we saw on TV what was happening in the rest of the country. I think eighty riots broke out on the night of the assassination. Arson, arrests, violence."

"But nothing in Atlanta?"

Mom shook her head. "Nothing. Calm. On Sunday I went with Carl and Cassandra to Spelman College to see where Dr. King's body lay in state. And then on Tuesday, a bunch of us met outside of Mt. Carmel and walked toward Ebenezer Baptist Church, where the funeral was being held. The throngs of people were unimaginable. Everywhere I looked, it was a sea of slow-moving bodies. Our group didn't get anywhere near the church, but we could hear the whole service because loudspeakers had been set up all over that part of the city.

"At times I felt a little wave of panic sweep over me when I thought of what might happen if the crowd turned violent. But it didn't."

"Man, Mom, you really took an active part in all the civil rights stuff."

"I did. It mattered so much to me. But I wasn't militant about it, not like Rachel was about so many things. I wanted peaceful resolution."

She looked weary with the telling of her life, so I suggested she rest in her bed and I'd bring her something to eat. She didn't argue.

As I was preparing a bowl of soup and cutting up some apples, I kept saying to myself, *Was that really my mother doing all the things these paintings showed?* Stuffing her face with food, miserable and questioning her faith, being furious with Rachel . . . waiting all those years for Daddy, hoping against hope that he'd love her again and then being surprised by his love, and then having to tell him good-bye and send him off to Vietnam. And marching in Selma, Alabama.

But there was something else. In a way, Mom was doing exactly what I'd expect her to be doing back then: caring about civil rights and peacefully protesting things, painting, talking to God, and dreaming about Robbie Bartholomew. Even taking that trip with Rachel to Europe had been something she had always wanted to do.

I had to spoon-feed the soup to her. Even though she protested, I could see a resigned thankfulness in her eyes as she took the first sip. She didn't seem to be getting stronger, and I didn't really want to hear from the oncology specialist. I was afraid he'd give me bad news, and I didn't have time for bad news. We were only in 1968, and I wanted Mom to gain back her energy and explain the other paintings and look through her sketch pad with me and paint out on the beach.

Several of Mom's sketch pads were lying on the floor in her bedroom. I picked up the one from her European trip with Rachel and opened to the first page while she nibbled on a cracker.

"There's something I don't get, Mom," I said. "If you hated Rachel so much at the time, why'd you agree to go with her to Europe?"

"It was your grandfather's idea. He was worried about me—gaining weight and all. He and Trixie could see I was miserable. And there was so much unrest in the States—things that were upsetting me, things close to my heart.

"I actually thought he was nuts for suggesting it, seeing as how Rachel was stoned half the time. But it was something I'd always wanted to do. I'd talked about it for years—practically ever since Mama died. It was my way of honoring her, and I thought it would be cathartic.

"And it was like one last desperate attempt for Rachel and me to get along. After all, she was the only one who knew everything about me—all about my family and my mother's problems and—oh, so much. Deep down I didn't want to give up on that friendship. She didn't either."

I thought again of Megan . . . the only person who knew all about me.

"This is you and Rachel on the plane, isn't it?" I asked, pointing to the first sketch.

She smiled. "Yes. I call it *Airplane Food*. We were flying from Atlanta to Paris, and already Rachel was driving me crazy, but then the stewardess brought our dinner. I just sat there and stared at the tray. My stomach was in knots—I was scared of flying, after what happened to Mama, and I was missing your father and, well, let's just say I couldn't eat.

"Then Rachel got that wicked little grin on her face and said, 'Watch this, Swan.' She took her fork and placed the tines under the icing on a piece of cake. With a flick of her fork, the icing flew off and landed in a perfect unbroken rectangle on my tray. We laughed so hard that our stomachs hurt."

I smiled to myself, imagining Mom and Rachel . . . those schoolgirl giggles bridging the distance between them, and that made me happy—for both of them.

"So the trip to Europe started off okay?"

Mom made a face and then gave a long sigh. "Well, I wouldn't go that far. It's a long story, sweetie. Probably not very interesting to you."

I flipped to a sketch in the middle of the pad. "Yeah, you're probably right. Just boring stuff like riots, people getting beaten. Your old everyday kind of thing." I glanced at Mom and she grinned.

"Okay, I'll tell you about it tomorrow. Not now. I'm just about done in."

"I'll let you sleep, Mom."

As I left the room, she called out, "Ellie?"

"Yeah?"

"Thanks for asking me about the paintings and the sketches. Thanks for being interested."

"You bet, Mom."

I went back upstairs to my bedroom and opened the door to the little covered balcony. Tonight, the sky was clear and stars were beginning to dot the horizon. I could see the white foam of the ocean lapping onto the beach, hear the constant low roar of the waves breaking, rushing to shore, receding. I could make out the almost-round moon. Hindsight came onto the balcony, winding in and out of my legs. Then she hopped up on the round white wrought-iron table, which was still warm from the day of sunshine.

I leaned forward, straining to hear beyond the roar of the ocean. I wanted to hear Mom's laughter, and Rachel's. I wanted to hear my own. Of course laughter—the true, good kind—doesn't appear on demand. But I enjoyed the peaceful night air and the chirping of the crickets and the faint smell of the ocean, and I physically felt my body relax—relax from the stress of caring for Mom, from wondering what the platelets were doing. I could relax too for the Mom and Rachel of the sixties, take a deep breath for them, and wish them well on their European adventure. I found it downright surprising that I could hardly wait to join them tomorrow.

When I came back inside, I automatically dialed Megan's number.

"Hello?"

"Meggie?"

"Ellie! Hey, there! How are you?"

"Fine. What're you up to?"

She sounded about to burst with happiness. "Timothy and I are just getting ready to go out."

"Oh. Well, good. I don't want to keep you."

"Ellie, what's up? You don't sound so hot."

"No, everything's fine. I'm a little bored sometimes, but that's okay."

"And? Help me out a little here, Ellie. You're playing Miss Enigmatic. I'm not good at that game, remember?"

"It's too long to go into now. I don't want to make you late."

She groaned. "Ellie, don't be impossible. Hold on a sec, will you?"

She whispered something to Timothy and then came back on the line. "Timothy says to take my time. We're not in that big of a hurry. Anyway, I'm ready early for once in my life. So go on. Out with it."

"It's nothing big. Things are fine with Mom. I'm just bored and she sleeps a lot and you can only take so many walks on the beach a day."

"Is your mom getting on your case, is that it?"

"No. Not at all. I almost wish she was. No, from the looks of her, she won't be getting on anyone's case for a long time."

"That bad, huh?"

"Meggie, it's kinda creepy to see her in a bathing suit. Makes you think she's . . ."

"She's what?"

"Dying or something."

"She's been a very sick lady. But if she were dying, your dad wouldn't have sent you there alone with her."

"I hope not."

"Listen, El. I think you are so brave. Think of how many people just refuse to even try to heal old wounds. I know it's not easy, but it's an important thing you're doing."

I sighed. "You sound like my counselor at rehab."

"I know I do. But I mean it. Look, I realize more than probably anyone else how much it's costing you to be there. I'm proud of you, Ellie. It's gonna be worth it. I really think it will."

I felt like Megan was pouring a relief remedy through the telephone lines, and it was seeping into my hands, my veins, my heart. "Thanks, Megan. Thanks. And you know what?"

"What?"

"You're right about Jamal and Jeremy's. I think I want to change jobs. Get something more in my line of interest—you know, helping at an animal clinic or something."

I could almost feel a perfect smile spreading across her face. "Excellent. That's a cool decision. What are you eating anyway, El? Is your mom drugging your vegetables?"

"Nope. I'm just taking lots of walks and thinking."

"Well, keep cool—don't overanalyze."

"Promise I'll try. I wish you were down here."

"Me too, Ellie. But this is about you and your mom. It'll be worth it; you'll see."

I road my bike to Harbour Town at ten o'clock and parked it outside Ketch Court, then walked along the harbor to the Quarterdeck Lounge. Ben's band was playing, and the tables were mostly full. I was surprised to see three kids from the church group. One of the girls, Sal, motioned to me.

Sal was what I'd call a pseudo tomboy. She seemed pretty athletic, at least from what I'd seen of her skills at touch football, but I got the feeling she was mainly interested in keeping her figure perfect (it was), her body tanned (it was), and her makeup just right (it was) so that guys couldn't help but glance at her as she flipped her thick brown hair over her shoulder.

"Hey, Ellie," she said. "Wanna join us?"

I didn't really. I hadn't expected to see anyone I knew except for Ben. But I acquiesced.

Sal asked, "You remember Tommy?"

"Hey, Tommy. Yeah. I think you gave me the bruise on my shin."

Tommy, who looked as if he should be on a poster ad for a lifeguard with his blond hair and tanned body and muscles everywhere, smiled and said, "Look who's talking. I was sore for two days."

"Hey, Ellie." This came from Sal's best friend, Samantha. From what I gathered, they lived in different states, but their families had met years ago at Hilton Head and now they vacationed here at the same time each year.

"So how do you like Ben's music?" I ventured.

Sal's face turned beet red. "I think it's sweet." She said *sweet* the way kids used the term, not like my mom calling something sweet . . . which meant that she liked it a lot. And maybe she liked Ben too.

Ben finished playing and came to the table. "Hey, Ellie-o. This is a nice surprise. My lucky night. Sal, Sam, Tommy, and Ellie." He turned to me and said, "I promised these guys they could come up to my place and play a hot and heavy game of Risk tonight. You're welcome to join us."

"Sure you are," Samantha said, elbowing Sal, "as long as you don't mind Sal taking over the world."

Risk was by no means my favorite board game, but I went along.

On the way back to Ketch Court, Ben asked me, "How's your mom? What did the doctor say?"

"We'll know about the platelet count tomorrow. But it wore her out to go to the clinic. She turned in a while ago."

I hung out with them for an hour and watched as Sal did indeed take over the world. Then Tommy asked, "Y'all wanna go frog gigging? I'm meeting Zeke at the dock in thirty minutes."

"That's gross," Samantha replied.

"Count me out," Sal added, then looked over at Ben. "I hope *you're* not gonna go with them. Pastors shouldn't kill innocent frogs."

"Nah, that's not how I get my thrills."

We walked down by the water, listening to it gurgle underneath the yachts. Tommy took off in his car, and I saw the girls look after him longingly, then giggle and say, "Bye, Ben. Ellie. We're gonna rent a movie. See ya Saturday."

We stood out by the harbor, and I told Ben about Mom's paintings and the civil rights things she'd been involved in and then about the sketch of Rachel and Mom in the airplane. And we laughed.

"If you want to come over tomorrow, Ben, you can hear all about Europe. Mom's gonna tell me about their trip."

"Well, take good notes. I promised Tommy and Zeke and a few other guys we'd go crabbing and then do some beach volleyball and stuff."

"You really *want* to hang out with them, don't you?"

"Yeah. It's part of my job. And I like it. A lot."

I couldn't think of a single thing to say, but Ben filled in the silence by asking, "Did you drive over here?"

"No, I biked. I locked my bike up next to yours. Or, should I say, next to the one you stole from my house."

He grinned. "Hey, I figure you can't ride six at once. Anyway, leave yours here and I'll drive you home."

Sitting in the passenger's seat of his old Honda, I noticed a file card taped onto the dashboard. "What's that?"

"It's my reading material," he joked.

"No, serious."

"Promise you won't accuse me of babbling?"

"Promise."

"It's a Bible verse I'm learning by heart."

"For seminary?"

"No. Just for me."

"Oh, wow. Now that's cool."

"Hey, Miss Sarcastic. You asked. I do it to keep from dwelling on things that don't get me anywhere."

"Like what?"

"Oh, girls, or drugs, or friends I used to hang with or reliving some of the stupid things I did when I was younger."

"You too?"

"Sure. Somebody told me once that if I didn't put good stuff in my big head, it was going to get filled up with a lot of junk. So I'm trying to pick appropriate things."

I read what was written on the card out loud. "'Forget the former things; do not dwell on the past. See, I am doing a new thing! Now it springs up; do you not perceive it? I am making a way in the desert and streams in the wasteland.' Why'd you pick that verse?"

"If you really want to know, it's because I'm twenty-seven years old and most of my life has been just one big royal screwed-up mess. And sometimes I feel completely bummed about it, and I get stuck thinking about the past. Then I read this verse, and it's like it jolts me back to the reality of now. It's a promise that I hold on to."

His voice was soft and sincere, and even though it had seemed to me that the new Ben was happy and sure of himself, sitting there in the car beside him I had a glimpse into a less confident part, one that reminded me of Ben, the rebellious teen.

"Okay," I said. "That makes sense. And does it help?"

"It does."

When I got out of the car, I closed the door, leaned through the window, and said, "Thanks for the ride, Ben."

He was staring at that file card. Then he looked at me, and the expression on his face was like a thirsty man on his knees, drinking water by a river. "You bet, Ellie-o. See ya soon."

Chapter 14

A carefree and unforgettable vacation . . .

—FROM THE BROCHURE ADVERTISING THE AMERICAN EXPRESS TOUR THAT ENDED IN THE ORLY CRASH, JUNE 3, 1962

We will claim nothing. We will ask for nothing. We will take. We will occupy.

—SLOGAN FROM STUDENT RIOTS, MAY 1968, PARIS

When I walked out to the kitchen at eight the next morning, I couldn't believe my eyes. Mom was sketching by the window, and she had both Grandmom Sheila's and her own sketch pads lying on the table in the family room and five or six of her paintings on the floor, propped against the table. She heard me come in and turned around, a charcoal pencil stuck behind one ear. Her eyes looked warm and green, alive, like a softly polished jade, and she was smiling, which was such a relief that I involuntarily smiled too.

And goose bumps popped onto my arms. Annoyed, I thought, *Why in the world do I have them now?* I realized it was because Mom was so excited about telling me about her European trip. She reminded me of a young girl who'd carefully arranged all her treasured baby dolls and wanted her mother to come and see them. I guess I was supposed to be the mother, coming into the room to approve of her hard work, and to be honest, it gave me a creepy kind of feeling.

"Morning, Ellie."

"Morning, Mom. You're up early! And you look like you're feeling better."

"I am. I had a good night's sleep and woke up feeling almost normal."

Mornings are my absolute worst time for being sociable, so it took real effort to say, "I'll get us some breakfast, and then we can head to Europe."

"Take your time, sweetie. I've already had a little orange juice."

Thirty minutes later, I was dressed and had fixed Mom a pot of tea, and put butter and jelly on toasted English muffins, which she ate with something resembling an appetite. I finished a bowl of cereal, had a cup of coffee, and cleared the table.

"Okay, fire away," I said, sitting down beside her.

She took Grandmom Sheila's pad, held it in both hands, and started talking as if she were a teacher. Or maybe a newscaster. Or maybe her matter-of-fact voice was a defense, so the tragedy wouldn't come and squeeze her heart.

"Well, the original tour was from May tenth through June 3, 1962, and the group was going to visit Paris, London, Amsterdam, Lucerne, Venice, Florence, and Rome. About forty-five people took a package tour arranged by American Express, which emphasized visits to the great museums of Europe.

"But many people on the trip merely flew to Paris and then went their own way. That was what Mama and Daddy did. They veered off a bit from the program because Mama wanted to see the Kunsthistorisches Museum in Vienna and the Prado in Madrid, and then of course she wanted to visit Scotland, since she was half Scottish."

She opened Grandmom Sheila's sketch pad, and a piece of writing paper fell out.

"Oh yeah," I said. "I started listing the different sketches, and then I got distracted and never got back to it."

"Well, let's finish the list, then," Mom said brightly, reminding me again of a little girl.

So we did. When we got to the last page of the pad, I asked, "Now why is this piece of paper ripped out and taped in the back of Grandmom's pad?" It was another sketch from Scotland with the Dwelling Place wall running across the page.

"Oh, that was Mamie's doing."

I knew from family stories that *Mamie,* which rhymed with *whammy,* was what French children called their grandmothers. My great-grandmother Evelyne was a hundred percent French and had insisted that her grandchildren call her by the French name.

"Poor Mamie was a bit nutty," Mom continued. "I guess I would have been too if I'd outlived both of my daughters."

"Mom, you're not making any sense."

"I'm sorry. It's just complicated. Let's see. Okay, first, the ripped-out page. That happened before I went to Europe. I went down to visit your great-grandparents, Mamie and Papy. Let's call them Evelyne and Ian, that will make it easier. And we'll refer to your grandmother as Sheila."

"Whatever."

"Ian and Evelyne lived on a plantation in Griffin, Georgia—you visited there when you were little. My father convinced me to ask my grandparents about some of the places we wanted to visit in Scotland, so I went. But I wasn't looking forward to the visit because Mamie—Evelyne, I mean—always scared me.

"The first thing she told me was that I was fat—except she said *grosse,* because she always spoke to me in French. She was excited about my trip, bound and determined that my French would improve. But when I finally got down to asking her about some of my mother's sketches, she took the sketch pad and started saying mean things about her."

Mom made her face hard and started speaking with a French accent. "'Your mother was trying to unearth her roots and understand why I was so crazy. Why I ruined her life. Terribly childish, blaming me for things.'"

"Was her accent that thick?"

"Oh yes. Even after living in the States for fifty years. I actually loved her accent. But what I didn't like was that she drank a lot, and that day, she kind of lost it. When I showed her this sketch"—she pointed to the ripped-out one at the back of the pad—"she was livid! She squinted at the sketch and was quiet for a moment, then she softly pronounced the words: 'The Dwelling Place.' Then she hit the pad with her fist and screamed about Sheila being such a child and Sheila trying to punish her again, even though she was dead. Then she ripped the page out."

"Weird," I said.

"Yes, weird. I grabbed the pad from her and begged her not to rip out the pages, and she said I was wrong to try to find out things about the past. Then she wiggled a finger at me, and I thought she looked like a witch from a Walt Disney film—thin, angry, wrinkled. She looked like this."

Mom picked up one of the paintings that she'd propped against the table. It was a small portrait that I hadn't noticed before. It really did look like a witch, maybe someone Mom had seen at a Halloween party—a frail-looking woman with gaunt cheeks and hair dyed too dark for a woman of her age.

"That's Evelyne?"

"Yes. She was beautiful when she was younger, but then she started drinking." The lines alcohol leaves were visible on her thin face. "I thought it always looked as though she'd closed her eyes when she was putting on her makeup, the way it was smeared on. She was high-strung, like a Thoroughbred. Unpredictable."

And mean. I thought my great-grandmother looked downright mean.

"Later, I taped the page back in. It was a very strange encounter. But I think the strangest part about it was that when my father had looked at the same sketch, he'd said that Sheila had been really happy and peaceful when she got back from the Dwelling Place. He hadn't gone with her—he was golfing at St. Andrews while she was hunting up her relatives.

"Anyway, as you can imagine, those incidents made me want to go on the trip even more. Like a big riddle. Mysterious, but fun to solve."

Now Mom took her own sketch pad from Europe, flipped past the first sketch of *Airplane Food* to the next one. "But it didn't really work out that way for me. It was a riddle, all right, but it wasn't much fun to solve. See, when Rachel and I got to Paris, we landed in the middle of the May '68 student revolution. If Daddy and Trixie had had an inkling of an idea of what was happening there, they would have never let us go."

"What *was* happening, Mom?"

She giggled, which seemed a little odd, seeing as we were talking about a revolution.

"Sorry. I just was thinking about Rachel and how she kept telling me I was a naïve child because I didn't understand what was going on. And I didn't really care. I just wanted to follow Mama's sketch pad. But Rachel thought she'd died and gone to heaven. She kept insisting that we were part of 'history in the making.' This is pretty much what it looked like."

She slowly turned the pages as she narrated. "Overturned cars everywhere, trash everywhere, graffiti everywhere, and in the Latin Quarter, students everywhere, especially at the Sorbonne, hanging out and giving political speeches about the rise of the proletariat. And barricading the streets. A sixties version of *A Tale of Two Cities*."

"Why were they so upset?"

"I don't know—it turned into a time for everyone, students and blue collar workers, and I guess just about anybody else, to air their grievances. And everything in the whole country was on strike. Banks, schools, post offices—so I couldn't get letters from your father—gas stations, you name it. And of course, no trains were working either. So we ended up being stuck in Paris for two long weeks." She made a face and repeated rather dramatically, "History in the making!"

"That's cool," I said, looking at a sketch of several posters that were plastered on a wall. "So what did y'all do for two weeks?"

"We were staying with a friend of Trixie's, Anne Dumontel. She was an American who'd gone to Paris for a semester's art class, met a Parisian, and never came back. Her husband, Jacques, was very involved in the revolution. He was a professor at the Sorbonne, where a lot of the action was taking place. And he had this student, Theo, who was one of the leaders. Rachel, of course, fell in love with him. She was always following Theo around."

She picked up a painting from the floor of Rachel and a very French looking young man.

"He's cute," I said, and Mom rolled her eyes.

He looked to me like a true bohemian. He wore his thick dark hair in a ponytail pulled back tight against his face so that his sharp, prominent nose and high cheekbones showed perfectly. His brows were dark and thick, and his expression was proud and seductive at the same time. He was small boned for a man, and not tall, only a couple inches taller than Rachel. In the painting, he was wearing a T-shirt and a pair of faded jeans and holding a poster with an angry slogan printed on it.

"That's when I met Anne's sons, Jean-Paul and his brother, Alain. You remember Jean-Paul, don't you?"

"Of course. He comes to visit almost every year."

"Well, he and his brother were thirteen and eleven at the time, and dear Jean-Paul kept me from going crazy while Rachel was off chasing the revolution and falling in love with a Frenchman. We were kindred spirits—two shy souls, lacking confidence but not lacking a dream. While Rachel traipsed about town with Theo, Jean-Paul took me to all the places Sheila had sketched in her pad."

"That was cool."

"Yes, we made quite a pair. Jean-Paul loved art, and he drew all the time, but he'd never dared to paint because he was afraid his mom, who was a fairly successful graphic artist, might be embarrassed by his feeble attempts. Anyway, I guess you'd say we bonded, and I convinced him to try it."

She flipped to a sketch of two boys and then picked up a painted portrait of the same two kids. "That's Jean-Paul at thirteen. What a cutie. He was so timid—his face would turn scarlet if you just looked at him. We had such fun together! And Alain, what a little mischief maker."

Jean-Paul had a long, thin face, inquisitive hazel eyes, and curly brown hair that fell below his ears. He looked as if he were straining to smile, and Mom had painted his face as if he were blushing. Alain's face was rounder, with bright blue eyes and blond hair and a smile so cute and charming that you wanted to reach out and pinch his cheeks.

While I was examining the portrait of the brothers, Mom flipped to a sketch of the student riots. It showed the streets jammed with young people carrying axe handles and what looked like torn-up pavement and wooden clubs, and you could almost hear them chanting furiously. Cars were turned over in the road, and students were climbing on top of them, pulling and piling old furniture on top of the cars. In the distance were riot police with helmets and clubs, and you could almost feel the tear gas pricking your eyes.

"It was one of the worst nights of my life. . . ."

There she went again, drifting back into a story that she told with such detail that I was riveted in my seat. But I don't think she even remembered that I was there.

We were all at the Sorbonne one evening—Rachel and Theo, Jacques, the boys, and I, along with thousands of others. Everyone had gathered around radios to hear the speech of General de Gaulle, the President of France. The students were already irate at his lack of response since the beginning of the revolution.

I was listening intently because, in spite of all my indifference, I had a feeling the words this man said were going to be explosive. And I was scared.

The students' anger grew as De Gaulle spoke.

"De Gaulle is an assassin!" "The French people will have the last word." "It's criminal, the way he is treating us!" "To the streets! To the streets!"

Jacques called his sons to him and said, "Boys, there's likely to be trouble tonight. You go home now with Mary Swan and Rachel." He looked imploringly at me.

I nodded. My throat was suddenly dry.

"No, Papa! I don't want to go home!" Alain protested. "I'm going with you."

"You can't come with me, son. Stay with Mary Swan."

"You girls can take care of the boys," Theo assured us. "You'll get them home safely. But you need to leave now."

Students were already beginning to pour out of the building and into the streets.

"It's going to be another demonstration!" Rachel shouted excitedly.

I could see in her eyes that she was ready for a fight. She joined in with other students and started chanting slogans wildly.

"Come on, Rachel!" I pleaded, catching her by the hand. "We've got to get the boys home."

"Quit panicking, Swan. Everything's cool."

I realized she had no intention of staying with me.

"Look, Rachel. I need you to help me. You heard Jacques. He wants the boys to go home now!"

"Then take them home, Swan. I'm staying."

I felt panicky inside. And furious. Rachel knew that I had no sense of direction. I'd never be able to get them back to the apartment at dusk with no map. "I don't know how."

"Don't be ridiculous!" Rachel mocked and turned to leave.

"I know the way!" said Alain confidently.

"It's true. We've done it before alone," Jean-Paul agreed, although he didn't sound very sure of himself.

The atmosphere inside the Sorbonne was like a teakettle about to boil over. I looked around for Jacques and Theo, but they had already disappeared into the crowd. I made up my mind fast.

"We're staying put. It's way too dangerous in the streets. I've heard that the riot police grab innocent bystanders and beat them. We'll be a lot safer here, guys."

Jean-Paul didn't argue; in fact, he seemed relieved.

But Alain started to protest, "I never get to do anything fun. *Ce n'est pas juste.* It isn't fair!" He gazed a bit longingly after Rachel, who was pushing forward with the other students, still chanting, one arm raised defiantly.

"Let's get to a phone. I'll call your mom and tell her we're staying here."

As the evening wore down, I sketched the inner courts of the Sorbonne in the fading light and rendered in detail several of the posters on the outer walls. In each sketch I tried to capture the frenetic energy around me. The noise from the streets was deafening, and occasionally we'd hear someone yelling in the halls, "Wounded comrade! Make room. Bring the supplies!"

Jean-Paul worked feverishly on his own drawing of the graffiti and the demonstration. We must have spent three hours this way, with Alain looking over our shoulders, giving us a running commentary of his thoughts.

Some time after midnight we went into the great lecture hall, took seats, and nodded off. It was Rachel who woke me.

"There y'all are! Thought I'd never find you."

"What are you doing here?" I mumbled.

"Getting ready for the fireworks! We're going to torch the Bourse!" she exclaimed, eyes shining.

"What?"

"There's a ton of students going over to set the stock exchange on fire. Can you hear 'em? They're yelling, 'Destroy the temple of capitalism!'" She was wiping something white around her eyes.

I sat up straight. "What in the world are you doing?"

"It's baking soda. Protects against tear gas. Put some on." She tossed a can to me. "And don't forget to take some lemon-soaked handkerchiefs. That helps too." She handed one to Jean-Paul, who was just rubbing the sleep out of his eyes.

"Are you nuts? Stay out of all that, Rachel. I'm keeping the kids here."

"Whatever you want, but I'm outta here. Just thought I'd give you the chance to be part of history in the making." She was gone before I could say another word.

"I've gotta use the bathroom," Alain complained. "I'll be back in a sec." And he trotted off after Rachel.

"All right," I said absentmindedly, feeling irritated again by Rachel's conduct. Jean-Paul had already closed his eyes, and I did the same. Then suddenly a terrible thought made me bolt wide awake and jump to my feet. "Jean-Paul! Quick! Come with me."

A quick check in the closest restroom revealed that Alain wasn't there. In the space of two minutes, he had disappeared.

"Oh, great! I bet he's gone with Rachel! Would he do that, Jean-Paul?"

The young boy nodded soberly. "Sounds just like him."

"Come on, then. Let's pray he hasn't gotten far."

The minute we got into the streets, I knew we'd made a mistake. I had never been a part of a riot, but Martin Luther King's funeral had given me a taste of what it felt like to be jammed in with a moving human mass. Still, that had been peaceful, and this was anything but.

Thousands of students were crammed together in the streets, shouting "To the Stock Exchange. *De Gaulle Assassin!*" They were building the barricades again. Pavement was flying, students were carrying axe handles and wooden clubs and iron bars, chanting, raving. In the distance I saw the riot police.

Rachel was nowhere in sight. I felt a knot in my stomach. How would we find Alain? He was small for his age, and though tough in spirit, his size was not an advantage in the midst of a riot. I cursed Jacques, Theo, and Rachel under my breath. Who did Jacques think he was, leaving his sons in the midst of a riot? At that moment I hated everything the students of May 1968 stood for. It was heady intellectualism and meaningless slogans.

But mostly, I was scared. "You need to turn around, Jean-Paul," I said, holding on to his arm. "Go back to the Sorbonne. It's dangerous out here. I'll bring Alain back."

"You'll never find him, Mary Swan. Look at the swarms of people. I'm staying with you. Anyway, there's no way to turn around."

He was right. We were crushed in a moving sea of bodies. Cold fear prickled my neck. The focal point of the students' wrath this night was the stock market, but many were meeting at the Odeon Theatre, just a few streets east of the Sorbonne. We were, in a sense, stuck.

Up ahead the police began spraying tear gas. The students screamed back insults. Some started pushing out of the ranks and moving toward the side streets. Young men jerked off their T-shirts and tied them around their eyes.

I managed to get the can of baking soda Rachel had given me out of my pocket. "Wipe spit around your eyes, Jean-Paul," I commanded. "Then pour on the baking soda. And hold that handkerchief Rachel gave you over your face."

He obeyed as we were jostled forward.

The students were responding to the police brutality by throwing bricks and pieces of wood. Police did not hesitate to beat them with billy clubs. A young man screamed for help and collapsed barely three feet from us, his face bloody. I thought I was going to throw up. I drew Jean-Paul closer.

And then I saw him. Alain was standing on the sidewalk fifty feet ahead of us, clutching his eyes and screaming. Grabbing hold of Jean-Paul, I forced us forward through the confusion, moving in Alain's direction.

Jean-Paul yelled to his brother in French, "Stay put, Alain! We're coming!"

When we reached him, tears were streaming down his face. "*Ça fait mal!* It hurts. It hurts!" he screamed.

Jean-Paul wiped his brother's eyes with the dampened handkerchief, and I took the can of baking soda and smudged the white powder around Alain's eyes. Then we were all hit with a new spray of tear gas. It felt like knives cutting at my eyes.

Alain started hyperventilating, gasping for breath. Jean-Paul tore off his T-shirt and ripped it in two, wrapping a frayed half around his younger brother's face. "Hold on to me!" he yelled.

"But I can't breathe! I'm suffocating! Help me!"

"Be quiet, Alain, and calm down. Breathe deeply and calm down."

I was surprised by the authority in Jean-Paul's voice, but Alain obeyed. I grabbed both boys, an arm around each of their waists, and began nudging us backward through the crowd.

I was terrified of the police, who were swinging their bats at anyone and everyone. In a panic, the crowd was dispersing down various side streets. I saw our chance to turn back to the Sorbonne.

"Come on, boys! Push!" We waded through the debris on the Rue des Ecoles and made our way into a side street, adrenaline pumping in my ears. We waited in the cove of a building and watched students overturning cars and pulling up pavement while the riot police tried to beat them back.

At that moment I felt the same fear and helplessness as I had years ago when Miss Abigail had taken me to a home in Grant Park where a drunken father was threatening his children with a knife. A slice of that evening slashed through my mind. I thought of Miss Abigail's calm prayers in the midst of a dangerous situation, and I prayed silently, *Dear Lord, you know very well that I don't want to be here. That I find nothing exciting about this riot. Protect us, protect the boys. Help me, please.*

As we ventured out again to Rue des Ecoles, attempting to turn onto Boulevard St. Michel and back to the Sorbonne, we were greeted by two members of the riot police. I shoved the boys behind me, yelling at them, "Get back. Run! Hurry!"

Suddenly Alain screamed at me, "Watch out, Mary Swan!"

I barely had the chance to turn around when a billy club came crashing down on my left shoulder. The force of the hit sent me sprawling, and I landed facedown on the pavement. I forced my knees to drag me onto the sidewalk as the crowd swept by.

From somewhere I heard Jean-Paul yelling, "*Arrêtez, Monsieur, s'il vous plaît! Elle est innocente!* She's innocent!"

And then I blacked out.

When I opened my eyes, the boys were hovering over me, tears on their faces. I groaned.

"She's alive!" Alain screamed dramatically. "She's alive."

"You idiot! Of course she's alive." Jean-Paul knelt down beside me. "It's okay now, Mary Swan. The riot police have left. Can you stand up?"

I closed my eyes to stop the sensation of everything wheeling around me. When I tried to sit up, an excruciating pain shot through my shoulder. "Wait a minute," I mumbled.

It felt as if my shoulder were broken. I grimaced when Jean-Paul tried to help me to my feet. "Let me sit for a moment. You're sure the police are gone?"

"*Oui,* for right now at least," Alain whimpered, rubbing his eyes furiously.

"Are you boys all right?"

"My eyes are killing me. Killing me!" Alain cried.

We stuck like glue to the buildings on our right as we hobbled, the boys' arms supporting me, back toward the Sorbonne. My head was swimming, my eyes burning, and the searing pain in my shoulder made me weak. At one point, I had to stop. I turned away from the boys and vomited.

"It's okay," Jean-Paul confided. "I've already thrown up twice."

A young woman came over to us, held me at the waist, and cried out to other students, "Quick, come help over here! Two young boys and a comrade are injured!"

"*Merci,*" I whispered. "Please, get the boys to the Sorbonne," I mumbled, half conscious. "Their eyes—the tear gas . . ." And I fainted again.

Somehow I was carried to the Sorbonne and placed on a cot in a room that had been turned into a makeshift infirmary. I remembered visiting it with Theo earlier in the day. The students treated me like royalty—or rather, much better, as a wounded member of the beloved proletariat. The boys' eyes were washed out with water and bandaged. They hovered over me through the night, looking miserable.

"Papa should never have left us here. We almost got killed," Alain repeated from time to time, until at last Jean-Paul hissed, "Will you please just shut up."

Sometime in the middle of the night a taxi driver offered to take me to the hospital, but the very idea terrified me. "Can you take us home instead?" I begged.

He smiled wryly. "I can try."

Ten minutes later, both boys were huddled beside me in the back of the cab, and somewhere in the midst of the streets of Paris, they fell asleep in my lap.

"Mom, are you making this stuff up?" I said.

She started and came back to the present. "No, I'm absolutely serious. For as nonviolent as Dr. King's funeral had been, this was the exact opposite, and it was terrifying. My shoulder was hurt pretty badly, but the boys were okay. Of course, we were still stuck in Paris, and I hated Rachel more than ever for dragging me into all the revolutionary activities. She didn't even think it was a big deal that I'd gotten injured. She said 'Swan, there are always casualties in revolution.' If I could have gone home, I would have—but, of course, there was no transportation. So Jean-Paul and I started painting."

I liked hearing about Jean-Paul as a shy thirteen-year-old. It warmed me deep down to realize that when he and my mother were out traipsing around Paris during the May 1968 revolution, they were both dreaming of becoming artists. And I knew the end of that story: they *had* both become artists. Jean-Paul was quite successful. One of the paintings at my parents' home was one he had done for Mom. And now I understood why he felt so close to her—sending her marble from Italy and fabric from Provence and bottles of fine red wine from his favorite French vineyards. She'd practically saved his and his brother's lives.

Mom picked up the last two paintings that were propped against the table and indicated one that showed the riot she'd just described. "Theo, the French student Rachel was in love with, convinced me that he could sell my painting of what happened that night. The final one is at the High, but this is what I worked on first."

Again, I was impressed with Mom's rendition of this riot, so alive and real.

She picked up the second painting and said, “And then I painted this.” It looked like the entrance to the Sorbonne, only the walls were covered with posters and graffiti.

“Did it really look like that?”

“Oh, worse. You can’t imagine all the posters that were plastered all over Paris. Some of the sayings were pretty clever.” She flipped to a sketch where she’d written a page full of French words. “That says *metro, boulot, dodo*—commute, work, sleep—same old routine. And that one says ‘No replastering. The structure is rotten.’”

I studied the sketches and paintings for a good five minutes without saying a word. Finally I commented, “But if you sold your first painting, that must have made all the hassle of the revolution worth it.”

“That’s what I thought. But, Ellie, nothing turned out as expected from the first day of my trip to the last.”

“Okay, keep going.”

“We finally got out of Paris. We had to skip Vienna and Madrid and Rome, which Rachel didn’t mind at all. Of course, I was terribly disappointed. We did go to Florence. This is sketched in the Piazza della Signoria—one of the most famous squares in the world, because of all the statues—fifteen or sixteen of them, all from the Gothic and Renaissance periods.”

“Oh yeah. You showed me this one at the hospital. What did you call it? Your first glimpse of male anatomy?”

Mom forced a smile, but her face turned about as red as Jean-Paul’s in the painting.

“How can that be? I thought you sketched nude models at your art classes.”

“Yes, we did. But they were always female.” She cleared her throat and said, “This is the Ponte Vecchio—the oldest and most famous bridge in Florence. That’s where I got the Italian faience bowl.”

“Yeah, the one we broke and you transformed into the table.”

“Exactly. And then we got to Amsterdam. We stayed at a Christian youth hostel in the middle of the red-light district, and Rachel met up with Theo, went to some party, and got high on some bad dope. The police came, and Rachel ended up sequestered with three other kids in a room that had been used to hide the Jews in World War II. Theo got busted and spent the night in a Dutch jail."

"Mom, you *are* making this up!" I accused, grinning.

Mom grinned back and said, "I am not. I promise it all happened just as I'm telling you."

"And what about the painting Theo was supposed to sell?"

"He hadn't exactly sold it. He'd had it framed and then he'd hidden drugs in the frame. But evidently the police had been tipped off, and when they busted the party, they took my painting. And so my very first 'sold' painting spent the night in jail too."

I laughed aloud. "That's pretty cool, Mom. I never would have expected you to get into so many adventures."

"It was all thanks to dear Rachel." She said it lightly, but—I don't know—she looked really sad. Then she brightened. "The best thing about Amsterdam was that Rachel and I made up."

"Oh, now that is good news."

"Yes, after that awful night and the drug bust, well, Rachel was pretty shaken up. She got a little more docile, and of course she realized that Theo was maybe not the right guy for her. So we spent the next few days doing typical tourist stuff, stuff Mama and Daddy had done. That was a big relief.

"We went to the Flower Market—you've never seen so many gorgeous tulips in your life—and we took a canal tour and went to the Anne Frank House and then I took her to the Van Gogh Museum."

"Van Gogh? Is *Starry Night* there?"

"Oh yes, you like Van Gogh, don't you? I can't remember if that painting is there or not, but I know you'd enjoy visiting the museum. It has I think over two hundred of his paintings and loads of his drawings. It's a small museum. Rachel loved it, and so did I."

"So what made y'all start getting along?"

"Well, it was actually because of the Van Gogh and the Rijkmuseum—the wonderful national museum. When I started explaining things about the different paintings, Rachel was impressed. She finally kind of tried to come into my world and see the things that interested me."

"Cool."

"And then she found your father's ring."

"What?"

"Remember? He gave me his class ring from Tech as an engagement ring. I'd kept it hidden from Rachel during the whole trip, but that night I accidentally left it out and she found it lying on my cot at the youth hostel. And she of course guessed it was Robbie's, and then she started asking me a lot of questions that I refused to answer. And then she got her feelings hurt, if you can imagine that. She said she couldn't believe that I would hide something as important as my relationship with Robbie from her—since she and I were best friends.

"And that shook me a bit, because of course I didn't consider her my best friend anymore. Maybe my arch enemy." Mom gave a little chuckle. "I couldn't imagine that Rachel Abrams, pragmatic, brilliant, beautiful, messed-up Rachel Abrams, still considered me her best friend.

"Anyway, she kept pressing me to tell her what was going on with Robbie, so finally I just lit into her and said something like, 'Why would I tell you about the most important person in my life when you'll just start quoting idiotic stats about Vietnam and accusing him of being a murderer? Wake up, Rach! I don't exactly feel like we have a lot in common these days!'"

"You said that to Rachel?"

"Something like that. I'm not proud of it, but I did."

"Heck, I think it was about time. Good for you, Mom. And how did she respond?"

"I thought she was going to start crying—she was fiddling with her love beads and saying something about how she knew we were different and that I didn't agree with her, but she was at least honest with me about her life. And our differences didn't make her stop loving me and thinking I was her best friend.

"Somehow we got through to each other and forgave each other." Mom blinked back tears. "Really, Rachel was the one who asked for forgiveness. That astounded me so much that I didn't know what to say. Then slowly my tears started coming and I threw my arms around her neck and we just sat there bawling.

"We finally talked about so many things that night—her drug problem and my weight problem and how my faith was making me seem serious and narrow-minded, and how that had scared Rachel and made her think maybe I was in a cult." She looked at me and said quickly, "I wasn't.

"Anyway, we sat on her cot in that youth hostel just bawling like babies and laughing at our awful, puffy eyes and crying again. And finally when we couldn't cry anymore, Rachel begged me to please tell her what was going on with Robbie and me. So I did. For the first time on our trip, we stayed up all night talking, the way we'd done so many times when we were teenagers."

She looked at her watch and said, "Good grief! I've been going on for an hour. You must be bored stiff. I'm sorry, Ellie. I got carried away."

"That's okay, Mom. I mean, it's all interesting stuff." I could have said that I was glad to be learning about her life, but I didn't. But as I went out to the beach while Mom sat on the screened-in porch, I felt satisfied that I would be able to report to Rachel and Megan and Ben and anyone one else who asked that I was getting to know my mother. Maybe I was even beginning to empathize with her.

Daddy had once said Mom was a person "with a personality that never stopped and a constitution that often did," meaning that she had never been very strong physically. Since I was athletic and sturdy, I had always seen her physical limitations as a sign of weakness. But maybe Daddy was right. Maybe Mom did have a lot of inner strength, which came through in a crisis.

And as I walked down the beach past the sunbathers and castle builders and novel readers, I felt something new. Admiration. For my mother.

Chapter 15

O Caledonia! Stern and wild,
Meet nurse for a poetic child!
Land of brown heath and shaggy wood,
Land of the mountain and the flood.

—SIR WALTER SCOTT

When I returned from my walk around nine-thirty that morning, I expected to see my mother sketching out on the porch. But she wasn't. She was sitting in a folding chair, those two sketch pads still in front of her, this time on the oblong white plastic table on the porch.

She glanced my way and said, "Would you like to finish looking at the sketch pads?" Then she gave a nervous little laugh, as if she were afraid I might refuse, and added, "Then you'll have it over with."

So of course, after I'd gotten a glass of ice water from the fridge, I came onto the porch and sat down beside her. She took Sheila's sketch pad and found another sketch of the Dwelling Place—not the one that had been ripped out. "Jean-Paul was the one who helped me begin unraveling the riddle of Scotland. Look at this sketch. What do you see?"

"I see a grassy field, a few sheep, and a low stone wall running across the field." There wasn't a human in sight. A pastoral scene. Period.

"Look more carefully at the wall," Mom said.

I squinted for a minute—the stones in the wall were small—no bigger than the size of a pea—but finally I noticed that there seemed to be letters of the alphabet sketched into some of the stones. I grabbed a pencil and a Post-it and copied down the letters in the order in which they appeared. "Okay. These letters were obviously meant to spell words, because Grandmom Sheila skipped a stone between several of them."

"Right." Again, Mom reminded me of a little girl. "So what does it spell?"

I read the words, obviously French. *"Demain dès l'Aube."* There was an accent mark over the second *e*, an *accent grave*, if I remembered correctly from my high school French. I laughed out loud. "That's kinda cool. Or just nutty. Grandmom Sheila was sketching French words on the stones of some old wall in Scotland."

"Yes, and Jean-Paul was the first one to notice it. I'd looked at that sketch pad for years and never seen it."

"Well, it's not exactly what I'd call obvious. You practically need a magnifying glass to see the letters."

"That's what Jean-Paul had done—gotten out a magnifying glass—and then he made me figure out the words."

"So what does it mean? *Tomorrow of the sunrise?"* I translated literally. "What in the world did she mean by that?"

"No, no! She put an accent on *dès*. See?"

"So that means . . ."

"Well, it means, tomorrow, *as soon as* the sun rises. *Demain dès l'Aube*. It's a very famous poem by Victor Hugo. French kids have to memorize it in elementary school."

"What's the poem about?" I'd read *Les Miserables* (in English, of course) and seen the musical twice. But I didn't know Hugo's poems.

"Oh, it's sad."

And to my astonishment, Mom began to quote the poem in French:

"Demain, dès l'aube, à l'heure où blanchit la campagne,
Je partirai. Vois-tu, je sais que tu m'attends.
J'irai par la forêt, j'irai par la montagne.
Je ne puis demeurer loin de toi plus longtemps. . . ."

She gave me a bashful glance. "I memorized it too, in honor of my mother—after I realized why she'd written it in the stones. The poet is talking about going somewhere, on a trip, first thing in the morning. At first you think it's to meet an old lover. But then it turns out that the speaker is going to place a bouquet of flowers on someone's grave—someone very dear to him, someone he calls with the familiar form of you—*tu.*"

"Oh, that is sad."

"Yes. Hugo wrote it after his daughter died." Mom said this reverently, as if she expected me to make a connection between Hugo's deceased daughter and my grandmother Sheila.

But once again, I was completely lost in my mother's story. I watched her for a few silent seconds, and then asked, "So why did Grandmom write that poem into the stones?"

"Well, to tell you that story, we have to go way back a lot further than 1968."

With both sketch pads opened to drawings of the Dwelling Place, Mom began.

"Your great-grandfather Ian and great-grandmother Evelyne met in Paris, during the First World War—not in the best of circumstances, I might add. You see, Evelyne was a prostitute, a very beautiful, very broken young woman—a girl, really. She was starving and living all alone. I think her parents were dead, she was sixteen years old, and she saw no other way to stay alive. But she got pregnant, which wasn't good for business. She gave birth to a baby girl and called her Laure.

Evelyne's 'colleagues' helped her care for the baby, and she kept working.

"Ian was stationed in Paris. He met Evelyne in a bar when she was eighteen and Laure was barely one. He knew what Evelyne was, but he fell in love with her and treated her like a fine lady. When he offered to marry her, she couldn't believe her luck. It was her chance for freedom and a future.

"But there was Laure. Evelyne was terrified that if she told Ian the truth, he wouldn't take her with him, so she told him that when her best friend, the baby's mother, had been on her deathbed, Evelyne had sworn to her that she wouldn't abandon the child.

"Ian said they could take the baby back with them to Scotland. He had a cousin whose wife had never been able to have children. Perhaps they would adopt her.

"And so it happened. Just like that. Ian brought Evelyne back with him to Scotland and married her, and Laure was adopted by his cousin Colin and his wife, Rosemary, in the Borders. Evelyne thought she'd always live close to Laure on Ian's sheep farm—the loving aunt who watched the child grow.

"But then Ian had the notion to move to the States and make a fortune in cotton—he'd already done it with wool. Evelyne begged him not to go. She told him she hated the States. But he was determined. And he said she was so young that she'd get used to it—she'd love it. And so she said good-bye to her little Laure, who was two and a half by then.

"Evelyne had died so many times in the arms of other men, wild, reckless soldiers, that her heart was already hard as rock. But this time she died another death. She left the child she loved, and she never breathed a word to Ian."

I blinked back tears.

"Evelyne went back to Europe two or three times a year. Growing up, I always thought that my grandmother Evelyne was going on all those exotic trips to get away from Papy Ian. But that wasn't it. She went to get away from America, maybe, but mostly to see Laure. She told Laure the truth when she was old enough to understand. And I'm pretty sure Colin and Rosemary found out at that time. They surely suspected something—apparently Laure looked quite a bit like her mother. But Ian didn't know. It was Evelyne and Laure's secret. They met in places and traveled.

"When your grandmother Sheila was born, oh, about three years after Ian and Evelyne were married, it was hard for Evelyne to love her. Sheila looked Scottish, even as a baby, with her red hair and green eyes, and for Evelyne, being reminded of Scotland was her curse, a wound that could never heal.

"Evelyne hated America, missed Paris, couldn't stand the food or the ways of the Americans. She drank too much. But Ian loved her, bless his soul. He did love her. And she loved him. But I wonder if he ever knew it.

"On one drunken night, Evelyne told him the truth about Laure. It broke his heart. He would have raised Laure. He loved her too. There was a fight and a reconciliation. And another baby was conceived. They seemed happy for a while, Evelyne and Ian and Sheila and baby Anne.

"But then, Ellie, when Sheila was around four years old and Anne just a baby, Evelyne took her two little daughters out for a stroll around the plantation. No one knows exactly how it happened—perhaps Evelyne left Anne in the baby carriage for a few minutes and took Sheila to look at something in the cotton fields. At any rate, when Evelyne and Sheila got back to baby Anne, she was already blue. Evelyne panicked, tried to revive her, and screamed at Sheila to run for help. But by the time Sheila got back with someone, the baby had died. Evelyne was holding her baby to her breast and wailing."

"How awful," I blurted out. "That is so, so awful." And to myself, I wondered, *Is there no end to the sadness in my family?*

"Yes. I can't even imagine it. I guess Evelyne just snapped completely after that and started blaming poor Sheila for Anne's death. So your great-grandfather Ian sent his little Sheila to Scotland to get her away from her mother. Sheila went to live with Colin and Rosemary and Laure, who was around ten at the time. My mother used to sit out on the stone wall and hold her dolly and just cry.

"But Laure was delighted to have her there, and she took care of her. They'd sit in the fields and Sheila would draw—she was an artist even back then. Sheila lived there for six months, maybe longer. She was Scottish in her heart, from her red hair to her green eyes to the strange Scottish accent she picked up in the Borders.

"When she had to leave, she missed Scotland in her heart. Over the years, every time she came back to what she called the Dwelling Place, she was peaceful and happy and less depressed. And one time, when she was a young teenager, Laure told her the truth—that they were half sisters. And Sheila told Laure the truth about Anne and the accident."

My mother flipped the pages to a sketch of the Dwelling Place in her pad—not the one with Rachel or the one of Mom and Rachel together, but another. In this third drawing of the stone wall, there was a woman—a lovely woman with long, dark hair—perched on the wall, wearing nice pants and an elegant but simple sweater. In the sketch she was looking out toward the fields, so that you could only see her profile. It was a perfect profile—a small, delicate nose, a high forehead, and full lips.

"This is Laure."

"She's beautiful."

"Yes."

"Is that when you met her—when you went to the Dwelling Place in 1968?"

"Yes. She's the one who told me that whole story about Evelyne and Sheila and herself. Rachel and I arrived in the Borders on June fourteenth. I literally felt a quickening in my heart as our taxi approached the Ettrick Hills. The grass was a brownish shade of green and sheep dotted the landscape and the trees were rather sparse and the hills smooth. I could see a river winding off to the left, and then we went over a narrow hill and looked down from above, and it was exactly what Mama's sketches looked like. There were crisscrossing stone walls and just a handful of sheep in each field, and some tall pines.

"I tried to focus on exactly what she'd sketched. It was nothing extraordinary, not nearly as breathtaking as the Edinburgh Castle or the ruins of Melrose Abbey, which Rachel and I had visited the day before. Those places had a haunted, ominous beauty. This scene was rugged but breathtaking in a different way. And as soon as we drove down into the little valley with the fields and the meandering stone wall and the dirt road leading to a simple wooden house, I felt protected, as if I were coming home."

I could tell Mom was getting overly sentimental, and I had a fluttering worry. I could almost hear Abbie's reprimand. *For heaven's sake, Ellie, why did you let her get so worked up?* But Mom seemed to be enjoying reliving her trip, even though it hadn't been carefree. And now she was at her final destination. So surely this would have a happy ending. Granddad JJ had said the Dwelling Place had had a calming effect on my grandmother.

"Uncle Colin—that's what I called my grandfather Ian's first cousin—greeted us, looking every bit the elderly shepherd he was, with fifteen or twenty sheep walking placidly in front of him and a Border collie at either heel. We went with him to the rustic two-storied house. Cozy, simple, inviting. I half expected to see a wooden sign planted in the earth proclaiming *The Dwelling Place*. But there was nothing.

"After he showed us our room, Rachel and I went out to the field and sat on the wall. Of course we'd brought the sketch pads, Mama's and mine, and we spent about an hour looking for any type of writing on the rocks—I'd shown Rachel what Jean-Paul had discovered—but we didn't find anything having to do with *Demain dès l'Aube*.

"The first night we were there, I asked Laure why my mother, Sheila, had chosen to come to this part of Scotland, and she told us all she knew about Sheila and Evelyne. She also explained that this spot wasn't really called the Dwelling Place—that was just a name my mother had made up for it.

"And that was the beginning of my unraveling more about my family. You see, Ellie, all of these things were just festering family secrets."

Mom stopped, got up, and stared out the big sliding glass doors toward the beach.

"Hey, Mom, you don't have to tell me anything else. I don't want to make you all upset. We can talk about it later. Or never. Whatever you want."

I guess she heard me, but she didn't acknowledge it. She just kept on talking, standing in front of the window, her face turned away from me.

"Ellie, it was such a relief for me to talk to Laure, to have our family's past out in the open, to find out that Evelyne intimidated just about everyone who knew her, to hear Laure say it was just a façade, that Evelyne had been so wounded and scarred by life that she coped through meanness. I've often thought it must have been absolutely terrible, a nightmare, for her to outlive her daughters. I don't know what I'd do if something happened to you or Nan or Abbie. It's hard enough just to see you going through difficult times and not be able to help." She turned to look at me.

I think Mom was holding out a line to me. I think she was trying to say, *We've talked enough about my life in the past. How about talking a little about you and me?* I could see a look of hope and expectation in her eyes. I had seen it before. And just like before, I looked right past it, looked over her head, picked up a sketch pad, and said, "You said this property isn't called the Dwelling Place. But Evelyne must have heard it called that, since she got so furious when you showed her Grandmom Sheila's sketch."

Mom acquiesced, as she always did, to my response. "This spot of land in Scotland was a very painful place for Evelyne, Ellie. It's where she lost Laure, her first daughter. And I think she felt like it was where she lost Sheila as well, when she sent her away after Anne's death. This place was one big hole in my grandmother's heart—a place of tragedy and guilt. I think that was why she got so upset when she saw the sketch, why she said that Sheila was still punishing her from the grave."

"But why did *Sheila* call this the Dwelling Place?"

"That first time she came to visit, she was a frail and wounded little girl. Colin and Rosemary and Laure loved on her, fed her well, brought some red into her cheeks. She went with them to the parish church in the village. The vicar was a lovely man, kind and wise, according to Laure. He was preaching on the psalms that spring, and Laure said that Sheila, young as she was, was captivated.

"She would ask the strangest questions, questions too hard for a little girl. She wanted to know what it meant to 'dwell.' Laure didn't know, but the vicar explained to Mama that when God dwells in your heart, it means you are safe and that He will never, ever leave you. He becomes your dwelling place—a place of shelter and caring and protection.

"Well, after that, Sheila called Colin and Rosemary and Laure's house and fields her dwelling place. Even the last time she was here." Mom brushed her finger lovingly over Grandmom Sheila's cursive at the bottom of the sketch. The Dwelling Place. Then she whispered with a catch in her throat, "I truly believe it was the one spot on earth where my dear mother felt genuinely at peace." She pointed back to the sketch.

"Anyway, after Laure told me the whole story that day in June, I went out after breakfast the next morning, took the sketchbook with me, of course, and found the very spot in the wall where Mom had written the words *Demain dès l'Aube*. Once again I looked at the stones, examining them closely to see if she had somehow carved the words to Victor Hugo's poem on them. But they were flat and bare.

"I knew then that I wouldn't find anything in the stones. The sketch was one more whisper of love from my mother to her baby sister. It made sense to me—Mama who was always drawing symbolism into her sketches. This sketch was her love letter to her sister—her way of placing a bouquet of flowers on her grave. And to me, it seemed it was a love letter to Evelyne too. Sheila chose Victor Hugo's poem out of love for her French mother."

I waited to see if Mom had finished with her story, if she was going to turn around and make another attempt at getting me to talk.

She did turn around, and said, "In Scotland, when I discovered these missing pieces to my mother's story, it made me miss her all over again. It made me hurt with the longing to have gotten to know her better, before it was too late. To have understood these things and assured her that she was safe and loved and protected in Atlanta too.

"And it made me want to go back to Atlanta and give Mamie Evelyne, frail, nutty Mamie, a long, warm hug and tell her that I loved her. I didn't know if I could really do it, but I knew I should try. She was all I had left of my mother."

"Did you do it, Mom? Did you ever hug Evelyne?"

"I did, Ellie. I ended up hugging her a lot before she died."

"Did she become less of a witch?"

I thought I saw a little sparkle in Mom's eyes as she said, "Well, she still had a long mean streak in her, but since I understood why, I guess my attitude toward her changed. I think the last years of her life were probably the best ones. I don't know if she ever forgave herself for losing her daughters, but I think she learned to appreciate Jimmy and me. And one time, I did give her my interpretation of this Dwelling Place sketch. When she saw for herself the title to Hugo's poem, well, I think something happened in that ole heart of Evelyne's. I think maybe she let herself believe that Sheila had forgiven her and loved her." Mom's expression was soft and relieved and yes, hopeful, as she looked at me.

I pretended not to notice.

"Rachel and I spent several days there, wonderful days, lazy days there at what had become for me a place of discovery of my family heritage, a place of reconciliation and hope, a place where I renewed my commitment to God and reaffirmed my desire to work among the poor and to paint. I even started the painting *The Dwelling Place,* the one at the High, right there, with my easel planted in the grass and the long low wall in front of me." She smiled at the memory.

"And most of all, it was where I made a commitment to Robbie, to love him and care for him and be the wife he needed. I'd gotten several letters from him by that time and heard some pretty awful things about what was happening in Vietnam. I wasn't exactly scared for him, but I realized that he wasn't going to just come back from war and be the same. I knew he would be tired and maybe even scarred on the inside when he returned, so I promised him there at that wall that I'd wait and be there and take care of him, and we would try our very best to make our lives and our work count for good. At that moment, the Dwelling Place meant healing for me, just as it had for Mama."

Again I thought she had finished her story, and again she stood up and walked back to the window. She pressed her forehead into the glass pane.

I let out a long sigh and said, "Well, that was another good story, Mom. Thank you for sharing it. I'm so glad that this part of the trip turned out better than you expected."

When she came back to the table and sat down, I pointed to her sketch of Rachel and her, sitting happy and carefree on the stone wall. "I like seeing the two of you like that."

"Yes." But Mom was not smiling or looking happy and carefree. She was looking at that sketch as if she distrusted it, as if what was drawn onto that piece of paper was not what really happened.

"And then you came home?"

"Yes."

"So you did finish the trip, really."

"Oh no. We left on the spur of the moment."

"Why?"

"Because I got the telegram."

"What telegram?"

"The one from Granddad JJ telling me that Robbie was missing in action."

"Daddy was *missing in action* in Vietnam? I never knew that!"

I don't think she even heard me.

"I'd been sketching out in the fields when Uncle Colin came out to find me. He had the saddest expression on his usually jolly face, and he handed me the telegram. As soon as I read it, I fell on the ground by the wall. It was so ironic—just the day before I'd recommitted my life to God and to Robbie and then, wham. I get a telegram from my father announcing another tragic event. I poured out my soul at that stone wall. I poured out everything that was inside me—and my, there was a lot of grief and anger and misunderstanding and fear and terror. Then I got flat on my face and just lay there, completely spent.

"And strange as it may sound, I suddenly felt a type of peace, that peace that always comes after I've poured out my heart to the Lord. Rachel found me there, and she came over and kept saying 'Oh, God, I'm so sorry, Swan. This can't be true.' But it was true.

"Anyway, we left right then. Oh, Ellie, your father had told me enough stories about the horrors of war that I didn't have one illusion as to what those words meant. Missing in action. Wounded, captured, tortured, killed." Mom pronounced each word slowly, a tone of finality in her voice. "And just like that, the field and wall in Scotland switched from being a place of healing for me to what it had always been for Mamie: a terrible place of grief and death and loss."

It was only ten in the morning, but Mom looked as if it were way past her bedtime and she was fading fast.

"I'm sorry, Mom. I'm sorry about all of it."

"Life doesn't always do what we want it to, Ellie." She closed the sketch pads. "But now you know the story. Do you mind if I lie down for a while? Then maybe we can take a walk or I can paint."

I felt an immense relief that the story was over. "That sounds like a good idea, Mom."

I took a long walk on the beach, contemplating my mother's most recent tale. Scotland I understood, but Vietnam? I was more than sorry. I was in shock. How could I have never known that my father had been missing in action for over a year? How could they have hidden this from me? Was I really so callous to my parents that they had never dared share this huge, angry interruption in their lives?

I kept picturing my mother by the stone wall, on the ground, crying out for my father. Here I was walking on the same beach that she and Daddy had walked on when they had discovered their mutual love. That was such a shimmering, happy picture in my mind—even as I imagined them kissing in the rain. That was the snapshot I wanted to paste in my memory. Not Mom on the ground by the stone wall, begging her God for some kind of mercy, not Mom doing this only one day after she'd promised God and Daddy that she'd hang on. I did not want to see that image, did not want to try and examine that coincidence.

Walking briskly, feeling the wet, hard sand under my feet, I chose to picture my mother laughing with Rachel and Laure, even as she longed for her own mother. I chose to picture her back in Atlanta, leaning over and hugging Evelyne, feeling as if she were hugging a skeleton with skin slipped over it, but hugging her all the same, out of some deep-down love. Then I tried, I really tried, to picture myself, hefty me, leaning over and hugging my shriveled-up mother, feeling her firm, unnatural chest on her bony frame.

Back at the house, I checked my e-mail, chatted with Nate, and read the *Journal* online. I felt antsy and went downstairs and listened outside Mom's door. It was cracked, and I peeked inside. Mom was curled up on her bed, eyes closed and breathing softly. I felt as though she were lying there completely naked before me. I knew so many things that I had not known only two days earlier.

For some odd reason, I got on my knees beside her bed. I was afraid to touch her—not because I was afraid of waking her, but because I was afraid that her skin would feel clammy and cool, like that of a dying person. I was glad she was asleep so that I could whisper to her, "Mom, I don't know what to say. I'm so sorry about all the hard things in your life. I'm sorry I accused you of having a perfect life. You just rest. You need all your strength to get better. Rest."

I bent over and kissed her lightly on her cheek.

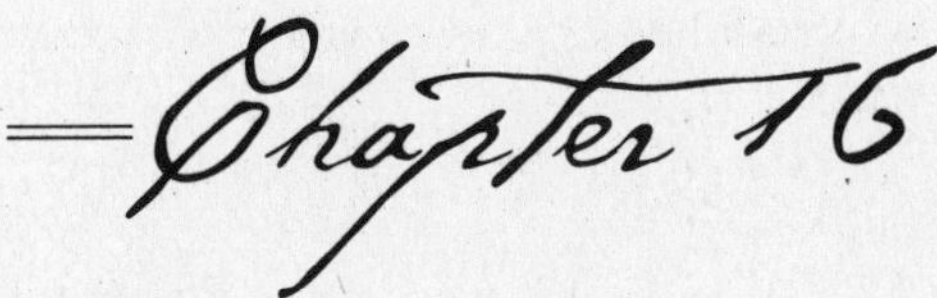

Chapter 16

Tomorrow morn, what time the fields grow white,
I shall set off; I know you look for me,
Across the forest's gloom, the mountain height:
I can no longer dwell away from Thee . . .

—VICTOR HUGO, *TOMORROW AT DAWN*

When I heard Mom get up and go to the bathroom around noon, I had already made lunch—a tomato and mayonnaise sandwich—and put it on a tray, which I carried downstairs and set on her bedside table. She was in her usual position, propped up in bed with a Bible opened across her lap.

"Oh, Ellie. Thank you, sweetie. You've fixed me a real feast."

"Hope you like it," I said, trying to read what was in her eyes.

"It's divine. You've turned into Florence Nightingale." She smiled softly. "And I'm so thankful that you're here."

I perched on the end of Mom's bed as she took a sip of lemonade.

"Dear, I hope you weren't too shocked about all those things I told you about."

"No. Actually I was amazed. I mean, your life was anything but boring. Man, Mom. You were part of 'history in the making.'"

I said it with such a deadpan voice that at first I wasn't sure if she understood. Then her eyes met mine, and we burst into laughter. I don't remember ever having laughed like that with Mom, just the two of us, sharing a personal joke. It felt so good that I tentatively asked, "What happened after Scotland, Mom?"

"Oh, it was so hard. I had to rush home. It was awful."

"You just packed up and left?"

"Yes, the very next day."

"Rachel too?"

"Both of us."

"And you've never been back?"

"Never."

"Is Laure still alive?"

"No, she passed away five or six years ago."

A hundred questions were rushing through my mind as she ate her sandwich. Finally I broached one of them. "How long was Daddy in Vietnam?"

"Almost three years." She winced. "Two years, ten months, and eleven days, to be exact."

"He was missing all that time?"

"Most of it."

"You didn't know if he was alive or dead?"

"No. And at one point we were sure he was dead."

"Why haven't you ever talked about it to us, Mom?"

"Oh, sweetie." She reached over and squeezed my hand. "It was too awful for your father. Too awful for both of us. Some memories aren't worth putting into words." She closed her eyes.

"Did you ever give up? Did you ever think he wasn't going to come back?"

She didn't answer at first. "I hung on to hope for a long, long time, but after two years had gone by, I pretty much gave up." Her voice cracked a little. "But not your father. They tried to yank everything good out of him, kill his soul. But they couldn't. He didn't give up."

She looked straight at me, her face suddenly a pasty white and all sparkle gone from her eyes, as if just the effort of remembering those atrocious months had wiped the soul out of her. "Ellie, it's not a thing he can talk about. We lived through hell, muddled through afterward, went on. And thankfully, God blessed us with you girls to help us heal."

Compassion for my parents flooded through me, like the sudden warmth of the sun I had felt on the beach earlier in the day after a cloud had shadowed me. "I'm sorry I made you talk about it, Mom."

She carefully wiped a napkin across her mouth and leaned her head back on the pillow. "No, don't be sorry. It's probably time to talk about things. It was an awful time in our lives, but even then there were good things that happened too. For all the sorrow, the questions, the hurt and fear, the day in Scotland when I thought I'd lost Robbie was the day that I knew I had gotten Rachel back. It is so strange and mysterious how life works, Ellie."

Then she wiped the expression of grief off her face, with one movement of the tissue across her eyes, so that when she started talking again, her voice was stronger. "Rachel was the one who assured me there were things we could do to help find Robbie. So of course, I didn't want to waste one second more in Europe. We left."

"And then what happened?"

"Oh, we wrote letters, we waited. I died, in a way. And in a way, I started living again. I plunged back into the work in the inner city. I shadowed Miss Abigail night and day. That became my purpose. I didn't paint much—after the drug bust in Amsterdam."

"Theo was quite a character."

"Yes." She shook her head. "I was so naïve. To think that one of my first paintings was used to smuggle drugs. It'll make a good story for the grandchildren."

"It's not such a bad one for the kids." We met eyes again.

"Yes. Heaven knows what happened to Theo."

The next question was going to cost me something, so I tiptoed up to it, stretched my courage, and asked, "And how did you stop binge-ing?"

She reached across the bed and squeezed my hand without meeting my eyes. "It wasn't easy. Nothing happened all at once. I talked about that problem with Miss Abigail. She's the one who convinced me to see someone."

"What do you mean by 'see someone'?"

"I went to see a pastor friend of hers. I guess he was a psychiatrist or a psychologist. All I know is that I met with him for a year, and I also met with his nurse, and Cassandra was a great help too. She knew something about eating disorders from nursing school. And of course, I came to understand that the monster that was eating me up had several ugly names, like grief and rage and bitterness. I learned it had nothing to do with food and everything to do with my family, my mother, my perception of life. Thankfully, counseling and inner city work helped me—and also the things Laure had told me about my family's past—and very gradually, that vice lost its grip."

I shivered involuntarily. Maybe that was what was happening to me. But it was too close to discuss, to examine with Mom. I got off my figurative tiptoes and purposely changed the subject. "Rachel had a rough time of it, didn't she?"

"Oh yeah. Both of us were messed up. It was a very hard time to be trying to figure life out. But we pulled each other through a lot. She was a saint about all the MIA information. She wrote letters to the government, got me contacts, helped the Bartholomews. It was very personal for her, Robbie's nightmare. I mean, of course, it was for me, but after all the awful things she had said, she really went to bat for him."

"And she got over the drugs and stuff? Settled down?" But that wasn't what I meant—those were the wrong words. Even now, I could never imagine Rachel as someone who had "settled down."

"I had my faith. Rach didn't. She was always on the outside looking in. She went to law school and then fell for Harold, much to my dismay. . . ."

"And you hung out with Miss Abigail and Dr. and Mrs. Matthews."

"Yes, I was never bored. I helped out at Mt. Carmel and did a few art classes down at Grant Park. I thought I'd try my hand at art therapy—something Mama had started. I knew your father would want me to keep on with life. So I tried. It wasn't easy. Not one bit easy. But I tried."

"It's pretty cool that Dr. Matthews is a doctor. He must have worked really hard to get through med school."

"Yes, he had a rough start, but he's quite an amazing . . . quite an amazing man. Helped his brothers and sister through college too." She spoke quickly, as if she wanted to get over the part about the Matthewses.

But I wanted to hear more. "And Mrs. Matthews became a nurse."

"That was even more surprising. If you could have seen her—the first time I met her—a skinny teen with a newborn in her arms. She wasn't even planning on going back to high school."

"She says you helped convince her."

"Hmm," Mom said. "It doesn't surprise me that Cassie would say that. But it wasn't just me. I certainly was proud of her, though. She finished high school and went on to nursing school."

"And when did she and Dr. Matthews get married?"

Mom faltered again. "Oh, in the fall of 1971, I think. About a year before your dad and I did."

"Man, they waited a long time. I mean, didn't you say that Dr. Matthews got back from Vietnam in 1968?"

"Mmm. Yes. They did take a while. He was in med school and well . . ." She looked out the window. "Would you mind heating up my tea, sweetie?"

I did mind, truthfully. I was so amazed and content to be having this conversation that I didn't want to budge. But Mom was earnest, and she was especially earnest about avoiding the subject of the Matthewses. So I went upstairs, warmed up her tea in the microwave, and when I came back downstairs, she had gotten up and was getting dressed.

She surprised me by saying, "Would you like to take a walk on the beach, Ellie—before the sun gets too hot? I was thinking that I'd really enjoy getting out."

I was equally surprised by my answer. "Sure, Mom. That's a great idea. I'd like that a lot."

The sky was overcast, the air fresh and warm, without the smothering heat that would come later. The beach was filled with sunbathers. It was low tide, and the sand was flat and smooth and sparkling where the ocean had recently receded. We walked slowly, Mom holding tightly to my arm, her green scarf billowing with an occasional gust of wind. She was wearing a long-sleeved white cotton Oxford and jeans, with the sleeves and pants legs rolled up. In a way, she resembled Audrey Hepburn, whom I'd always considered beautiful but so tiny and slim she might break at any moment.

"I feel better today, Ellie. It's the air of the ocean. The rest. You being here." She held onto my right arm, leaned heavily into me. "You look better too. Peaceful."

We walked along in silence, but for once, it was not an awkward silence.

"How did you know you would paint, Mom?" I asked at length.

She didn't say anything for a long minute. She just looked out at the glistening ocean. Then she stopped, bent over slowly, and picked up a tiny perfect clam shell. "I don't know how it is for others. For me, it was such a strong feeling. Something I had to do . . ."

"A passion."

"Yes," she said, looking down at her long, slim fingers. "It was what they were created to do, it always seemed to me. Hold a brush. I knew it, but of course, many times, I didn't believe it. I painted, but after the art scandal and Robbie in Vietnam, I was ready to abandon everything. But it was always so strong, the longing, the desire. It was how I expressed myself."

I looked down at my hands—they looked like Mom's, except that mine were pudgier now—long fingers, narrow across the palm, strong nails. Most everything else came from Daddy, but I had Mom's hands.

She took hold of my arm again and said, half as a question and half as a statement, "You've always known what you wanted to be too, haven't you, sweetie?"

"Me?"

"From the time you were a tiny girl, you loved animals. But you were never content to just hold them and love on them. You wanted to fix them. Remember the baby squirrel you nursed back to health? And that bird that Mr. Boots had caught. Brought the poor thing to you in his mouth, and you saved the little sparrow. I think you've always known. It takes time for dreams to mature, for us to mature and move into them. Sometimes the road gets bumpy."

"It was bumpy for you, wasn't it?"

She nodded as the tide rolled over our toes. "Terribly bumpy at times. But the Lord just kept bringing circumstances and people into my life at just the right time to encourage me to keep going.

"For example, there was this big ceremony at the High Museum the fall of '68—a few months after the telegram about Robbie. October, I think. France was offering the museum a bronze casting of Rodin's famous sculpture *L'Ombre*—you know, *The Shade*—in memory of the Atlantans who died at Orly in 1962. All the families who had had loved ones on that plane were invited to the ceremony. Your Granddad JJ spent a fortune on the event. Trixie helped organize it. The French ambassador to the United States made the presentation. Of course, I attended.

"Something struck me that day. Broke my heart. You know, when an artist's heart is broken, sometimes that's the best time to paint. And so I did. I went back to Mama's atelier and painted *Letters From Vietnam*."

I knew that painting because it was at the museum. It showed a woman from the back, sitting at a desk with many letters opened all over it. She was holding a telegram in one hand, and covering her face with the other, obviously weeping.

"But, of course, the things I did back then just sat in my atelier for years and years, gathering dust. Until one day the Lord worked it out. He worked out the painting and the inner city. And of course, He brought your father back."

I involuntarily let go of her arm as we turned back toward our house. "Mom, it's not God doing all that. It was you and coincidence."

"No, Ellie, it was the Lord. I know it was Him."

"How do you know? That's insane." And before she could reply, I said, "It's hard to talk to you about things, Mom, because you always bring God into it. God does everything for you, it seems. Well, He hasn't helped me too much, and I'm not wild about Him. Leave Him out of the story."

She sighed heavily. "I can't. He *is* my story."

"Well, sorry to say it, but He's not mine. I don't want to twist my life to make it all go back to 'God this' and 'God that.' I just want a nice half-normal life."

She touched my arm softly but didn't say a word.

We were standing in front of the Hamilton House, and Mom's shoulders were sagging, and once again I winced at the contrast of her thin frame and the way her reconstructed breasts filled out the cotton Oxford. My words had been arrows; I had injured Mom. Immediately I felt regret—not just guilt. After all, I had asked her about these things. How could she leave God out of it, when in her mind, He was in charge of every event in her whole life?

"Sorry, Mom," I offered lamely.

She touched my arm again in reply. I'd made a feeble attempt and she had accepted it. Somewhere inside, I felt the stirrings of hope. We had talked about important things. Maybe Hilton Head's sun was melting the ice between us, melting my frozen heart. At least it was a beginning.

While Mom napped in the early afternoon, I stretched out on the chaise lounge in my bedroom with a pencil and paper in my hands. I had always liked to figure things out on paper, like a math problem. I wanted to see what I was up against. So I started writing names and approximate dates down on the paper while I carried on a conversation in my mind, analyzing my family:

1917 Evelyne—my French great-grandmother—has illegitimate child, Laure

1919 Evelyne marries Ian from Scotland after WWI, takes Laure with them to Scotland. Ian thinks Evelyne is raising the baby for a dead friend

1920 Laure is adopted by Ian's cousin, Uncle Colin, and wife, Rosemary, who couldn't bear children—they live at the Dwelling Place (sentimental name my grandmom later gives the property)

1923 Ian leaves for USA with Evelyne—she is heartbroken

1924 Grandma Sheila born, Evelyne sees her as stealing Laure's place

1924–1929 Evelyne is miserable in the US, travels to Europe (but *not* Scotland) often to see Laure

1929 Anne is born after Evelyne confides to Ian about Laure

1930 Anne dies, Evelyne blames Grandmom Sheila

1930 Sheila sent to DP for six months, starts sketching there, loves DP, becomes friends with Laure

1930s–1962 Sheila goes back to DP on several occasions, lastly on the trip in '62, sees Laure. Happy. Sketches *Demain dès l'Aube* in stones—memorial to Anne

1962 Sheila dies in Orly crash in June

1963–68 My mom, Mary Swan, wants to follow Sheila's sketch pad around Europe and find out about the Dwelling Place and Evelyne and Sheila's reactions to it

1968 Goes to DP in '68 with Rachel—talks to Laure and "gets it" about *Demain dès l'Aube*

1968 Has watershed spiritual experience at DP—Mom promises to live for God and wait for Daddy

1968 Telegram ruins everything. Daddy MIA. Rachel and Mom leave DP. DP signifies loss to Mom. She never goes back.

I concluded that Mom needed to go back because she wanted to close something. She'd had a spiritual high, but then everything had come crashing down on her. Heart healed, heart broken. If she needed to go back there, I wanted to get her there. Suddenly it was more than a family obligation. It was my mission. We had to get to the Dwelling Place. *Before it was too late.*

Mom peeked her head into my room a little while later and said, "I feel like painting, Ellie. Not just sketching, but painting. Isn't that just grand?"

"It is, Mom! It's wonderful. May I help you get the easel out?"

"Sure, we'll put it in the family room by the window. It's the perfect spot for inspiration, looking at the beach."

As I went to gather her supplies, I was still thinking about her painting *Letters From Vietnam* and the one of the riots in the Latin Quarter—she called it simply *Mai Soixante-huit,* as that wild month of May 1968 was known in France. Both of them were hanging in the High Museum. The raw emotion she'd displayed in each painting did not leave the viewer indifferent. I wondered what raw emotion Mary Swan Middleton would paint today, sitting there in her white button-down and jeans, a scarf wrapped loosely around her bare skull.

At around five that afternoon, as she sat painting in the family room, Mom asked, "Ellie, do you think you could help me get my stuff out on the beach? I'd love to work on this painting with my feet in the sand, the way I used to do down here."

Pleasantly surprised, I said, "Of course, Mom."

In only a few hours, her painting had already begun to take a shape, a soul, yes, the beginnings of that raw emotion. The painting showed the beach and the ocean, peaceful and calm, a bright sky with the sun's rays turning the ocean into a million tiny shimmering sapphires. But far out in the ocean there was a dark, foreboding cloud. The painting was obviously just in its beginning stages, but I felt immediately that it would become something fine and important, perhaps her best work to date. I chided myself on my silly emotional response to the colors on her canvas as I carried it downstairs and out onto the beach, stretching wide and smooth before me. Mom's chair sat firmly on the hard sand, the easel equally firmly planted in front of her. I put a small wrought-iron folding table beside her where she set her paints and palette.

"Perfect, Ellie. Oh, it is absolutely perfect!"

I agreed. "I'll just take a little walk and be back soon."

"Take your time, Ellie. I could stay here forever."

The sand was still warm from the sun, the tide coming in, the seagulls scattering in front of me as I walked briskly down the beach, far from the ocean's reach. I was thinking about Mom's family, all the secrets, and then I started thinking about Ben and feeling rather aggravated with myself for the way my mind kept replaying the last scene of our biking episode, with his hands covering mine. I must have walked for fifteen or twenty minutes, maybe even thirty, concentrating on every encounter I'd had in the last week with Ben.

Suddenly it was as if God covered the sky with His hand, and the peaceful late afternoon blue turned to a shadow of gray. It took me no more than ten seconds to register that a storm was brewing, coming up quickly from the east, but by the time I'd turned around to head back to the house, big slow raindrops had already started falling from the sky. I broke into a jog and then a full-out run, imagining Mom feebly trying to gather her paints and easel in the midst of the storm. The rain increased in intensity, the big drops becoming small pelting ammunition.

By the time the Hamilton House came into view, I was sopping wet and my lungs were burning. Mom was standing in front of the oil painting, bald-headed, her shirt and jeans soaked and her face turned upward, catching raindrops. Her eyes were closed, and she was smiling.

"Sorry, Mom. The rain came out of nowhere," I gasped. "Here, let me help you."

She took her paintbrush and dabbed it on the canvas and said, "Oh, don't worry, Ellie. I love painting in the rain. It reminds me of happy memories." She seemed completely oblivious to the fact that the rain was going to ruin her painting.

"Mom, let me get the painting inside. Quickly. After all, it could be your next masterpiece."

She began slowly picking up her paints and brushes. I gathered the painting in one arm and the easel in the other as we made our way back to the house.

"Don't worry, Ellie. Oil and water don't mix. The rain can't hurt the canvas or the paint. You'll see, Ellie. The rain will be an important part of making this 'a masterpiece.'" Mom smiled at me, her face wet and glistening.

I fixed her a cup of tea while she changed, after I had secured the painting on the easel in the family room. Sure enough, it looked unharmed.

"She's had one of the hardest lives of anyone I know," Rachel had said. *"But she isn't complaining. Not even with cancer eating up her body."*

No, my mother wasn't complaining. My mother was a painting in the storm, convinced down to the last fibers of canvas and the last drop of paint on the brush that the rain was an important part of the making of a masterpiece.

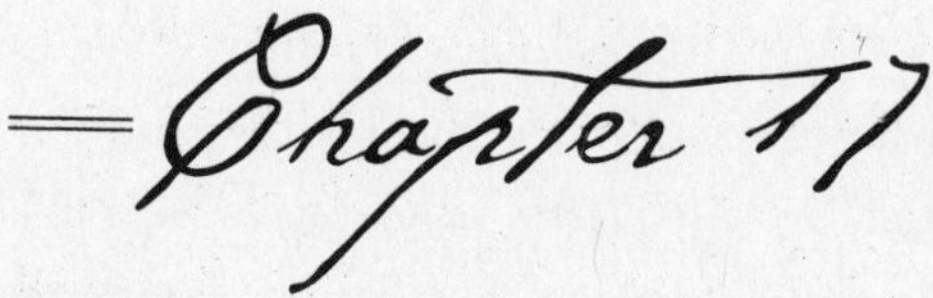

Vietnam has always been my teacher. . . . I went with all the answers and left with only questions.

—LAURA PALMER, *SHRAPNEL IN THE HEART*

Later in the evening, after a light supper of soup and crackers, I was lying in bed, listening to the rain and watching the Braves game on ESPN. Mom came into the bedroom and I glanced over at her, motioning with my eyes for her to join me. She climbed into bed beside me and we snuggled under the covers, the rain on the roof making a slapping sound that contrasted with the screaming and applause as the Braves scored a run in hot Atlanta.

We watched the game in complete silence. Once Mom got up, and when she came back in the room she was carrying a bag of Cheetos and a glass of Coke.

"Here you go, sweetie."

"Thanks, Mom." I wasn't about to tell her that I was in the process of giving up junk food. Not when, for the first time in the ten days I'd been with her, she felt physically well enough to do a simple motherly chore she had done so willingly for so many years.

"What inning?" she asked when she was back in bed and munching on a Cheeto.

"Top of the seventh. Braves are trailing the Mets by two."

“ ’Bout time to bring in Smoltz,” she said.

“Hey, Mom! Since when are you up on baseball?”

She patted my hand. “Way back before the Braves were worth much, your granddad would take Uncle Jimmy and Aunt Lucy and me to watch them in the brand-new stadium, soon after they came to Atlanta. Those were very happy times.” Then she said as an afterthought, “Your father and I usually take in a few games every season.”

I didn’t exactly feel accused, but I did find it surprising that I’d never noticed how much Mom knew about baseball, how happy she seemed to be watching the game with me and making comments about her favorite players.

By ten o’clock the game was over—the Braves had won—and Mom had gone downstairs to bed. At least I thought she had. But as I was undressing, she knocked on the door and poked her head in.

“You okay, Mom?”

“Yes. Fine. But I, well, I thought I’d let you read these letters—one of your father’s letters from Vietnam, before he was MIA and then—well, another one. Don’t worry—there are just two of them—the ones I keep in my Bible. The others are back in a box at the house on Beverly.” She placed the letters on the bed. “I just thought it would help you get a picture of that time—what your dad was living through.”

“Why do you keep them in your Bible, Mom?”

“Just as a reminder. Sometimes when I feel discouraged, I take out these letters and read them, and I remember that the story isn’t over yet. No matter what it looks like. It isn’t over.”

She gave me a kiss and said, “Good night, sweetheart.”

I wasn’t sure I wanted to read Daddy’s letters, wasn’t sure I *ought* to read them, to hear Daddy’s tender words to his Swannee. The first letter was written on thin paper, and Daddy’s cursive was tiny and cramped, as if he couldn’t get his thoughts down fast enough.

June 6, 1968

Sweet Swan, my Goose,

How I miss you! It is like hell here. I keep counting the days. 340 till I see you again. Imagining you at Hilton Head, walking beside me, holding me, well, it's what keeps me half sane. Thinking of you and then being around Amos. Thank goodness for Amos.

I've told you about him—my radio man. He keeps me singing and laughing and praying. You'll meet him one day, Swan. Never knew a deeper guy than good ole uneducated Amos. Big—probably 6'4". Blackest skin you ever saw. He says I'm freckled and scrawny, and compared to him, well, I guess I am. He's twenty and already married and has a little girl and another baby on the way. The way he talks about his Linda and little Susie, it makes me miss you all the more. I can't wait until we're married and sharing a nice bed together and trying our hardest to make some kids. . . .

He's one of only two black men in my platoon. From LouEEZiana, as he pronounces it, a sharecropper's son. He came from a family of eleven kids, and all of them worked from dawn till dusk in the fields. Didn't get any schooling from the time he was thirteen. But he loved to read and kind of just educated himself, and he sounds like a born preacher to me.

Amos's older sister was beaten during the Freedom Rides of '61. Clubbed with a baseball bat in Montgomery, Alabama. He joined her for the summer of '64 in Mississippi, helping the poor. He rode a bus to Washington to take part in Martin Luther King's march last year.

And last week he went back under fire to pull out a wounded soldier. I don't know how he didn't get his head blown off, but he's here. And he's a real comfort to me. When the men are getting depressed and fearful, he'll just start singing that song, you know, "We shall overcome someday . . ." I know it sounds funny, it being sung over here in the trenches. But somehow it gives us hope.

Amos is a mystery to me, Mary Swan. He's got some kind of deep-down peace. Doesn't complain. Just does the nastiest chores and somehow gets the men to come along. God put him in my unit for a reason. I think it was to give me the courage to keep going.

The men in my platoon are as varied as you can imagine. Good men, some so young. Two are only seventeen. Danny, Fort, Eddie, Jim, Gerwin, Dick, Gene, "Limbo," Amos, Tucker, Roe, Billy, JD, Daft . . . I could write a chapter about each one. It's strange how quickly you learn about others, how strongly you bond, how essential trust is on the field. For us—the ground troops—everything is intense, how we fight and how we live when we're not fighting. We come to the field naïve, and (if we're honest) afraid, and then we grow up fast. Way too fast. Jim told me last night, "You've got to squeeze a lifetime into a few months—just in case you never get another chance to live."

It sure is mixed up over here. Every man I know is counting every day. But the problem is that so many aren't making it past the first month or two. We can see that this war isn't going to be won. We want to leave. It is a terrible burden in a soldier's heart, to let yourself begin to question your superiors. . . .

June 10, 1968
Swan, sweetheart,

I'm hurting in my heart tonight. Three of my men, boys all of them, died today on a stinking hill. We pulled Roe and Tucker to safety and were going back for the other three when they opened up again with fire. And we lost them. I lost them. Three boys who'd never been away from home before they went into the military. Scared young boys. How I hate this war!

I wish I could really describe what it is like here. I go to bed afraid lots of nights. And I don't think I'll wake up the next day. Amos doesn't seem afraid. He chides me and says if I have God in my life, I'd better enjoy His peace that passes understanding; otherwise what's the point of having it? He's right, I'm sure, but many nights my stomach is in knots.

And you have to concentrate really, really hard on the task at hand and do it almost without thinking so as not to lose hope. So as not to say to yourself, "What the hell is the point of all this death?" Sometimes the threat of Communism and all the big political words and speeches seem like an empty chasm in the laughing mouth of Satan.

June 13, 1968
Dearest Goose,

I got your first three letters, finally. I think I've read each one a hundred times. Amos said, "If ya don't quit holding those letters they're gonna disintegrate in yore hands, boy." But holding them, keeping them in my pocket, makes you seem so much closer. I need to feel you close, sweet Swan.

Thank you for the cookies. When I shared them with the guys in the platoon, well, two of them started crying like babies. Said their moms used to bake them the exact same cookies. When we stop long enough to think, we're all so homesick we can hardly stand it.

I'm sorry about Paris. We heard something about the riots. I'm sorry it's been so difficult to be with Rachel. Don't get down on yourself, sweet Swan. We've seen Rachel changing for several years now. Hang in there.

The other night Amos and I were talking about our lives back home. He said Linda was the "pertiest" gal in the whole school and he fell in love with her in seventh grade. He had to quit school after that, but she kept going and he was afraid she wouldn't want anything to do with him if she got an education and he didn't. But she loved him. I think they knew they were right for each other at the age of fourteen or fifteen. That's one thing we have in common. I knew right away when I met you that you were the one I wanted to spend the rest of my life with, Swan. That seems like so many worlds away now. I pray you'll still want me when I get back.

I told Amos how for as long as I can remember, all I wanted was to follow you around for the rest of my life. He thought that was funny, and he laughed when I told him that I gave you my class ring as a temporary engagement ring. He says he didn't have any money to get a ring for Linda either. Finally got her something real simple and cheap. "I'd be mighty proud to give her my class ring," he told me. "That would prove I'm educated." Amos is always asking me about what I've studied. He reads anything he can get his hands on.

"You're one of the most educated people I know," I told him. "You know the Bible and you understand people and life."

June 17, 1968
Dear Swan,

My sergeant, Rick, calm, cool-headed Rick, died today—in the hospital.

We ran a mission two days ago, and it turned really bad. We were shorthanded, fighting with fewer men than ever before. My men and I, we were all stuck on this mountain and just about as good as left for dead. We knew our chances of getting out of there stunk to high heaven. So we just hunkered down together. Amos was out there encouraging the troops, manning the artillery. A couple of the boys were crying.

JD and Daft were hurt awful bad. Bleeding to death. There was a pungent smell of death everywhere. I had run over to haul JD out of the crater the artillery shell had made. I vomited when I saw his face—his ear was missing. I'd just pulled him behind the boulder and was running for Daft when the mortar hit me. It threw me in the air and flopped me down twenty feet away. I knew I was a goner. Still, I had the soldier's instinct to scramble, to try to find cover. But there wasn't any cover, and the enemy was coming in hard. That's when I looked up and saw ole Amos coming for me. Foolish boy, sweetest man I've ever known, coming at me with his amazing stubborn determination. He picked me up and said, "You ain't gonna die, boy. Ain't gonna let you die. Come on, Robbie, gotta git you home." But he was crying, sobbing when he saw me all twisted and the other boys just lying there dead. Rick was running out to help us both when the mortar struck him from behind, blew him in the air. He came down in a heap, and Amos set me down and went and got Rick.

"We's in a mess, Amos," Rick was saying, spitting up blood. He looked at me. "Gonna meet my Maker today, Amos, just like you been saying. I'm ready. But you go on, don't you give up, boys. You can make it, Robbie. Go on, think of Swan. And Amos, you get home to Linda and Susie. You hear me . . ."

And they were shooting around us and Rick was bleeding and gasping for air and dying. And we were pulling him to shelter and he was saying to just leave him to die.

We got him out and finally the helicopters came in and rescued what was left of us, took the wounded to the hospital. But Rick didn't make it. Died this morning.

I was shaken up but not really injured. Gene said it was my stinkin' luck to get blown up to the sky and fall back down in one piece. "If you'd lost an arm or a leg, at least you'd be going home." He did lose a leg and he's on his way home, soon as he's strong enough to travel.

Oh, Swan, I'm so sorry I always write about such depressing things. It's just that everything is really bad. But never forget the most important thing, Goose. No matter what, no matter how bad things seem, I love you. I'll always love you.

Your faithful Boy Scout and lover,
Robbie

It didn't seem like the news from Vietnam could get much worse, so it was with hesitation that I picked up the second letter, one thin sheet of onionskin paper, written again in Daddy's small slanted cursive, but written slowly and deliberately, because there were ink spots where he must have stopped to consider his next words. The paper had been torn and taped back together, and the tape was now yellowed. There were several smudges that looked to me as if a teardrop, a perfect teardrop, had splashed onto the paper and washed some of the writing away. I set the letter on the bed in front of me, smoothed it out carefully, and just looked at it. Finally I picked it up and began to read.

Sweet Swan, precious lady,

How I wish you didn't have to read this letter! How I've prayed against it! How I've imagined another happier scenario. A long, long life with you beside me, in my arms. But it is not to be. I am not here any longer. I've already gone over to the other side, and you know, sweet Swan, that I am not suffering there. So now it's you who has to bear the burden of the pain. You who wake without hope, you who must pick up pieces and start over.

Letters are strange things, aren't they, Swan? I am dead as you read but alive, so very much alive, as I write. And in this heart of mine, I tell you there is a love as big and wide as that ocean that stretched before us at Hilton Head. There is a wild man bursting with energy to show you his love. Begging for time to live our love together. Begging the Lord for time.

I am alive, and my heart is aching with the pain of loving you. The distance, the separation, the longing to reach out and say the things that will make you smile. Your all-American Boy Scout. I hope you will always smile when you think of me. Don't think of what the war did. It cannot really take me away.

But Swannee, my lover and friend, I am not coming back to live our dreams together. I am so very sorry. I am not coming back, and you must go on. You must live for both of us. And you must BE. Be yourself with all the God-given talent He has stuffed inside you. Use it, Swan! Go on with it! You can!

I know you don't want to think of this, can't imagine it now, but let yourself grieve and then, dearest one, let yourself love again. Mourn and cry and hurt, but go beyond it. If God did not plan for us to share life together, then He must have someone wonderful picked out for you. Don't be afraid. Don't feel that you are betraying me. It breaks my heart to write it now, with me so very alive and well and longing so desperately for you. But do it, Swan. Let yourself love again.

My love for you will last
into eternity.
Robbie

I held the letter to my chest and cried real tears for my mother and father. I cried as if I didn't know the end of the story, didn't know that Daddy had, obviously, finally made it home. I sat there in a trance for ten minutes or more, unable to escape from the vivid, violent images that flashed through my mind. Finally I shook myself, got out of bed and stretched the way Hindsight does after a nap, and stood with my head resting on the windowpane in my bedroom.

The words on these pages were written by my father, of that I was sure. But the sense of the words, the violence and death they represented, seemed to belong in a movie, not in my parents' real life. Not here, where, when I closed my eyes, I could hear the calming drone of the ocean punctuated only occasionally by a gull's cry and a frog's chirping and the rush of the tide onto the shore.

Chapter 18

Soldier, rest! Thy warfare o'er,
Sleep the sleep that knows not breaking;
Dream of battled fields no more,
Days of danger, nights of waking.

—SIR WALTER SCOTT, *SOLDIER, REST!*

I didn't sleep well. I tossed and turned and dreamed of Vietnam and Daddy lying face up in a rice paddy, and Mom reading his letter, the one that announced his death and encouraged her to get on with life. When I awoke, I lay in bed for a long time, just letting my parents' lives soak into my spirit.

I was mad at God. Furious with Him. This was the God of love that my parents trusted intimately? Why had He made them suffer so terribly? Why had He ripped apart their worlds? Even though they had eventually been reunited, there would always be those ugly wounds of confusion, of pain, of death. Why, why, after all the heartache, had Mom and Dad chosen to keep believing in this God?

They didn't see Him as indifferent, or far off. They saw Him as a personal God, one who was "intimately acquainted with all their ways." I remembered memorizing that verse from the Psalms when I was a kid—and hating it.

He knew about their scars; He had allowed them to happen. How could they believe in that kind of God? And how could believing in a God who would let your mother die in a plane crash and you suffer with an eating disorder and your fiancé be lost in Vietnam and come home with an eye missing and big, ugly raw scars, how could believing in that kind of God bring you peace and joy and hope and love?

And if He knew about their scars, He knew about mine. Right on the tail of my anger at God came a surging anger at Mom. Again. Anger at her for swallowing this naïve belief in an all-caring God, anger because it was her faith that had made me agonize about what was wrong with me—she could accept the accident, but I never could. But I didn't want to dwell on those feelings, not with Mom so close, not with conversation finally beginning. It surprised me that my rage was still so close to the surface. I wanted to bury it deeper or, better yet, chase it away.

I'm not sure if it was my emotional state or the fact that I wasn't eating much, but I suddenly felt a terrible gnawing in my stomach. I looked at the clock. Almost ten. I went to the bathroom and threw water on my face, then I padded out into the family room where Mom was seated, painting.

"Morning, Ellie. I fixed you some breakfast."

"Morning," I yawned. An English muffin and a cup of coffee were sitting on the kitchen counter. "Thanks, Mom."

She turned around and smiled. "It's my pleasure—to finally feel like doing something."

I walked up behind her, looking over her shoulder at the painting, and for some reason, as I stood there, I let my chin rest lightly on her head and my hand rest on her shoulder. She brought up her hand, the one not holding the brush, and patted my hand. A split second of intimacy.

"Looks great, Mom. Keep working."

I shuffled back to the bedroom, and that's when I heard her sneeze.

A little ordinary sneeze that struck terror in my heart. I rushed back into the family room, fully expecting to see blood gushing from her nose.

She looked up. "Honey, are you all right?"

"Yeah. Yeah, um, I just got a little worried when . . ."

"Oh." She smiled. "When I sneezed. I understand, but don't worry, all is fine. It was just a tiny little sneeze. I feel fine."

She looked fine, much better than fine, so I just nodded and went into the bedroom, chiding myself that the gore of Vietnam was causing me to project things into the present. I had not checked my e-mail the day before, so I turned on the laptop, watching the color come to my screen. I downloaded my messages and then unplugged the laptop and brought it into bed with me. While I nibbled on the English muffin and sipped my coffee, I read my e-mails.

Dear Ellie,

My brother and I are having a good time together. Mrs. Rose says hurry home, the cats are fine but she's lonely. She says to tell your mommy hello from her. You can say hi from me too. I hope she is feeling better.

Turns out that Mark likes looking at the web sites too and he isn't so bad in chess. I still beat him every game, but he doesn't get as mad as when we were little. I took him to the Varsity—I paid for it all. Then we walked around Piedmont Park and I saw some of the girls you play softball with.

I went to a Braves game last night with Mark. Smoltz came in in the 8th and won it for them. It was way cool.

Guess what? Mark doesn't have a girlfriend anymore. He's a pretty nice guy. Maybe you'd like to meet him.

Oh, I forgot to tell you that Mrs. Rose said a big black man came looking for you yesterday. Isn't that funny how she says it?

Bye,
Nate

Dear Ellie,

Mom has reserved the church. Timothy has been gone all week, so I've been out hunting dresses after work. I wish you were with me. When you get back, we'll go together.

Ellie—I'm scared to death. I hope he really loves me. How will I ever really know? I wish you were here so we could talk. I'm having all these dark thoughts. All of a sudden I don't trust Timothy anymore. For no reason. Well, for the same reason as always. I don't trust any man.

I hope I don't drive him away.

Lots of love,
Megan

Dear Ellie,

Hope everything is going okay at the beach. I just wanted to tell you thanks for being there with Mom. I know you had to rearrange your schedule at the last minute and it was a pain.

Thanks for doing it. Tell Mom hi from all of us. Tell her Bobby drew her a picture to put on the fridge. Homemade finger paints. The biggest mess you ever saw. Not a good idea to do with a one-year-old! Then he wanted to do one for you too. So they're both waiting here on MY fridge.

I've been wondering, Ellie. Is dark blue still your favorite color?

Love,
Abbie

Dear Ellie,

Hope everything's cool down there—or hot. You know what I mean. Panthers won on Wednesday night—barely. We missed you. Jan is not "in her element" as catcher (that's how she puts it—you know Jan). But if things keep going okay, it looks like we're in line for regionals again. So get your tan (ha, ha!) and hurry back.

Hope your mom is doing better.

Ciao,
Sharon

Hindsight had hopped onto the bed and was pushing her claws into the side of my thigh, obviously annoyed that my laptop was occupying her rightful spot. I carefully set the computer on the bed beside me and picked her up, holding her under the tummy and gently scratching her between the ears. After an initial scowl, she settled in my lap and began to purr.

Reading the e-mails made me long to get back to my little apartment and see Nate and Mrs. Rose and the cats. I wanted to play a good game of softball with the Panthers and help Megan pick out a wedding dress—or at least talk about her wedding worries while we sipped our coffee at the Flying Biscuit. I even had a fleeting desire to stop by Abbie's house and see little Bobby and his artwork.

But I still had ten days at Hilton Head with Mom.

I decided to call Daddy, and dialed his number at work. His secretary answered and put me through. "Hey, Daddy, how are you?"

"Ellie! Good! How are you doing?"

"Fine. Mom and I are doing fine."

"Yes, I talked to your mother a little earlier this morning. Sounds like she's feeling stronger, even painting a little."

"Yeah, she is. I mean, she tires very quickly, but at least she gets up some. She's walked once or twice on the beach and she's painting. She even fixed me breakfast this morning."

"Wonderful."

Then I whispered so that Mom would not hear, "But she's got a cold, Dad."

"Oh. She didn't mention that to me."

"It's nothing—just a sniffle, but she sneezed this morning. I know it sounds stupid, but that scared me. What should I do?"

Daddy cleared his throat, then said, "I don't think you need to do anything, Ellie. Except make sure she stays out of the rain. She told me how wonderful she felt painting in the rain, but that's not what she needs."

"I'm sorry, Daddy. It was my fault. I was walking, and when I got back, it was pouring and she was already sopping wet."

"Ellie." Daddy's voice took on a rare stern tone. "Your mother is an adult. She chose to stand there in the rain; it wasn't your fault. I'll call her later and remind her of the doctor's orders. Don't worry."

"Okay, Dad. I'll try not to." I thought it was time to change the subject. "How's work?"

"Okay. Got approval for a few new projects near Grant Park—ones that will favor the residents who've been there for years. What about you—not too bored? Mom says that Ben Abrams has come over a couple of times."

"Yeah. We go for bike rides. It's been good to catch up with him."

"That's great. And just remember—what you're doing for your mother is making a difference."

"I hope so. Anyway, are you gonna come down soon?"

"I'm taking off some time next week. I'll see you on Wednesday night, late. I have a meeting and then I'll drive down."

"Daddy?"

"Yes, Ellie?"

"I . . . uh . . . I can't wait to see you."

"Me too. Thanks, Mae Mae, for everything."

"Bye."

I had been one second away from asking him about Vietnam. Even on the phone, hearing his voice, I was picturing him in his army uniform, young and hopeful at first, until almost daily, all the hope was rubbed out by death. Grim, horrible death. I wondered if it were true—if even now, thirty-five years later, he thought about it all the time, the terrible things of Vietnam.

A gruesome scene from a movie flashed before my eyes, and I wondered what my father's years of missing in action were like—if Daddy had lived through what those POWs had, if he'd been locked in a bamboo cage, hanging above the ground, deprived of food and water, tortured, gradually losing his mind. I understood suddenly why you would never talk about all those things, why you would never be the same, how you would maybe either go crazy or spend the rest of your life desperately trying to create something clean and good.

What had it been like when he had finally gotten home? Did Mom still love him, with his missing eye and his ugly red welts and all the internal wounds that must have festered for so long? Did I have the right to ask these questions? Maybe when Daddy came down to the beach next week, we could take a long walk and he would tell me the truth.

I thought about Mom's paintings, still propped at various places in the family room. They showed doubt. Doubt and anger and disappointment and despair. Every one of those emotions struck me as absolutely necessary and real. Not perfect, not smooth or easy or flattering.

Mom was real with God, and I was almost positive she was that way with Daddy. And Rachel. And given the time, she'd probably move into that type of relationship with Ben—no longer the mother-protector-savior figure, but a "fellow traveler" or something, she'd probably say. But she couldn't be real with me, because I kept her at arm's length.

I thought about it long and hard. There were only so many people you could let get that close. I'd let Megan in. Period. She was the only one who deserved to be let in, who had shown me she could be trusted with the rotten things in my life. Thinking about these things made me miss her, and I dialed her number a few minutes later.

"How are you, Meggie?"

"Okay." Her voice was flat.

"Having doubts, girl? I got your e-mail."

"Yeah. But not doubts about Timothy. He's great. It's me. It's me, Ellie. I don't want him to go through life with a possessed woman. Possessed or obsessed or something. You're the one with the big vocabulary."

"Why are you feeling like this? What started it?"

"The mirrors."

"Oh."

"It's just my trying on the wedding dresses and looking at myself in the mirror, always looking at myself, and always hearing the sales ladies saying the same thing—almost whispering it to my mom. 'She should be a model. She's perfect.' I'm not perfect, Ellie! I am so screwed up. When I hear that, all the old memories come back, and I want to get out a hammer and smash mirrors again. I know it's insane. The poor women are only trying to sell me a wedding dress! I thought I was past this. Poor Timothy."

"But Meg—haven't you talked to him about all of that?"

"He knows some, but I'm afraid to get into all of it. I'm afraid he'll see how weird I am and not want me anymore. But if he only finds out later, he'll leave then and it'll be worse."

"You have to talk about it again, Meggie," I stated emphatically. "Talk.. Timothy loves you."

"But I don't know how to bring it up."

"Believe me, Meggie, I understand. It may sound crazy, but I feel the same way with Mom. I don't know how to really talk. We've started, but . . . it's like walking in minefields in Vietnam. You're afraid it'll suddenly explode in your face. I couldn't have anything else explode in my face, Meg. I couldn't live through that again."

"Ellie, will we ever be over this stuff?"

"I dunno." I paused and then blurted out what was on my mind. "Megan, it's hard to hear about some of the awful things Mom and Daddy have been through."

"Like what?"

"Oh, so much. Vietnam, for sure. It's all running around in my head. The war and Mom's family problems and her eating disorder and civil rights and then my accident. It gets confusing. And on top of all that, Megan, she's got a cold."

"Well, call her doctor. Tell him."

"Dad knows. He said not to worry."

"Then don't. Chill. One day at a time. Eat your vegetables and chill."

"Yeah. I'll try. Thanks. You too, okay?" I wished I could reach through the phone and give Megan a hug, do something to get her mind off mirrors, off the past. "Hey, did I tell you that Ben Abrams is down here? You know, Rachel's son?"

"Yeah, you mentioned it in an e-mail."

"He's gotten all religious, which is kind of a pain. But he's pretty cool to be with too."

"What is that supposed to mean, Ellie?"

"Nothing. Who knows? Anyway, Meggie, stay away from the mirrors. I'll be home in a week or so. We'll look at dresses, and I'll tell you that you look fat and ugly in every one, if you want."

"Thanks, Ellie." She gave a little chuckle. "I'd like that a lot."

When I hung up the phone, I went and stood in the bathroom beside my bedroom. It was a big room with marble floors and a huge mirror all across one wall above two nice sinks. I leaned in close and examined my face. It was losing that bloated look that had been there since I'd gained all the weight. The scar, though, had not changed. It still ran from my left ear down to my mouth, still was oddly smooth and red; my mouth still curved down unnaturally. I pulled my hair in front of my face, as I'd done a thousand times as a girl, so that the lower left side was concealed. I lifted my eyebrows seductively, looking deep into my green eyes.

"Who will dare to look beyond this face? Who will forget the scar?" I had thought of it a hundred times—breaking a mirror, any mirror, shattering it as Megan had done. But breaking it carefully, if that was possible, so that only the bottom left corner was shattered. So that when I looked into it, the scar was lost in the shattered glass and everywhere else was my true reflection.

I leaned over the sink, resting my elbows on the marble counter and stretching the skin on my face with each hand, pulling it hard, so that my mouth lifted and the scar seemed to fade into my normal skin. I tried to imagine Megan standing beside me, both of us reaching into the looking glass of our lives and trying to repair something. Instead, the image that flashed into my mind was of Mom and Rachel, sitting on a stone wall in Scotland, dangling their legs and smiling, carefree at last.

I found the dog sniffing through the trash that had spilled out of the big trash urn outside of Publix grocery store when I was taking my shopping cart back to the car that Saturday afternoon. He had no collar on, and when he heard me approaching, he turned around, his tail tucked tight between his back legs and his eyes filled with fear. He was young, probably no more than a year, and still had a puppy look about him. His eyes were the color of rust, perfectly matching his long furry coat. His face was that of a Brittany spaniel, although he was a bit larger than typical for the breed. I sized him up in an instant: a beautiful, mistreated mutt.

"Hey, fella," I said, holding my hand out. "I won't hurt you." I opened a box of crackers I'd purchased and emptied some onto the concrete in front of the dog. Without hesitation he began gulping them down, barely taking time to chew.

"Come on, pups. Come on," I called. He stood far off, watching me suspiciously as I unloaded the groceries from the cart into the trunk of Mom's Mazda and then returned the cart to the spot marked for it. "Come here," I cooed, holding a few crackers in my hand.

He followed me to the car.

"Come on in, pups. I won't hurt you, fella." I opened the passenger-side door, pushed up the seat, and placed crackers on the backseat.

The dog approached hesitantly, legs stiff, and poked his nose in the car, his tail wagging tentatively. He reached with his head and was able to retrieve a cracker with his tongue. But the others were impossible to get without actually stepping into the car.

I whistled softly. He looked over at me, wagged his tail again, hesitated. He scrambled a little and then hopped into the car and snatched the crackers. When he'd finished them, he looked back at me, wanting more. I complied. Then I shut the door and went around to the driver's side and quickly hopped in. The dog was standing on the backseat, hunched down and trembling.

"It's okay now, pups. Don't you worry." He lost his balance when I drove out of the parking lot, and then I saw him peeing on the leather upholstery. "If you sit down, it'll all be easier, silly mutt."

I drove straight to the animal shelter. I'd been there several times before. It was called the Hilton Head Humane Association and was located, of all things, on Humane Way, near the Cross Island Parkway. It took me a good fifteen minutes to get there, and by that time, the dog was whining pitifully.

I picked him up and carried him into the small building. "Found him by the trash cans at Publix," I explained to the woman at the front desk.

"Oh, the poor thing. Look at him. Pitiful."

"Have you had any calls for a lost pup?"

"Not a one. He's pretty, ain't he? Skinny as all get out, but pretty, with a soft coat and sweet eyes. Hey, fella. Want to stay with me awhile?" The woman looked up at me.

"I was thinking I'd take him home with me. You could give me a call if anyone stops by asking about him."

She nodded. "Sure. I'll do that. But don't expect no call. One look at him, and I can tell you the story. His owners brought him to the beach, got tired of dealing with him, and left him at the grocery store. Ain't no one gonna be calling for this boy."

I borrowed a few towels and a sponge and cleaned out Mom's car, spraying it with some type of ammonia solution. Then I put the mutt in the backseat again, with strict instructions to be a good dog.

When I got back from the grocery store, Mom was seated in front of her easel, painting, as she looked out the window in the family room toward the beach. I pulled up a chair and sat down beside her. "I brought you a surprise, Mom," I said.

"A surprise?"

"Yeah." I handed her a pint-sized carton of Midnight Cookies and Cream.

"Oh, Ellie! Thank you." She scooted her chair back and grabbed my hand. "Looks delicious. I'll fix a bowl for each of us."

"Sure," I said. "I'll be right back." Two minutes later, I was leading the trembling dog, complete with the leash and collar I'd purchased at the animal shelter, over to where Mom sat at the family room table.

"This is actually the surprise I was talking about!"

"Ellie! Oh, what a sweet, sweet puppy. Look at him. He reminds me of your Uncle Jimmy's dog, Muffin, that we had when I was a girl." She came and knelt by the dog and started petting him on the head. He trembled slightly, tail stuck between his legs, and then began licking Mom's outstretched hand.

"I checked at the animal shelter. No one has reported a missing dog. Found him outside of Publix."

"Oh, isn't he a sweetie?"

I knelt down beside Mom, both of us petting the dog, and asked, "Can we keep him, Momma?"

Mom looked at me with a sudden glimmer in her eyes, a soft smile crossing her face. I had asked the same question a dozen times as a girl, when Trixie and I would return from one of our visits to the Humane Society, nervously exhibiting the stray cat or dog we'd brought home with us.

There were tears in her eyes when Mom answered, "Yes, sweetie. We'll keep him. Of course we'll keep him."

We dubbed him Rusty, for the color of his fur. He remained quiet and trembling for all of ten minutes. Then he devoured all the food we set before him. When Hindsight came into the room, tail held high and twitching slowly, Rusty began barking furiously. Hindsight spat and hissed and hopped onto the couch, and Rusty slid across the floor, sticking his nose up at the cat, tail wagging, body wiggling, hair standing on his back. Hindsight swatted him in the nose with a paw, and he howled as if he'd nearly been killed and skulked off to lick his wounds. And Mom and I laughed hard. Together.

That's when I decided to put Mom's paintings back in the garage closet, safely protected from the livestock. Mom helped me stack the paintings carefully as I made seven trips up and down the steps.

On my sixth trip back into the family room, Mom was caressing one particular painting with her eyes. "I think I'd like to keep this one out, down in my room," she said.

It was the last painting in Mom's chronological order, and it was as strange as *Red Diaper Babies* and *Addiction*. But I didn't ask her about it because she looked as if she might start crying again. And I was afraid if she started crying, her cold would get worse. So I took it down to her bedroom and set it on the vanity, where she could look at it when she was lying in bed.

Thirty minutes later, Hindsight had retreated to the bedroom, and I was sitting on the floor in the family room, my back against the wall and Rusty's head lying across my lap. Mom had stretched out on the couch. As I stroked the mutt, I tossed out a question, hoping to sound curious but not too prying. "So, Mom, why do you want to go back to the Dwelling Place?"

She didn't answer immediately, so I added, "Is it because of how you left it, in the summer of 1968—with the telegram and Daddy missing? Do you want to go back now that things are better?"

Mom turned on her side, readjusted her scarf, and asked, "You really want to know?"

"Yes. Sure I do."

"I wanted to go there for you, Ellie. Not for me."

"Why in the world would you want it for me? I don't care about it." I spoke too quickly, defensively.

"I thought maybe if you went there, heard the history, knew the lives of the people, maybe you'd be more interested . . ."

"In what?"

"In God."

"Oh, Mom. Not that again."

"I'm sorry I haven't known how to make you see Him, Ellie. I tried in my own way and I failed. I know the Lord doesn't need my help. I guess I was just conniving again. All these years I've prayed that you'd see the truth, if not through Dad and me, then through someone else. . . ."

Through someone else. Her words brought me up short. But Mom was still talking.

"The Dwelling Place isn't a place, sweetie, it's a person—the Lord." She turned her eyes to me hesitantly. "I know you don't like me to talk about it, but—" she shrugged and gave a half smile—"you did ask."

"You're right, Mom. I asked." I wanted to change the subject. One glance at my watch, and I knew just what to say. "Hey, I've gotta get to the church—I promised Ben I'd come early to help him get things ready for the cookout. Do you want me to fix you something for dinner?"

"No, sweetie. I'll be fine. I hope you have a wonderful time."

"You'll be okay here, with Rusty and Hindsight?"

"I'll be more than okay. I'll be happy as a bug in a rug." She did look happy, sitting on the couch with her knees pulled under her and an oversized sweater—probably one of Daddy's—pulled over her skinny shoulders. "I was hoping to paint the sun setting."

"I'll have my cell phone with me in case you need to reach me."

"Perfect. Now go on and have a grand time. And tell Ben hi."

When I left the house fifteen minutes later, Mom had taken my place on the floor and was cradling Rusty's head in her lap and humming a strand from a Brahms lullaby.

We walked from the church out onto the beach, and the kids, about twenty of us in all, started a game of touch football. After thirty minutes of hard playing, I was dripping with sweat and called out, "I'm taking a break."

"Aw, come on, Ellie. Don't stop now. We need you." This came from Sal.

"I'm beat," I huffed. I grabbed a bottle of water and took a long gulp, smiling to myself as the kids tumbled on top of each other, the girls squealing when touched by the boys. They seemed so innocent, so simple and pure. But I knew from Ben's stories that some of these kids were dealing with pretty heavy problems. Parents splitting up, drugs, abortions. I wished their lives could always stay as innocent as they seemed at that moment, with a football and a beach and a lot of laughter.

Ben was cooking hot dogs and hamburgers on a makeshift grill. I came up beside him and asked, "Why do you do this, Ben?"

"Do what?"

"Take care of these kids. What's in it for you?"

He threw a few hamburger patties on the grill and listened as they sizzled over the coals. "Oh, Ellie, I'd think you of all people would understand why I do it."

I almost said something sarcastic, then stopped.

"When you've made as many mistakes as I did as a teen, and then you find something else, well, gosh. I feel it's a vocation, a calling, to give back—to maybe in some small way help the kids I'm around learn to make wiser choices and to grab onto God earlier. That's why I do it, Ellie-o."

"Ben, the eternal rescuer," I teased.

"Hey, you were rescuing long before I cared one iota about it. All those poor animals locked in cages with a bunch of other miserable animals. You have it in you too, Ellie."

I looked at him in surprise. "Did Mom say something to you? Did she call and tell you about Rusty?"

"Who? Rusty? What are you talking about?"

I looked at him sheepishly. "I, um, sort of rescued a dog today—found him at Publix, sniffing through the trash."

Ben laughed. "You see?"

"I only rescue animals. I'm hopeless with people relationships. I'll leave those to you."

He didn't respond, just continued turning the hamburgers.

I looked over my shoulder to make sure none of the other kids were around, and then confided, "It's just that every time I start thinking that I might have something in common with Mom, I get this awful hard feeling inside, and then bad memories flash through my mind and I want to lash out at her. And what I see, again and again, is shattered glass and fire and big, ugly scars."

Ben cocked his head. "You've got so much rage in you, Ellie. You've got to forgive if you're ever gonna get on with life." He ignored my scowl and continued, "Look, I had a ton of anger too, especially after Dad left Mom, and I thought he'd ruined my life. I was eaten up with it. Everybody has to deal with what's inside."

"You make it sound easy, Ben. It's not. It's awful. Anyway, I was just a little kid. So why is it all my fault if I'm carrying around this bitterness? Why can't it be their fault? Mom's particularly? She should bring up the past and talk about it with me."

He shrugged. "If you wait for other people to initiate, even if you're convinced they're the ones in the wrong, you may wait all your life. And then all you get is one huge mound of bitterness and rage to lug around with you."

"It's not like I want to lug it around, Ben. It's not like I haven't tried. They told me the same kind of stuff in rehab. They made me make lists of things that made me feel rage and bitterness and then burn up those lists and let them float away into ashes. But it still comes back. Maybe I can still be a vet, have a life. But I'll always, always be scarred. That will never change. We tried. Five excruciating operations, and I'm still scarred."

"Don't you get it yet, girl?"

I didn't answer.

"Don't you see how 'being scarred,' as you put it, has made you sensitive to other people's pain? You aren't out to impress people. You are near to the brokenhearted, Ellie, because you've been broken-hearted."

He said it so convincingly, so enthusiastically, that I almost believed him.

"Ellie, you know when I started 'smiling all the time,' as you put it? It was when I finally accepted the fact that I was short, with a prominent nose and a quirky personality. These were things I couldn't do anything about, so I finally figured God was going to use them for good. I decided to trust Him to do His job, to make something out of Benjamin of the Obnoxious Olfactories, and boy, did I feel relieved."

I couldn't help but give him a half smile, hearing the cynical nickname he'd given himself as a teenager, and remembering how I'd started calling myself "Ellie of the Perpetual Pout" when I was with him. I had the strongest urge to reach over and touch him—his hair or his face—or to run my finger around the contour of his smiling mouth.

"If you let Him, God will use your accident for good too. You're already halfway there, Ellie—you've got a tender heart."

I scowled at him.

"No, I'm serious. Think of Rusty."

At that moment, Sal and Samantha came up, with Zeke chasing behind, and bumped into Ben, so that one of the burgers flew off the spatula and into the sand. They started giggling in their silly way, and then a few other kids came over and scrounged through a big cooler and began tossing Cokes to everyone, calling out, "Think fast!" as the icy cans went sailing through the air.

Samantha spread out three big beach blankets, and someone grabbed a guitar, and the kids sang a catchy chorus as their blessing for the food. And all the questions and anger I'd felt at different points during the day just left me, washed away, like footprints in the sand, and I felt happy, almost lucky, to be a part of this group on a warm summer night at Hilton Head.

Later, as I listened to them singing around the campfire and watched Ben, I remembered why I liked him when I was a little girl. He was a short teenager with long black curly hair and cold blue eyes. He had been every bit as odd as I was, and even as a child, I'd felt sorry for him. He didn't fit in.

Now here he was, completely at ease with these virile boys with deep tans and broad shoulders, and perfect-figured long-legged girls, all of whose eyes were glued to him, listening almost in spite of themselves. He brought out his Bible and opened it to the book of Isaiah. He read an entire chapter and then said, "Tonight I want to talk about the real Jesus. The one the Bible says 'was despised and rejected by men,' with nothing to attract men to him. Jesus wasn't beautiful as we define beauty. He drew men to himself through love. . . ."

Sitting there, watching him in the dimming light with the fire casting shadows across his face, I could not deny the radical change in Ben Abrams. Those icy eyes had changed, had melted, and were now imbued with warmth and laughter, imbued with love.

I thought, *This is how Jesus must have looked*. It wasn't His physical appearance that drew people to Him. It was His eyes, His love, His complete acceptance of himself and of those around Him that made the difference.

Ben was showing me Jesus.

Chapter 19

Just like me, they long to be
Close to you.

—HAL DAVID

In spite of my thoughts and feelings of the night before, I didn't decide to go to church the next morning because I wanted to hear more about Jesus. When I awoke at nine-thirty after spending a rather restless night with Rusty whimpering beside my bed and Hindsight pouting on the chaise lounge, I decided to go to church because I wanted to see Ben. It just happened—one day I was riding behind him on a bike trail in Sea Pines, and when I caught up with him, I could no longer look him in the eyes without my palms growing clammy and my face turning red.

Mom was delighted to join me, so I drove us the mile and a half to church and parked the Mazda underneath the oaks. We arrived just as the service was beginning, and both of us were surprised to see that the sanctuary, which must have held at least three hundred people, was pretty well filled, so much so that we climbed the steps to the balcony.

Ben was sitting up front, next to the pastor. He looked a bit out of place in his jeans and white polo and navy blazer beside the other staff members in their suits and ties. But when he stood behind the pulpit to give a prayer, he seemed perfectly at ease. I don't know if he saw us, but I found myself having difficulty concentrating on anything in the service except him. I felt proud of him when the pastor baptized two teens from the youth group, though Ben would doubtless have reminded me that he wasn't the one who had rescued them—it was God.

I could tell that Mom was thrilled to have me sitting beside her in church, as I had done for all those years as a child. It did seem familiar and right to be there this morning—not for God, but for my mother and for Ben.

Ben came home with us afterward for lunch. Rusty greeted us at the door by leaping in the air and planting paws on my abdomen. Then he spied Ben and began barking, if not ferociously, nonetheless convincingly.

"It's okay, boy," Ben said softly, squatting down and holding his hand out toward the dog. It took at least five minutes before Rusty would approach him. Eventually, he gave Ben's hand a sniff and then a lick. But when Ben stood up, Rusty fled into the kitchen, tail flattened between his legs.

"Ellie, the rescuer," Ben said, almost reverently, and he gave me such a warm, sincere smile that I could think of nothing in reply.

Hindsight sulked in a corner and hissed whenever Rusty stuck his nose under the chair where she was hiding. Already three long scratches on his nose testified to his losing battle. But that was all he was losing; he'd completely won Mom and me over.

Ben followed Rusty into the kitchen, and this time he sat down on the floor and whistled softly as Rusty eyed him suspiciously. "Is he house trained?"

"Yeah, he does fine. Hasn't peed anywhere but outside so far—well, since the ride home in Mom's car, anyway. But he isn't the easiest dog to take on a walk. He about jerked my arm out of socket this morning. I don't think we made any friends with the way he was carrying on and waking everyone up on a Sunday morning."

Ben had scooted over toward Rusty and was petting the mutt, which had plopped down right beside him and was enjoying having his head scratched. "Well, you've made a friend now," he said to Rusty. But when he winked at me, I felt heat rise in my cheeks.

Ben and I biked from the Hamilton House to Harbour Town, and after we'd locked up our bikes in racks outside of Ketch Court, we walked out to the harbor and got ice cream cones at the little shop beside the lighthouse.

"Wanna climb to the top?" Ben asked.

I shrugged. "Why not?"

So we walked inside the candy-striped structure, bought tickets, and climbed the winding steps to the top. We stood looking back across the harbor toward the buildings in the distance.

"It's gorgeous up here," I said. "The view is perfect. Almost as perfect as when Daddy and I would watch the sun set from the balcony of your condominium." I began to tell him of those memories. I must have talked for twenty minutes as we leaned over the railing, letting the gusts of wind blow our hair in our faces.

He turned to me suddenly and asked, "You know what I think is the most beautiful thing at Hilton Head?"

"Could be a hundred things. Everything is beautiful at Hilton Head."

"True. But the most beautiful thing is the way your face lights up when you talk about watching the sun set right behind this lighthouse."

I must have blushed, because he added, "Really, it's great to hear you talk like that. You're coming back to life, girl. You and Swannee both. You're remembering happy times with your family. And I think you're making some good memories with your mom."

"Yeah, maybe. I just hope the memories will stay happy. I hope she doesn't up and die on me down here."

"Oh, Ellie." He put his hands on my shoulders. "Don't think like that. Just appreciate each day."

We climbed down the stairs and walked back toward the shops. Without consulting each other, we sat down in a couple of the red rocking chairs. We rocked back and forth in silence. I was watching a particular gull that was busily pecking at something on one of the yachts in the harbor.

After a time I ventured, "You seem preoccupied, Ben."

"I do? Sorry. Yeah, I kinda got lost in thought. No big deal."

"What's bugging you?"

He ran a hand through his hair, pushing it away from his face. "It's Sal. She's all torn up. Her folks are splitting up, and she knows this may be their last family vacation at Hilton Head—at least with them all being together. She's heading back up east with her mom in a few days. I'm worried for her, Ellie."

"It must be hard to have all that responsibility on you," I said. "I mean, the kids probably admire you and turn to you for counsel. And you have to figure out what to say."

"Exactly. It is hard."

"Do you think you should mention something to her parents? Do they know what she's thinking?"

"I doubt it. They're so caught up in their own problems, I don't think they have a lot of energy left to see what's happening to their daughter."

"Does she talk to you?"

"Some. Mostly she confides in Samantha—who then confides in me. They're all so fragile, Ellie. Life is fragile. It needs caring for, and most of these kids just don't get what they need. They get good educations and nice vacations and the latest in computer technology and cell phones, but they're screaming out for something more." Ben himself looked a bit fragile at the moment. "At least I was."

"What were you screaming for, Ben?"

"A point. I wanted there to be a point to life. You know, Ellie, deep down inside, I wanted your mom and dad to be right about things. I wanted their babble to make sense. My parents' lives sure didn't make a whole lot of sense. Your parents, I don't know. They had something different." He stuffed his hands in his pockets. "Maybe it sounds egotistical, but I guess I want these kids to see that in me. I want them to wonder what makes me tick."

"They probably do," I said, thinking, *At least I do*. "Can I ask you something, Ben?"

"Fire away."

"Do you really think faith makes your life better? The more I learn about Mom and Daddy, well, it seems to me that my parents' lives have gotten worse because of their faith. Their lives may be intriguing, but they don't seem very easy or . . . I don't know . . . fair."

Ben was quiet for so long that I thought he had nothing else to say, but eventually he wrinkled his brow as he met my eyes. "I guess it all depends on how you define *better,* Ellie. I admired your parents' character. I could tell they had the big questions of life settled. Once you have the big questions settled, it makes the living out of the daily junk a lot easier to accept." He squinted his eyes, ran his hand through his hair again. "That's what I mean about having a point to life. If the whole point to life is to make it easy or fair, well, it ain't gonna happen."

"No, you're right. I don't mean easy. I want my life to have a purpose, but there's a difference in having a hard life, with the normal difficulties everyone has, and having a tragic life. I'd say Mom and Daddy's life has been tragic. And that doesn't seem fair."

"Why not?"

"I'm not explaining myself well. What I mean is, if they trust in God and then so many awful things happen, worse than what happens to most people, then how in the world can they keep believing in this God? It seems like they'd catch on that their belief doesn't work." I crossed my arms over my chest. "Yes, that's what I mean."

"That's a great question, Ellie-o. You should ask your mom and see what she says."

"I don't want to ask my mom. I'm asking you! You don't babble." Then I whispered, "I'm scared, Ben. I'm scared that you are all just believing in a big myth. I'm scared that it might kind of be intriguing to me, but I don't want it—not if it's something that has ruined the lives of people I care a lot about."

Ben opened his mouth as if he was going to say something, and I watched while a dozen expressions played across his face. Finally, he reached over and touched me on the shoulder. "Keep wrestling with it all, Ellie. Keep wrestling. Don't believe in anything just because someone else tells you to. I have no doubt that God is big enough to convince you of His authenticity—without the need of any of our babble."

He wrinkled his brow again, started to say something else, then changed his mind and said, "I've gotta get to the Quarterdeck. Thanks for lunch and the bike ride."

He walked the two hundred yards from the red rocking chairs to the Quarterdeck Lounge, and I sat there wishing he would turn around and look at me with a smile on his face. I wished he would say, somewhere out of the blue, "Ellie, you're a hard woman to love. But I'm gonna try."

When I got back to the house, I found Mom planted in the family room in front of her easel. Rusty was lying contentedly at her feet. I peered over her shoulder at the beach scene on the canvas, observing the sunset, shells, and a series of footprints near the water. More to be polite than out of real curiosity, I asked, "So whose footprints are you painting?"

She beamed up at me. "That pair, you see, the ones that stay right along the edge of the water? Those are mine. And the others, the ones that start out so small and then disappear into the ocean and then reappear down the beach, only bigger, those are yours, Ellie." She looked back at the painting. "You know, sometimes we expect things to be wrapped up neatly at a certain time, and then they aren't, and we lose faith. But then, like the footprints there, something reappears, something is changed, healed. The story really wasn't over. It's like that verse in Isaiah about building up the ancient ruins and restoring the cities that have been devastated for generations."

As she talked, my rage returned. I didn't let my face betray me, though. I just mumbled, "Cool, Mom. I'm gonna take a walk."

I stalked down the beach so fast, with my fists clenched so tightly, that people stared at me—a broad girl wearing a tank top and old gym shorts, her long hair stuffed under a baseball cap and an angry frown on her face.

Mom was painting a syrupy picture of our footprints on a beach with the sun setting—a happy ending in her mind. She would convert her little Ellie and the whole family would finally be in the fold and then she could die in peace and the sun would set and it would be just like in the movies. Sad, but oh, so good. A tragic but somehow happy ending.

But I didn't want that ending! I wanted Mom alive and well, I wanted to be able to argue with her, to disagree and laugh and cry and talk. I could feel the fury pounding in my temples. I'd never been one for aerobic walking, but I was working up quite a sweat. I ended up near the Beach Club, which was still crowded with sunbathers at five in the afternoon. By then I had slowed my pace and splashed in the ocean in water up to my thighs.

I spied Samantha and Sal sitting under a parasol, laughing, their slim, tanned legs curled up under them. I considered just walking on past, as if I hadn't noticed them, but then Sal turned my way and saw me.

"Hey," I said, approaching them tentatively. "Whatcha up to?"

Samantha shrugged. "Nothing much. Just hangin'." She looked over the top of her sunglasses, patted the towel beside her, and said, "Have a seat."

I complied.

"Want a Coke?" she asked.

"No, thanks. I'm fine. Or maybe just a sip of water," I added, spying a bottle in their little half-opened cooler. "Did I interrupt something?"

I thought about what Ben had said about Sal. She was sitting on her towel in her bright pink bikini, her brown hair twisted up into a loose bun, aloof, self-sufficient. *And, no doubt, miserable.*

"Nothing interesting," she said. "Just boy troubles."

"Oh, you've got them too?"

"Why? You know about boy troubles?" This came from Samantha.

The way she asked reminded me of high school, of girls who in their offhanded, snobby way hinted that it was surprising, even astonishing, to think that a guy might like a girl with a face like mine. I thought of playing my favorite strategy game called "humiliate the enemy," but knew Ben would never stoop so low.

Instead I said, "Oh, I've had my share of problems. So do you have a crush on one of the guys in the group at church? Some of them are pretty cute."

"Yeah, that's right. Tommy's hot. Real hot. Right, Samantha?" Sal elbowed her friend.

"Oh, shut up. It'll never work out with him. We live too far apart."

"Well, at least he's better than the guy you left back home. He was a real jerk. Yeah, Ben would approve of you liking Tommy."

Samantha looked disgusted. "Do you have to get approval from Reverend Ben for everything? You just have a crush on him, Sal."

She flashed, "Oh, come on. I do not. He's practically twice my age. But he's pretty cool. Anyway, Ben likes Ellie."

She said it so innocently, as if it were just one more tidbit of silly teenage gossip, that I was taken completely off guard. I felt my face grow hot, but I didn't say a thing.

"Well, Ellie. What do you think about Ben? He's cool. Are you dating?" Sal pried.

"Ben and I have known each other since we were babies. That's all."

"Oh no. That's not what Ben says. He likes you," Samantha confirmed. "He likes you a lot."

I gave them an annoyed look. "C'mon, girls. No more gossip. Leave Ben and me out of it. We're friends."

They exchanged a knowing glance and grinned.

"What?"

"Ben says whenever you hear a girl say 'we're just friends,' it means she's hoping for a lot more."

"You're crazy," I snapped.

"Maybe," Sal said, "but he's always philosophizing about love. He's trying to keep us virginal—you know how straight he is."

"Yeah, well, he's too late for you," Samantha giggled, and elbowed Sal again.

"Shut up!"

I stood up. "Look, I gotta go. No more gossiping, girls."

"Ben thinks you're beautiful. He's said it twice. If a guy says a girl's beautiful, that means something."

"He said I was *beautiful*?" I couldn't help asking. "No one thinks I'm beautiful."

"Oh, you're way wrong, Ellie. He just says it like that. 'Take, Ellie. Beautiful Ellie. She's given up her job to help her mom.'"

"He just means he thinks what I've done is beautiful, self-sacrificing. That's all."

"Say what you want, Ellie. We know what we heard. Anyway, do you like him?"

I sighed, staring down at them. "Of course I like Ben. It's great to see him again, and he's really changed. But I just *like* him. *Get* it?"

"How's he changed?"

"He used to be wild . . . and miserable."

"Yeah, he told us all that. And so were you. Y'all go together, Ellie. Face it."

I got a stupid grin on my face that wouldn't go away. "I'm gonna keep walking, guys. See ya later. And stop gossiping!"

When I got back to the house, Mom was still sitting in front of the easel. She was humming lightly to herself and dabbing bright globs of yellow paint onto the canvas.

"Hello, Ellie, dear," she called without turning around.

"Hey, Mom," I answered nonchalantly. Inside I suddenly felt happy. This was how I'd found Mom on many days when I'd come home from school—painting on the sunporch, humming quietly, so caught up in her work that I was almost an afterthought. Gratitude washed over me. She didn't need me right now, and I needed time alone, to get my thoughts toward Ben under control.

I grabbed a bottle of water from the fridge, took a long drink, and then headed for the shower. I came out, towel-drying my hair, and stood beside the easel.

"It's good, Mom," I said, which actually was true. I felt kind of guilty about judging it as a sentimental painting.

"Thank you, Ellie." She breathed in deeply, then slowly let out the air, as if she were in a doctor's office. "It's a start. I can't tell you how marvelous it feels to be holding a paintbrush again."

I pulled a chair from the table over beside her and sat down. "Tell me when you really started painting, Mom. When you had exhibitions. When people started buying your work."

Mom laid down her brush, seemingly pleased with my questions. "Oh, you must remember, Ellie. It wasn't that long ago. You were at least ten, maybe twelve, when I left for my first exhibition. Well, no. My *first* exhibition was in 1971, and it was a fiasco—I just showed one painting, but it nearly destroyed me."

It must have been a truly distasteful memory, because Mom scrunched up her nose, then rubbed her forehead and cleared her throat.

"Anyway, I didn't show my paintings again until 1985. I was invited to speak in Washington, D.C., of all things—at the National Gallery. They were doing an exhibition on art from 1968 and showed three of my paintings—actually the three that are hanging in the High Museum now.

"But then things happened, and I didn't paint much, and it wasn't until—let me think—the spring of 1991 that I exhibited my paintings again—and had one or two decent reviews. That's when I sold two paintings. I was astounded. I'll never forget what it felt like to hold that first check in my hands . . . twelve hundred dollars. It seemed like play money, maybe something I'd won in Monopoly.

"And then I started having more exhibitions. You probably remember that—your dad and I getting dressed up and going to cocktail parties and mingling with people who were interested in my art."

"Yeah, I remember that. It always seemed really glamorous."

"I guess that part of it does sound glamorous, although at most exhibitions, I'm so nervous I start perspiring in my fancy gown." She smiled. "Most of the time, painting is just hard work. But when you work for something so hard, dream of it for so long, think it will never happen—well, I'd say it's a million times better than glamorous." There was a passion in her voice that I hadn't heard in a long time. "It's fulfilling and thrilling and finally, it's a vocation, a calling. You do it because it's what you're supposed to do, and some days you feel like doing it and some days you don't. But you keep on."

"Like anybody else's work."

"Sure. Who has a really glamorous life? No one I'd want to emulate. No, I didn't become a painter to have a glamorous life. I did it because I *had* to paint, as I told you before. That's all."

I'm not sure what made me change the subject from the relatively safe topic of painting to the controversial one of family, but I found myself saying a bit defiantly, "Yeah, maybe you didn't want a glamorous life, but I always thought you needed to have a perfect life. I'm not talking about your career as an artist; I just mean as a mom. You wanted everyone and everything to be perfect. And I didn't fit in."

She looked startled. And hurt. And for a moment, unsure of what to say. "I'm sorry, Ellie," she stammered. She looked down at her hands. "It's one of the biggest problems I have. Trying to make everything be okay—for your father, for you girls, for me. It's just that things were so bad for so long that I thought maybe I could create a place of peace. I tried so hard. I didn't know it seemed like I wanted perfection."

"Well, it did! At least to me!" This came out harshly. "It was awful, because everyone else at least tried to fit in, but I didn't. And then I got burned, and I was even further from perfection, and you couldn't deal with it. You wanted me back the way I'd always been, and it wasn't going to happen. I wasn't going to fit into your nice neat package. I was scarred."

Mom started to cry, then forced the tears away. "Keep going, Ellie. I want to hear this."

"Mom, look at me! Look at my face! Five excruciatingly painful operations, and still it's just this scarred, ugly face. And don't tell me it's not. You haven't lived with it! You haven't been stared at all your life."

"I'm sorry, Ellie."

"It's not enough! It's not enough when the whole reason I'm this way is your fault!" It came out so loud and angry and quickly that we both looked absolutely shocked.

She didn't say a thing, didn't make any excuses, didn't even cry. Her eyes were wide, astonished. "You've never forgiven me, have you, Ellie. After all these years, it's still a big, ugly raw wound."

"How could I forgive you, Mom, when you talked like it was God's will, and He was gonna make everything fine? How could I forgive you when you wouldn't even admit it had happened? You sugarcoated it like everything else in your life with religious phrases and hope, and you made it sound like God was answering all your prayers for me and everything was going to be perfect again. But it wasn't. It was lousy and awful, and you just seemed to me like a hypocrite. You didn't take any of the blame, any of the pain. You just prayed it away!"

All of this was said so quickly, in a run-together sentence of sobs, that I was perhaps more amazed than my mother. She was holding her head in her hands and brushing her hands through the scarf so that it eventually slid off down her neck, and her bald head was there and her sunken cheeks and her green eyes, full of tears.

"I don't know what to say, Ellie. I'm sorry. It isn't enough, I know." She looked like Rusty—frightened, wild, backed into a corner. "Forgive me."

I felt sick to my stomach. I didn't want to lash out anymore. Heavy silence hung in the narrow space between our two chairs. Nothing in me wanted to reach over and touch her hand, and she made no effort to move toward me, as if she was afraid I might strike out again.

"Do you want to talk about it now?" she asked finally in a slight, quivering voice.

"No. No, not now."

We sat in complete silence for a very long time, neither of us sure what to do next. My face felt tight and hard. I couldn't look at Mom, and I stood up awkwardly and said, "I'm going to my room for a while."

"Okay, Ellie," she said heavily. I left her there in front of her painting of the sunset, raw and wounded.

I shut the door to the bedroom and flopped down on the chaise lounge, trying to decipher what was pulsing in my head. Rage and relief. Confusion and guilt. Rusty had stayed in the family room with Mom, and Hindsight, seeing her chance to regain stolen territory, pounced into my lap, scratching me slightly with her claws to show her complete disapproval of our new boarder. I stroked her fur, suddenly hungry for Cheetos, but I was not about to go back into the main room and face my mother.

I paced back and forth in the spacious bedroom, then went out onto the little balcony. I wanted to do something with the anger. But I didn't have any of my old familiar things to fall back on—no baseball to toss in the air, no food to stuff in my mouth. I switched on the TV and let it drone in the background.

Then I saw *National Velvet,* which I'd brought with me from my parents' house and set inside the wicker étagère. It was one of my favorite books as a child, and I knelt down and took it out and leafed through its worn pages, imagining young Velvet riding on the black-and-white stallion she called the Piebald. If only I could slip back into the skin of innocence and ride away into my childhood. Far away from now. I could not face the present.

Stuffed inside the book were two letters from Mom, the ones I'd grabbed out of the desk at home, both still in their envelopes with their flaps torn and the glue worn off. I sat down cross-legged on the floor, placed the book back on the shelf, and stared at the envelopes, as if I were daring my mother to float out of them and into my life.

I thought they'd both be from that horrible month in the summer of 1990 when I went to camp, but I was surprised to see that one was postmarked 1997 and addressed to Miss Ellie Bartholomew at the Alpha Rehab Center.

I couldn't remember Mom writing me at rehab. Of course she must have, but I didn't remember it. And I wondered why I had saved this letter. I was so mad at Mom during those months that I'd have expected to have tossed any letter from her in the trash can, unopened.

I halfheartedly picked up the other letter, the one written to me at camp. I didn't want to open it. I was afraid to see Mom's writing, afraid that the letter was full of babble and that her babble would only add fuel to the fire.

I felt stuck—stuck in my bedroom while Mom sat stuck in her chair, neither of us daring to approach the other. I whispered a string of angry expletives to myself and took the first letter out of the envelope.

June 22, 1990

Dear Ellie,

I miss you, sweetie. Thank you for the letter. I'm so glad you got to ride the horse you wanted. Yes, it is different to ride in the Western style saddle. I've always thought it was almost like cheating on a test—you don't have to post or anything. You just sit there. But don't tell your counselor I said that!

Guess what? I have a surprise waiting for you when you get home. Only one week now. I hope you will like it. I'm really excited about it, and Abbie and Nan say it's cool. It has something to do with your room, but I won't tell you what. And I don't think you'll be able to guess.

Daddy sends "tons of hugs and kisses"—his words exactly, and Abbie and Nan send their love too.

I love you, Ellie Mae Mae, the world's sweetest girl.

Momma

I gave a little gasp and then covered my mouth with my hand. The scene that flashed in my mind was crystal clear. I was ten, freshly home from camp, and Mom and Nan and Abbie were walking upstairs with me to my bedroom, Nan's hands over my eyes.

"Don't peek, don't peek!" she squealed.

And then I was in the middle of my room, my eyes wide with surprise and getting wider every second and a big smile spreading across my face. While I'd been away at camp, my mother had painted a mural of all my animals on the walls of my room. That first glance at my room was ten times better than opening the biggest present under the Christmas tree. It was magic.

I don't remember if Abbie and Nan stayed there with us, but I remember how I walked around and around my bedroom, running my hand along each wall, touching each animal, Mr. Boots and Jinx and Daisy and Fluffy Fury and Shadow and Sally and Bonnie. Finally, after a long mesmerized minute, I turned to my mother and hugged her fiercely and said, "Oh, Momma. It's perfect. It is so, so perfect. Thank you, thank you, *thank* you. I love it!"

I remember Mom beaming with happiness, and I remember that it *had* been perfect. Forgotten were camp and the mean girls.

Mom had painted the walls just as if we were outside in the backyard, with the flower beds full of pansies and primroses, and the dogwood trees in bloom, and the sky a deep blue with a few clouds floating near the ceiling. Mr. Boots was sitting on a bench sunning himself, and Jinx was swatting at a goldfish in the pond, and Daisy the dog was standing on her hind legs, leaning on the magnolia tree in our backyard and barking up at Shadow, the gray witch cat. And Bonnie was there, on another wall, her ears pricked forward, looking over the door of her stall in the Abramses' stable.

Throughout the years, Mom added to the mural each time a new animal came our way—whether it was the bird I'd rescued from Shadow's mouth or the baby squirrel I'd found when Daddy cut down a dead tree or yet another puppy that Trixie and I had gotten at the Humane Society. Every animal that ever sojourned at the Bartholomew house made its way onto the walls. I had loved that mural, loved those walls, loved the fact that Mom had painted them for me.

And then I had hated them. Hated them because they represented my mother.

"Are you sure you want to paint over all this, Ellie? It's like your own private museum up here. I've always loved your room." I could hear Megan's

question even now, as we brought the cobalt blue paint upstairs into my room.

And my cruel reply, *"If you don't want to help, then leave. I don't want anything in this room to remind me of my mom!"*

I had tried to paint my mother out of my life.

But she had tried to paint me *into* hers, from the time she had lovingly created a menagerie on my walls right up to the present where she was sitting in front of her easel, painting my footprints in the sand.

One short sob escaped from my mouth as I set down that letter and reached for the one Mom had written to me at rehab.

August 4, 1997
Dear Ellie,

I don't really have much to say. Life just goes on. I guess I could say I miss you, and that would be true. I miss you as a person, as my daughter. But I don't miss what our lives had become, your anger and seeing that hate in your eyes and the way you refused to talk. I don't miss the terrible feelings that went through me.

Maybe they were hate too; you said in your last letter that you thought I hated you. You accused me of saying cruel things and trying to brainwash you and a lot of other things that were not so pleasant to read.

I used to be afraid of hate. The emotion scared me. But I've come to understand it as a welcome warning.

Thank you for writing out your feelings. Ellie, I love you, no matter what. But I confess that over the last months I've felt rage and helplessness and hate and, well, as if I might just go crazy—with worry, with anger, with grief.

Daddy and I are seeing a counselor—the same one we saw when Daddy got back from Vietnam and then after your accident. Maybe with all of us seeing counselors, we'll get the help we need. Make no mistake—we all need help.

We plan to come up at Thanksgiving.

Love,
Mom

In one blink of my eyes, I knew why I had kept that letter, why it was tucked in beside the one from camp. I saw myself lying sprawled across my bed in my little room in Annaton, New York, reading this letter and thinking, *My mother is telling me the truth.* And I remembered that I had written her a letter expressing some of the rage that was in me and that the letter turned out to be one long page filled with expletives. But that too had been my effort to start telling her the truth about what was inside. Rehab had been all about learning to tell and hear the truth, so when that letter came from Mom, somewhere inside my closed-up heart, I felt something new and fresh; I felt hope.

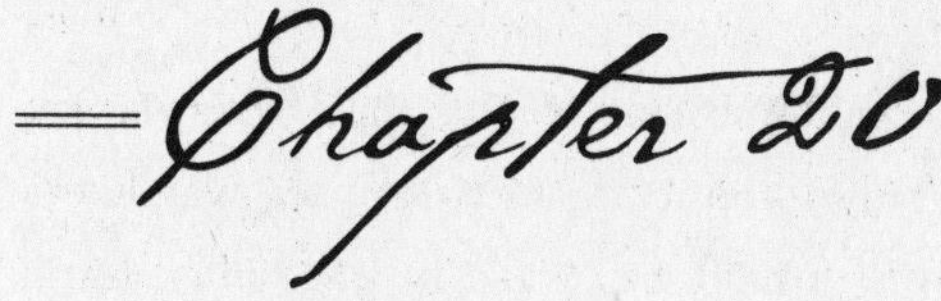

Chapter 20

Today, baseball is the only major sport that doesn't limit itself within the framework of time, and perhaps that is one reason its appeal transcends all others. . . .

—ANGUS G. GARBER III, *BASEBALL LEGENDS*

No replastering, the structure is rotten.

—SLOGAN FROM STUDENT RIOTS, MAY 1968, PARIS

I stared out the bedroom window, my feet tucked under me where I sat on the chaise with Hindsight in my lap. Probably no more than twenty minutes had elapsed since I had cloistered myself in the bedroom. It wasn't even dark outside. It was dusk—a time of day I often found depressing, when the sun has set and the sky is gray and heavy. I shivered. I felt afraid and immobilized. I didn't know what to do next, so I picked up my mother's letter to me at rehab and read through it again. It didn't sound like my normal mother. No babble, no encouraging phrases. She sounded mad. And firm. And relieved—relieved that I was gone because I had made her life a living hell, and she had finally admitted she didn't know what to do.

She was right. I had been awful. As awful as Rachel had been all those years ago. Or probably much, much worse. I had laughed when I found out I was expelled from school, and then I had sneered at Mom and said, "Shocked you to death, didn't I, Mom? Well, it's all your fault! You screwed my life up, and that God of yours can't do one thing about it!"

I squirmed as I remembered how I had treated her. The raw emotion with which Mom had written about me in that letter was like a scalpel scraping the dark blue paint off the walls in my room. Mom loved me. She loved me and hated me and lost her mind over me and gave me up and held on to hope. And now, now she was beginning to get me back. No wonder she had been so happy to paint the footprints. No wonder, when I had been so awful to her for all those years.

And I had been awful to her thirty minutes ago.

I closed my eyes, exhausted. I was trapped in this room, trapped at the beach, just as surely as Mom had been trapped in Paris with Rachel. No escape.

It occurred to me then that Ben would say there was a way to escape—if I would just walk out into the living room and forgive my mom and let her forgive me. If I would let go of rage and bitterness, tell her why I had those feelings, I was pretty sure Ben would say I would at long last escape the past.

It took me at least fifteen minutes of deliberation before I could get up the nerve. After stroking Hindsight's coat until I had literally rubbed her the wrong way and she hopped to the floor, I picked up the letter as if I could hide behind it, *wanting* in fact to hide behind it, and opened the bedroom door.

Mom sat in the chair in the family room, her back to me. She was not painting. I thought she might be dozing, for her head was bent down. Dozing or praying. I made some noise closing the door so she would turn around. When she did, I saw that she had been crying. There was no pretext in those green eyes when she looked up at me. What I saw there was resignation.

I stood a few feet from where she was sitting and said the words I had practiced in my mind. "Sorry, Mom." I could not make any other words come out of my mouth, and I could not look at her. I just stared at her painting, and I wondered briefly if she was going to have to paint my footprints going back off into the water again.

"Ellie," she said at length. "I understand that it angers you for me to try to make things 'perfect,' as you say. I'm sorry it seems like I'll only love you if you believe the way I do." She closed her eyes, reached for my hand, and grasped it without looking at me. "Please forgive me for projecting that to you. I love you, Ellie, just as you are."

I tried to move closer to her, but I couldn't. I tried to force my mouth to say the words, "It's okay" or "I forgive you" or "I believe you, Mom" or "I'm sorry too for being so angry at you. I think I just chose to forget all the ways you tried to help me and how awful my accident was for you." But nothing came out of my mouth.

Forgiveness. Boy, was that something that Mom and Daddy preached in our house when we were growing up! Asking for it and giving it. Not just a superficial "I'm sorry" from me with an "It's okay" from Nan, but a true "change of heart"—meaning we wouldn't do the bad thing anymore. I got pretty good at faking sincerity about being sorry and about forgiving too.

But I didn't want to fake it anymore. When I asked for forgiveness, I wanted it to be true. I wanted the rage to leave.

"Ellie, can we please just talk? I need to hear what you think. It hurts, but hurting isn't the worst thing in life. Hurting because of the truth is probably the one thing that helps us heal. So tell me the truth. Tell me what has been locked up in your heart. Please just come sit here and tell me."

She was holding out her arms as if I were a three-year-old and she needed a hug. It seemed like a small miracle that I actually moved forward, became unstuck, went to her, knelt before her chair, and wrapped my arms around her.

"I'm sorry, Mom," I whispered, this time meaning it. "I'm sorry for everything. Everything. It's me that was wrong. It was all my fault."

"Shh, not all your fault, Ellie. Never." She patted me as she said it.

"But I mean it, Mom. I *am* sorry. The real kind of sorry. I need you to forgive me for, for all my anger."

I could hear the thumping of her heart, my ear pressed into her chest as it rose and fell. She stroked my hair, softly, for at least five minutes and then whispered, "I do forgive you, Ellie. I do. For everything. Can you forgive me? I know it won't erase the past, but can you forgive me?"

I thought about it, thought of Ben's words, of my anger and rage, of the way Mom had always seemed to pray hardship away. I didn't answer for what must have seemed an eternity to Mom. But I couldn't be flippant. I needed to carefully consider what I was forgiving. Not so much for Mom as for me. So I could remind myself that I had let it go of my own accord. Freely. Out of love.

Finally I whispered, "I forgive you, Mom. I really do."

She bent down and kissed me on the top of my head and we must have sat there for five or ten minutes. When she let go of me, I stood up, and she stood beside me. We just naturally held each other's hands, staring out the window where the sky had gone black and the moon was a bright white dot far off in the distance and the stars, a handful of them, were winking at us from heaven.

It had lasted all of ten minutes, but our brief exchange felt as long and wide as Hilton Head's sandy shores. After I had fixed us a salad, which we ate on the porch, looking out to the beach, Mom said, "Ellie, would you mind taking me to hear Ben at the Quarterdeck? All of a sudden I feel like getting out."

My mouth must have fallen open. "Why, Mom, that was exactly what I was going to suggest."

She squeezed my hand. "Then let's do it."

I helped her put on her wig and watched as she carefully applied makeup to her face—the first time she'd made the effort since I'd been with her. She chose a pretty pale green T-shirt that brought out her eyes, and she wore it out over a pair of Capri pants. The makeup and the nice clothes and her wig transformed her again into my regular mother. I realized then that perhaps she had been this thin and tired for a long, long time but had only recently let it show.

I drove us the few miles to Harbour Town and parked the Mazda in a spot near Rachel's condominium. We walked through a passageway to where the harbor opened before us, the boats resting peacefully on the still water.

"This is the one your father always wanted to buy," Mom said, pointing to a yacht named *The Ramblin' Wreck*.

"I could see one of Georgia Tech's biggest alums sailing the seas and drumming up support on *The Ramblin' Wreck*," I laughed and then we both started singing, "I'm a Ramblin' Wreck from Georgia Tech. . . ." Mom's laughter was high and tinkling and mine low and hearty.

She put her arm through mine. "I see that Gregg is gathering the troops," she commented. Gregg Russell was a singer who had performed under Harbour Town's Liberty Oak for the past fifteen years. His nightly outdoor concert was geared at children with plenty of subtle adult humor to keep parents entertained too. As we strolled by the long benches overflowing with children and parents, he was singing a song about how to drive your parents crazy on the way back from the beach.

"Remember when I followed his advice one summer?" I commented.

"Yes, and it worked. I thought I was going to strangle you if you didn't quit chanting, 'Are we there yet, are we there yet?'"

"And remember when we went on the dolphin cruise? Took the boat that's sitting right there . . ."

". . . and we didn't see a single dolphin and you were heartbroken . . ."

". . . so Daddy took me back the next day and there were dozens of them around."

"Yes. Robbie always did like to spoil his little girls."

We walked arm in arm beside the shops. "Do you feel like looking in any of them, Mom?"

"I'd like to go into Nan's Gift Shop—it was always my favorite, I guess because of its name. You and Trixie preferred the clothes shops." We entered Nan's Gift Shop and walked over to the pottery section.

"Oh, look, Mom! A lighthouse pitcher!" I carefully picked up a tall blue pitcher with the Harbour Town candy-striped lighthouse painted on it. "I'm going to buy this for you!"

"Ellie! Don't be silly. It's expensive." But she sounded delighted.

"You're worth it, Mom." I was surprised at how naturally, how easily those words flowed from my mouth.

The walls in the gift shop were decorated with posters and prints and paintings and numbered watercolors of scenes from Harbour Town, all with pretty price tags attached. "You should paint the lighthouse, Mom, and sell it down here."

"I have done that, Ellie. Several times."

"Oops—I guess I didn't notice." We both giggled, happy, unaffected laughter. I paid for the pitcher, and we left the shop. In one hand I held the bag with my purchase; the other I draped around Mom's skinny shoulders. We walked alongside the harbor, past the lighthouse to the Quarterdeck Lounge. As soon as we opened the door, we could hear Ben's gentle voice singing "Desperado." My palms grew sweaty as we took a seat and Ben looked over at us with a smile.

Mom and I ordered Shirley Temples, which made us giggle again, especially when the bartender raised his eyebrows and commented, "Wow, girls, you sure you can handle something that stiff?"

Mom batted her long eyelashes and said, "We've got connections.

The lead singer in the band promised to drive us home if we get hammered."

I shot Mom an I've-never-in-my-life-heard-you-talk-that-way look, and she raised her eyebrows and shrugged, and we both giggled again.

To my delight, Ben sang "Hard Woman to Love," and I whispered to Mom, "He wrote that one. For Rachel. Just listen to the words."

Mom whispered back at the end of the song, "He's absolutely right. She *is* hard to love."

I gave a long sip on the straw, finishing my Shirley Temple, and said, "I can't believe you'd say that about your best friend."

"What are best friends for if we can't tell each other the truth? Anyway, she'd say the same thing about me. In fact, she's told me that a hundred times. Only she doesn't say I'm hard to love. She just calls me a silly scatterbrained girl and says I'm impossibly naïve. But it amounts to the same thing."

When the band had sung a few more songs, Ben leaned forward and said into the mike, "We're taking a fifteen-minute break. Don't go away." Then he set down his guitar and came over to our table.

"Hey, girls! This is a nice surprise. Swannee, it's great to see you up and about. And you look fabulous."

"I think fabulous might be a little farfetched, but I'm feeling much stronger."

"Leave it to Ellie-o and her French cuisine."

I stuck out my tongue, and he brushed my cheek with the back of his hand. "It's great to see you here together. Hey, I finish in about an hour or so. Wanna come by the condo afterward?"

"I don't think I'll last that long, but Ellie can if she wants."

"No, I'll get you home, Mom," I replied too quickly. But I wanted to go to his place with the moon shining bright and the soft music drifting over the boats and the smell of hope in the warm night air.

Mom and I walked out behind the Quarterdeck onto the long wooden pier that stretched its way into Calibogue Sound. Young lovers strolled hand in hand, a group of teens stood bunched together, laughing, couples walked behind their children who were licking ice cream cones and swirling strings with plastic fireflies in the air. We bought ice cream cones—Midnight Cookies and Cream—and then perched on the railing, just like two teenagers.

"What do you want to ask me, Ellie?" Mom said after her cone had disappeared and she was wiping her mouth with a paper napkin. "Is there something you want to talk about right now?"

I crunched on the cone and let my legs dangle over the railing. Here it was, the perfect opportunity, without rage or accusation. So I said, almost in a whisper, "I want to know about my accident. I want to know what really happened, because maybe what I remember isn't right. How'd it happen, Mom?"

She slid off the railing, encouraging me to follow. We walked in silence back toward the lighthouse, toward the shops and restaurants of Harbour Town, and then Mom began to talk.

"It was an afternoon in November. I was upstairs in our bedroom, talking on the phone with someone. You were playing with Mr. Boots and Daisy out in the backyard. Abbie and Nan were still at school. I remember you coming upstairs and asking if you could get a drink, and me nodding yes. I thought you'd just get a glass of milk. Well, it was very cold outside, and I guess what you wanted was hot chocolate. So you got the milk out and the pan and then you tried to light the stove, and I assume you couldn't get the clicker thing to light. You must have let the gas run for a while, sweetie. And then, I guess you finally got it to light—only it exploded. I heard a loud noise and I called down to you, but there was no response for a long moment. Then you started screaming the most awful blood-curdling shrill screams, and when I got to the kitchen, there you were, on fire. Your face, your hair—and your scarf. You were wearing an old wool scarf around your neck and it had caught fire. . . ."

She swallowed hard and sniffed. "If you hadn't had the scarf around your neck, the fire would have simply singed your hair and your eyebrows. But that old scarf just lit up and by the time I got there, it wasn't just your hair on fire—it was your clothes—and . . . and your face—and the fire got out of control. I grabbed the first thing I could find, which was the curtain on the kitchen window, and wrapped it around you, trying to smother the fire, but my skirt caught on fire too, and it was spreading and you were screaming and so was I. . . ."

"Momma . . ." I said softly.

"Somehow I got that fire out—I don't know how—and I don't remember what I did next—I think I called the emergency number, and then I just held you and cried. I was afraid you were dying. Then the paramedics came, and I rode with you to the emergency room at Piedmont. And I'll never forget on about the fourth day, when you were all wrapped up and in a coma in the burn unit, that the doctor came and told me that you were going to pull out of this. And he said that I had acted quickly and done what I should. But, of course, I always blamed myself. . . ."

I had a huge lump in my throat. "You put the curtain on me?"

"Yes."

"What about the person in the white sheet?"

"What person in the white sheet?"

"Somebody . . . the person who saved me."

"There was just you and me and the curtain, Ellie." Mom looked confused. "The white lace curtain that I wrapped around you to put out the fire."

I swallowed hard twice. "That wasn't how I remembered it, Mom."

"What do you remember?"

"It's always confusing. I remember wanting you to come downstairs and help me get something to drink. I was cold, and I wanted some hot chocolate. I called to you, but you wouldn't come, so I turned on the stove and it exploded. I was crying for you. And I see it again and again and again, me screaming for you, me on fire, and I can't find you. And then the big white sheet—the ghostlike figure in the big white sheet coming toward me. And I was afraid, and then everything went blank. And then I kept having those nightmares about the fire and the white sheet."

Mom's soft expression had grown strained—not angry, not accused, but as if she could physically feel my pain. "Is that what you remember, honey? Is that what you think? You don't remember that I wrapped the curtain around you, that for a second we were both on fire? By the time I got there, your clothes were in flames. I threw the curtain over you. I never abandoned you, sweetie. I was always there."

"It was you, Momma?"

"I was panicking inside, but somehow on the outside, I knew what to do. *Smother the fire, smother the fire*. That's what I kept hearing. It took me a few minutes, but I got it out.

"I hated your nightmares, Ellie. It seemed so unfair for you to have to keep reliving it. The nightmares went on for several years, and then, well, I thought they'd gotten better. You didn't cry out at night. You didn't talk about them anymore."

"Why didn't you tell me these things ten years ago, Mom?"

She looked confused, and her eyes filled with tears. "Ellie, we *did* talk about it—so often that you'd put your hands over your ears and go running from the room, saying you didn't want to hear it. We talked as a family, we talked with your pediatrician and the plastic surgeon and the counselor. Why do you say we didn't talk about it?"

"I don't ever remember you saying one word except that you were praying for me. That lots and lots of people were praying for me. You'd come into my room at night and hold my hands and pray."

"Yes, I did that too. And after a while, we gave up going to the counselor. You refused. You screamed and raged and blamed us."

"Why didn't you make me go? Why did I win?"

We were standing by the rocking chairs. Mom looked almost relieved to find two that were empty, and sank down into one while I took the other. I could barely hear her next words.

"I don't know. All I can say is that we tried, Ellie. I'm so sorry that it doesn't seem like it to you. And I can understand you blaming me. I blamed myself a thousand times. I was upstairs on the phone with a lady who was always going on about her problems. I should have hung up when you came inside. But you knew how to get a drink. And I never imagined you'd try to light the stove. You were six years old. You knew better than to try to light it by yourself. Believe me, I've relived it and blamed myself a hundred times. I guess I finally realized I had to let the guilt go, and let you go too. I couldn't change any of it.

"Ellie, I have to say it was a relief to give it up, to forgive myself. But I never meant to diminish your pain or to make you think I didn't care or act like we'd just pray the pain away." She reached across to my rocking chair, where my hand was resting on the arm of the chair. "I hated the distance between us."

I looked at her bony fingers covering the soft, pudgy flesh on my hand, thought about the stark contrast, the way Mom's blue veins were so prominent in her hand and how the veins in mine were barely hinted at.

"Some of my distance over the years wasn't just about being mad, Mom. You know, after I got kicked out of school and everything and after rehab, I just thought if I kept my distance, I could maybe keep from embarrassing you anymore."

"I wasn't embarrassed, Ellie. Or maybe I was a time or two, but that was never the main emotion. Heartbroken. Mad—even furious. I cried and prayed and wondered like every parent what I'd done wrong and what I could have done differently, but I always wanted you back."

"I thought you wanted the pretty little six-year-old back. Not me."

"Oh, Ellie. I *did* want things to get better, easier, but I didn't expect your scars to just magically go away. I hated having you go through the operations. I would have kept you just the way you were. I know you think you have terrible scarring, but Ellie, do you remember how much worse it used to be? Don't you remember all those 'before and after' pictures the doctors took?"

I shook my head no. But then for a split second, I thought I saw the flash of a light bulb in my mind, something stirring in my memory.

"You always said you admire the way Daddy and I love each other," she continued. I don't just love him in spite of his scars. I love him because of them. Because he has been courageous enough to go on. To survive and go on. And that's how I love you."

But she looked miserable. "I can see how if you thought I had abandoned you, it would just infuriate you to hear me pray and proclaim that God was answering prayers. Oh, Ellie. I'm so sorry! We should have insisted on seeing the counselor more often, even when you hated it.

"All I can say is that we tried, sweetie. I'm not saying we did it the right way, but we tried. And you didn't talk. You were so angry. I never gave up on you or stop caring and loving, but I stopped trying to communicate. It was just too painful to see your anger and always be saying the wrong thing and making things worse. But I always cared. Do you believe me?"

Probably at least once every few minutes I had to force myself to keep my mouth shut, not to say something inappropriate, to simply listen. It reminded me of a game we used to play as a family. Each of us had a set of plastic clowns that could be hung one by one onto a base, making a sort of clown tree. The goal for each turn was to put your clown on without the whole structure toppling over. Round and round we went, each of us carefully studying the hanging structure of clowns, picking the spot where they would balance, swing gently but not topple.

Our conversation was as fragile as that clown tree. I was sure that at any minute I would say the wrong thing and it would all fall down.

So you just start over again. Don't get mad, Ellie! Just try again. That was Daddy's admonition every time I'd pouted when my clown was the culprit that caused the collapse.

I wanted Mom and me to build something stronger than a tree of plastic clowns. So I said, "I do, Mom. I do believe you." My throat had gone dry, and I was blinking back tears. All I could do was squeeze her hand. But inside my heart, I felt something good and strong, something I had not felt in a long time. I felt thankful.

Later, after the shops had closed and tourists had vacated the sidewalks and the main sound we could hear was the water lapping against the hull of the boats, we stood by the big Liberty Oak and watched the night.

"I wish your life had been easier, Mom. I wish you hadn't had to go through so many awful things."

"I wouldn't change my life, Ellie. It was awful to go through, but I wouldn't change it. I lived and learned and loved, and it has been worth it."

"You say that as though now you're just gonna curl up and die and go to heaven."

"No, I won't give up. This is all part of the journey, sweetie. The journey is as important as the destination. God has given me so much."

"Quit saying that, Mom. He hasn't! He's messed up your life! I would change my life in a second if I could. Maybe you wouldn't change Daddy's missing eye and all the scars from Vietnam or my face, but I would. I would change it all if I could."

"Yes. I imagine you would. I know you don't agree, but this is how I see it—it's not suffering for no reason, Ellie. All the things that have been hard and even terrible have been a chance for me to cry out for help, to admit I didn't have the answers or the strength to find them, and to watch God work."

She paused as if expecting me to respond.

When I didn't, she continued, "I never would have *chosen* to go through it, Ellie. And yet . . . what would I have had to say to all the women who have come to me with stories of pain if all I had ever known was bliss? What would I have been able to give in my paintings if it were just a superficial splash of colors on a canvas? Our pain gives us energy. Oh, sometimes it defeats us, but God has made the human spirit to fight. To want to live.

"I can't explain it, but I know it is true. When I held my friends after their losses, I thanked God that I had known pain, had felt terrible loss and grief and despair. Now it's the cancer. I will walk through this too. It's not like I'm the first person to have to deal with sickness. It's part of life.

"I know you think I'm just 'babbling'"—she gave me a little smile—"but I have to say one more thing. Suffering has made you beautiful. You don't want to see it, but I can tell you it's true. You have a sensitivity, a gentleness beyond your tough exterior. You look at eyes and expressions and hearts. You hold the innocent kitten and the old mangy dog. You care about the neighbor who's afraid of terrorists and dear, eccentric Nate. These are the real moments of life, and you have embraced them. This is what is important."

I don't think Mom could see that I was blinking back tears. "But, Mom, I haven't embraced *you*! I've hated you inside for all the wrong reasons. I've pulled away from the family and not shown you love. How can that be good?"

"There's another element besides love and forgiveness and acceptance, Ellie—it's time. And we cannot predict the time it will take. All we can do is keep walking forward and trust it will come. The time will come."

We turned from the harbor, and I glanced back toward the Quarterdeck Lounge before walking in the other direction with Mom.

She must have noticed that quick glance, because she said,

"Sweetie. I can drive home. I'm a big girl." She gave me a mischievous grin. "You go visit with Ben if you want. He seems kind of lonely. And you young people can keep later hours."

I nodded without saying a thing and handed her the keys. I watched her walk to the car, and then I looked out into the night. The moon seemed to have moved closer in, so that it was big and low on the horizon and very bright, just as it should have been when a mother and a daughter were talking late into the night and learning to forgive.

The time will come. Yes, Mom was right about that. It had finally arrived.

When I got to the Quarterdeck, Ben was packing up. It was a little after eleven. He grinned when he saw me. "Hey, you decided to stay. Great. Tell Swannee I'll be with you in a minute."

"Um. Mom went on home. She sent me along to enjoy the night life. Is that okay?"

"Of course it's okay. Great. Get Louis over there to give you a Coke or something. I'll be there in a sec."

Ten minutes later, we were walking to the condominium, each of us holding onto the handle of the guitar case in between us.

"I don't like to leave my guitar there. I like to keep it with me . . ."

"In case you get lonely?"

He looked surprised. "Yeah. How'd you know?"

I shrugged. "You either spend your time with a bunch of spoiled rich kids or with the guys in the band, who seem nice enough, but not exactly like you. So I'm just thinking you might get lonely every once in a while. Anyway, I seem to remember that your guitar was always your best friend."

"You remember that, do you, Ellie?"

"Yeah. I remember lots of things about you." I felt myself blushing and asked quickly, "Are you ever lonely in New York, Ben? Do you have a girlfriend? Do you hang with normal people, or do you stick with a super religious crowd?"

He chuckled. "You and your questions, girl. Well, no, I don't have a girlfriend. As for other friends, I've got every type. Religious, as you say, and also atheist, gay and straight, black and white. You name it. Anyway, I'm not lonely in New York.

"Down here at Hilton Head is another story. I'm so glad you and your mom are here, or I'd probably wither a little. I mean, as you said, the kids in the youth group are great, but they don't always want me around. Take Sal, for instance. I need to go see her."

I felt a stab of jealousy. "What's up with her?"

"I told you she's not doing so well. I said I'd come by and we could talk. Take a walk or something. But it's not the easiest thing to convince her to open up to her youth pastor."

I wasn't so sure about that.

"And the guys in the band don't particularly like hanging with me. So I can get pretty lonely." We'd reached the condominium, and he held the door open. "But, hey, you're here. How much longer are you staying anyway?"

"A week or so."

"I'll miss you when you leave."

"Yeah, me too."

For a split second, I felt awkward. Then Ben asked, "Wanna sit on the balcony?"

"You bet. One of the most gorgeous views in the world."

"And I've got just the right thing for you—Miss Shirley Temple." He brought me a tall glass of lemonade.

"Freshly squeezed, no doubt."

"Exactly. By yours truly."

I settled into a low chair on the balcony. Ben leaned against the railing and asked, "What about you? Who keeps you from being lonely?"

I told him about Megan and Timothy, and Nate and Mrs. Rose, softball, the animal shelter. He just listened and nodded periodically, and I noticed again how his eyes were piercing, yet warm.

When I paused, embarrassed by my monologue, he commented, "Someday I'd like to meet your friends, Ellie-o. They sound pretty neat."

Again I felt an awkward pause, and I searched for something to say. "So have you talked to your mom since you've been down here?"

"Yeah. She called the other day—checking up on me. Good ole Mom. There's something I've learned from the parents of the kids I work with. Most of them really do love their kids, even though a lot of times they don't know how to show it. My parents and yours are no different. They really do want the best, you know."

"Yeah, I know. Or I guess I should say, I'm finding that out."

"It was great to see you and Swannee together. You seemed to be having a good time."

"We were, Ben, and all because I followed your advice." I paused. "I forgave my mother."

He got a big smile and gave me a high five. "Way to go, Ellie-o."

My face got hot when his hand touched mine.

"We talked about my accident for the very first time. Well, no. It was the first time I remember. And we both remained calm and tried to understand each other's point of view."

"And?"

"And I learned some things."

"Such as . . . ?"

"She never abandoned me. She was the one who put out the fire. And she's always blamed herself for the accident. And mostly, it was an accident."

His back was against the railing, and I looked over his shoulder to where the lighthouse was in the distance with the moon bright above it. "Maybe you're right, Ben. Maybe something good can come out of it now."

"I'm proud of you, Ellie." Our eyes met, and we held each other's gaze for a long moment.

I could feel the sexual tension on that balcony and could read something good and strong and fiery in his eyes. Desire. I wanted him to move toward me, to hold me close so that I could feel his heart beating. But he stayed back against the railing, hair falling down on his shoulders, one foot propped on a low chair. He wanted to come over to me, to touch me. I knew it. And I also knew that Reverend Ben, as Sal had called him, would never cross his self-imposed lines. He would stay firmly planted in his place. But it pleased me that he wanted it. It pleased me a lot.

He finally broke the long silence by saying, "I wanna get you something. Then I'll drive you home." He left the balcony, then reappeared a moment later with a book. "Here. I've been meaning to bring it to you." It was a dog-eared copy of *From Screwed Up to Awesome*.

"Thanks," I mumbled. "Looks like you've read this a couple of times."

"I've lent it to a lot of kids."

"Lost kids like me."

He grinned. "Kids looking for answers—like you."

"Is that what I am to you, Ben? Just another kid to save and reform?" I knew it was a mean question—or a loaded one.

But Ben wasn't taken off guard for a second. In fact, he surprised me by saying, "No, Ellie-o. You know good and well that you'll never be a project to me. Don't try to put a guilt trip on me because I won't take you in my arms and kiss you. I would if I could. But I can't. You're too important to me for that. You're a rediscovered friend, a potential soul mate." He grinned shyly. "Give it time, girl. Just give it time."

He drove me home. I opened the door to the car, started to get out, then turned to him and gave him a quick kiss on the cheek. "Thanks for the ride, Ben."

As I curled up on my bed, I thought how one day could truly make a difference. How a decade of hurt and misunderstanding and anger and cruel actions toward my mother could somehow be forgotten in a day.

No, not forgotten, not swept away, but something. Forgiven.

Mom hadn't changed. She was still the same sweet, sentimental, talented woman she'd always been. But I had changed. I had decided that it was worth it to stick around and begin to build back our relationship.

And then there was Ben. Good, patient, wise, kind Ben. But no matter how I tried to make him good and kind and keep him at an arm's length, what I was really thinking as I drifted off to sleep with his book tucked under my pillow was that someday I wanted sexy, wonderful Ben Abrams lying here beside me. I didn't know how much time that would take, but I was willing to wait.

Chapter 21

There's nowhere I'd rather be
Than here with you
Beneath these stars
And this old tree. . . .

—GREGG RUSSELL, SINGING AT HARBOUR TOWN UNDERNEATH THE LIBERTY OAK

I woke up the next morning feeling happy—more than happy, hopeful—about my relationship with my mother, about the ability to forgive, about Ben Abrams. It was a luxury to lie in bed and turn over our conversations in my mind and not feel angry. Mom said she had gained relief from letting guilt and anger go, and that seemed likely for me too.

Hindsight was curled up in bed beside me, in the possessive way she'd adopted since Rusty had shown up. She was purring, pleased with herself.

"I think I'm purring too," I said to her out loud, and then I closed my eyes and tried to hear Mom's and Ben's words again, tried to relive the moments each phrase was spoken, and that felt like a luxury too. It felt like the loud smacking sound when my bat makes contact with the ball or like a long gulp of Coke after a hard ball game.

I felt as though I were tiptoeing carefully around each kind word they had said, considering it, inspecting it, deciding if this could be true. It wasn't that I'd never received compliments before. But I had always believed they were pitiful attempts to bandage my terrible scar, to cover something that couldn't be covered. *You're just saying that because you feel sorry for me.*

But on this morning, the memories were bright, they were good. I could accept them. That made me shiver a little. Acceptance. Could it possibly be as simple as Ben was claiming? Maybe I wasn't going to have to settle for a mediocre life, struggling to find a way to prove myself. Maybe there was something more.

I took the book Ben had given me out from under my pillow and started reading. It turned out to be a modern translation of the Gospel of Mark. It actually made the Bible seem fresh and new and appealing. I had gotten to the second chapter, the part about Jesus healing a paralyzed man, when the phone rang. I grabbed it quickly, not wanting to wake Mom.

"Hey, Mae Mae. How are you this morning?"

"Good, Daddy. You'll never believe what I'm doing."

"What?"

"Reading the Bible."

He whistled low. "Wow. To make Mom happy?"

"No. Not at all. We're having some good conversations, but I picked up the Bible on my own."

"Well, that's . . . that's good . . . and surprising. Not at all what I was expecting to hear."

"And what *were* you expecting to hear?"

He chuckled a little. "Well, from what your mom told me last night, I thought you might be telling me about Ben."

"Daddy! What did she say?"

"Not much. Just that you were meeting him after he finished up at the Quarterdeck."

I rolled my eyes. "Don't start getting ideas. Didn't she tell you that he invited both of us over and she was too tired to go? Mom's just trying to be a matchmaker."

He was still laughing. "I figured as much. Don't worry, I know better than to get involved in women's stuff. But I'm pleased to hear y'all are having a good time. Mom sounds so much better."

"She is, Dad. The past few days she's been painting a lot, and we've taken walks, and she's eating more."

"Good. Thanks so much, Ellie." He cleared his throat, and then his voice didn't sound jovial. In fact, it was a little strained. "How's her cold?"

"Oh, I think it's fine. It doesn't seem to be bothering her now."

"Ellie, I talked with Dr. Marshall this morning. He's gotten the latest blood tests back, the ones from the oncologist on the island. He's a bit concerned."

"About what? I just told you she's doing lots better."

"I know, Ellie. I can tell that your mom is feeling a hundred percent better. But the platelets are still low . . . dangerously low. I think the doctor may want her to have another transfusion."

"Oh." I felt blood draining from my face just thinking about that word. "When?"

"I've made an appointment for Thursday."

"Down here?"

"Yes, I'm coming down Wednesday—so I can take her."

"Does Mom know?"

"Yes, we talked about it last night. She's not worried, honey."

"Are you telling me everything, Dad? Mom and I are getting along now; we're talking about stuff. Important stuff. So please don't hide anything from me. Is the cancer back?"

"The truth is that there is no sign of cancer. The low platelets are because of the chemo and the hemorrhaging. If the doctor is worried about other things, he hasn't told me yet. Promise."

"Okay, Daddy. I'll take care of her."

"Thanks, Ellie. And don't worry. Everything's going to be okay. See you in two days."

I hung up the phone, my bright mood a little diminished. *Don't worry*. I flicked on the computer to get my mind off of our conversation. When I checked my e-mail, I was relieved to see a note from Nate and one from Megan.

Dear Ellie,

Mrs. Rose said to tell you thank-you for the pretty postcard from the beach. We each got our postcards yesterday and I like getting things from you in the mail like that.

We want to meet Rusty and that made us happy to know about him. Do you think a dog will be okay here with all the kitties? Mrs. Rose said he sounds like a sweet dog, but she is a bit worried.

I will give you the names of web sites that Mark has shown me. I miss Mark.

Don't worry about your sister Abbie. I don't think she is the one poisoning the cats. Yesterday she came over to visit me and brought Bobby. We sat on the floor and I worked a puzzle for him and then we played with my plastic dinosaurs. He is a cute little boy.

Tell your mommy hello from me.

Nate

Hey Ellie!

It was so great to talk to you the other night. I am actually feeling a lot better about everything. And you will be proud of me. Tim and I talked about my fears, most of the bad things in the past (including the mirrors), and even my penchant to "medicate through shopping." Isn't that the phrase they used in rehab?

Timothy didn't freak out at all.

I may have found THE DRESS but will not make a final decision until you've seen me in it and assured me that I look big, fat, and ugly.

Cool that you and your mom are talking. Tell me more about Ben.

Love Meg

Mom was still in bed dozing when I poked my head into her room. "How you feeling?" I asked.

"Just a little tired. Otherwise fine."

"Did we overdo it last night?"

"Surely not! I wouldn't trade last night for the world. Being with you at Harbour Town, looking in the shops, hearing Ben perform, talking. It was perfect. And today, I'll just have to take it a little easier." She made a face. "Who would think that a stroll by the harbor would wear me out? I'm about ready for this body to get stronger."

"Me too. Hey, Dad called a little while ago. He told me he's coming down on Wednesday."

Her face lit up. "Yes, it'll be wonderful to have your father here with us for a few days."

I smiled. "Yes, it will. In the meantime, what can I bring you for breakfast?"

"How about some orange juice and a cup of tea?"

"And an English muffin?"

"You've got me figured out."

I brought a tray with her breakfast on it down to her room and perched on the bed beside her as she ate.

In between bites, Mom asked, "How was Ben?"

"Oh, fine. He was sorry you didn't come."

"I'll bet."

That remark caught me off guard, and when I looked up at Mom, she had a sly grin on her face.

"No, I'm serious."

"Thank you, Ellie."

"We're just friends, Mom. Don't you start gossiping too."

"Gossiping? Who's gossiping?"

"You said something to Daddy. He told me." My face felt hot. "Just please don't tell Rachel that Ben likes me—don't start dreaming things up, Mom. Okay? Promise?"

"Cross my heart and hope to die, stick a needle in my eye."

I rolled my eyes. "You and Rachel sound like a recording sometimes. Anyway, I have something more interesting to ask you about. Did you really mean what you said, about wanting to go to the Dwelling Place for me? You really don't care about going anymore? I thought you needed to go there for yourself—you know, because of how you left it—the telegram and all the bad memories."

"Of course I would love to go back, Ellie. It's very important and near to my heart. But you're even nearer. That's what I meant. The trip to Europe was a chance to spend time with you."

I considered that for a moment and said, "Okay. That's cool. And so now when you think about Scotland, you aren't upset or depressed or anything?"

"No, Ellie. Now when I look at the sketches and my painting, I get a full feeling in my chest. I can't really explain it. Not sadness, though. A feeling that life is turning, a sphere, and the longer I live, the more I can see how the different slices of that sphere fit into place. Some of the slices are still missing, that's for sure. Maybe I'll never know how they fit back into the globe this side of heaven. But your father came back. That piece is there." She let out a long sigh.

"You know how the Bible says that the sins of the parents visit the children. I guess since I'd been exposed to a series of secrets, depression, betrayal, lying, I thought it was time to break the cycle. There are things we pass on to other generations. We don't mean to, don't want to either, but it is so much a part of us that it just happens. Evelyne poisoned my mother with the things that happened to her, and it just continued.

"At the Dwelling Place, I finally understood about all the secrets. And I don't know. It gave me hope. Miss Abigail used to quote a verse from Isaiah: 'Your people will rebuild the ancient ruins and will raise up the age-old foundations; you will be called the Repairer of Broken Walls, Restorer of Streets with Dwellings.' Over the years, my family was in the process of being repaired. I needed to learn that in 1968 when I was trying to discover who I was—apart from my mother, and because of her too—what my purpose was in life. I wanted that for you too, Ellie."

She looked at me as if she expected an answer, so I said quickly, "I'm glad you learned those things, Mom. And that you told me about them—even if we never get to Scotland."

I thought about our conversation as I cleared away the breakfast dishes, took them to the kitchen upstairs, and loaded the dishwasher. I was still thinking when I got back to her bedroom. But Mom looked so tired I decided not to ply her with more questions. Instead, I asked, "Want to paint?"

"No, not yet. I think I'm just going to be lazy and stay in bed awhile. I'm sorry, Ellie."

"No prob, Mom." I said it lightly, but in truth, I wished she could find the strength to paint.

Mom stayed in bed all that day, which alarmed me, especially after what Daddy had said on the phone. I took two walks on the beach, and each time I came back in to check on Mom, I was hoping she'd say that Ben had called and was coming over. Then I grew irritated with myself for having those thoughts.

She finally got up around six o'clock. I'd been out with Rusty, touring the neighborhood and once again having my arm practically pulled out of its socket. When I got back, Mom was upstairs, sitting on the couch. She was still wearing her pajamas and had the green scarf tied neatly around her head. Her old sketch pad was opened on the floor in front of the couch. She leaned over and retrieved it just before Rusty planted a dirty paw right where it had been.

"Hey, boy," she said, scratching him behind the ears as he panted. "Looks like he enjoyed the walk."

"Yeah, he did." I got some lemonade from the fridge and brought a glass out for Mom and one for myself. I sat beside her on the couch. "He's especially fond of the little Schnauzer on Red Woodpecker."

"Mmm," Mom said, still petting Rusty but obviously lost in her own thoughts. "I've been thinking some more about your question, Ellie. About why I wanted to go to the Dwelling Place. The other thing—the most important thing—was the promise I made to your father there—before *and* after I got the telegram that he was missing. I promised him in my heart that I'd wait for him. It was one of the most difficult promises I've ever had to keep."

"I can believe that. He was gone for a long time, and you didn't even know if he was still alive."

"Yes. There were some very hard things going on in my life," she said, nibbling her lip. "Things that just about wore me out emotionally. And then your dad was found. Of course, I was so surprised and shocked—we all thought he was dead. I was excited to see him, of course, but scared too. Still, I carried in my heart the storybook endings I'd read all my life, and I still believed in them."

She kept hesitating, as if she wanted to say something else. Finally she whispered, "But it wasn't like that, Ellie. He was wounded—physically, mentally, emotionally. He wasn't the same man I had been in love with."

"Are you saying you didn't love Daddy anymore?"

"I didn't *feel* love, Ellie."

Hearing her admit that made me sit up straight on the couch. "How did you start loving him again?"

"I didn't do it very well, and certainly not all at once. I said to God—I probably yelled at Him—'I give up. You win. I cannot do any of this.' I just went in and threw a fit before the Lord."

I couldn't help but give a sad smile, imagining the scene.

"Miss Abigail was the one who got through to me. I poured out my heart to her once again in the sanctuary of Mt. Carmel, and she said, 'Mary Swan, no one can force you to surrender. You can hold on to all those painful things and die inside, or you can let them go. Only you can decide how your fiery trials will affect you. Will they draw you to Jesus or turn you away? Will you accept His scars, His sacrifice, or will you go through life bearing your own scars? I promise you, Mary Swan, if you give them to Him, He will make something beautiful of them.'"

I felt my heart skip a beat, hearing Mom say those words about fiery trials and scars, but I could tell she wasn't connecting those things to me. She was remembering what Miss Abigail had said to her.

"Miss Abigail could be very convincing, Ellie. I gave up my dreams a hundred times. And God gave them back to me. I'd promised Robbie I'd wait, and I did, so I was counting on God to help me love him again.

"It's one of life's paradoxes—how fighting and surrender go together. I had to give up first, and then gradually God gave me the strength to fight for Robbie and me. We took our time, a long time, to get reacquainted, to get counseling."

"And love came back?"

"Not right away. At first I just felt sorry for Robbie. I was heartbroken, grieving, confused. It wasn't the romantic reunion you see in the movies. He was so disfigured and weak. He spent months in physical therapy and counseling. I didn't know what would happen. I was terrified.

"We waited over a year before we got married. By then, things were much better. It still was hard, but . . ."

She was holding the sketch pad in her lap and touching the pages of that stone wall in Scotland. "I guess the only way I survived all that . . . the only way I've survived anything, was by having the Lord as my dwelling place. I know it's not what you want to hear, but it's the simple truth. That's what my journey in Scotland confirmed for me. I didn't know it at the time, but those days in Scotland gave me a glimpse of what reconciliation and peace and hope could look like. Mama had found something, so had Rachel and I, and then I'd promised to hang in there for Robbie. Scotland prepared me to hang on."

I put my arms around her and gave her a hug. "Are you sorry you married Daddy, Mom?"

"Of course not. Not now. Ellie, God honored our commitment. He let love grow again. I learned that it was worth it to sacrifice what you want, even what you think you *have* to have, to wait for something better. It doesn't really make sense to our human way of seeing. But eventually, the heart accepts what the mind chooses. I chose to love your father again, and he chose to trust in my love.

"It was a gamble, they said—everyone, especially our parents, who loved us both. But I didn't think it was gambling. It was trusting in the promises of God."

"You're both fighters, Mom. That's how you made it."

"No, I tell you, Ellie, we made it through surrendering. It was one of the biggest lessons of my life." She leaned her head back on the couch and closed her eyes, and a single tear slid down her cheek. Sitting there beside her, one arm laced through hers, I took my other hand and wiped the tear away.

"All along the way, I had to surrender my art. I wanted to be known, to prove myself, to show I was as good as my mother. But it never worked out the way I planned. The first time was that silly art scandal in Amsterdam. Imagine, I thought my work was getting noticed when really it was just being used to smuggle drugs!

"And then again in 1971 when my painting caused such . . . such problems . . ."

I couldn't let that ambiguous statement slide past again, so I interrupted. "What do you mean? What's the deal with your painting in 1971?"

Her face reddened, and she shook her head. "It's not something I want to talk about right now."

I was annoyed. She was telling me everything else; what was the big deal with this? But I didn't press, and she seemed relieved to go on with her story.

"I just kept having to let it all go. I am *so* thankful now, Ellie, that God did it His way. I never would have been able to handle the schedule and renown of an artist's life when I was a young mother. And your father needed me so much too. At times I was resentful, or bitter or just depressed, but every time I took it before the Lord, He showed me the way. And then poof, after all those years, He opened the door.

"Every hard thing I've been through has been worth it. Even the worst things, like with your father and . . ."

"And what?"

"And with you. When you were burned and disfigured, I blamed myself, and I would have done anything on earth to change places with you. I can't think of anything more anguishing than to watch your own child suffer. It was even worse than wondering if Robbie was being tortured in some POW camp.

"All we could do was hold on and pray and love you as best we knew how. I knew you were mad and rebellious. I didn't blame you. I hated making all those curfews and grounding you. We tried and you bucked us, and I would go to bed crying. But even there, it was another lesson in surrendering. I had to give you up. I couldn't control you. And I couldn't make God make everything easy for you."

She was completely worn out with talking, her eyes glazed with tears.

"Shhh. You don't have to talk anymore now, Mom. Thanks for telling me all that. I know it wasn't easy." Then, in another impulsive moment, I said, "You did okay, Mom. You did okay after all."

I tucked Mom into bed, literally, around nine o'clock and went to my room. Hindsight glowered at Rusty as he wiggled his body over to the bed, begging with his eyes to hop in beside her. She reached out a fine-tuned claw and swatted at him.

"Come here, Rusty," I cooed softly, leading him by the collar into the kitchen. "You sleep here, buddy."

I closed the door to my bedroom and got into bed. I felt a headache pulsing in the back of my head. So much information, so much emotion. I was completely drained, so I switched on the TV and watched a ball game. I barely remember zapping it off around midnight and curling up under the covers.

At first I thought the knocking was in my dreams. When I finally woke up and realized it was coming from rocks being tossed at my window, I felt a moment of panic. It was pitch black outside. I fumbled for the clock. 2:45.

I could barely make out my name being called. "Ellie. Psst. Ellie."

I went out on the little balcony and stared down toward the street.

Ben was looking up at me. He was shaking, crying, his face a ghastly white.

I ran down the stairs, out into the driveway, and whispered, "Come in, quick. Ben, what is it? Are you hurt?"

He followed me inside as if in a trance, plopped on the couch, and rested his head in his hands.

"Are you hurt?" I repeated.

He sighed, sat up, pushed the hair out of his face, and said, "Not me. Not me. I told you I was worried about her, and then I didn't do anything. It's all my fault."

I felt my body tense. "What are you talking about?"

"Sal. She . . . she swallowed a whole bottle of her mom's sleeping pills."

"Oh, Ben, no. And you found her?"

"Yeah. Samantha called around ten and asked me to help her look for her. We found her crumpled up out on the beach behind the house, with a note in her hands." He raised his eyes. "But she was alive. She's alive. Oh, God, thank God, she's alive."

Ben looked small and ghostlike and fragile. He was crying softly, and I sat down beside him and hugged him fiercely and tightly, hugged him so I could feel his heart pounding and feel the tears on his face falling on the nape of my neck. I felt his arms come around me, holding me, holding on for dear life, felt his tears soak into my nightshirt.

"Oh, Ellie, I'm glad you're here. I'm sorry. I didn't know what to do. Who to see."

"Shh," I kept saying, stroking his hair as if he were Rusty. We held each other for another moment, then Ben sat back, wiped his hand over his face, and breathed deeply.

"Where is she now?" I asked.

"At the hospital on the island. Her parents are with her, and Samantha too. I told them I'd come back later."

He went to the bathroom and washed his face and hands while I made him some coffee. Gradually a little color came back to his face. But he kept saying, "How could God let this happen? How could He let her do it after all we'd talked about? This isn't making sense. This isn't right."

Ben Abrams, bright, clever, devout, and kind Ben, Ben who was so sure of himself and his faith, looked as if all his neat philosophies and religious phrases had been shattered like the mirrors in Megan's house.

"There are no easy answers," he kept saying. "I'm not cut out for this job. I should have caught on quicker. Gosh, Ellie, if it weren't for Samantha, Sal could be dead. I saw all the signs. I even saw the resolve and then the peacefulness. It was all staring me in the face, and I didn't get it. I shouldn't have this job."

I put my finger over his mouth. "Shh, Ben. Don't think about all that right now. You need to rest."

In my mind, as I got him blankets and took him downstairs to the extra bedroom, the words throbbing in my temple were déjà-vu. I wasn't seeing Ben there. I was seeing Megan, her face white and her hands bloody.

"Get some sleep," I said.

He nodded, like a little kid who was worn out. As he took the blankets and pillow from me and went into the bedroom, he looked back at me, eyes filled with tears. "Thanks, Ellie. Thanks for being there for me."

I went back upstairs and into the bathroom. My hands were shaking as I turned on the spigot and let water rush into the marble tub. I took a long, hot bath, keeping the water running the whole time to make sure that he couldn't hear my sobs.

When I finally got into bed, I lay there, wide-awake, seeing Ben shaken and pale, then seeing Megan, and then Ben again. I must have drifted off to sleep for a moment because suddenly I was dreaming. In the dream I saw Jesus, standing on the beach holding Ben in His arms. But Jesus was looking at me, His body scarred, His eyes full of love. And in the dream I could hear Him saying to me, "Suffering, surrender, beauty, redemption."

Then I was awake again. I sat up in bed. I had the firm conviction that Ben was going to learn something vital from this near tragedy and that, until he could stand on his own, God was going to hold him through it. And He was going to hold me. I was astounded by these thoughts, by this revelation that suffering could be working for good. Ben didn't know it was happening; he was sound asleep. But I saw it, and I didn't sleep a wink for the rest of the night.

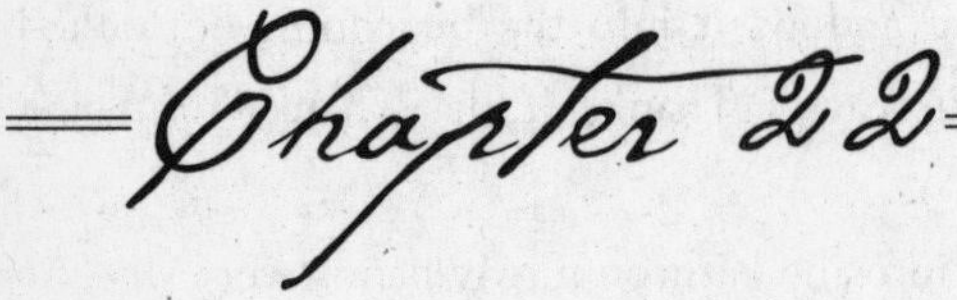

The future will only contain what we put into it now.

—SLOGAN FROM STUDENT RIOTS, MAY 1968, PARIS

I must have dozed off around seven and then woken with a start, remembering Ben. I threw on my shorts and T-shirt and came out to the family room, where Mom and Ben were deep in conversation.

"Thanks for being there for me last night, Ellie-o," Ben said when he saw me, forcing a smile across his otherwise somber face.

"Of course. Any word about Sal?"

"Yeah, I called the hospital a little while ago. She's stable. She'll pull through."

Mom was pushing a piece of bacon around on her plate, obviously with no intention of eating it. Rusty sat at her side, tail wagging eagerly. She broke the bacon in bits and dropped them on the floor as she said, "Poor girl. Sometimes life is so complicated."

We spent the morning inside, all three of us. Ben played a game of solitaire, Mom eventually went over to the easel and started painting, and I cleaned up the kitchen. Then I scrounged around the game room downstairs until I came up with another deck of cards and joined Ben at the table in the family room. After we'd played three rounds of double solitaire, numbly, calmly, grateful for something simple to do, we both got up and came over to where Mom sat in front of the window, painting the ocean.

"You're amazing, Mom. I don't see how you do that. You look out, get an idea, and put it on the canvas. It's right. What inspires you?"

She dabbed her brush in a little glob of bluish paint. "A sad movie, a beautiful sunrise, a snippet of truth being tossed out in the air. Creation. Anger. Anything that needs me to use my senses. But lots of times, it's pain."

She looked over at Ben, and he nodded, and we sat there in silence.

Perhaps the pain of learning about Sal had inspired Mom to paint, but it had also zapped her of what little energy she had in reserve. She left Ben and me in the family room, proclaiming that she needed to lie down for a little while. That was nothing new, and yet the way she said it made me look at Ben with raised eyebrows, and I saw a flicker of worry cross his face.

"Let her sleep, Ellie," he reassured me when she was downstairs. "We're all completely spent, and she's an artist. She admits that hard things pierce her heart. She needs rest."

Ben left for his condo sometime before noon, and I went down to Mom's room to call her for lunch.

"I think I'll eat down here," she said with resignation. "Do you think you could close the curtains, please? It's a bit sunny for me."

She was sitting in bed, knees pulled up under the covers, looking across the room to where she'd placed the lighthouse pitcher on her vanity. "I can't decide where to display this. Upstairs, I guess. But it would look cute on the sunporch at home too. At any rate, Ellie, thank you for the gift. I'll treasure it always."

It pleased me that she liked the pitcher, but I didn't like the way she seemed to be drawing into herself, overly sentimental. And I especially didn't like the way she kept looking at the strange painting that was sitting right beside the pitcher. She got tears in her eyes when she saw me staring at it.

"I painted that while your father was missing." Her face was strained. "A lot of things can happen in two years."

Her bottom lip was quivering, and her eyes were absolutely liquid.

"Listen, let me get your lunch, Mom," I said quickly. She didn't object.

When I brought her a cup of soup and some crackers and set it beside her bed, she had not moved an inch. She was still just staring straight ahead at that painting.

"When you were in rehab, I used to just sit and stare at this painting and some of the others, and I'd cry and want to roll up in a ball and die. Daddy decided that dwelling on all the sadness from the past wasn't exactly helping me deal with the present, so he packed up all these paintings and brought them down here."

Wanting to "roll up in a ball and die" was exactly how she looked to me at that moment, and I wanted to grab the painting and run with it under my arm onto the beach and throw it like a Frisbee out into the ocean. I sat down on her bed once again.

She took my hand, and she squeezed it so tightly that I winced a little, surprised by the strength in those fragile looking hands. I scooted back so that my back was resting against the headboard, and I watched my mother look at her painting. This one also had the Dwelling Place wall rambling from one side to the other, but nothing else in the whole painting resembled in any way the peaceful pasture in Scotland. There was no lamb in the top corner, or any other sheep, for that matter. Instead, there were a lot of angry people, people fighting, on either side of that wall.

At first I thought that it was a depiction of the Civil War, a modern day civil war. Then I realized it wasn't the Civil War, but civil rights. On one side of the stone wall, there were mostly blacks, with a few whites sprinkled in, and on the other side there were only whites. And everyone looked angry. Many of the figures held up clenched fists and had open mouths, and you could easily imagine the obscenities coming from them. Draped across the stone wall were the bodies of Martin Luther King, Jr., and several other men and women who had apparently died defending civil rights.

"This is why I stopped painting what you called 'bold, gutsy' stuff."

"This painting?"

"Yes. The final copy of it."

"But it's really good, Mom. Even the rough draft."

"I know it's good, Ellie. That's the whole point. It was too good."

"You're not making any sense, Mom."

"This is the painting I was talking about, the one I did in 1971. I even won a prize for it. But it was extremely controversial."

"So? That's cool, Mom. You made people think."

She looked as if someone had taken a carving knife and sliced into her soul. "I suppose you're right, but . . . you know me, Ellie. I don't enjoy controversy. Especially when it yanks people apart. I like unity."

She seemed to be referring to something very specific, but I had no idea what she meant.

"What do you see in this painting, Ellie?"

I didn't hesitate for a second. "Hate."

She gave a painful little groan. I glanced at her, and all she said was, "Go on."

"Well, it looks like whites hating blacks and blacks hating whites, a lot of confusion, and a few people trying to step in and help."

She sighed. "Yes, and who's winning, Ellie? Can you tell?"

I honestly had no idea. The fight looked pretty equal, the numbers of people about the same on either side of the wall. "Beats me."

"So you can't tell either." She sighed one more time and said, more to herself than to me, "I thought I'd made it crystal clear. I thought they'd get it."

"Who?"

"The people who commissioned it, the people who reviewed it, the viewers . . ."

"Nobody got what you were trying to say?"

"No. It was supposed to be a wall of hope, Ellie. Hope for civil rights as it had been hope for me and my family. That's why I chose the Dwelling Place wall. Of course, no one else knew its significance, but that didn't matter. The point was the larger symbolism. See there, Ellie? The bodies of Dr. King and the others are draped over the wall, and the weight of their bodies is causing the stones to crumble down, little by little."

Sure enough, when I examined the painting, I could see places in the wall where stones had come loose and were lying in little heaps on the ground.

"The process of breaking down the wall isn't quick, and yes, it's costly. People die. But there is hope that one day the wall will disappear and the people will be unified, getting along in spite of their differences, richer because of them.

"I was young and naïve, Ellie. The media made this painting into a huge political statement. They turned it all around. Made it propaganda. It almost cost me my whole career as an artist. And it cost me other things—even more important."

"What do you mean?"

She shook her head as if to say, *Let's drop it*.

And I *would* have dropped it—I really would have—if I hadn't suddenly noticed something that made goose bumps shoot all across my arms. Mom had put Carl Matthews in the painting. Even though I had only met Dr. Matthews once, and this painting was made over thirty years ago, I had no doubt that the young man standing a few feet from the stone wall was Carl Matthews. He was standing between a tall white man whom I recognized as Mayor Ivan Allen and another black man who looked vaguely familiar to me, someone involved in Georgia politics.

"Mom," I blurted, "you're talking about the Matthewses. This painting cost you and Daddy your friendship with Carl and Cassandra. This is the reason you haven't seen them in so long!"

I probably sounded excited, as if I'd found the last word to fill a crossword puzzle, but immediately I realized that my enthusiasm was completely out of place. As soon as it was out of my mouth, I wished I hadn't said it.

She nodded, looking miserable. "When I saw this painting on the floor upstairs the other day, it just brought back such hard memories. The other paintings remind me of difficult times, but this one is like a gaping wound."

My head was pulsing with the words, *Ellie, do something! Don't let her go on and on about this.* It was probably Abbie's conscience screaming into mine. But Mom was still talking, and I thought she needed me to listen.

"Your father was missing for over two years, and during that time the things that kept me alive were helping at Mt. Carmel and painting. I took classes, got to know the artsy crowd in Atlanta. I suppose it was heady stuff. I showed the things I was doing to a group of politically minded Atlantans, people interested in the future of the city, and they got the idea of commissioning me to paint something that would symbolize the future of the civil rights movement. And they wanted it to be displayed before the city elections that fall.

"It was a few months after Carl and Cassie were married, a few months after I'd been her maid of honor and cried with happiness as they walked down the aisle as husband and wife. They were two of my best friends, Ellie. If I hadn't had Carl and Cassie and Miss Abigail and Rachel during those months when Robbie was missing, I would have sunk into a very deep and dark depression.

"I was so excited about this painting. It was the first time I'd actually been commissioned to do anything. I hid out and painted in my mother's atelier for three weeks straight. I couldn't wait to show Carl and Cassie. But when Carl saw it, he begged me not to exhibit it. He said it was too controversial—it would do more harm to the black community than all my years at Mt. Carmel had benefited it.

"I just didn't see it that way. I thought it would make people think—just as you said. So I sold the painting to the group that had commissioned it. But Carl was right. It was very polarizing.

"I'd never seen Carl as angry as he was when a photo and review of my painting appeared in the *Atlanta Journal*. He came over to my house—I was living at Granddad JJ and Trixie's—and he threw the paper on the kitchen table and yelled at me with some kind of righteous anger burning in his eyes. We had a fight, Carl and I. I tried to apologize, but he didn't want to hear it."

"Did you think you were wrong, Mom?"

"No. I saw it as a difference of opinion."

"And for thirty years you've never been able to forgive each other? Over a painting?"

Mom teared up again. "It wasn't that simple, Ellie. The painting won a prize and got a great deal of media attention, which heated up the political race even more. And all kinds of rumors started flying around. Carl was working night and day, between doing his residency and helping at the campaign headquarters. In the end, his candidate—the man beside him in the painting—didn't win. The man who was elected appointed a judge in the Georgia appeals court who was much less enthusiastic about civil rights. I think Carl always blamed me for my part in the whole affair.

"We talked once or twice after the election. We each tried to explain our position, but it always ended up in an ugly shouting match. We're two of the most peaceable people in the world, and there we were, screaming at each other. I tried to talk to Cassie too. We might have worked it out, but then your father came back right at that time." Mom closed her eyes as if imagining the scene.

"When Robbie got back, he was in terrible shape, and suddenly all my attention had to be for him. I didn't have any emotional reserves to deal with the fiasco of the painting. Carl knew that. Cassie saw it. But they didn't step in. They didn't stick up for me. They didn't help me with Robbie. I thought I might lose my mind caring for him, and they never even called me."

I heard a bitterness in her voice that sounded fresh and strong, as if she were recounting a misunderstanding that had happened only a few weeks ago.

"They felt betrayed, and I felt betrayed. Betrayed! Because of a painting! How can a painting cause people who are best friends, people who have been through so much together, people who love the same God, how can it cause them to stop talking to each other? One misunderstanding that just grew and grew and grew.

"The army had put Carl through med school, so he owed them a few years. He was sent to Texas. Daddy and I were married in 1972, and Carl and Cassandra didn't come. We didn't see them again for probably eight years. Then Carl was offered a position at Grady Hospital, and they moved back to Atlanta.

"I was pregnant with you at the time. Cassie and I got back in touch; she even visited me at the hospital when you were born. A month or so later, she and Carl came to visit, but—" She sighed miserably. "I could read the disappointment in his eyes. He made a comment that hurt my feelings so much. He said, 'I never thought you'd be living in a fancy white neighborhood, Mary Swan.' I tried to explain, but the old wounds were still there. We exchanged angry words again. In the end, we just chose to stop seeing each other. We chose to lose touch.

"It must have broken Miss Abigail's heart—she was so close to all of us. She never preached to us, but I'm sure she prayed a lot."

Mom was sitting cross-legged on the bed with her arms out to each side—almost as if she were in a lotus position. But she wasn't meditating. She was holding a tearful conversation with her painting, and I might as well have been invisible.

"I've thought about it a thousand times, thought about how Rachel and I eventually patched things up. She asked for forgiveness and forgave me, and she's not even a Christian! But not Carl. He wouldn't forgive me."

"Oh, Mom. You're getting yourself all upset. Please stop crying. I shouldn't have let you keep this painting down here." This time I did get off the bed and plucked the painting off of the vanity. I took it out into the hallway and set it on the floor. Then I went back to Mom, removed her scarf, and helped her under the covers.

She was dabbing her eyes and nose with a tissue. "I'll be okay, Ellie. I'm sorry. It's my last story, and it's the worst because nothing is resolved. Not really."

"Shh. Mom. Shh." I racked my brain to think of something positive to say. "Remember that you've been talking with Mrs. Matthews. Surely that's progress. Everything will be fine. Daddy's coming tomorrow. Please don't think about any of those paintings anymore. It's all my fault. I should never have brought them out. Please just forget about them. Please try."

Again I had the terrifying impression that I was the mother, tucking the frightened child into bed, reassuring her, chasing away the nightmares with soft words. I shivered as I left the room and turned out the light.

I picked up the painting, marched into the garage closet, and shoved it onto the shelf with such force that another smaller painting fell onto the floor. I felt a headache starting as I stooped down and picked up the fallen painting and set it back in its place. Then I stalked out onto the beach, surprised at the depth of my anger. I had thought I'd gotten rid of it, but here it was again, pulsing in my head, screaming for attention.

I was cursing myself for having found all those paintings in the first place and then cursing myself for having the stupid idea of displaying them all over the house. But then I thought, *It was thanks to these paintings that Mom and I started talking. That was a good thing.* And I was remembering the way I'd grabbed *National Velvet* from the bookshelf in my old room and stuffed those letters from Mom into the book, and how that quick, almost thoughtless gesture had allowed me to read those letters down here at Hilton Head. I'd read them right after I'd been cruel to Mom, and then that had precipitated my forgiveness of my mother.

I turned those things around in my mind and saw one other incident. The Humane Society fund-raiser and my meeting with the Matthewses. I considered the irony of the situation—renegade Ellie helping to patch up a strained relationship between Christians?

I collapsed onto the shore, digging my fingers into the sand. I had never believed in what my parents called God's sovereignty—that Somebody up there knew all about what was going to happen in your life before it happened. I believed in coincidence, and I believed in scheming. But when I considered the timing of each of those recent events, well, I felt perplexed. The way they fit together seemed to be just too big of a coincidence to be, well, a coincidence. Maybe it was a well-crafted plan, a twisted plot of Mom's to have me discovering truth down here at Hilton Head where I was yanked away from my support group and forced to face this junk on my own.

But I knew as surely as I was mashing the wet sand in my hands that Mom had not planned this. She had not contracted cancer so I'd meet the Matthewses at a party and tell them about it. She hadn't cancelled our European trip so that I'd come to Hilton Head and find those paintings or read those long forgotten letters or meet up with Ben again, Ben the reborn friend.

If I thought about it in my reasonable, scientific way, I came up with only one person who could possibly have foreseen all this. Maybe this big and powerful God of Ben's and Mom's *had* orchestrated this whole thing. Maybe, as Ben said, there were no coincidences with God.

Maybe He was the director of the orchestra or the painter of the finished work or the tapestry maker or any other metaphor I wanted to choose. Sitting in the sand, I settled on a different image. Maybe He was the umpire in the softball game of my life, and maybe I wasn't going to strike out at all. Maybe it was a full count and with the next swing of my bat, the whole game was going to change.

I felt afraid, a tiny, scary, falling-into-thin-air feeling in the pit of my stomach. Ben had said, *It was weird, like God was after me.* Yes, that's what it felt like. The God of the universe was after me, placing His hand on me, forcing me to rearrange my stance, to concentrate on the ball, to swing at it with confidence.

Why are you trying to get me, God? I yelled in my mind. *Leave me alone. I don't want you! I don't need you!*

It was that anger again, that throbbing anger that made me want to reach for a ball to hurl or a handful of pills to swallow or a box of doughnuts to stuff in my mouth. Wasn't it enough that Megan and I were trying our very best to get over our addictions, that Mom and I had forgiven each other, that Ben and I were talking about spiritual issues? Weren't these things enough?

As I argued in my mind, I could almost swear I heard a sound above the noise of the ocean. Not just a sound, but words. I stood up and waded into the water, waded far out past where the waves crashed on the shore, as though I thought if I waded out far enough, those words would suddenly become intelligible. And they did. This is what I heard, standing in the ocean. I heard it as clearly as I had when I was ten years old and we had sung the chorus in Sunday school: *for the earth will be full of the knowledge of God as the waters cover the sea.*

Mom had been resting fine all day, so when she asked if we could go out onto the beach near the end of the afternoon, I thought it was a good idea. I suggested setting up her easel in the sand, but Mom said, "I don't think I'll paint, Ellie. Let's just take the chair. You go on a walk. I'll just watch the sunbathers and the gulls."

It was late in the afternoon, but the beach was still crowded. I didn't really want to walk. I kept thinking about Mom seeming so weak again, about Daddy's phone call, about the platelets and the transfusion, about Sal's brush with death, about how upset Mom had been just a few hours ago, and somehow it just seemed like I should turn around. I couldn't explain it at the time, but later, of course, I would call it another of those coincidences that wasn't really a coincidence at all.

As I walked back toward the Hamilton House, I smiled at the different people sunning themselves. Many I had noticed throughout the week, families who were renting nearby houses. I was concentrating on a sailboat struggling in the ocean—it was windy—when I got back to where Mom was seated. At first I thought she was dozing. Her head was bent down, the big straw hat covering her face. But there was something wrong with the way she was sitting. Unnatural.

Then I saw the blood. A dark stain in the sand.

"Hey, Mom! Hey!" I ran to her side, knelt down in the sand. Blood was literally pouring from her nose. I cupped her head in my hands and watched with horror as her eyes went back in her head.

"Hey! No way, Mom, come on!" I slapped her lightly in the face, then took her by the shoulders and shook her. There was no response. "Mom, hey, Mom! Wake up! You are *not* allowed to die right here on the beach. Do you hear me? You can't do it with no warning at all. You've been through a lot harder things than a simple nosebleed. This is *not* your time!"

I picked her up, surprised again at the featherweight of her body, and held her there, screaming, "Help me! I need help! My mother is dying! Please, is anyone a doctor?"

In just seconds, four or five men and women surrounded me.

"I'm a doctor," a young man said. He took Mom from me and laid her down on the beach and tossed a cell phone to his wife. "Call an ambulance. Get them here at once." He was holding a yellow beach towel over her face, and I watched as a bright red spot seeped into the material. "What happened?"

"She's had complications from chemo—she had a double mastectomy seven months ago and then I think eight rounds of chemo. And a couple weeks ago a nosebleed turned into bad hemorrhaging because of low platelets. But she was okay. She's going to the hospital for a transfusion tomorrow. . . ."

"How long since the platelets have been checked?"

"Five days."

He was listening to her heart. "There you go, ma'am. Keep breathing. Keep breathing."

His wife came over. "The ambulance is on its way—it'll meet us at the road."

The doctor lifted Mom up in his arms and carried her up the beach. Two minutes later an ambulance appeared, and Mom was placed on a gurney and rushed inside. I was standing outside the door, looking at her limp body, now draped with a white sheet as two medics worked feverishly to stop the hemorrhaging.

"I'll ride in the ambulance with her," the doctor said. Then, almost as an afterthought, he asked, "What's her blood type?"

"I don't know."

"Well, find out and call me on my cell!" he yelled as they slammed the doors to the ambulance.

"I'll take you to the hospital," his wife offered.

"Thanks," I said numbly, feeling as if I couldn't quite get my breath, watching the ambulance pull away and trembling with cold fear. "I need to call my dad."

I ran inside the house, grabbed my cell phone, and called Daddy. When he answered, I spit out a string of words in a voice that sounded as if it belonged to a terrified child. "Daddy, I'm on the way to the hospital. Mom started hemorrhaging. What's her blood type?"

He groaned. "It's O positive."

"Come down here, Daddy. Hurry! Come down."

"I'll be on the next plane to Savannah. I'll be there tonight, Ellie. Just stay calm."

I went down to Mom's room and got her purse and then gathered up all the little brown bottles of prescription medicine—five different ones—that were on her bathroom counter. I threw on a pair of jeans, found my purse, locked the animals in the house, and called Ben on his cell phone.

"Mom's hemorrhaging. She's on the way to the hospital. A lady's driving me there. Oh, Ben, I don't even know if Mom's alive. I don't know . . ." I was sobbing into the phone.

"I'll be right there."

Ben arrived at the beach house so quickly that he ended up taking me to the ER at the Hilton Head Regional Medical Center in his car. The doctor's wife called her husband and gave him Mom's blood type, and then she drove in front of us.

I vaguely remember Ben helping me to the reception desk, Ben taking me to the waiting room, Ben holding my hand, Ben getting me a cup of coffee, Ben trying to make conversation, Ben jumping up to meet the young doctor when he appeared in the hall, Ben and the doctor assuring me that Mom was receiving excellent care, and Ben leaving me to go back to the Quarterdeck.

Then I was alone. Mom's purse was sitting there beside me on the metal chair. At times when I was really bored, I'd read the contents of my purse—the grocery ticket, the stub from a Braves game, the bulletin from the Humane Society. But it was not boredom that caused me to empty Mom's purse and rummage through her things. It was fear. If I didn't occupy my mind, I would sink into panic.

Mom's purse held lipstick and blush, a wallet, her medications, the bulletin from the Baptist church service, keys to her car. And no brush. Of course not—she didn't need one for her bald head. I unsnapped her wallet and leafed through the little plastic pages. She had pictures of all of us stuffed in those small compartments. There was this really old family photo—the last one we'd had done in a studio, when I was around twelve. Mom, Daddy, Abbie, Nan, me.

Then there were some more recent pictures: Abbie and Bill in their wedding attire. Bobby at six months and a year, Nan and Stockton sitting on a boat. And then me. Except no one else would ever know it was me. It was taken from the side, and I was squatting down, dressed in my softball uniform and catcher's attire, the face mask pulled over my head. On the other side of the little plastic page was a snapshot of me with Hindsight—another one that Nan had taken last year.

Mom had stuffed a little piece of wrinkled paper in between those two photos. When I removed the wad of paper, I saw my handwriting on it.

Dear Momma,

Happy birthday! I love you soooo much! Thanks for talking to me at night by my bed. Thanks for fixing my favorite meal. Thanks for letting me keep Patchwork—I know he'll be a good kitty. I hope your exhibition goes really well. I am going to be praying for you.

Ellie

Immediately I was transported back to my eleven-year-old body, could feel myself holding Patchwork, an oversized calico stray, and waving good-bye to my mother. I had loved my mother, and I had prayed for her. Those words were sincere—straight from a young girl's heart. Maybe they were the last kind words I'd ever written my mom. For some reason, they were precious enough to have been tucked inside her wallet for ten years.

"Oh, Mom," I whispered, cradling that piece of paper in my palm. "Don't die now. Please, please hang on. Give me another chance to show you I love you and to pray for you."

Then I closed my eyes and thought, *Dear God, let Momma live.*

Chapter 23

Greater love has no one than this, that one lay down his life for his friends.

—JOHN 15:13, NASB

Hours later, I was still sitting in the metal chair in the waiting room, my head in my hands, when someone touched me on the shoulder. I looked up, saw Daddy, and jumped to my feet to embrace him.

He held me tightly, almost fiercely, and whispered, "They've got the bleeding under control. She's having a transfusion right now. Oh, Ellie. Dear Ellie."

He grasped my hands, and it was then that I realized my shirt was covered in blood, just as Daddy's had been at Piedmont Hospital a few weeks ago.

"You already saw a doctor?"

"Yes. Mom's been admitted by an internist. He thinks they'll keep her in the hospital here a few days at least—probably a week—until she's strong enough to go back to Atlanta."

We sat there in silence, and after a while I think I dozed off. Later Daddy brought me some coffee.

"Ben called. He's driving back here to pick you up. I'll spend the night here with Mom. You go on back to the beach house. Try to get a little rest."

"Daddy, I don't want to leave you here. I don't want to leave *her*. Not now."

"I know. But I think it's going to be okay. You can come back tomorrow."

"I could just give Ben the keys to the house. He could take care of Hindsight and Rusty. I can stay with you."

"We'll see, Mae Mae. We'll see."

Daddy leaned over, elbows on his knees, and was very quiet. I knew he was praying, so I kept still. But inside, my heart was racing and my stomach was cramping.

I went to the restroom and washed the blood from my hands and arms. Daddy had bought me another T-shirt at the hospital gift shop so I could take off the bloodstained one. I threw water on my face, for the third time, and tried to breathe deeply. When I went back to the waiting room, Daddy was sitting up straight and gave me a little smile.

"There, you look much better."

A little while later, I asked, "Daddy, how can you seem so calm? Are you really feeling that calm on the inside?"

"Oh, Ellie, of course I'm worried for your mom. It tears me up to see her going through all this." He took my hand and said, "Let's just say that if I didn't have rock-solid faith in moments like this, I'd be a lot more worried. There's not much I can do right now except pray."

"Prayer doesn't work, Daddy! It didn't work for me. When I was in rehab, I bet you had a ton of people praying. I bet they were praying that I'd be indoctrinated to your beliefs at that rehab place. But look at me!"

Daddy turned to face me and took my other hand in his too. Then he smiled the kind, wise smile that showed his dimples. "Yes, look at you, Ellie! Just look! You're alive again. You're my feisty daughter who wants to live, who is fighting for her mother, who knows how to confront life. You're pursuing a dream, you're studying, you're using your brain and your heart, and you've come back to us. Ellie, my prayers have been answered. Every single one."

"I still don't believe like you and Mom do."

"That was never one of my prayers. I don't want you to believe 'like I do.' I don't want you to do it for me, or like me. I just pray that God surprises you with who He is along the way. And I think He's doing that, Ellie. I think He is."

Later, Daddy suggested that we go to the hospital cafeteria and get something to eat. It was while we were sitting side by side at a little table in the cafeteria that I told him, "Daddy, Mom let me read two of the letters you wrote to her from Vietnam. Well, one was from Vietnam and the other one . . ."

"The other one was what I wrote for her to read if I didn't make it back."

"Yes, how did you know?"

"She keeps those letters in her Bible." He put an arm around my shoulder and said, "Vietnam is something I don't talk about, Ellie. I don't know any of the soldiers who survived 'Nam who want to talk about it." He reached over and held one of my hands tightly. "And everything you've seen in movies or read about POW camps is just about true. You don't need to know any more details."

I scooted my chair even closer to his and buried my head in his chest, and he put his arms around me and held me. "I'll tell you one thing, though, Ellie. I'll tell you about Amos."

"Your radio man? I read about him."

"That's right." Daddy was quiet for a moment, reverent. "I'll tell you what Amos did for me. It was on yet another mission that turned rotten. June 19, 1968. We were surrounded by the enemy, and we knew we were in big trouble.

"A grenade exploded not far from me—that's how I lost my eye, got all the scarring on my side. It ripped me up pretty good, but I was still conscious. I had a flashing thought of Mary Swan and all that we would never know together.

"Suddenly Amos was there, crying and saying, 'You're gonna live, man. You're gonna git back to your girl, and God's got some other work for you. He told me so.' And he started dragging me through the rice paddies, bleeding all over me from a wound to his head. He pulled me to some underbrush, and we could hear the soldiers around us.

"Amos told me to lie perfectly still and look dead. And he draped his huge body over mine, protecting me, hiding me, while the enemy drew closer. We didn't know if there were two or twenty of them. We lay as still as we could, and then their footsteps came closer, and Amos's breathing got awfully heavy. A soldier came right up to us, took his gun, and fired one shot. I felt Amos's body go limp above me. It was over. I waited for the same treatment, but the soldiers left. I lay there crushed under the weight of the greatest man I'd ever known and wept until the sun went down and the night engulfed me. I had no idea how I would survive. But I knew I had to—because that was the only way to make Amos's sacrifice worth it."

I literally felt sick to my stomach, imagining too well the scene.

"It was Amos's faith that pushed me on. I was determined to make it back to love Mary Swan as much as he had loved his wife. He had decided that my life was more important than his. I don't know how he decided that. It came from way down in his soul, something that was so strongly rooted there, that in that moment of fear, it never wavered. Something happens inside a man when he witnesses a deliberate act of sacrifice, when his life is saved through another person's willingly handing over his own life.

"It marked me for the rest of my life, Ellie. If my life was worth saving, then it was worth living, and I was going to live it right."

I couldn't bear to look at Daddy. He patted my hand and took a bite of his sandwich, and I didn't say a thing.

"When I came back from Vietnam, I was a broken young man. I had survived on my faith and Amos's and on the dream of being reunited with your mother. I never once doubted her love for me. I couldn't let myself even imagine that she'd given up. Coming home to her was all that mattered in my life, and I did it.

"But right away I knew things had changed. Here I'd survived the worst possible hell I could imagine, and I stepped back into a country that treated me like I was an embarrassment and a fiancée who didn't know how to help me. But God was still there. And just as surely as He changed our hearts long ago, He changed them again. And the more we spent time together, the more Swannee said the love grew. It grew. She learned to love me again." He shook his head. "It wasn't easy, Ellie. It was a miracle that we didn't take for granted. She knew how fragile I was. And we got it back, together."

I swallowed hard, then hugged Daddy around the waist and said, "I'm so glad you did, Daddy."

Back in the waiting room, I fell asleep with my head leaning hard against my father's wide shoulders, his arm holding me securely to his chest. I dreamed of Vietnam and of a stone wall and of a long, wide beach.

When I awoke, I asked Daddy, "What happened to your ring?"

"My ring?"

"The class ring from Georgia Tech—the one you gave Mom before you left for Vietnam. I've never seen it."

"We left it at the Wall," he said.

"The Wall? You mean the wall in Scotland?"

He looked confused, then shook his head, with a sad little smile curving his lips. "No. We left it at the Vietnam Veterans Memorial in Washington, D.C. That wall."

"Oh."

"Your mother was invited to exhibit her three paintings from 1968, the three that are at the High now, at the National Gallery. I went with her, one of her very first exhibitions, 1985. Rachel kept you and Abbie and Nan.

"We got there a day early—on purpose, of course. We wanted to visit Arlington Cemetery and the new memorial. It had been dedicated in November 1983, but this was our first visit, and frankly, we were both nervous."

"Nervous?"

"Memories. So many memories, Ellie. The Wall sits just down a slope off to the left of the Lincoln Memorial. I've been back several times now, and there is always a Vietnam vet at a little table before you get to the Wall selling MIA bracelets, and I always buy one after I've searched through them, looking for names of soldiers I knew."

I could tell that Daddy was drifting back into time, rummaging through the rooms of his mind to find a table stacked with MIA bracelets.

"Every bit of that long black granite wall is covered with names: 58,209 of them. When you're standing there, you look to your left where the Wall rises to an apex at its beginning, and then to your right as it turns a corner, and it looks like it's going to continue forever. Every day people go there and leave notes and flowers and other mementos of testimony to those men and women who gave their lives in the war America hated. The Wall has let them grieve." Daddy looked me in the eyes. "The Wall helped me to grieve too, Ellie."

"It's awful, Daddy. A long wall of suffering and pain."

"Yes. Suffering and pain. But also healing."

"Healing? How?"

"I don't know exactly. But I felt it, as so many others have. The Wall lets us cry over our terrible losses and mourn and grieve. And heal. I took my medal and a letter I'd written to Amos and left them at the foot of the panel, right under his name. Then I touched his name and rested my head against the warm granite. It sounds silly, but I think I was trying to hear his heart beating again.

"And then your mother unfastened the gold chain she was wearing around her neck and put my class ring from Georgia Tech beside my medal and the letter. Amos had always wanted a college education, and that was our way of giving it to him."

"What kind of medal was it, Daddy?"

"It was a Purple Heart, honey. But I left knowing without a doubt that it belonged to Amos, as did my ring and everything else. I owed him my life. As I looked one last time at Amos's name on the black granite, what I saw was my face staring back at me. *Life* staring back at me. My life—beyond the interminable list of names, beyond the blackness, the death, the despair."

I considered his story, felt the heaviness of it, and knew every word was true. But I had to ask him, "Daddy, didn't you ever feel sorry for yourself or angry at God for the things that happened?"

I think Daddy could see right through my question to my heart, and he put his arm around my shoulder, squeezed me tightly again, and said, "Oh, Ellie. Of course I felt angry and depressed and sorry for myself and a thousand other emotions. If I hadn't gotten help from a lot of other people, I'm pretty sure I wouldn't be here. I know what it's like to want to give up, Ellie. I'm so glad the Lord doesn't answer my prayers the way I want. If He did, I wouldn't be here and neither would you.

"I have to choose to stay here, in the present. I have to choose to not let myself drift back, not to let my mind replay horrible scenes, not to let my thoughts spiral me down into self-pity. Sometimes it's a hard choice."

He talked softly but with certainty. "Ellie . . . do you remember the thank-you game we used to play?"

I nodded silently, reliving one of the many times that I'd climbed into Daddy's lap when he'd gotten home from work and was sitting in his big La-Z-Boy chair out in the den.

"*I hate my scars, Daddy.*"

"Yes, I know, Ellie. Sometimes I hate mine too. But then I try to think of things in life that I love. I find one and I thank God for it. Can you think of things you love, Ellie?"

"I love you, Daddy, and I love Momma."

"Then let's say thank-you for that. Let's thank God for your parents."

We closed our eyes and I had my little hands folded together, and Daddy's thick hands covered mine, and we said thank-you.

"Anything else?"

"Mr. Boots and Jinx."

Again we closed our eyes and continued the process until I'd thanked God for all the animals and people in my life.

"And what about you, Ellie? What can you thank God for about you?"

I thought for a long time. "I like my hair and my eyes. . . ."

I remembered it all, the cozy feel of the armchair and me snuggled beside my father and how my heart seemed happier after we finished recounting the things we were thankful for.

"I still play that game, Ellie. Only it's not a game at all. It's a choice. And I don't know how to explain it, but *saying* thank-you to the Lord ends up by making me *feel* thankful. I am so very, very thankful for life."

Ben arrived around midnight. I thought Daddy looked relieved as he shook Ben's hand and entrusted his little Ellie to Ben. That was how it seemed. I slept the whole way back.

When Ben let me off at the Hamilton House, he asked, "Do you want me to stay here, Ellie? I can sleep downstairs again."

I shook my head. "Thanks, Ben. But no. You've got enough to do. I think I just need to be alone."

"Call me in the morning," he said as he turned to leave. "If you hear anything else about your mom. And . . . well, just call me. I want to know you're okay."

After he left, I checked on the animals and then I walked out on the beach. The tide was coming in, almost up to where Mom had been sitting in the chair, and the moon was bright. Someone had thrown sand over the spots of blood—there was just one small patch that had not been covered up that I could make out in the shadows—and the beach chair was folded up and lying by the path that led back to the house. Mom's towel was wadded up and tucked into the chair. I could see that it was covered in blood. Her straw hat was lying upside down with a few seashells in it to keep it from blowing away. Seeing it flopping there, I felt tears sting my eyes.

I reached down, removed the shells from inside and then picked up the hat and put it on my head, first twirling my hair together and stuffing it underneath. I rolled up the legs on my jeans and sloshed into the ocean. The water was warm from the day's sun. I stood perfectly still for a long time, my hand on top of my head, holding the straw hat so it wouldn't blow away with a gust of wind. I stared out into the endless expanse of water.

I was being rocked by the low roar of the ocean, its ebb and flow, hypnotized perhaps with the constant motion—the motion that Mom had said would never betray her. And then in the gentle roar, I started hearing those words again, about the earth being filled with the knowledge of God. Something that felt warm and strong, something that felt like love, came washing over me as surely as the tide was washing over my toes. A feeling, and yet more than a feeling. An assurance, a peacefulness. When I felt those things, I was scared. A good kind of scared, the way you feel when chills start shooting through your body, and you are cold and then the chills turn to warmth, because suddenly, amazingly, things start making sense and you see the other side. You turn the corner in your mind and then, what was only in the mind goes down and settles in the heart.

Something was settling in my heart.

Then I kept hearing two other words in my mind, words that Mom and Daddy and Ben had used in recent conversations with me. Words that Jesus had said in my dream: *surrender* and *sacrifice*—the kind of words you wanted to nail to a cross. Unnatural, unattractive words that made me want to cover my ears and run screaming, as I had done when I was a girl when my parents had tried to talk about the accident and my scars. For now I remembered it. Now I could see the little girl in tears, the little girl angry.

And it came to me in a sudden rush of pain. It wasn't my mother who wanted to get her beautiful little six-year-old Ellie back. Mom had loved me just as I was, with all of her raw and real heart emotions.

It was *me*. *I* was the one who had wanted it, who had run from the room because I couldn't bear to hear the truth, that *that* Ellie, the Ellie I knew and loved, the Ellie that was *me*, would never come back. I had never known how to grieve my loss.

Inside I had been the same. My mind still worked as fast, my eyes still perceived as quickly, my heart still hurt for the lonely, my hand still reached for the stray kitten. But never, ever again in my life would I be that beautiful strawberry blond Ellie with the piercing green eyes and the bright smile. Never would others look at me the same way.

That was the chasm I had fallen into. That was the reason for the angry blue paint on my walls. I had always blamed my mother, but standing there on the beach and staring out into the horizon, I finally admitted the truth. I was the one, after all these years, who could not accept the scars.

Much later, I walked back to the house, carrying the beach chair and towel. As soon as I opened the door, Hindsight and Rusty greeted me, all wiggles and hisses, but the house felt strangely empty. I put the bloody towel in the downstairs sink to soak in cold water. I climbed the stairs and walked into the family room. Mom's stuff was everywhere, her sketch pads lying on the couch, her easel set up with the painting of the footprints, her paintbrushes still covered with various shades of color, her green scarf draped over one arm of the chair. I touched each thing, cleaned the brushes with turpentine, called Daddy on the cell phone, and cried with relief when he reported that Mom was sleeping peacefully. I took a long, hot shower and then I fell into bed, exhausted, and slept hard, deep—a deeper sleep than I'd slept in two weeks.

The fresh air of morning made the sand cool as the tide traced its pattern back and forth. I observed the way my feet sank into the sand, leaving a momentary footprint that sprang back as soon as I lifted up my foot. It was a stormy day, and the ocean was mad. Very few people were on the beach.

About twenty feet away, a father was digging in the sand with his son, a child of about five or six. They were making a drip castle, near the ocean's edge, using the water from their hole to drip sand onto the structure. The castle looked warped and medieval. The little boy was carefully placing miniscule Lego men on the ramparts, and the father was busily digging a moat around them.

Then the boy stood up. Something caught his attention—a gull or a pelican—and he started off toward it. The father was leaning over, one whole arm descended into the moat as he extracted the dripping sand. His back was to the ocean, and he didn't notice his child rushing out into the waves.

That kid's old enough to know better than to run out into the ocean when the waves are that high, I said to myself.

The father had still not noticed what his son was doing. Suddenly the little boy fell down and a wave crashed over him. I started jogging toward the boy, my heart beating faster, when the father looked up, jumped up quickly, and scooped his little boy out of the water.

"Hey, Scottie! What are you doing! You know better than to go out there in those waves. It's dangerous." The father's voice was stern, but he picked up the boy gently and held him tight.

I passed by and raised my eyebrows and gave a little smile.

The father's nod to me lasted half a second. But it changed my life.

In his eyes, I saw the glistening of tears, and on his face was a look of immense relief and overwhelming love as he carried his son away from the ocean and set him down in the sand. The boy was crying and saying, "I'm sorry, Daddy."

I started jogging, then running, for five or maybe ten minutes, putting distance between myself and the father with his son. The beach ahead was deserted.

I fell to my knees, right there in the sand, by the ocean's edge with the wind howling and the breaking of the waves roaring around. I screamed, "I'm sorry! I'm sorry, Father! I'm sorry! I should have known better. I *did* know better than to light the gas stove. All my life I've been blaming Mom—and really blaming you, when all you have ever wanted to do is scoop me up in your arms and protect me. When all you have ever had for me is love."

All this I screamed out loud in great heaving sighs. Tears sprang to my eyes. Not just a few stinging tears that I could brush away, but whole rivulets of them, falling down my face into the water. If someone had seen me, I'm sure he would have thought I was a shipwrecked woman who had been tossed on shore. I was kneeling in the sand, my hands planted in front of me, and I was heaving, crying, begging for something I had refused to receive all of my life.

Forgiveness.

"Forgive me, change me. Please don't let the scars be for nothing. Make it worth it! Oh God, please just make all this mess worth it."

You are worth it, Ellie. I love you.

The words seemed as audible as those of my dream. I heard it so clearly that I stopped crying and turned my head upward toward the gray sky, still on all fours, and looked, expecting maybe to see Jesus there with His outstretched palms reaching to me. Expecting to see the scars in His hands and touch them, like doubting Thomas. I got off my knees and sat in the sand, sopping wet with perspiration and seawater.

I waded out into the ocean, pulling my knees up high, walking heavily as the water weighed me down in my shorts and T-shirt. "I give up, Lord. I surrender. Take my life and make it whatever you want."

I was far out in the ocean now, and the waves were crashing around me. I stood up, facing the beach. I lifted my head toward the heavens, lifted my arms high above my head. As a wave crashed over me, as the water stung my eyes and I came up gasping for breath, I was laughing—deep, joy-filled laughter. I could hear the pastor at the little Baptist church on the island saying the phrase he'd repeated on Sunday each time he'd baptized one of the youth. *"Buried with Him through baptism into death and raised to walk in newness of life."*

I was clean.

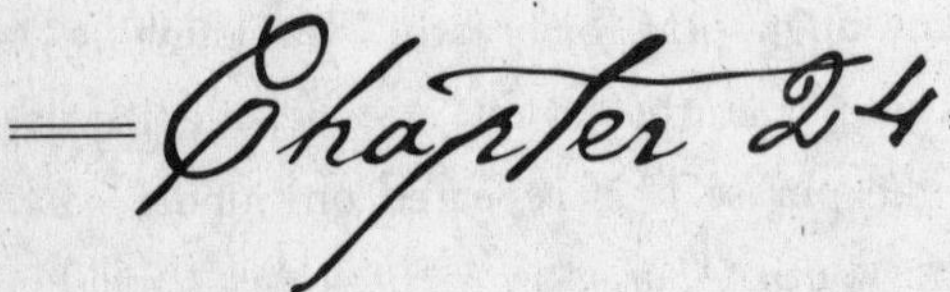

Chapter 24

Underneath the paving stones, the beach!

—SLOGAN FROM STUDENT RIOTS, MAY 1968, PARIS

I will give you a new heart and put a new spirit in you; I will remove from you your heart of stone and give you a heart of flesh.

—EZEKIEL 36:26

I don't know how other people feel after they've gone from what Ben called screwed up to awesome, but I just wanted to be alone. I came into the house and removed my clothes—I would always afterward refer to them as my baptism clothes—and took a hot shower.

Before I could truly be alone, I needed to check on Mom, so I called Daddy. His voice on the other end of the line sounded fairly upbeat.

"She rested well through the night. The transfusion has helped, and they want to keep her here awhile—until she's stabilized. She says to tell you thank-you. She keeps saying, 'She saved my life. Ellie saved my life.'"

"You know Mom and how she exaggerates."

"I know, Ellie. And I also know, according to the doctors, that your mother is not exaggerating. Ellie, you've had an intense couple of weeks. Try to get some rest."

"I will, Daddy." Somehow, it was not yet time to tell him of my experience on the beach—it was too fresh, too personal. "I'll come see her tomorrow. Call me if anything changes."

"Yes, I will, Ellie."

I fed Hindsight and Rusty, in separate rooms with the doors closed. Then I made a cup of coffee and was about to get the modern translation of the Gospel of Mark when the phone rang. I hesitated for a moment, not wanting to answer, but I decided that Mom's condition was too fragile to ignore a call.

"Hello?"

It was Ben. "How are you doing? I tried to call earlier, but there was no answer, and then the phone was busy."

"I was out for a while, and then I called Daddy. Mom is doing better."

He gave a long sigh. "Thank the Lord. And what about you?"

"I'm okay. I'm good, Ben. I just want to be alone right now, but maybe we could do something later. Do you have a meeting with the youth?"

"A few of us are going by to see Sal—her request. She's back at the house here at Hilton Head. Then I'm free till I go to the Quarterdeck around seven."

"You know what I'd really like to do? Could we eat at Café Europa? It's my favorite restaurant, and I haven't been there yet this summer."

"Sounds good to me. I'll make early reservations. Pick you up around five-thirty."

"Thanks, Ben."

"Okay, I'm off to see Sal. Pray for me if you think of it." Then he was silent for a second. "Oops—sorry, Ellie. I didn't mean to babble. I'm just so used to asking people to pray. . . ."

"It's okay, Ben. Don't worry about it. And I will."

"Will what?"

"I will pray for you."

It started storming hard, with thunder and lightning and pelting rain, all of which terrified Rusty. He hid under the family room table, and then, when I lay down on the couch with a cup of coffee, he plopped down by my feet, his tail occasionally smacking against the wooden floor when I cooed to him sweetly. Hindsight was completely unimpressed and perched on the kitchen windowsill, watching the storm with such a blasé attitude that I was sure she was mocking the dog.

Daddy was right. The stress of the past two weeks had exhausted me, and I fell into a light slumber.

In the afternoon, as the rain turned to a drizzle and the sun tried to poke its head through the clouds, I went down to Mom's bedroom and began to pack up her things to take to the hospital the following morning. I had finished putting her clothes in the suitcase when I came upon her old Bible lying on her bedside table. I stared at it long and hard. The dark leather cover was smooth and worn; there was the fading mark of a mug on it where she must have accidentally set a hot cup of tea, and a little piece of leather was missing in the top right-hand corner. Standing there, I flipped through its onionskin-thin pages, most of which had lost their gold-edged tinting. A few pages were ripped slightly. On many of the pages, Mom had underlined words and even whole passages in different colors of ink, and she had written little notes out in the margins, occasionally adding the date with a short explanation of why these verses were important to her at that point in her life.

I thought to myself that this Bible looked a lot like my mother: worn, well used, much loved, and I wondered if one day my life would somehow seem as significant as hers did in that moment. I went to my bedroom to retrieve Daddy's letters from Vietnam and placed them back inside the Bible, in between Psalm Twenty-two and Psalm Twenty-three, and as I did, tears sprang into my eyes.

I held that Bible to my chest and then I felt my chest constricting, getting tighter and tighter. These were not tears of confession or worry or compassion. These were tears of love for my mom. Once again I felt chills shoot through my body, starting in my scalp and racing down the nape of my neck and settling into the tightness in my heart.

Later, as I was going through the closet in Mom's bedroom, I came across some of my old clothes—things I couldn't wear after I'd gained all that weight. I pulled a blue jeans dress from the closet and tried it on. It actually fit. Granted, it was only one size smaller than what I normally wore now, but I felt satisfaction and even pleasure putting it on. I had definitely lost weight.

I rarely wore a dress or skirt, but suddenly I decided that I would wear this to the restaurant—not so much for Ben as for myself. Somehow it felt right that I'd be dressed differently on the day when I had become different.

At five o'clock, I started getting ready. I leaned forward, throwing my hair over my head and brushing it so that when I flipped it back over my shoulders, it was full and shiny. Then I went into the bathroom and searched through the drawers till I found a small tube of liquid foundation, which I carefully smoothed over the scar. I applied a soft green eye shadow and finished up with mascara. Finally I dabbed some pink gloss on my lips. As I looked at my reflection in the mirror, I liked who was looking back at me.

"Wow," Ben said when I opened the door for him. "Wow, Ellie. You look great."

I blushed. "It's just the dress."

"No, it's everything. It's your face—you're beaming, like you've been watching reruns of the sun setting behind the lighthouse all day long."

We both laughed.

"Actually, that's kinda like what I have been doing."

"Really? When it's rained the whole day?"

"Yeah. I'm serious. I'll tell you about it at dinner. But first tell me about you, Ben. Are you okay—I mean after what happened to Sal and then to Mom?"

He didn't say anything for a moment, and we both got into his car. As we headed out of Spotted Sandpiper, he said, "I dunno. I'm all right, I guess. Let's just say I'm at the point where I can believe that somewhere in the future God will use all my questions and fears for good." He looked over at me. "And for right now, I'm just letting Him hold me up until I can get back down and walk on my own."

I was astounded by his words. They reminded me so much of my dream, with Jesus cradling Ben in His arms—and again, I was sure that it was not a coincidence.

Café Europa sat right behind the lighthouse and beside the Quarterdeck Lounge. I loved the food there, and I especially enjoyed the view of Calibogue Sound from the restaurant's glassed-in porch. I waited until we'd been served our appetizers—for me it was the Vidalia onion tart and for Ben the oysters—to bring up the subject of my morning beach experience. "I did something strange and wonderful today, Ben."

"What?"

"I told God I was screwed up and asked Him to fix me."

His eyes grew wide, and he leaned across the table toward me. "You did?"

"Amazing, huh? And don't worry, I did it the right way—not for Mom or Daddy or you or anyone else. I did it for myself. I admitted it all to Him."

Ben's face changed from surprised to a subtle smile and then a wide grin. "Man, Ellie! Wow! That is way cool. Now I know why your face looks so . . . so radiant."

We talked nonstop for over an hour, and I found myself smiling and laughing my deep-down laughter so often that I grew embarrassed. But Ben wasn't bothered by it. At one point, he leaned so far across the table that our noses almost touched, and he whispered, "For being Ellie of the Perpetual Pout, something has surely changed in you, girl."

I couldn't keep from giggling as I said, "I hope so, Obnoxious Ben. I hope so."

After dinner, which Ben insisted on paying for, he looked at his watch. "I've got fifteen minutes before I need to be at the Quarterdeck. Wanna take a walk to the pier?"

"Sure." I was thinking about how I had done the very same thing with Mom only a few days earlier. "Hold on a sec, Ben. I want to check on Mom."

"Of course."

When Daddy reassured me that she was fine and resting, I clicked off the phone and said to Ben, "I'm going to see Mom at the hospital tomorrow and then head back to Atlanta."

"Yeah, I figured that might be the case." We didn't say anything for a few minutes as we walked out to the end of the pier. Then, leaning against the railing, he said, "It's been fun having you down here, Ellie. You and your mom."

"Yeah." I hopped up on the railing and perched there, looking out to the sound. "We might get a flaming sunset tonight after all."

"That would be appropriate."

That gave me an idea. "Could I borrow your keys and go up to the condo, just to watch the sun set? I promise I'll come back and listen to you afterward."

He laughed. "You can stay up there as long as you want. It won't hurt my feelings. You've already heard just about everything I know how to sing." He handed me the keys.

I slid off the railing and stuffed the keys into my pocket, not wanting to leave the pier, not wanting to leave Ben. "I'm actually a bit nervous about going back home, for a lot of different reasons," I said finally.

"That isn't surprising. You've had a very strenuous couple of weeks—good things and bad things and so much to think about. And you've changed. . . ."

"And I quit my waitressing job."

"You did?"

"Yeah, I called in this afternoon to give them my notice. I told them I'd help out through the end of July if they need it, but after that, I'm done."

"You're making decisions left and right."

"I hope they're good decisions, Ben."

He put his hands on my shoulders and looked me straight in the eyes. "Ellie Bartholomew, I guarantee you that you'll never regret the decision you made this morning."

"I'm gonna believe you on that one, Ben. I really am." I had a huge ball in my throat, this sensation that I couldn't swallow, that if I did, I was going to sob or something. I wanted to say, *Ben, I'm afraid of leaving you. I want you to be there with me to walk through this new chapter in my life. Can't you see it? You're the one I need.* But, of course, I didn't say that. I just asked, "When do you go back to New York?"

"Near the end of August. School doesn't start till mid-September, but I promised Mom I'd help her with a few things at her apartment."

"What a nice son," I said.

Ben looked at me, we both smiled, and I could tell that he knew I meant it. It took me a moment to ask just one more question.

"Will you stop by Atlanta on your way back to New York?"

"You couldn't keep me away."

We were still standing out at the end of the pier, and it seemed like it would be the most natural thing for him to reach out and take my hand. It was what I wanted. But he didn't. Ben was my friend. *We're just friends, just friends, just friends*. I could hear my words and see the smile on Sal and Samantha's faces.

I left Ben at the Quarterdeck and walked back past the shops and the Liberty Oak and the yachts and the red rocking chairs to Ketch Court, climbed the three flights of steps, and let myself in. I walked through the den with its comfortable couches piled high with pillows and opened the sliding glass doors that led onto the little balcony with its view out over the harbor. I sat down in one of the low chairs, propping my feet on the round glass table, and I waited. I waited with my eyes opened, watching the wide sidewalk below where families pedaled by on bikes and joggers ran by perspiring and a gull perched on the sail of a yacht. I watched the sun's descent, the bright haze behind the clouds. Eventually the clouds lifted so that my view was of a pale blue sky and a bright white light that slowly turned deeper yellow and then orange; then, finally, for a few seconds, it settled right behind the lighthouse and beckoned to me. With a smile on my face, I applauded God and His creation and then whispered, "This is very good."

Around nine I walked back to the Quarterdeck, ordered a Coke at the bar, and sat down at a little table. Ben smiled and nodded to me when I came in, and from then on, I could tell that every song he sang was for me. After a while he said, "This song is dedicated to a good friend of mine who's made a very important and very hard decision."

He started singing "Desperado." I closed my eyes and listened to the words of the slow, haunting ballad, and I got a few tears in my eyes as he sang the last line:

"You better let somebody love you . . . before it's too late."

I knew very well that he was not hinting at a relationship between the two of us. It was his way of acknowledging that I *had* finally let Someone love me. *Before it was too late*.

He drove me home around eleven. We sat in the car talking for probably an hour, and then, as I was getting ready to get out, I said,

"And don't worry about me. I'll keep doing the right things. I'll read the Bible. I'll even find a rockin' church with a cool youth pastor."

He smiled at that and asked, "Can I pray for you, Ellie?"

"I'd like that. I'd like that a lot."

So he did—a gentle, sincere prayer.

"Keep in touch, Ellie." He leaned across the seat and gave me a hug and kissed me on the top of my head. Like a friend. And a brother. Yeah.

"Bye, Ben. See ya around."

Rusty awakened me the next morning, yapping excitedly from the kitchen. When I padded into the family room, I found him standing on his back legs and barking at a squirrel that was perched outside the kitchen window, completely unperturbed.

"You nutty dog," I laughed. "How in the world am I gonna keep you in my apartment in Atlanta?"

I took him out for a walk, came back in, and wished I could be fixing Mom a cup of tea and an English muffin. I had no appetite at all. I did not want to leave Hilton Head, for a hundred reasons. Mostly I felt protected here, in the island's carefully maintained wild beauty, with the ocean to rock me and the beach to offer her shores for long walks and Ben to ride bikes with me and answer my questions.

I took my last walk on the beach, slowly, appreciating the simple pleasure of sun on my shoulders before reluctantly turning back to the house. I remembered my conversation with Daddy in the hospital and whispered a thank-you prayer. "For this, dear God, for your creation, for life here at Hilton Head, and for my family, I thank you."

I packed up Mom's little Mazda with her suitcase, the easel, the paints, the incomplete canvas of the footprints on the beach, the two sketch pads. I shut Rusty in my bedroom while I coaxed Hindsight into her cage. She protested with a look of disdain and displeasure. When I'd set her in the passenger's seat, I went back in and got Rusty. He wiggled and barked and jumped into the car, refused to sit down, and planted his legs stiffly on the leather seats. I stuck a copy of the Eagles' Greatest Hits into my Walkman and listened to "Desperado" over and over again as I drove to the hospital.

Daddy met me in the hospital parking lot, having agreed to baby-sit Rusty and Hindsight while I said good-bye to Mom. He grinned when he saw me and gave me a kiss. "Some things never change. Ellie, my little vet."

I almost said, *But some things do*. Instead, I pecked him on the cheek and said, "I'll be back in a little while."

"Take your time."

"I brought you a few gifts, Mom," I said and handed her the scarf and the wig and her Bible.

"Just what I was hoping for!"

"How are you feeling?"

"Pretty good. I'd give anything to go back to the beach house with you, but the doctor is adamant. I'm to stay put."

"Yeah, I heard. It was kinda strange and sad packing everything up. Any idea when they'll let you out of here?"

"I'm supposed to have another transfusion tomorrow, and when I'm feeling strong enough, they'll send me back to Atlanta."

I found that my heart was beating rather insistently, rapidly, as I contemplated what I wanted to say to my mother. After a few moments, I forced myself to spit it out. "Mom, I, uh, I have something to tell you. But first you have to promise me something. You have to promise me that you won't give up and die after I say it. You have to keep fighting."

Mom wrinkled her brow and frowned. "Ellie, why do you say that?"

"Just promise first. You'll see."

"I promise. What is it?"

"I, uh, I believed. You know, I said I was sorry and then asked God to fix me—and I meant it."

She looked astounded, but I didn't pause. I had to say it fast. "I didn't do it for you or Daddy or Ben; I didn't do it because I thought you were going to die. I *do* think God used a lot of things in the past few weeks to get my attention, but I did it for myself.

"And, also . . ." I cleared my throat. "I just want to say again how sorry I am for all my bitter years. I finally get it. I couldn't forgive myself, couldn't let go and grieve and go on with life. But now I can."

"Oh, Ellie."

We embraced, and she started crying, of course, but I thought that after all we'd been through, it was just exactly the right response.

"Promise me, Mom, you'll get stronger. This isn't the time to fold your arms over your chest and say, 'Well, all my lambs are safely home' and go to heaven."

Mom squeezed my hands and actually laughed. "Ellie! You and your ideas! But I promise." Before I got up to leave she said, "And I am so proud of you, for everything, Ellie. Not just for your believing. For everything."

Telling Daddy was easier than telling either Ben or Mom. He just hugged me and held me and whispered, "Ellie, that's the sweetest gift you could offer your mother. A gift. And I know you didn't do it for her or for me. I know you took a long time and made that decision all by yourself, for yourself. That's one thing we were never afraid of, Ellie—that you'd be a hypocrite!"

I kissed him on the cheek, glad to leave my parents smiling, glad, without an ounce of cynicism mixed in. I was just beginning to get my first glimpse of the rest of that verse, the one that said that God causes everything to work together *for good* to those who love Him. This, at least, was very good.

So I drove back to Atlanta with the windows down and the cat hissing in her cage and the straggly red dog standing stiff-legged in the backseat with his head leaning between the two front seats, trying to keep his balance.

When I parked in front of the apartment complex, I could see the drapes parted in Nate's apartment and Nate sitting by his window. I had sent him a brief e-mail the night before, saying I was coming home. He got a big smile on his face and waved at me, then came downstairs and walked outside.

"Hey, Ellie! Glad you're back." I opened the car door, and he bent down and gave me an awkward hug. "Can I help you with your things?"

"Sure. Thanks. Maybe you could take Hindsight's cage and carry her inside. I've got my hands full with Rusty."

Nate leaned through the opened rear window and tried to pet Rusty, but the mutt backed against the far door and began barking furiously. "Hey, fella. I don't know how you're gonna like our place here. All we've got is cats." Then he picked up Hindsight's cage and said, "Come on, Ellie." He was grinning almost in spite of himself, like a little kid with a secret.

I frowned a little and asked, "You okay, Nate?"

Immediately he changed his facial expression, looked worried, and said, "Sure, why?"

"You're acting weird."

"Oh, well. You'll see."

I attached the leash to Rusty's collar, and he bounded from the car, yanking me along with him. "Here, can you please unlock the door?" I handed Nate the keys and gave Rusty a sharp tug on the leash. We walked upstairs.

Nate opened my door, stepped inside, and set down the cage. Then he came back out and said, "Let me hold the dog. You go on in."

I flashed him a look, but he was smiling like a kid again. He took Rusty's leash and the dog sank down, tail stuck between his back legs, barking. Nate knelt down beside him and kept repeating over and over in that little-boy voice of his, "Now that's no way to treat your new buddy, is it?"

I went into my little den, turned around, and blinked. "Wow! Would you look at this?"

The walls in the den had been repainted a light shade of blue, with white trim on the baseboards and cornices. There were dark-blue-and-white-striped curtains in the windows; beside the blue leather couch was the crate I used as a magazine rack, only it had been painted dark blue also and then covered with decoupage articles about the Braves. A few issues of *The Humane Society Review* and the Braves magazine, *Chop Talk*, were lying in the rack. A quilt from my room at my parents' house was draped across the couch, adding color, and a tall leafy, sturdy-looking plant—I have no idea what kind—sat by the window. The apartment smelled like fresh paint.

"There's more!" Nate enthused. "Abbie did it all. She's been working on it since you left. That's why she kept coming over. First she was taking measurements for the curtains and stuff, and then she started painting."

My room had been sponge-painted in dark blue, with plenty of white showing through so that it was not too somber, and three of my favorite Braves posters hung on the wall above my bed in big glass frames. There was a new modern lamp on the little bedside table, along with a framed picture of Megan and me taken right before a game at Turner Stadium last year.

On the other wall were about ten or twelve different pictures, all in identical black frames. In each one, I was either holding or standing beside one of my pets, starting with Mr. Boots when I was only three or four and continuing right up to a picture of me with Hindsight. Most of the photos were just old snapshots. I grinned as I saw Mr. Boots and Daisy and Patchwork and Jinx and the others.

"Wow," I said again. "This is really neat."

"She planned it all for when you'd be in Europe. Then when you went to the beach earlier, well, she had to hurry. She came every day. And I came over and baby-sat Bobby. I sat on your couch and read him books and built with his blocks while she painted."

"Nate! Thank you!" I tried to imagine my thin, pregnant sister painting my walls and entrusting her one-year-old son to a man she had classified as "really weird" only a couple weeks ago. Dear Abbie.

Sitting at the foot of my bed was an old cedar chest I recognized from Mom and Daddy's attic. Abbie had refinished it and set my softball trophies and medals on top.

An envelope with my name on it lay on the bed. I picked it up, still in a daze, and took out a postcard of Turner Stadium. On the back, Abbie had written: *Happy birthday, Ellie! (A little early) I hope you like the little redecorating touches. It was fun doing it. Feel free to change anything—except not the drapes. Those took me forever. Love, Abbie*

When I went back to the den, Nate was sitting on the floor petting Rusty, and Mrs. Rose had come in and was sitting on the couch stroking Hindsight.

"Mrs. Rose!"

She scowled, "You're back, Ellie! It's about time!" But when I gave her a hug, she softened and said, "We're all so glad you're home. But I don't know how in the world we're going to get all the kitties used to Rusty. He seems a little feisty."

"Don't worry, Mrs. Rose," Nate volunteered. "Ellie will know what to do. She always does."

After I'd unpacked, spent an hour with Nate and Mrs. Rose, and let Rusty romp in Piedmont Park for thirty minutes, I locked the dog in the apartment, left Hindsight with Mrs. Rose, and drove to Grant Park. Abbie and Bill lived not too far down the street from Mt. Carmel Church. I parked the car and walked up the steps of their house, hesitated for only a second, and knocked on the front door.

Abbie opened it and looked genuinely surprised and pleased to see me. "Hey, Ellie. I didn't think you'd even be back from the beach yet. Daddy said you left late this morning."

She still looked thin, and her tummy was even rounder.

I gave her a hug. "Thank you, Abbie. Thank you sooo much. My apartment is beautiful. It's a great birthday present. I can't believe you went to all that trouble just for me."

"Oh, whew. That's a relief. I really hoped you would like it." She flashed me a smile. "And I enjoyed doing it. I really did. Knowing you like it makes it all worth it."

"I love it. It's great."

"Can you come in for a sec? Bobby's still asleep—he usually doesn't take such a long nap, but it's actually been a blessing."

I followed her inside, and we sat in the small den.

"How did Mom look today?"

"Not too bad. Weak, of course, but I think she'll be home in a few days."

"Poor you. It must have been awful to go through all that with her."

"Lots of things were pretty intense during the last week or so. But there were some pretty great moments too."

"Really?"

"Yeah. Mom and I talked a lot, and stuff just happened, Abbie."

"What kind of stuff?"

"Oh, it'll take me a while to figure it all out, but"—I had to say the rest before I chickened out—"I, um, just want to say I'm so sorry, Abbie, for being so mad and mean all these years."

It was all I could get out, but she understood.

She gave me a hug, so that I felt her hard belly against mine and she whispered, pulling my hair off my neck, "Ellie, I forgive you. Of course. But I want you to know something. I fixed up your house as a way of letting you know that we love you. You do fit in this family. We need you, Ellie. I'm sorry that you didn't feel as though we did for so long."

Later, after Bobby had woken up from his nap and drunk a cup of apple juice, Abbie put him in the stroller, and we walked up the street to the Mt. Carmel Church. I hadn't been inside in years.

"Do you remember the paintings that are here?" Abbie asked.

"Kinda—you were talking about them last year."

I followed her into the sanctuary, and she led me to the front, where a painting hung to the left of the pulpit.

"Oh yeah. I remember Mom telling us about this one. It's Oakland Cemetery, and that's Dr. Matthews kneeling over in the field." As soon as I'd said his name, I thought of Mom's tears and the other painting, the one that had ended their friendship.

I was still thinking about that when Bobby started crying. Abbie leaned down to pick him up, and I said, "Let me hold him, Ab. You're carrying enough weight these days."

She looked surprised and thankful as I hoisted little Bobby on my hip, and we walked down to the fellowship hall.

"Ella Mae and Mom," I whispered as we stood in front of my Grandmom Sheila's painting of my namesake holding Mom as an infant. "Mom really loved Ella Mae, didn't she?"

"Yep. A whole, whole lot." Then Abbie reached over and touched me on the shoulder and said, "She loves you a whole, whole lot too."

I smiled at her. "I know, Abbie. I know that now."

Chapter 25

On April 8 [1974], a crowd of 53,775 crammed into the Atlanta Stadium hoping this would be the night that [Hank] Aaron would make them witness to another dramatic milestone in baseball's grand tradition. . . . At 9:07 P.M., Aaron took his first swing of the night. It was the only one he needed. He delivered [the] fastball over the wall in left field. . . . There it was: [homerun] 715! Yet it fails to convey the enormity of the task achieved. . . .

—ANGUS G. GARBER III, *BASEBALL LEGENDS*

It's absolutely perfect," I concluded when Megan stepped out of the dressing room a few days after I returned from Hilton Head. "It is so *you*. Simple, unpretentious, and elegant. Of course, nothing can keep you from looking like a fat slob, but hey, it's pretty good."

I loved seeing Megan laugh. I especially loved the way she stared at herself in the full-length three-way mirror and looked genuinely happy and at peace.

"Do you really think it's the right one?"

"I am absolutely positive, Meggie. It's the right one."

"Okay, now you have to help me pick out the bridesmaids' dresses. You will be my maid of honor, won't you?"

"Of course. I was afraid you weren't going to ask!"

"I've decided on the color—teal. Everyone looks good in teal, and you'll look gorgeous—it'll bring out your eyes."

"First week in November, right? Maybe that'll give me time to lose some more weight."

"Sure it will. You know, Ellie, with all the good things going on in your life now, I'm sure you'll be back down to your high school weight by the end of the year."

"I don't know about that, but I plan to try really hard. My goal is to be at one thirty-five before I get married."

Megan shook her head. "Ellie! I've never heard you talk like that before! Are you and Ben getting serious?"

I laughed. "Nope. But I figure if I set my goal for the wedding, maybe I'll catch a man along the way."

"I know you will, Ellie. I can't wait to see the wonderful guy you end up with."

We decided to stop at the Flying Biscuit for a late breakfast, and we both ordered tofu. That sent us into a giggling fit, and as I sat there watching the delight and silliness in Megan's dark eyes, I knew I was witnessing yet another small miracle.

The apartment felt like home to me, and I had no real desire to leave it again. Every single change Abbie had made pleased me. But Daddy was bringing Mom back from Hilton Head, and I didn't hesitate for a second to offer to stay again at Beverly. Hindsight and Rusty, of course, came along. The next four days were spent keeping them apart and watching Mom rest and keeping all visitors away.

It was in early July, at least a month after the whole saga of the nosebleeds and hemorrhages, that Daddy returned from his daily visit to the oncologist with Mom and announced, "The platelets are at fifty thousand!" They remained stable for the next week, and I think the whole family let out a collective sigh of relief. It was great to see Mom feeling stronger, even if all she did was walk down the stairs once a day.

When I answered the door on Saturday afternoon, I was caught completely off guard to see Carl and Cassandra Matthews standing there.

"Ellie!" Mrs. Matthews said warmly and reached for my hand.

"Hello, Ellie," Dr. Matthews said in his deep soft way, his eyes smiling kindness onto me. I could not imagine those eyes flashing anger or hatred or mistrust, especially not at my mother.

Daddy appeared before I had a chance to say anything. "Carl. Cassandra. Thank you for coming over." He welcomed them into the house and led them directly out onto the sunporch, where Mom was tucked on the wicker love seat.

Dr. Matthews walked over to her quickly, knelt down, and enveloped her in a warm hug. "Mary Swan. Dear, dear Mary Swan."

I saw Mrs. Matthews pucker her lips and cover her mouth with her hand, and her eyes filled with tears. Daddy slipped a strong arm around her shoulders, and they both watched from a distance as Mom and Dr. Matthews spoke.

"Carl. Dear me, Carl. Thank you for coming. I'm so sorry for all the lost years."

He placed a finger over her mouth and said, "Shh. Mary Swan. It is all forgiven. I'm sorry too. We humans can be a stubborn bunch." And his voice cracked a little. "To think of all the time I wasted . . ."

I felt out of place and turned to quietly leave the room, but Mrs. Matthews saw me and held out her hand, saying, "Oh, Ellie, stay with us. My goodness, if it hadn't been for you, we'd still be living in our separate worlds."

And so I stayed. The afternoon passed into evening and the sun began to set and we were still out on the porch, eating Chinese takeout that Daddy had ordered and laughing comfortably together. I heard story after story of Miss Abigail and Mt. Carmel, and then Carl and Cassandra told several hilarious stories about patients they'd had at Grady, and Daddy talked about a few embarrassing incidents in his career as city planner.

It was when I had taken my second helping of cashew chicken and rice that Dr. Matthews asked me, "Ellie, how long ago was your last skin graft?"

I shrugged, feeling self-conscious for a split second, then glanced over at Mom.

"Her last one was almost ten years ago, Carl."

"You know, they've made a lot of progress in plastic surgery in the last ten years. I have a colleague, a good friend whom I respect greatly as a surgeon, who specializes in facial reconstruction. I'd be happy to set up an appointment if you'd like."

It was natural to look to my parents for their input, but almost immediately I knew that I was the only one who could answer. They would not try to influence me. They had made that choice a long time ago.

"I guess it wouldn't hurt to talk to him," I said. "Let me think about it." Then I added, "Thanks." And I *did* feel thankful for Dr. Matthews's concern, his professional wisdom. I felt thankful and not one bit resentful or bitter.

When Rusty put his head in Cassandra's lap, eyeing her pitifully, she laughed and said, "I don't know where dogs learn that look, but Baily—the little yellow Lab puppy—has perfected it already. Jessie says there's not one thing in the whole wide world she can do about it. When he looks at her like that, she always gives in."

The Matthewses left a little after eight. Daddy saw them to the door, then came back to Mom and gave her a long hug. "Did that wear you out too much, Fat Goose?"

"Oh, Scout, you know it didn't. You know it was . . ." And her voice faltered and cracked. "It was like a dream coming true. A day I won't ever forget. Thank you, Robbie." Then she looked over at me, her eyes full of love, and said, "Thank you, Ellie. Thank you." She kissed Daddy softly on the lips, and he scooped her up in his arms and carried her upstairs to their bedroom.

Later, after I'd fed Hindsight and Rusty and loaded the dishes into the dishwasher, I walked out into the backyard and sat down on the little bench and breathed in deeply, smelling the sweet fragrance of magnolia blossoms.

A few days later, I insisted on taking Megan and Timothy to dinner as a celebration for their engagement. I was still working at Jeremy's till the end of the month, but for this special occasion I chose a new restaurant in Midtown that had gotten the reputation of being shabby-chic. In fact, the whole restaurant was decorated with furniture restored from the Goodwill. After we'd enjoyed a strange combination of "new American cuisine," Megan and I left Timothy and went to the rest room.

The ladies' room was papered in a luxurious red material and had an old porcelain sink with brass fixtures and an antique mirror above the sink. I stepped into the stall and closed the door. Two seconds later I threw the door open and grabbed Megan's arm, dragging her back in with me. "This you've got to see."

All the walls inside the stall were made up of mirrors. But not just plain, big flat mirrors. They were broken pieces of mirrors glued on the walls in a mosaic.

Fortunately, no other woman entered the ladies' room while we were there, or she would have thought we were nuts, Megan and I holding on to each other in that tiny room and laughing and crying and reaching out to touch the mirrored walls, and me whispering to Megan, "Isn't this absolutely perfect? Prophetic!"

I moved back to my apartment during the second week of July. I had stopped by Abbie's to put in a load of clothes, since my washing machine wasn't working, and we'd taken Bobby out to the park while I was waiting on the clothes to dry. We walked back to Abbie's house without saying much, but when we got to the little yard, I let Bobby down out of my arms and asked, "Are you hanging in there, Ab? How long has Bill been gone?"

"Almost a week this time. To tell you the truth, I'm getting a bit tired of his traveling. It's not his fault, but I just can't seem to get much rest."

"When does he come back?"

"Tonight."

"I've got an idea. I don't have to work till tomorrow night. Let me take Bobby back to my place. You and Bill can have a nice reunion—just the two of you."

"Are you serious, El?"

"Sure, if you think Bobby won't mind." I knelt down and looked at his bright round eyes, his rosy cheeks. "Would you come visit Aunt Ellie, Bobby? You can see Nate and meet my kitty and puppy."

Bobby's eyes got even bigger. He looked up at his mom, and Abbie asked, "Would you like to go with Aunt Ellie?"

He got a big grin on his face and went toddling through the house to get his bear.

"I don't know. He's never spent the night with anyone but Mama and Daddy."

"Nan kept him once, didn't she?"

"Just during the day. He wakes up at night sometimes. And his diapers are gross. I'll warn you—he's a handful."

"Don't worry. Between Nate and Mrs. Rose and me, we'll be fine."

I was actually quite astounded by my offer—astounded and pleased. We spent the next thirty minutes packing the car with more stuff than any one-year-old could possibly need—a playpen and a fold-up kind of bed and a car seat and a huge diaper bag and a bag full of baby food and bottles and a long list of instructions.

I was chuckling to myself as Abbie explained everything, thinking, *This cannot be that hard!*

"Thanks, Ellie. Thanks a ton."

"Don't worry, sis. I'll call if I have any problems!"

"Do you know those people over there sitting in the stands?" Sharon asked in between the second and third inning of our game a few days later.

"Who?"

"The couple over there waving to you."

I squinted, shielding my eyes from the sun, and looked in the direction Sharon was pointing. Then I laughed. "Ha! Well, look at that! My parents and grandparents have come to watch me play."

After the game, I went into the stands.

Trixie was smacking away on her gum and greeted me with, "JJ said you had her out at home—that ump stinks."

"Well, at least you still won, dear," Mom said. She was wearing a Braves baseball cap and a Braves T-shirt that she'd tucked into her Capri jeans.

Daddy gave me a hard pat on the back. "Way to go, Ellie. Great job. You go on and celebrate with the girls. I'm gonna get your mother home now, before she gets too tired."

"Oh, Scout. I'm fine. I feel fine."

"Look, Goose, doctor's orders. Don't overdo it."

Trixie stood up, adjusting her wide-brimmed yellow straw hat and looking back at Granddad JJ. "If you're so sure that Ellie had her out, why don't you go down and talk to the ump yourself, JJ!"

Granddad frowned and said, "I have half a mind to do it, Trix. Never seen such a lousy excuse for an umpire."

"Oh, now, let's not cause a fuss, not with everything having ended up just fine," Mom commented.

They were still talking about my last play and arguing like little kids when I turned and went back down to the field.

I was completely surprised by the party a week and a half later. I thought I was going over for a simple birthday dinner with Mom and

Daddy, and I was actually looking forward to it. But when I walked in the door, there was the sound of people whispering and then someone, Nan probably, saying, "Shh, here she is!" and then a loud chorus of "Surprise! Happy birthday, Ellie!"

Gathered on the sunporch were Mom and Daddy, Nan and Stockton, Abbie and Bill. Nate was holding little Bobby in his arms, and Mrs. Rose was engrossed in conversation with my talkative neighbor, Mrs. Elliott. Granddad JJ and Trixie were laughing with Dr. and Mrs. Matthews. Megan was holding onto Timothy's arm with one hand and holding out her left hand toward Mom so that my mother could inspect the ring, which she was doing with plenty of *oohs* and *aahs*.

Uncle Jimmy was out back grilling steaks, and Mom had put bowls of potato chips out on the picnic table. One bowl was heaping with Cheetos, with a sign in Megan's writing: *For Ellie only*. There were bottles of Coke and a pitcher of Trixie's extra sugary iced tea and a big pitcher of lemonade with a little card in front that said *Freshly squeezed*. When I saw that sign, it made me think of Ben, and I got a little twittering in my stomach.

Abbie had made a big sheet cake and decorated it like a baseball field, and the paper plates and napkins were ones meant for a kid's birthday party, with *It's a hit!*, *That ball's outta here!*, and *Grand Slam!* printed on them along with bats and balls and baseball caps and pennants. She had a big blue candle in the shape of a *2* and placed beside it a candle that looked like a baseball bat standing straight up, so that together the candles represented *21*.

Before I could say anything, I was swept into the group, and soon we were eating and laughing and chatting. Propped on an easel over to the side of the sunporch was my twenty-first-birthday painting, the one with Hindsight sitting on my lap. Beside that one was another easel holding the much smaller painting of the footprints at the beach, still incomplete.

"I promise to finish it soon," Mom whispered to me, but I thought that it was just as good as finished. The essentials were there—Mom's steady footprints by the ocean and mine, small, disappearing and then reappearing right beside my mother's. And a setting sun—an unfinished sunset that I could tell was going to be breathtaking.

After dinner everyone sang "Happy Birthday" to me, and I opened an enormous present that turned out to be ten boxes, each wrapped within another, the smallest holding a check for a sizeable sum and a card that everyone had signed, which read "to help tide you over till you become a vet." We all had big scoops of Midnight Cookies and Cream with cake, and then Trixie announced that we were going to play a game called "Name That Pet."

She or Abbie had apparently gone by my apartment and brought over all the framed photos of me with the animals, and they were all displayed on the sunporch. Trixie explained the rules, "Now y'all. The one who can come up with the most correct names of these animals that Ellie and I rescued, well, there's a real nice prize. No cheating!"

Of course, Trixie and I were not allowed to play. Mrs. Rose went up to each photo, picked it up and held it within two inches of her face and kept asking Nate, who was standing beside her, "Is this one Hindsight, Nate? I don't know any of the others, but I do know that cat. Shoulda brought my glasses."

Nate was patiently saying, "No, Mrs. Rose. You haven't gotten to the one of Ellie with Hindsight yet. See, Ellie's just a little girl in these first pictures."

In the middle of the game, the doorbell rang, and Daddy rushed out to get it. "Mae Mae, look who's here!" he called.

Rachel and Ben came into the house. "Hey, kid!" Rachel said. "Sorry we're late! Ben drove up from the beach and picked me up at the airport on the way here, and the traffic was awful." She gave me a quick hug. "You look great! I love the sapphire in your eyebrow. And your dress is darling!"

I was, in fact, wearing the blue jeans dress I had found at the beach house.

Rachel bustled out onto the porch calling out, "Swannee! Swannee, where are you? You silly, scatterbrained girl! You said the party started at *seven*, not *six*!"

I think my face turned three shades of crimson when Ben said, "Hi, Ellie" and gave me a kiss on the cheek. "I wouldn't have missed this for the world." Then he handed me a wrapped gift and whispered, "Wait till later to open it."

Back in my little den around midnight, I sat cuddled on the floor, leaning against the couch with Rusty's head in my lap. Hindsight was sprawled on the couch, purring. I ripped the paper off of Ben's gift and just smiled. It was a copy of my favorite Dr. Seuss book: *Marvin K. Mooney, Will You Please Go Now!*

I had begged to have it read to me so many times as a little kid that I had memorized it. Did Ben actually remember that? I opened the cover and laughed aloud. Several of the words in the title had been crossed out and replaced, so it read *Ellie Bartholomew, Will You Please Come Now! By Benjamin Abrams*.

I turned the pages and slowly read Ben's message to me. In every place that Dr. Seuss had said *go*, Ben had crossed through it and written *come*. And every time it said *Marvin K. Mooney*, it now read *Ellie Bartholomew*. And inside the back cover was a long envelope: Ben had sent me a plane ticket to fly up and see him in New York near the end of August.

I hadn't forgotten his words to me at Hilton Head. *Give it time.* Sitting on the floor reading that book, I knew that whatever was ahead, it would definitely be worth the wait.

On a slight incline of immaculate grass outside the High Museum of Art stood the bronze statue of Rodin's *The Shadow*—the gift from France, given in 1968 as a memorial for the 1962 Orly plane crash. A low marble wall beside the statue, in the form of a semicircle, was engraved with the names of the victims of the crash. I remembered as a girl seeing this stone marker, reading the names, and wondering about Grandmother Sheila.

On this warm July afternoon, Mom and I stood side by side, her arm holding mine. We were looking past the marble marker and the statue, past the huge ginkgo tree that was giving us shade, up over the hill to our left where the Atlanta School of Arts, the Alliance Theatre, and the Symphony Hall were housed, our backs turned away from this section of Peachtree Road known as Colony Square. It was part of Midtown, and Daddy always said that the Arts Center had acted as a catalyst for commercial growth there. I thought the Arts Center had been a catalyst for our family too.

Then we started walking to our right, making our way to the museum, admiring again the bright white building with its curving forms. Once inside, we climbed the winding corridors to the second floor. I had asked Mom to come with me to the High Museum. I needed to go there with her, since we definitely weren't going to Scotland. We were all—Mom's family and friends—waiting, kind of collectively holding our breaths, and praying that Mom's platelet count would stay up and that she truly would be getting stronger.

But that day, as we stood in front of her paintings, I was determined not to worry. I just stared at the paintings with her, lacing my arm through hers as she rested her head on my shoulder. Once again I studied the low stone wall bisecting *The Dwelling Place*. Once again my eyes were drawn to the little lamb standing stiff-legged in the top right-hand corner.

"So what is the lamb looking at?" I asked Mom.

"You really don't know?"

"No idea."

"She's looking at her mother. She sees her down the hill, and in another second she'll be cantering toward the wall, leap over it, and stand content beside her."

I was speechless.

"I found my mother at the Dwelling Place, Ellie. I found her there. More than any other place. And I wanted you to do the same."

I tucked my arm more tightly in hers and tried to clear the lump out of my throat. "I've already found you, Mom. Now it's okay."

Rachel had said I wanted to know how Mom did it. How she survived her life and became a respectable, peaceful woman, a blessing in society. I marvel that the answer was in front of my eyes the first time I considered the question. It was in her painting *The Dwelling Place*.

I am so literal, it is hard for me to see metaphor, but finally I understood. That lamb was looking for its mother, and there was a surprised expression of relief when it found her—found her literally, yes, but Mom meant it symbolically, a tumultuous trip through the heart. Mom survived because she had the Dwelling Place in her heart. She could go there anytime she wanted and be refreshed by streams of cool water.

And so could I. The Dwelling Place was a specific spot, I suppose, or rather a moment in time, when I allowed God into my heart. But the Dwelling Place is also a journey, and I will be on this journey forever—for the rest of my life, walking, running at times, stumbling, no doubt, toward the future, which time and God will reveal. It is a place where there is forgiveness—given and accepted—where wounds can be healed, where families can enjoy each other and can speak their minds and be appreciated. Mistakes are made. And accidents will happen. But in the end, it's all worth it. *I* am worth it.

I'm sure of that now.

Acknowledgments

A writer's life lessons cannot but creep into her stories, and I am thankful that the Lord has permitted me to learn about surrender, sacrifice, and *dwelling*. Hard lessons, learned through tears, but indelibly marked on my heart. It is my prayer, as always, that my words will somehow inspire my readers to pursue the path of faith, seeking until they find.

I owe a huge *merci* to two people:

Dave Horton, Editorial Director at Bethany—I trust your expertise, and I know *The Dwelling Place* is a better book because of it.

Lora Beth Norton, my editor, who encourages me with good counsel and good humor. We've never met, have only spoken on the phone twice, but our friendship spans ten years and goes past the limits of cyberspace into eternity. You are brilliant. Thank you, thank you, thank you. . . .

And my thanks to many others:

My parents, Jere and Barbara Goldsmith.

Mom—who had her own bout with breast cancer after I had begun writing this book. Courageous and determined, you came through this trial with your typical positive attitude and are still jumping your horse, among a hundred other things. Thanks for finding the time to take me around Atlanta and help me in so many ways with research and publicity.

Dad—thank you, as always, for being so enthusiastic about my books, for tending to the practical matters, for all you have taught and shown me. Go, Georgia Tech! I love you both so much!

My grandmother, Allene Goldsmith—for taking me to the Humane Society many times when I was a girl and allowing me to rescue homeless cats and dogs, and for rescuing countless ones yourself and giving them dignity.

Beau—our very own rescued mutt, who served as inspiration for the dog in this book.

Valerie Andrews—breast surgeon and precious friend, thank you for your detailed medical advice and for the way you spur me on in my pursuit of God.

Tyler and Kim Huhman—vet and research scientist—Tyler, thanks for the veterinary advice, and Kim, thanks for our priceless, lifelong friendship and for all those memories of flute lessons and days at the barn with our nutty mares!

Laura McDaniel—thanks for driving me around Atlanta and sharing breakfast at the Flying Biscuit Café and doing a hundred other things to make my life easier on both sides of the Atlantic, and of course, thank you for being a wonderful lifelong friend who knows how to encourage and pray.

Margaret DeBorde—precious friend and owner of a darling yellow Lab puppy, thanks for your help in the field of rehab.

Catherine Schiltz—with whom I had the privilege of walking through your courageous battle with cancer in Montpellier—you always encourage me in my writing, *merci*.

Trudy Owens—soul mate, pre-editor, prayer warrior. Don't know what I'd do without you. Thank goodness for the telephone and e-mail!

Cathy Carmeni—dear friend and "truth speaker." How I miss our prayer times together! Thanks, as always, for the editing advice.

Odette Beauregard—dear friend, you are really "family"—and a tireless encourager. Hurry back to France!

Cheryl Stauffer—my new teammate and friend in Lyon. You're also a gifted editor and a real techie!

Louise Adamson—as always, your life of service and sacrifice inspires me. Thank you for sharing with me your miracle stories of the inner city.

Mary Stuppy—who graciously allowed me to walk in unknown and unannounced and gave me a tour of your home on Spotted Sandpiper, and Margaret Samples—who did the same for me in Ansley Park.

Dale and Jo Patterson and Rich and Mary Gartrell—for being willing to provide valuable—and sometimes painful—information about the Vietnam War.

Jean-Claude Cohen—for providing information about May '68 in

France and for being a great neighbor for so many years. You, too, Josette!

Jill Steenhuis—gifted artist and fellow Atlantan-in-France, thank you for helping me understand the artist's inner eye.

My brothers and their spouses and children, Jere and Mary Goldsmith, Katie, Chip, and Chandler; and Glenn and Kim Goldsmith and Will—your lives inspire me in ways you may never know! Thank you for all the long-distance calls, the love and support, and the new Web cam!

My uncle and aunt, Alan and Jay Goldsmith—lifelong cheerleaders. Way to go, Uncle Alan. Congrats on your new novel!

The whole Musser gang: First, the world's greatest in-laws, Harvey and Doris Ann—thank you for twenty years of love and encouragement and, most recently, for rescuing me from the cold by coming over to France and insulating my "writing chalet"! All my brothers-in-law and sisters-in-law, and all my nieces and nephews, too—every one of you is a priceless jewel. And especially Sadie—for the miracle of your life, for your courage and the beautiful young lady you are, thank you for modeling to all of us what real healing looks like.

All those who work so hard at Bethany House Publishers—thank you.

My publishing friends on this side of the "pond": De Groot Goudriaan, Johannis Verlag, Lunde Forlag, and Editions Vida—many thanks for your enthusiasm and encouragement, and for the opportunities you've given me to reach out in Europe.

Others who gave of their time and knowledge: Eileen Smith Bettig, Debbie and Tim Sharold, Anne Moore, Louis Ross, Janet Crawley, Bet Freed, Anthony Jones, Beth Knox, Wayne Rogers.

My faithful readers who write to encourage me and tell others—thank you.

And of course, my sons, Andrew and Christopher, the world's greatest teens—who cheer me on when I'm down, give me lots of helpful insights (not to mention much appreciated backrubs!), and bring me great joy.

And to my husband, Paul—always to you, my greatest thanks—

faithful, funny, strong, kind, wise, and a whole lot of other things I won't mention here. Here's to another delightful twenty years!

And finally, to my Lord and Savior, Jesus Christ, who has been redeeming the broken things in my life for many years now. Without you, I can do nothing.

A Delightful and Engaging Novel

FROM AN

Acclaimed Author

Two-time Christy Award finalist Stephanie Grace Whitson writes a powerful and touching story. A widow seeking to escape the past and restart her life travels to Paris, France, in search of what she might have been. Traveling with her daughter, Mary Davis seeks to discover what is truly important in this life. Will she be able to reconcile the past and find a new future?

BETHANYHOUSE